THE PATRIOTS OF FOXBORO

To Ed,
A very nice person,
Best regards,
[signature]
9-30-09

**Other books by
Award Winning Author Jay Carp**

The Gift of Ruth   2003

The Gift of Ruth—Large print   2008

Cold War Confessions   2007
USA Best Books of 2007 Award Winner

THE PATRIOTS OF FOXBORO

JAY CARP

River Pointe Publications

© 2009 by Jay Carp

Published by River Pointe Publications
Milan, Michigan 48160, USA
734-439-8031

All rights reserved. No part of this book may be reproduced or transmitted
in any form or by any means, electronic or mechanical,
including photocopy, recording, or any information storage and
retrieval system, without permission in writing from the publisher.

Publisher's Cataloging-in-Publication

(Provided by Quality Books, Inc.)

Carp, Jay.
   The patriots of Foxboro / Jay Carp.
   p. cm.
   LCCN 2009930420
   ISBN-13: 978-0-9817258-1-9
   ISBN-10: 0-9817258-1-3

    1. Vietnam War, 1961-1975—United States—Fiction.
2. Soldiers—United States--Fiction. 3. Vietnam War,
1961–1975—Conscientious objectors—United States—
Fiction. 4. Young men--United States—Fiction.
5. Post-traumatic stress disorder—Fiction.   I. Title.

PS3603.A768P38 2009   813'.6
                                  QBI09-600095

Interior design and composition by Sans Serif Inc.
Cover design by Barb Gunia

Dedication

No author works alone and in a vacuum. There are always distractions, disputes and disasters small enough to lure the author away from his or her task. Fortunately, or unfortunately, I had guard rails to keep me on track, but certainly not on schedule, while I was writing.

The first guard rail, was my wife Hazel Eunice Peabody Proctor. She is a saint without a name day; she exerts much more of a yearly influence. Hazel has put up with my procrastinations and my negative prayers (also known as swearing) patiently while pushing me towards my computer. She is the one that must bear the blame for this book being published.

My other guard rail concerned my thoughts towards our younger generations. They have always been handed the problems that older generations have not been able to solve. Younger generations were never given choices or asked their opinions; they were just handed these legacies.

When they did inherit war from their elders, they bore the brunt of the carnage. I often wonder if this is the best that we can do for them? May the older generations finally learn how to get along so that the world is peaceful and the word "war" becomes completely, and utterly, defunct.

This book is dedicated to my guard rails, my wife and all of the younger generations yet to be.

1

When Katie Oldfield carefully drove her car off the asphalt road and onto a narrow dirt lane, she realized that her long journey was almost over. Weariness, not elation, welled up inside of her, as she was tired almost to the point of being cranky. The trip had begun seven days earlier over 3,000 miles away. She had started in San Luis Obispo, California, and she was ending in Foxboro, Massachusetts.

It had been a hard trip for her both physically and mentally. She was the only driver and her companions were her four and a half-year-old son, Tyler, and her two cats, Bonnie and Clyde. She had to take more pit stops than she had really wanted but there was nothing she could do about that. The cats required medication to keep them quiet and she and Tyler had to eat, stretch, and go to the bathroom. However, those stops did considerably lengthen her driving day. She was exhausted by the time they pulled into a motel at night.

And while she was driving she kept asking herself if she really knew why she was making the journey. Katie had left Foxboro just after she had gotten married almost a dozen years ago and she had not been back except for two short visits.

She was aware that she was returning to the place where she had been born and raised but she was not sure what to expect when she got there. She realized that she had changed as she had gotten older, as had her family and her friends, so she knew she was not returning to her past. However, since becoming a widow five years ago, her life had taken on a sullen murmur that she did not like and she wanted to change the melody.

Now, after her seven days of continuous driving, all she had left to travel was a distance of a few hundred feet. As the car was turning off the pavement she stepped on the gas pedal because she wanted the car to speed up. In her haste to reach her final destination, Katie had bypassed several rest stops and, as a result, she had a problem. She needed to get to the bathroom in her grandmother's house quickly.

However, the dirt lane was so rutted and uneven that she was immediately forced to slow the car down because of the heavy jolting.

"Shit," she muttered aloud softly, "I've got to get to the john. This is awful, I don't want to pee my pants." No sooner had she spoken those words then she looked in the rear view mirror to see if Tyler were sitting upright in the back seat. She tried not to swear in front of him and there were certain words he was not allowed to say. She called his name softly and, when he didn't answer, she assumed he was sleeping.

While she drove, she kept opening and closing her knees and drumming her fingers on the steering wheel. "Come on, come on," she muttered as she passed several small homes on either side of the lane. She came close to missing the driveway that she was looking for because the light was starting to fade and the entrance was almost hidden by untrimmed lilac bushes. When she did spot the opening she swung the car off the lane and, with the bushes scraping against the sides of the automobile, she drove up the short driveway close to three wooden steps that led to the front porch. The house was a tiny, one story, wooden home that had seen better days a long time before Katie parked her car.

She opened the front door, and looked into the back seat to see Tyler stretched out and sleeping. "I'll be back, Tyler, but right now I have to go."

She didn't even try to shut her door as she bolted out of the car and climbed the porch steps. As she was crossing the porch to the front door she was jiggling her legs and fumbling for her keys at the same time.

When she got to the door, she put the key in the lock but it wouldn't turn the bolt. "Oh Granny, how many times did I ask you to get this damn lock fixed?" She wiggled the key and the tumblers finally lined up, allowing the bolt to move.

"Thank God." She dropped her purse on the floor as she ran down the hall to the bathroom. Much to her relief and satisfaction she did not have an accident. When she finished, she was in a more relaxed frame of mind and she recovered her composure as she came back to the front porch. Her son was still asleep on the back seat and Katie stood on the porch of the house her grandmother had lived in for all of her adult years. She shut her eyes and took a deep breath, inhaling the cool air that was the forerunner of the colder weather to come.

Katie began to weep as she remembered her last two visits. Her grandmother and she had been even closer after Katie's mother had passed away and she wished so much that her mother and grandmother were on the porch with her now.

Her first trip back had been after she and Mike, a Lieutenant in the Navy stationed in San Diego, had been married a year. They had made a quick trip to Boston and they had managed to see her father, her stepmother, and her brother over that weekend; that had been a pleasant trip.

Her second visit was made under entirely different circumstances. Her family was not home as her father and stepmother were traveling in Europe and her brother was living in Canada to avoid being drafted. At the same time, she and Mike were having marital problems.

It was at this low point when a neighbor of Grandma Barker, her mother's mother, called to let Katie know that her grandmother had just been placed in a nursing home. She flew to Massachusetts immediately. When she arrived at her bedside, her grandmother's disease, Alzheimer's, was so bad that she didn't recognize, or even acknowledge, that Katie was there. After a few days of trying to get through to her grandmother, Katie sobbed, kissed her goodbye, and left. She waited for what she knew was inevitable.

Two years later, Katie was reminded of the anguish of that visit when her stepmother wrote and told her of her grandmother's passing. Katie was inconsolable. The people she loved, those who had raised and guided her from the time she was a child, were leaving her. She wanted them to stay on earth for her sake. Her grandmother's death made her feel lonely and vulnerable.

It was some time after her death that Katie was notified that her grandmother had left her small house in Foxboro to her. That was when she began thinking of leaving California and going back to Massachusetts. While she was growing up, her grandmother's house had been filled with love and pleasant memories, so different from her present state of affairs. She was realistic enough to know that her memories of her past were behind her forever while her future was what she must face. Without even realizing it, she was looking for a new starting place and her grandmother's house, with all the love it had held in the past, gave her hope that she could bring order and serenity back into her life.

Katie Oldfield had just returned to the town of Foxboro, where she had been born and raised.

***

Foxborough, Massachusetts, is situated midway between Boston and Providence, Rhode Island, about nineteen miles from either. Hardly anyone writes the last three letters of the original spelling under which it was first incorporated in 1778. The town was named in honor of Charles James Fox, a British statesman who was sympathetic to the goals of the revolutionary colonists. Foxboro was a way station on the Old Post Road that ran between Providence and Boston and, for almost two hundred years, it went almost unnoticed by both capitals, both states, and, indeed, the rest of the nation.

During the mid 1960s and 70's, Foxboro was a town of less than ten thousand inhabitants. Like all other small New England towns, it had a distinct personality based on its geographic position and the ethnic background of its inhabitants. During this time it was not a bedroom town for either Boston or Providence. The people who worked in Foxboro were the same white, Anglo-Saxon, Protestants and Catholics, who also lived in Foxboro. The largest employer, by far, was the Foxboro Company, which designed and manufactured commercial pumps, valves, and gauges for oil companies and heavy industries all over the world.

The Company, as it was referred to by the townspeople, was a big firm and it employed hundreds of workers. Two brothers, the Bristols, owned it and they both lived in large houses in Foxboro. They were good to their employees and they were paternalistic, giving each employee a ham at Easter and a turkey at Thanksgiving. If their products and their business had not been so successful their business style would certainly have been considered old fashioned.

What was old fashioned was the layout of Foxboro. When the town was first incorporated, activity had been centered on Foxboro Common, an area set aside for Foxboro residents to graze their livestock. All the main roads, in their New England way of meandering, led from outside Foxboro, to the Common; it was the hub of all the crooked spokes. Businesses and churches and the Post Office clustered around the Common and, until the arrival of automobiles and multi-lane highways, the Common was the heart of Foxboro.

In the decades after the horse and buggy disappeared, progress began to change the town. The rectangular Common became a one way rotary traffic lane to keep the center of town from becoming completely congested. Malls were built on the outskirts and large stores drew businesses away from the Common. This left small stores, Mom and Pop enterprises, in the middle of town struggling to stay open.

All of these changes were gradual and were not noticeable as they were occurring. The net result was that, although Foxboro did have physical changes since its incorporation, the inhabitants were still about as feisty as the original settlers.

Indeed, there are many Foxboroites who are proud to announce that they are the fifth or sixth generation of their family who have lived in Foxboro without ever moving to another town. That they have never sought "time off for good behavior" seems hard to believe, but New Englanders are sometimes difficult to understand.

The changes that did occur in Foxboro were not unique to Foxboro alone. Over the years, progress changed every city and town in Massachusetts to some degree. However, there was one event that took place in Foxboro that was remarkable only to that small town. It became the home of a National Football League team, the New England Patriots.

The Patriots started life as an American Football League team in 1959 as the Boston Patriots. However, the Boston Patriots had a shortcoming that no other football team operated under; they had no permanent home stadium. They were a band of gypsies who played on any level field they could find. Over the years their home games were played at Harvard Stadium, Fenway Park, Nickerson Field, and Alumni Field.

Throughout the time that they had no home stadium, the owner of the team tried to negotiate with both the Commonwealth of Massachusetts and the City of Boston to find a resting place for his professional stalwarts; however, nothing was ever resolved. Finally, after one especially bitter negotiation between the City of Boston and the Patriot owner during which they could not agree on a price for an abandoned city dump that was available, it looked as if the Patriots would have to shift their franchise to another state. In 1971, through a series of business judo maneuvers that kept the team in Massachusetts, the Boston Patriots changed their name to the New England Patriots and they moved out of Boston.

The solution to a home stadium for the Patriots was reached in, of all places, Foxboro. A man by the name of E. M. Loewe owned a harness racing track in the town along with a large tract of land adjacent to the track. For years, he had paid taxes on the racetrack but, because he and the town were continually arguing over the zoning of the empty land, he refused to pay the taxes on it. Thus, according to town records, he owed Foxboro a substantial sum of money.

Mr. Loewe, being an astute business man, and knowing what the problems of the Patriots were, came up with an astounding solution. He met with the Foxboro Board of Selectmen and told them he would donate the disputed land to the town of Foxboro if the town would agree to certain conditions. Once the town had ownership of the property, it could lease the land to the Patriots for 99 years and, under this long-term agreement, the Patriots would be able to entice a brewery, for the advertising and the right to sell their products at the games, to construct the stadium.

This was a win, win, win, and win situation. Riches were generated from smoke, mirrors, and lawyer's fees. Foxboro would win with an American Football League team in their town and a stadium that would become their property after 99 years. The Patriots would win with a stadium that was theirs to use at no cost to them. The brewery would win with millions of dollars of free advertising to offset the cost of the stadium. Even Mr. Loewe would win because of his conditions for donating the land.

His first condition was that all of his back taxes for the land he was to donate be cancelled and annulled. The second condition was that the stadium parking lot, which was nothing more than an extension of the track parking lot, be paved with asphalt. His third condition was that he would retain the parking concession for all the cars that parked in the stadium parking lot during the football games. The stadium seated over 60,000, so, in essence, Mr. Loewe had converted land that had lain fallow into a gold mine.

Everyone who was involved in these negotiations was pleased with the outcome. The town fathers were happy that fame and fortune would be coming to Foxboro, The Patriot owner changed the name from the Boston Patriots to the New England Patriots and they were delighted to have a permanent home. The Schaeffer Brewing Company executives were satisfied that the advertising they received in their brand new Schaeffer Stadium would offset their construction costs. While Mr. Loewe was content in having performed a public service and, at the same time, in picking up a little pocket money.

So, the Patriots moved to Foxboro and were warmly welcomed with open arms by the inhabitants of Foxboro.

The New England Patriots received more attention moving from Boston to Foxboro than did Katie Oldfield, a native of Foxboro, when she made her return from California.

2

Katie Oldfield, born and christened Katie Givens, was thirty-four years old, a widow, a mother, and a working woman. Since the unexpected and violent death of her husband, her attention was almost completely focused on her immediate daily activities, events, and problems. Her life left her little time for reminiscing and she subconsciously preferred it that way. There were events and things that Katie didn't want to think about or dwell on. It was only when something out of the ordinary occurred that her thoughts would leave the present and return to her past.

Long after Katie had reconciled herself to her grandmother's passing, she received a letter from her grandmother's attorney that was totally unexpected. The attorney informed her that her grandmother had left her house to Katie; and that totally surprised her. She knew that her grandmother was not wealthy and she had assumed that the house had long ago been sold to pay for some of the medical costs her grandmother was charged when she went into the nursing home. The letter stated that, as an attorney, he needed some legal information from her to complete the paperwork and to transfer the deed to her.

Katie had been sitting in a chair, looking at the lawyer's letter and gazing into the past, when the phone started to ring. It rang four or five times before she came back to the present. She picked it up and heard her neighbor, and best friend, Brenda ask, "Katie? I wasn't sure you were home from work and your phone rang for quite a while. Were you sleeping?"

"No, I wasn't sleeping, just daydreaming."

Brenda gushed, "Oh, maybe that's a good sign, you must have had a good time. You know why I'm calling, I want to hear all about your date last night."

Katie chuckled, "Brenda, you are an eternal optimist. Tyler's taking a nap so why don't you come on over. I'll make some coffee and we can talk."

Brenda Quinn breezed in with some home made cookies she had just taken out of the oven. She stood almost six feet tall and was lean and lanky with long, flaming red hair, freckles, and a button nose. Katie was of average height with a fuller figure, short, curly black hair and a quietly attractive face. They made a startling contrast when they were together, which was quite often. They had known each other for three years, they shared their daily experiences, and they couldn't keep a secret from each other. They were both unattached and, while Katie accepted that status, Brenda fought against it. For the last six months she had been trying to get Katie to go out double dating, hoping it would change both of their situations.

Brenda nibbled on a cookie and sipped some coffee, "I'm sorry my date and I didn't catch up with you last night but he had car problems and we ended up being towed to a garage. Tell me all about last night. Did you like Sam, your date?"

"Brenda, don't ask. This guy, Sam, was the worst man that you have ever fixed me up with. At least the others had the courtesy to introduce themselves and ask my name before they tried to get me into bed. I don't know why men think that widows automatically are begging them for sex. This guy had more arms than an octopus and he spent a long time trying to convince me that he should be my very own personal sperm donor. Last night's date was a total, absolute loser.

"I also think that this experiment to fix me up with a blind date is about over. I have had enough of men whose veins are filled with boiling testosterone."

"Katie, I am so sorry. Sam seems so pleasant at work that I thought it would be a good match. I know what you mean about men. The minute they hear that I am a divorcee they cluster around with their divining rods ready to go dousing. To Hell with all of them. When I see Sam tomorrow, I'm going to really ream his ass. He has no right to treat you, or any other woman, that way."

"Don't bother, Brenda. It doesn't make a bit of difference to me because I'm not going to see him again. Let's drop the subject; besides, I have much more important matters to discuss with you."

Katie leaned forward and handed Brenda the letter she had received from the attorney. Brenda read it carefully and then returned the letter to her. "It looks like you have inherited a house. Which of your grandmothers is this?"

"Grandma Barker, my mother's mother. It's a small house down a dirt road near the Neponset Reservoir. It's really not too far from the center of town. I loved Grandma Barker, she was a perfect grandmother. Whenever I went over to her house to visit, we would cook and sew together and she would treat me as an adult. She rarely said, 'No' to me and, if I did something wrong, she and I would talk about it. She knew about children and she loved me.

"God, she was great and, after my mother died when I was eight, she never showed me her heartbreak, she just became better for me. I was so hurt and bewildered and she protected me with her love. My mother was her only child and she must have been devastated, but she made it a point to hide her pain from me. She was so brave and caring."

Katie stopped talking for a few minutes, her thoughts steeping in the past, and then she continued, "You know, now that I think about it, it's odd. My father's mother, Grandma Givens, she's really a good person but she doesn't have the warmth that Grandma Barker did. When I went to visit Grandma Givens, there were rooms I was not supposed to go into. Sometimes, Grandma Givens would ask me questions and then continue to talk even before I answered the question. She would ask what I was doing in school and ask what grades I was getting. If they weren't A's she would give me a lecture on doing better. She always took the time to point out what good girls should do, and what bad girls shouldn't do.

"Grandma Barker never asked about my grades and never mentioned good girls or bad girls. Come to think of it, there wasn't any room in her house that I couldn't go into. You know that I can't ever remember cooking anything with Grandma Givens. I guess it doesn't matter now, does it?"

Brenda spoke up immediately. "Of course it matters, you silly goose. Both grandmas have raised you and influenced you, for good or for bad. I would give anything to know something about my own grandmothers. I have nothing, I have no family history. I was adopted from an orphanage when I was thirteen by an elderly, childless couple. They were loving people who raised me from childhood until I was an adult. They both passed when I was twenty-two; they are the only family I have ever known. I don't have the memories you do. I wish I did."

She remained quiet for a while before asking, "Are you going to sell your grandmother's house?"

"I don't know what I'm going to do. I have to think this through. Lately, I have been having all kinds of thoughts and ideas. I'm not sure of what I'm doing or where I'm going; it's a feeling I don't like.

"As you know, living here in San Luis Obispo is marvelous. The sunshine warms both my body and my spirits. Along with the blue skies and the pleasant breezes I can't think of a more agreeable place to live.

"However, I do miss having the four seasons I was raised in when I was young. Fall, with its colorful leaves, crisp nights, and tangy apples, keeps popping into my mind; and, even though the winters could be nasty cold, I miss them a little.

"I've been thinking of all the unfinished family business that I need to address. I need to make peace with Grandma Givens, my father, and my brother, Mark. I want Tyler to meet his family and get to know his ancestry. Every child should be aware of his or her background. It's important. You can't move forward without knowing about your past.

"These thoughts have been on my mind even before I got this letter and now they are being pulsed as if they were in a food blender. I used to be so close to my family and now there is a gulf that I need to bridge. It's both comic and sad how old you have to get before you learn what life really is about."

**

Until her mother died, Katie Givens was raised in an atmosphere of love that every child deserves. She was the first born and her father absolutely doted on her. He considered her the cutest, smartest, nicest child in the world. Her mother had to caution him, many times, that there might be other contenders for these very same accolades. He was never convinced otherwise. She was wreathed in parental love.

However, there was more to it than just their love for her. Her mother and father made it a point never to have a bitter disagreement or an argument in front of Katie. Whatever squabbles they had, and they had their share, took place in private, away from her. They kept her world gentle and tranquil.

They tried to do things together as a family on the weekends. Every Sunday morning they would go to the early service at St. Mark's church. In the afternoon they would go to the Moose Hill Wild Life Sanctuary in Sharon, or the Stony Brook Bird Sanctuary in Norfolk, or the zoo in North Attleboro. The acres and acres of Christmas lights she saw at the La Salette Shrine in Attleboro dazzled Katie.

Grandma Barker lived close by and a phone call was enough to either set up, or cancel, a visit. Grandma Givens lived in Malden, an hour's drive away, and visits had to be scheduled ahead of time. Although she was treated nicely at Grandma Givens, Katie was glad that she saw Grandma Barker more often. Children are as sensitive to adult attitudes as barometers are to pressure.

Katie's world was shattered when her mother died giving birth to her brother, Mark. She went from adolescent unawareness to the brutal reality of grown up emotions. Her first reaction centered on the loss of her mother. In the beginning, she couldn't understand why her mother didn't come home along with her new brother. She clung to Grandma Barker who came over to take care of Katie and her new baby brother.

Through the next few years, as Katie grew older and tried to reconcile herself to the fact that her mother was gone, she began to notice that her father had changed. He was much quieter and more reserved. They did not do much together anymore and they completely stopped going to church. Her father paid hardly any attention to Mark. It was Grandma Barker who took care of Mark with Katie's help and they both showered him with the love his mother was not there to give. Katie quickly grew to adore her younger brother. He would trail her around the house and, in his childish voice, call her, "Sis."

When Katie was eleven, her father took her aside one day and told her that he was going to remarry. He explained that there was a woman who lived on their street and he had gotten friendly with her recently. She was a widow, a school teacher who had been Katie's teacher when she was in the third grade. They both needed companionship and, now, they were going to wed. He told Katie that he hoped she could get along with his new wife and learn to love her.

Katie was not as surprised as her father thought she would be. Grandma Barker had been telling her that, eventually, her father would get over his loss and that his life would continue. He was still young and it would be natural for him to try to find another companion. Without understanding it completely, Katie could accept what Grandma Barker told her.

Her future stepmother, Helen Schultz, soon to be Helen Givens, was a pleasant woman. She had no children of her own and she had always been attentive to and interested in her students. Katie had kind memories of Mrs. Schultz when she was her teacher.

After the marriage, when she moved in, Katie and she were cordial and friendly with each other. Katie especially liked the fact that her new stepmother gave Mark her complete love and affection.

However, there were two consequences of this new union that Katie couldn't fully understand. The first was that Grandma Barker never came over to their house unless she was invited. She was at the house often, but the arrangements were more formal, she just didn't come and go as she had in the past. Helen wouldn't think of preventing her from visiting her grandchildren, but there were changes in their lives at the Given's home. Mark was starting to go to school, her father and stepmother worked, and Katie was growing into her own world. She missed her grandmother's informal visits and called her on the phone every day. The second was that, after a while, she felt that her father wasn't paying enough attention to her and Mark. He was much more focused on the new woman in his life. They didn't do as much as a family as Katie would have liked and there was not an easy feeling of togetherness when the four of them went somewhere. It wasn't that the two children were disregarded, it was just that her father gave her and Mark a lot more "do's" and "don'ts" than they had ever had before. Katie felt that, in trying to please Helen, he was isolating himself from her. Not fully understanding the nuances of emotions, Katie began to resent the bond between her father and her stepmother. Her resentment didn't fade until after she had experienced the same emotions later in her own life.

When Katie graduated high school she enrolled at Boston University. Because of the way she felt, she elected to live on campus in the dormitories rather than commute on the trains that ran between Boston and Providence. After she graduated, she got a job as a librarian in one of the university libraries and moved into an apartment in Boston with two other women.

3

Being a parent and raising a child is a long, slow, irreversible process. Unlike any other species on the planet, it takes humans well over a decade to begin to mature. It is a long process fraught with peril. Parents conceive their offspring, bring their helpless child into the world, and protect and nurture them until the child grows up. Although the goal of the parents is simple, reaching that goal can be difficult. To raise a healthy, happy, well-adjusted child seems easy, especially since the child relies almost solely on its parents for guidance and love. However, being a perfect parent is impossible and the best any human can hope for is to be a good parent.

That is true because being a parent is only one of the many responsibilities adults face in their daily lives. Their attentions and their intentions are constantly being changed and challenged as they go about the business of living. The pressures and stresses from work, financial worries, other personal relationships, and world events often cause them to make rash judgements. Because parents have human frailties, parenting decisions can often times be off kilter or wrong. Add to this the fact that the playing field is different for each child as some children need more guidance and attention than other children. It is easy to see how parents can, without realizing it, stray from their goals.

John Givens fell into this trap. He was a good father to his first born, Katie, but he was not a good father to his second child, Mark. Yet, John Givens was completely unaware of the differences in his attitude. If he had ever thought about it, he would have insisted that he had treated both his children in the same way. From his point of view, he was correct, as he had tried to apply the same principles and the same discipline to each.

Despite what their father thought, Katie and Mark were brought up in completely different atmospheres. Part of the reason was that Katie and Mark had different personalities and they developed in different ways. Katie's problems never were at odds with her father's values while Mark's problems eventually led to a conflict between them.

More important though, was that John Givens, the father of Katie, was not the same John Givens, the father of Mark. The death of his wife, while giving birth to Mark, along with his problems at work, had embittered him. It was also true that, subconsciously, he held Mark responsible for the death of his wife.

John Givens was the third generation of Givens born and raised in Foxboro. He was an only child. While he was growing up, his father, William Givens worked as an engineer at the Foxboro Company while his mother, Alice, stayed at home and raised him. Although neither of his parents were strongly religious, both of them were upright and, in their own ways, grim. His mother was a fallen away Catholic who didn't attend church. She used her discipline and the Ten Commandments to raise him in her own home-schooled church. His father left John's spiritual background to his wife while he concentrated on the boy's physical upbringing. Exercise, discipline and determination were within his domain. As a result, although John was of average size, he had a stout and stubborn personality.

Starting as a youngster, John's father made sure that his son had duties and responsibilities commensurate with his age. By the time he was thirteen he had a large newspaper route and that quickly taught him the value of money. He learned about the stock market from his father and he soon had his own portfolio. He developed a remarkable capacity to pick stocks that made money.

Like all sons who are raised in close contact with their fathers, John grew to admire and adore his father. He unconsciously patterned himself after his Dad and picked up many of his habits.

Just before Pearl Harbor, his father, a West Point graduate who didn't stay in the military, went back into the army. He had been working at the Foxboro Company and could have claimed an exemption based upon his work but he felt his duty was to the Army. John Givens was swept up in the fervor of World War II, and when he was sixteen, he quit high school and joined the Company working in one of their laboratories. He was impressed with the way people worked together to get their jobs done. There was never any criticism of the government or of the war effort. Everyone seemed driven by only one goal: WIN THE WAR.

After he turned eighteen and was drafted into the army, he volunteered for the paratroopers but was turned down because of his eyesight, which was not good enough to aim a rifle but was sufficient to read piles of paperwork. He ended up in a warehouse in New Jersey issuing rations and clothing for overseas units. The war was nearly over in Europe when he got word that his father had been killed in action. His father's sacrifice was burnt into John's emotions for the rest of his life; especially when he contrasted it with the dull job he had been assigned. He became adamant about honor, duty, and country.

When he was discharged from the army, John returned to Foxboro and, instead of finishing school, he elected to return to work at the Company. He went back to the same mechanical lab where he had assembled and built pumps under the auspices of the engineers. He worked hard, learned quickly, and soon became one of the most dedicated employees at the Foxboro Company.

After he had been at the Company a few years, he met his future wife, Alice Barker, just after she was hired as a secretary for the head of his laboratory. She was a tiny blonde with a marvelous sense of humor and a zest for life. Since she had the same first name as his mother, she immediately caught his attention. She was the perfect opposite to the quiet, subdued John and they were immediately attracted to each other. Their courtship was happy and short and they soon married. They bought their own house in Foxboro, settled in together, and a year later Katie was born.

Those few years, from the time John first met Alice until just before Mark was born were the happiest years of John's life. He and Alice nestled and nested together and both reveled in awe over their daughter Katie.

Before Katie was born, her mother had a helter skelter, slap dash approach to religion; she usually showed up at St. Mark's Church for Christmas and Easter. John was more than content with this arrangement because he had had no formal religion during his upbringing, just his mother's observations and declarations. However, after Alice became pregnant, Sunday morning early service was an absolute must. John was also content with this arrangement because he felt that, for a child, any religion was better than no religion. They became faithful parishioners and went to church every Sunday.

This arrangement worked until after Katie's fourth birthday when, after church one Sunday, John was approached by three men who asked him to join the vestry. He told them he would consider their kind offer and give them an answer in a few days. After they got home and Katie was taking a nap, he told Alice what had happened and then he said, "We have a problem. I've never been baptized in any church and I've been taking Communion with you and Katie ever since we started going to St. Mark's.

"Should I get baptized now? If I do, they would probably withdraw their offer once they knew that I have been taking Communion under false pretenses. Should I keep quiet? If I do, I would become a vestryman under false pretenses; however, no one would know that I haven't been baptized. You have to decide what you want me to do."

They talked about what to do for quite a while before Alice decided that she would be embarrassed if her friends found out that John had been taking Communion all these years without being baptized. She asked him to join the vestry and never mention this minor detail. John had no problem with complying with his wife's wish; he quietly joined the vestry and stayed until his term as vestryman ran out after his wife's death.

Their married life was a quiet joy. They had youth, health, and the desire to please their partner; these are the basic bricks of marriage that the mortar of love cements into a wall of happiness. However, through no fault of his own, John began to have problems at work. One of the graduate engineers in his laboratory noticed a prototype pump that John was designing on his own. The engineer carried the idea to their upper management as his own design and he was immediately hailed as a brilliant innovator. John was angry and upset when he discovered that the engineer was claiming that the pump was his own design. What was worse though, was that there was nothing he could do about it. The engineer in question had covered his tracks by copying John's preliminary sketches into his own notebook in much more detail than John's sketches. In business, no one would take the word of a technician over the word of an engineer.

It got worse for him. A year later, the engineer who had stolen his idea was promoted to be the head of the laboratory. His new boss was aware of what he had done and he knew that John would not forget or forgive what had been done to him. As a result, he made John's life miserable by continually checking on him and micromanaging him. John felt trapped. He was a married man who had not finished his formal education and gotten a degree; getting a new job would be difficult. There was nothing he could do except continue on his present job while feeling anger and humiliation.

John's grief and pain over his wife's death, coupled with his negative feelings about his work, carried him down a path of loneliness. It was not that he felt sorry for himself; it was that he was trying to isolate himself from the pain of ordinary life. He became more reserved in his dealings with everyone, including his children. He just seemed to withdraw from everything and, while he did succeed in insulating himself from more pain, his new attitude began to give him a hardening of his intellectual arteries. Gray faded away until everything became either black or white. John did not realize it but his capacity for tolerance was slipping away.

What did help him get through his long, painful nights was that he again became interested in following the stock market. At first, he just tracked the rise and fall of the market without risking any of his money. He soon realized that he was making money theoretically and he began to buy and sell stocks and bonds on a small scale. His acumen was uncanny; he began to amass a large sum of money.

It was at this time that he met Helen Schultz. John had gone shopping at Shaw's Supermarket in Sharon one day and, when he came out of the store, it was raining heavily. The wind was blowing the rain hard, making for a chilly, nasty day. As he dashed for his car, he noticed that the car parked beside him had a flat tire on the driver's side. It was pouring so hard that he didn't notice anything else until he got inside his own vehicle. He looked over and saw a woman sitting in the car with both of her hands on the steering wheel. He spent a few minutes straightening out his wet clothes and the wet paper bags; when he looked up again the woman was still sitting there alone. He hesitated at first because he didn't know if someone was coming to her aid or not. After another short wait, John decided to find out if she needed help.

He rolled his window down and he motioned for her to do the same. When he saw her face he thought that she looked familiar. He asked, "Do you need help?"

She replied, "Yes, I'm stuck. I've got some frozen food and I need to get it home."

"If you want, I could drive you home."

"I'd hate to inconvenience you."

"It's really no inconvenience and I'd be glad to help you out. Where do you live?"

"In Foxboro, on Phyllis Road."

For the first time in this conversation, John was surprised. He said, "For heaven's sake, I live on Phyllis Road, so it's no inconvenience. Here, let me help you."

They loaded her groceries in his car and they drove the short distance in silence. When they passed his house he pointed and said, "That's where I live. Where is your house?"

She replied, "I live about six houses further down. Katie Givens lives in that house, you must be her father. My name is Helen Schultz. I was Katie's third grade teacher. I thought you looked familiar but I couldn't place you."

"How is Katie?"

"She's fine Mrs. Schultz. Which house is yours?"

She pointed it out and John parked the car in her driveway and helped carry the groceries into the house. She made him a cup of tea to warm him up and they sat and chatted for a while. When he was ready to leave, he told her that he would take care of her flat tire and then he asked for her car keys. She protested, but not too hard, and handed him her keys.

John drove home and called the mechanic that he always used at Joe's Gulf Station. He arranged for the tire on Helen's car to be fixed and, about three hours later, he drove the car back to her house. She came to the door and, when he handed her the keys, she invited him inside.

"I've made some coffee and sticky buns. Sit down and tell me how much I owe you for getting the tire repaired."

"Nothing, Mrs. Schultz. I was glad to help out. The tire had a nail in it but it's been patched and it is just as good as new."

They sat down and this time they had a long, comfortable conversation. It was then that John found out that Mrs. Schultz was a widow. As he was ready to leave, she said, "Just a second, Mr. Givens. I want you to know how much I appreciate your help. Whether you'll take my money or not, this is for you." With that, she handed John a double layered chocolate cake that had "THANK YOU" printed in white frosting across the top.

John was touched by her gesture. He had not expected any kind of a reward and her thoughtfulness was appreciated. So much so, that when he got home he asked Katie about her third grade teacher. Katie enthusiastically described how kind she thought Mrs. Schultz had been. This made John Givens begin to think about her. He was not a person who enjoyed wallowing in unhappiness or loneliness but now, after more than three years, it was time to put the past down and pick up the future. With this in mind, John called her two days later and, after chatting a bit he said, "Helen, thank you for the cake and the thought that it represented; I really did appreciate it."

Then, he paused a second and asked, "Would you care to join me at the Lord Fox and have a drink?" He waited, almost holding his breath, for her response.

"John, I would enjoy that but there is something that you should know. I am a recovering alcoholic; I don't drink alcohol if that is what you were suggesting."

John immediately replied, "Oh, I'm so sorry---," and then his voice trailed off and he stopped talking. He felt very foolish. He hadn't been aware that Helen was a recovering alcoholic. Would she think that he was apologizing for suggesting that they go for a drink or for the fact that he didn't know that she was a recovering alcoholic?

He heard Helen laugh and reply, "You don't need to apologize. I will be glad to go with you. I just wanted you to be aware that I don't drink alcohol."

They went to the Lord Fox and had soft drinks. Each asked questions and each answered questions as both were looking to leave their individual islands of loneliness. Their conversation wasn't deep and personal, that would come later; they were just searching for compatibility. They lingered so long that they also had dinner at the Lord Fox.

That was the beginning of their weekly dates. They stretched over many months and John began to appreciate Helen's warmth and charm. Especially when, after listening to him talk about his problems at work, she suggested something that he had not considered himself.

One time, he had finished telling her how his boss treated him and how unhappy he was, when she asked, "John, didn't you tell me that your investments were doing well?"

"Yes, they are. I've put together quite a little nest egg."

"Have you ever thought of leaving the Foxboro Company and spending your time taking care of your own investments? At least you'd be free from going to a job you don't enjoy any more. I don't know the money amounts but think about it. You'd probably be happier on your own if you left your job."

After going over the pros and cons of her suggestion he realized that he would be a lot better off both financially and personally if he left the Company. When he gave his notice, he had the small satisfaction of hearing his boss try to entice him to stay by offering him a large pay raise. It was an offer that was easy enough for John to refuse.

He started tending his financial garden from a desk in his cellar and soon his growing season was long and his harvest was bountiful. He became a much happier man. He began to enjoy his new lifestyle and it dawned on him how important Helen was to him and how much he needed her. He asked her to marry him and his second love started to bloom.

John's love for Helen Schultz was different from his love for Alice Barker. First love is an instantaneous conflagration while second love warms to the same temperature but much more slowly. Both sear the soul and bring happiness to the person lucky enough to find the magic potion. Love is the basic building block of life, yet we humans don't understand it. It brings us bliss but we have no idea where it comes from. We crave love but we don't know when it will enter our lives and we are miserable without it. Love is an addiction given by the gods that allows mortals to aspire to a higher, sweeter life.

***

Grandma Barker's house was on a cul-de-sac located near the center of town. There were only eight or nine houses grouped together and they were all small and old. Their owners had lived in them for years and they were friendly with one another: it was a tight knit community within a community. Together, they had banded together to resist progress and it was only in the recent past that all the houses had been forced, by court order, to connect to Foxboro's water and sewage systems. They had grumbled about giving up their wells and their septic tanks but they were pleased to be connected to the benefits of civilization.

Katie arose early the morning after she arrived. She had unpacked the car the evening before, fixed a simple meal for Tyler and herself, taken care of her cats, and then fell into her grandmother's bed and fallen into a deep sleep. The drive, along with her thoughts, had left her exhausted. She woke up and lazed in bed for a few minutes, thankful that she didn't have to drive that day.

After a while she got up and walked slowly through her new home. She peeked into the small bedroom to check on Tyler and then she walked into the living room. The furniture was a set of crimson, overstuffed, sofa and chairs. Katie always thought of them as "Italian Bordello." Nevertheless, they were now hers as she had decided to keep all of her grandmother's furnishings.

The kitchen, where she went to make coffee, was stark. Grandma Barker's work area was made up of a stove, a refrigerator, a sink, a kitchen table with mismatched chairs, cupboards with mixed china, and a collection of pots and pans. "Colonial Hodge Podge" was Katie's description of the place where her grandmother had prepared so many delicious cookies and meals. Katie loved this kitchen.

She made a pot of coffee, got Tyler's breakfast ready for him when he awoke, and then poured herself a cup and went out to sit on the porch steps. The chilly temperature was refreshing. She wanted to breathe some fresh air and think. She got to do the former but not the latter. As she stepped onto the porch she saw two women coming up the driveway. One was tall and old and the other was short and old, both were about the age of her deceased grandmother. Each of them was carrying a pan at chest level.

"Oh, my God," Katie thought to herself, "Mrs. Connors and Mrs. Buoni. I haven't thought about them for such a long time. Oh, I'm so glad to see them." They had been Grandma Barker's friends and neighbors for years and they had known Katie all of her life.

She ran down the driveway to greet them, kissing each one and hugging them despite the pans they were carrying. When the confusion of greeting each other was over, they sat on the steps and drank coffee.

The shorter woman, Mrs. Connors, said, "Katie, we heard that you might be coming back to live in this house. I saw your car pull in yesterday and I called Alma immediately. We are delighted that you came home. We miss your grandmother and we hope you'll stay in her house forever. I brought you some sweet rolls for your breakfast and Alma made you a casserole for this evening. It is not much but we wanted to show you that we remember your grandmother and that we love you."

Just then Tyler awoke and called for his mother and the women went inside to see him, talk to him, feed him, and fuss over him. Then, they settled in to reminisce and talk. After they chatted for what seemed a few minutes to them but was really two hours, Mrs. Connors asked, "Katie, what are your plans?"

"I really don't have any solid plans. When grandma's house became mine I decided to come home. I want to get in touch with my family because my brother, my father, and I have gone our separate ways. I want Tyler to have a family as he grows. I don't know really, I just felt like I was drifting and I'm looking for a safe harbor."

Mrs. Buoni nodded and said, "I'm sure you know that your father refuses to even acknowledge your brother. Your dad never forgave him for going to Canada during the Vietnam War instead of going into the army. When Mark finally came back to Foxboro hardly anyone cared where he had been or what he had done. He wasn't the only young man who objected to the war. The one person who didn't forgive him was your father."

Katie answered, "You're right, Mrs. Buoni, my father never understood why Mark wouldn't fight for his country. However, it goes deeper than that. I've always had the impression that he somehow blamed my mother's death on Mark. From the time Mark came home from the hospital my father has been distant and aloof towards him. He never approved of anything that Mark did; he gave him no encouragement. At least that was what Grandma Barker said and I think that she was right."

Mrs. Buoni was gossiping about a subject she both enjoyed and had talked about many times before. She quickly replied, "That's what your grandmother told us also, and Arlene and I think she was right. But who can tell about what goes on in other families?

" Mark came back to Foxboro after your grandmother died. Once he got settled, Arlene and I had him over to our houses for dinner several times. He was very close to his grandmother and he felt bad that he didn't get to see her before she passed. He seems so polite and so pleasant and yet so sad. I do hope your family can get together and resolve your differences."

"Oh, I do too, Mrs. Buoni. I want them to meet Tyler and I want him to meet them. We all need our families for love and support.

"How long has it been since you had Mark over your house?"

"Come to think of it, it has been a long time, months maybe. However, whenever he sees either of us he will have the driver of his truck toot the horn and Mark will wave to us."

"The horn on his truck?"

"Yes, didn't you know? He works as a laborer for the Foxboro Highway Department."

Katie was surprised by this information and she answered, "No, I never thought about him working; it never crossed my mind. It's obvious that he would have to have a job of some kind to support himself.

"I wonder what my father thinks about that? More important, I'm sure poor Helen is caught in the middle. My heart goes out to her. She has not had an easy life."

Mrs. Connors answered her question. "Your father tries to act as if Mark Givens is not in Foxboro; but it really doesn't make too much difference as he and Helen just became snowbirds and they now spend six months in Florida and six months in Massachusetts."

"Darn, I didn't know that. When do they leave for Florida?"

This time, it was Mrs. Buoni's turn, "Katie, they left about two weeks ago. They won't be back for almost six months."

Katie shook her head. "My timing has been all around perfect. It didn't dawn on me that Dad and Helen would be in Florida for the winter. Well, when they return, they'll be coming home to me instead of my coming home to them. That's not exactly how I wanted it but that's the way it's going to be. However, it won't be a surprise to them as I'm sure Grandma Givens will notify them after I call her. Coming home is more complicated than I expected it would be."

***

After Mrs. Connors and Mrs. Buoni left, Katie sat on her front steps thinking over what they had said about Mark. She was his older sister and they had been very close as they both grew into a world that had been distorted by the death of their mother. She had loved him, protected him, and understood him. Being estranged from Mark was something that Katie never thought would happen.

Yet, their last meeting had been so painful that Katie had avoided thinking about it. It had been over six years ago but she knew that both she and Mark still carried the pain and the damage inside; she felt very strongly that it was time to talk about it. The confrontation had taken place when her husband had directly imposed himself in a discussion they were having. That was the last time that the two had any contact with each other.

Mark had arrived at their apartment in San Diego, early on a Sunday morning, unannounced and unexpected. Through no fault of his, he came at a bad time as she and her husband, Mike, had been having domestic problems for a long time before Mark even showed up. What had started off as a happy marriage had bogged down into a quagmire of discontent.

The Friday night before Mark's surprise visit, Mike told Katie that he was going to be in a golf tournament all day Saturday and Sunday. Katie said that was all right with her but that he had said that this particular weekend he would help her install some new shelves in one of their closets. Mike flared up saying that he was tired of being bossed around and that he needed some relaxation. Katie did not respond and the rest of the evening Mike watched television and drank while she sat in the kitchen and read a book.

Saturday morning she fixed breakfast for both of them and he was gone until almost midnight when he came home drunk. That was when she and Mike had a bitter argument about their marriage. Sunday morning, while she was fixing breakfast and Mike was sleeping, her front door bell rang. When she opened the door, Mark was standing there.

Katie was surprised and delighted. She gave him a big hug and kiss. "Mark, Honey, where did you come from? What are you doing here? Come in, the coffee is just about ready."

As she was pouring him a cup, he asked her, "Sis, have you heard from Dad or Helen recently?"

"No. Why do you ask?"

"Because he and I had a disagreement and he ordered me out of his house."

Katie was stunned. She asked, "What are you talking about?"

"Listen. I'm getting close to eighteen and soon I'll be getting my draft notice. He is for my going into the army, I'm against it. We had a fight about the war and I told him that I wasn't going to go to Vietnam. I said that I would go to Canada before I got my draft notice. We were both angry and Dad got so mad that he ordered me out of his house."

Katie was shocked; she didn't know what to say. She poured herself a cup of coffee while she thought over what Mark had told her. Finally, she asked, "Why, Mark? Why? Why would you be willing to leave your country rather than fight for it?"

"Sis, that's just it. I don't believe I'm fighting for my country. I love you, I love Foxboro, I love our country; there's nothing that I'm against. But we shouldn't be in Vietnam; we are killing too many innocent people along with our enemy, whoever the enemy is. We are ruining Vietnam, carpet bombing it and spraying it with chemicals, and for no reason that makes sense. Not to me. I don't want to kill anybody or add to the destruction so I am going to go to Canada instead."

Katie was bewildered. "Oh, God, this is so new to me. Mark, I have to think. Dad really ordered you out of the house?"

"Yes, he really did. He said that his father had died fighting for this country and that he himself had been in combat in World War II. He said that he was ashamed to have a son of his that wouldn't fight for his country. I didn't mean to offend him but I feel as strongly against this Vietnam War as he feels in favor of World War II."

Suddenly, Mike's voice interrupted them. He had been listening to the conversation. Loudly and angrily he shouted, "And I totally agree with him. What the Hell are you doing here if you can't defend your own country? You peaceniks have no idea of what is really going on in this world. You'd sell America short and allow the god damn Commies to take over our government. I'm proud to say that I've bombed the shit out of those yellow Commie bastards.

"You have no idea of what you are talking about. There's not one real man in that whole bunch of you Canadian fairies. I'm sick of you candy-ass cowards."

Katie and Mark turned around to see Mike standing in the doorway in his pajamas. His hair was rumpled and his eyes were bloodshot. Mark replied, "I came to say goodbye to my sister. I'm not afraid to fight for what I believe in but I won't fight for what I don't believe in. That's why I'm going to Canada."

"Well, you goddamn sissy don't let the doorknob hit you in the ass on the way out. I consider you one of those Commie peaceniks and I don't want you in my apartment. I'm going to take a shower and you had better be gone by the time I am dressed or I'll throw you out." With that he turned and went back into the bedroom.

"Sis, I'm not doing this because I'm scared. I am but that's not why I am going to Canada. I don't want to kill someone because our government isn't doing the right thing. Why aren't more people asking, 'what are we doing there in the first place?'"

Katie went over to Mark and kissed him on the cheek. "Mark, I'm so sorry. Mike had no right to intrude in our conversation. This is strictly between you and me. He and I are having problems and I'll deal with him later.

"I'm glad you came to say goodbye but I hate to see you go. I don't know what to think or say, I don't know if I agree or disagree. I do know that we all owe something to our country. That's easy to say, I'm not in your shoes. Only you know what your conscience is telling you.

"I love you and I will miss you."

They hugged each other and both brother and sister cried. Katie walked Mark to his beat up automobile and she waved goodbye and cried until the car was out of sight.

When Mike got out of the shower, he and Katie got into a battle royal. Katie told him that whether he agreed with Mark or not, Mark deserved to be treated courteously. Mike shouted back that maybe she was soft on Commies just like her brother. She screamed that she didn't think her brother was making the right decision but, right or wrong, he was her brother and Mike should not have sworn at him or ordered him out of their apartment.

Mike got so mad that he came around the counter towards Katie and raised his right arm as if to slap her. Katie calmly picked up a butcher knife and pointed it at him. He stopped a few feet in front of her. "Drunk or sober, don't you ever try to strike me. Ever. I won't stand for it." She took the knife and drove it, point first, into the wooden kitchen table.

The argument ended with Mike storming out of the apartment to play golf and get drunk while Katie stayed in and cried.

4

The first few weeks after Katie returned to Foxboro she was busy trying to get her life settled. She applied for a job at the Foxboro Public Library and started work almost immediately. Both Mrs. Connors and Mrs. Buoni constantly fought for the job of baby-sitting Tyler when Katie couldn't be home, so she had no problems in that regard. When she wasn't at work, she was busy cleaning her new home, which was, in reality, an old house badly in need of attention and repair. The property had been benignly overlooked by a real estate management company since her grandmother went into a nursing home and both the inside and the outside of the house had been neglected. Inside, she and Tyler were safe from the elements but Katie had the feeling that the house was dingy and the paint had faded; outside, the gravel driveway was rutted, the garden was overgrown and the bushes needed to be trimmed. There was much work needed to restore the house.

Along with the concerns about her new home, Katie was disappointed when she returned to Foxboro and found that her father was in Florida with Helen. She had hoped that her fence mending would begin between herself and her father and then spread outward to include Mark. However, after talking with Mrs. Buoni and Mrs. Connors, she realized that her original ideas were not practical. If her father wouldn't even acknowledge that his son lived in the same town, the divide was deeper than she realized and she would have to change her approach.

She also discovered that reestablishing herself in the community was a slower process than she had anticipated. Getting a job and placing Tyler in school was relatively easy. Settling the details of her grandmother's will and establishing a pattern to her life took a lot more time. In a complete oversight, she had not taken into account the condition of her grandmother's house and she spent almost all of her spare time working to make the inside cozy and warm. The whole house needed cleaning and painting, inside and out, and, because of neglect and age, major maintenance was also required. Even though it was a small house, washing and painting the inside walls, which became her first project, turned into a large project. The weather was beginning to be too cold to work outside and Katie decided that she would have to let painting the outside go until spring.

After the initial inrush of activities settled into a pattern, Katie called Grandma Givens and found that she was in an assisted living home in Malden. One Saturday afternoon Katie and Tyler drove to Malden to visit her. Katie was shocked at the changes to Grandma Givens. Instead of the cool, aloof, elegantly dressed woman she remembered as a child, Grandma Givens was a frail, stooped woman who sat in a wheelchair with a shawl draped around her shoulders to keep herself warm. She had to be reminded that Katie was her granddaughter and she kept referring to Tyler as "Mark."

When Katie got back into her car she wept because of her grandmother's plight. She felt heavily that the present time was chipping away at her childhood memories. She baked cookies and visited Grandma Givens at least once a month always taking Tyler with her. Katie inherently felt sorry for her father, she knew that he had to be upset and worried about his mother's deteriorating condition. She was almost a little remorseful that she considered him too harsh in his attitude towards Mark.

That was when another fact became obvious to her. Her father's attitude towards Mark would take much more than a song and a dance to change. He was adamant, hard-nosed, and absolutely inflexible about Mark going to Canada to avoid the draft. Any reconciliation, if there were to be one, could only happen if her father changed his outlook and accepted what had happened; and Katie wasn't sure whether he could, or even would.

Realizing that she had underestimated her father's inflexibility towards Mark, Katie began to reexamine her own relationship with her father. When she was younger they had been very close but, unlike Mark, she had never challenged his authority. From the time she left home for school and then marriage, their feelings had varied from closeness to coolness. Now, there was a gap between them and, what made the gap worse, was that neither of them had ever talked about their feelings for each other.

Her mood, when she finally established a routine in Foxboro as a widow, was nothing like the mood she had when she left Foxboro as a bride.

***

By comparison with her other concerns, her job at the library was relatively easy and satisfying. The head librarian was a woman who had held that job for almost thirty years and Katie remembered her from the time she was a young girl taking books home. The rest of the staff was friendly and pleasant and Katie soon found herself enjoying her job.

Working at the library was interesting because the librarians had a preview of everything that was taking place both in their community and inside their local government. Working for the town they heard all of the planning that took place within the town hall and working for the public they heard all of the gossip that took place within the town. The staff knew that Katie's brother had gone to Canada to avoid being drafted, and they knew that, sometime after President Carter's amnesty declaration, he had returned to Foxboro. They also understood that he and his father were not on speaking terms, and they knew that her brother now worked for the highway department. They were also aware that Katie was a widow who had returned to her grandmother's house. Katie was more than a little uncomfortable with all that was known about her but everyone knew everyone else's business at the library and that was the way it was.

Even so, there were small mysteries that, no matter how hard they tried, even the librarians couldn't solve. Katie's sister workers pointed out one of the most intriguing mysteries shortly after Katie joined the staff. The librarians nicknamed him "Mountain Man" because he was a tall, thin man who had long hair kept in a pony tail, and a beard and mustache. The staff knew that he worked for the highway department because he often came in immediately after work, wearing his Foxboro highway department uniform. The staff also knew his real name, Thomas Booker, and his Foxboro address, but they preferred to call him "Mountain Man."

The only other thing they knew was that he was a prolific reader.

He would come in with a few of his own books, work for an hour or two, and then read books on history, music, science, or fiction. He was polite, patient, and completely uncommunicative. He would answer any question he was asked but it would be the shortest possible explanation. The staff decided that he was going to school somewhere and he came to the library to do his home work; however, they couldn't get any insight into who "Mountain Man" was, where he came from, or what his background was. It was obvious that he wanted it kept that way. They would try to engage him in conversations but he never nibbled at their banter bait. To a group that was curious about everyone and everything, he was a total enigma.

Katie got to know him by sight and even checked out his books several times but she didn't try to strike up a conversation. She believed that he was entitled to all the privacy he wanted and she didn't try to intrude. She only wished that her personal circumstances were as shrouded as his were.

During the time it took for Katie to get her home cleaned and to establish a routine to her life, she wondered how to get in touch with her brother. So much had happened since their last meeting when Mike had ordered him out of their apartment. That had been years ago and Katie was well aware that, since then, she had changed considerably. She was sure that Mark had also changed and that he might not want to see her again. She thought over several plans and scenarios and was still hesitant to do anything when Mark solved the problem for both of them.

Early one rainy morning, Katie was sitting in the kitchen drinking coffee and making a grocery list when she heard the engine of a heavy vehicle pull up beside her house. She heard a horn toot once. Puzzled by the commotion, Katie went to the window and saw that an orange dump truck with the Foxboro town insignia on its door, was parked in her front yard. There were two men in the cab both of them had beards, mustaches, and long hair. She recognized the driver as "Mountain Man" but she couldn't tell who the other man in the truck was except that he was waving at her.

Katie ran to the door and threw it open. The man who was waving yelled, "Sis! Sis!"

She started to cry. "Mark? Is that you inside that beard? Oh, oh, come here and let me hug you." They embraced each other, rocking back and forth, and neither of them spoke for a few seconds.

After a while Katie stepped back and said, "Mark, I am so happy to see you. I want you to meet your nephew, Tyler. Why don't you and your friend come in for a cup of coffee?"

"I don't know if we can stay, Sis. We're not supposed to use our trucks for personal errands. Let me talk to Tom, he's the one who would get in trouble if we got caught."

Mark walked back to the truck and soon returned with Tom. He said to Katie, "Tom says it is important for me to visit with you. If there is any trouble, he will handle it. Tom, meet my sister, Katie Oldfield."

As Katie shook his hand he said, "You're the new librarian? I didn't realize that you were Mark's sister." He smiled and added, "You certainly don't resemble each other."

Katie replied, "Until either I grow a beard or he shaves, I'm not sure anyone can really tell. Both of you, come in right now."

Tom sat and listened while Katie and Mark seemed to be continuously talking at the same time. Katie roused Tyler and brought him into the kitchen. Tyler was overcome with seeing two bearded strangers and he sat next to Katie and was quiet. His mother had to prompt him to reply to any of Mark's questions.

Soon Mark said that they needed to go to work and, after promising that he would return for dinner in a few days, he and Tom got back into their dump truck, backed out of the driveway, and drove away. Katie was so happy that she hummed and waltzed all day.

The next two months were pleasant for Katie and Mark as they both began to bridge the gap that separated them. The reconciliation started slowly. Mark came over to dinner once a week after work. He would sit in the kitchen talking to Katie and Tyler as she prepared their meal. When dinner was finished, he would do the dishes and clean the kitchen while she prepared Tyler for bed. Mark would read to Tyler and, after he was tucked in, Mark and Katie would sit in her kitchen, drinking coffee and talking.

At first, because of the painful memories of their last meeting in San Diego, their conversations were about their present work and their daily activities. Because they had lost contact for so long, neither wanted to goad or gore the other by mistake, so they kept to safe topics. It was Tyler, with his childhood innocence, who dispelled the awkwardness. Tyler quickly got over his shyness of meeting a bearded man and he and Mark fell in love with each other. When Tyler saw Mark, he would yell, "Uncle Mark," and run to him with open arms. Mark would raise him up, hug him, and they would play together until Katie needed Mark for something. Having her son and brother together pleased Katie and the warm feelings among all of them melted their reservations.

Soon, he was coming over in the evenings to help with washing the walls and the painting. One evening, as they were taking a break, Katie asked him, "Mark, I've been meaning to ask you, how did you know I was home? I was trying to think of how to get in touch with you when you showed up in that truck. How did that happen?"

"Very simple. Mrs. Buoni called me and told me you were in Grandma's house. At first, I kept telling Tom about it and he kept telling me to come over and talk to you; I kept hesitating. One morning, he told me he was tired of me talking about whether I should intrude or not and he just drove over here. I was so happy he brought us together that I bought him a beer after work that day."

A few evenings later Katie and Mark were sitting in the kitchen drinking coffee and eating a piece of blueberry pie that Katie had just baked. Mark had been quiet for a while before he said, "Sis, I'm so glad you and Tyler came back. I've missed you so much. I just wish you weren't still mad at me."

Katie was surprised at his statement. "Mark, what are you talking about? I'm not mad at you. I've never been mad at you. Where ever did you get that idea?"

"I don't know, exactly. When I got to Canada I never heard from anyone and I know that Dad was angry with me, so I assumed everyone else was also mad."

Katie replied, "I was never mad at you but I was always confused about what happened between you and Dad. He won't tell me about it and I don't want to put Helen in the middle by asking her, so I really don't know. That's one of the reasons I came back. It hurts me to think that you two are strangers to each other."

"Sis, it's a long story."

"Listen to me Mark, it's Friday night. I've got a freshly baked pie and a pot of coffee, and I'm searching for peace of mind. I don't care how long a story it is; I need to hear it. So, start."

"Well, OK, but it may not make sense because it's a jumble inside my head." Mark sat for a while pushing a blueberry around with his fork. Then, he took a deep breath and continued, "Dad and I were never close. He always kept me at arm's length. When Helen came to live with us you both tried hard to close the gap between us. Even though I tried to be a good son there was nothing I could do to gain his affection; and I really tried hard.

"Even before you left Helen did her best to change Dad's attitude. She gave me all of her love and, for me, she is the mother I never had. I love her. She tried but Dad never did warm up to me, and all I ever wanted was just some love and attention.

"By the time I started high school, my own outlook and attitude began to change. I began bumping into the adult world outside of my own family. I went over my friends' houses, saw how they lived and treated each other, and I began to compare their families to mine. I also began to hear about something that I had not paid attention to, the Vietnam War.

"My best friend was Jacky Taylor, I don't think you ever met him. He was a year older than I was but we were in the same class. He was always laughing and joking, we were inseparable. God, I haven't thought about him in years; we were so close back then."

Mark paused, and then resumed talking. "Anyhow, I enjoyed going over to his house. His mother and father and Jacky and his older brother, Billy, were always busy doing things as a family. Billy joined the army and I was over at their house when the family was notified that Billy had been killed in action in Vietnam.

"It was awful. From that point on, the laughter stopped. Jacky's mother did nothing but weep, his father cursed, and Jacky wanted revenge against 'those communist bastards.'

"He dropped out of school, got a forged birth certificate, and joined the marines. A year later, he was also killed in action in Vietnam. I went to his house to offer my condolences to his mother and father and they were like zombies. I'm not sure they even knew who I was."

Mark stopped speaking.

Katie knew that his memories were sour. In an attempt to give him some relief she said, "I knew Billy but I don't think I ever met Jacky. Those deaths and that family must have weighed heavily on your decision to go to Canada."

Mark replied, "Sis, it was awful. I wasn't even seventeen and I had lost my best friend and saw his family embalmed in sorrow. I never really thought of the Vietnam War as good or bad politics. That was too big a picture for me.

"All I knew was that I didn't want to hurt or to kill anyone or anything. Yet, what I saw on television was that we were spraying the country with Agent Orange, we were killing enemies and innocents alike, and we were turning Vietnam into a hellhole. I saw that horror and felt its effects in Foxboro. That was the only way I looked at Vietnam.

"At the same time, the tension in our house began to get worse. We would watch the news at night and, as the protesters got more vocal, Dad would get angrier and angrier with them. He really believed that we were fighting the Communists and that we had to win. We absolutely had to defeat them. He would shake his fist at the television and swear at the 'idiot peaceniks' that didn't support our country.

"Of course, he knew about the deaths of Jacky and Billy. In a town as small as Foxboro everyone knew. Those deaths made him even angrier. He would watch television and mutter that we ought to use nuclear weapons and really defeat the commies, that it was either them or us.

"After that Sis, I can't honestly remember the details of what happened or why. Don't forget that was what, over eight years ago?

I know that Dad felt that anyone who didn't support the war was a traitor and I have always felt that I was a disappointment to him. Dad was a veteran of World War Two and past commander of the Foxboro American Legion. He expected me to be more of a hawk.

"As the casualties mounted and the fighting got more bitter, Dad became absolutely intolerant towards anyone who suggested we get out of Vietnam. I began to lose my temper when he kept saying we should use more force. He could have been right, he could have been wrong; the only thing I knew was that my best friend was dead. I was a teenager and didn't understand any of the politics; all I saw was that it had ruined the Taylor family.

"As I look back on it now, I think that one of the reasons we couldn't even discuss the war was that we were looking at it from different sides. Dad was interested in the politics that got us there and the threat it posed to our way of life. I was looking at the devastation of the villages and the lives of the people, both in Vietnam and in Foxboro.

"Helen was caught in the middle. If ever a stepmother should be made a saint it should be her. From the moment she stepped into our house, she and I had an open, honest relationship between us. She gave me her love and she did her very best to change Dad. She tried to calm him and get him to be more tolerant, but nothing would change his mind. She made as much of an impression as spitting in the Sahara desert. She did everything she could and I love her for that. Despite Helen's attempts, he just wouldn't, or couldn't, stop raging at the 'peaceniks' and me for defending them.

"As I approached the time when I would have to register for the draft, a friend of mine told me that he was going to Canada to avoid military service. I hadn't thought about what I was going to do but I knew that I would have to do something.

"One night, Dad was particularly obnoxious about the 'peaceniks' and me for not knowing what was good for our country. I got angry and told him the first thing that came to my mind; that I was going to go to Canada. That's when he threw me out of the house. That's what happened and Dad has not spoken to me since."

Katie, who had been leaning forward as she listened, sighed and said, "Mark, I'm so sorry. I didn't realize that your life was so painful."

"Dad can be stubborn but I never saw him as intolerant as he was with you. I've had my share of problems with him but nothing like yours. Until Mom died he was a perfect father and I have much fonder memories of him than you do.

"You're right about Helen. I have come to admire and love her as much as you do. She has never discussed any of this with me and I am sure that's because she doesn't want to appear disloyal to Dad. She does love all of us, but as Dad's wife, she has to be careful of what she says. It must bother her to see our anguish.

"What you said about you and Dad makes me unhappy. You both deserve better from your father and son relationship. Hearing how Dad treated you, I'm surprised you came back to Foxboro at all."

"Sis, I'm like you, I had to come back. First, my life in Canada wasn't very good. I went there as a scared kid without completing my high school education. I ended up doing menial jobs and scarcely able to make ends meet.

"Worse, for me, was the attitude of most of the other Americans who lived in Toronto. In their own way, they were just as intolerant as Dad. They were extremely critical of our country. I wasn't, I just wanted the war to end. I was kind of a loner in a foreign country.

"Besides, I was homesick. I wanted to make peace with Dad and be with Helen and hoped that, eventually, you'd come back to Foxboro.

When I read in the Foxboro Reporter that Grandma Barker had died, I knew that, sometime, I had to come home."

"Mark, how the devil were you able to read the Foxboro Reporter in Toronto?"

"Easy, there were four of us from Foxboro and we chipped in to buy a subscription to our hometown newspaper. Anyhow, when I got back I got a job with the highway department. Although Dad won't talk to me, I do see Helen occasionally and we have lunch together. She never talks about Dad but I am sure that she tells him about our meetings. Anyhow, she told me about you and where you were living."

"Mark, if you knew where I was this last year why didn't you get in touch with me?"

"Sis, I thought that you were angry with me like Dad is. Besides, Mrs. Connors and Mrs. Buoni told me that you might be coming home to Grandma Barker's house. I just kept hoping and praying that you would be returning."

Mark leaned across the table and took Katie's hand. "Sis, I made my choice and I'll live by its consequences, however, I need you and Helen to help me. I need guidance. I don't want Dad mad at me. All I want is peace and happiness and love. Is that asking for too much?"

Katie was almost startled that her brother was wrestling with the same questions that she was. She leaned across the table and gripped his hands, "No Mark, you're not asking for too much. You're looking for the same things in life that I am. Maybe we'll find them, maybe not, but you and I will give it one Hell of a good try."

It took Katie a long time to fall asleep as she wrestled with heavy thoughts of her father, her brother, and what her marriage had been.

5

Two months after she started working at her first job in Boston Katie met Mike Oldfield. It was at a party that she saw a handsome, young man wearing the dress white uniform of the United States Navy. When they were introduced, his good looks and his quick-witted charm immediately attracted her. He was an Annapolis graduate, a RIO (Radar Intercept Officer) on a jet fighter bomber, and he had just returned from a tour of duty in Vietnam. Lieutenant Mike Oldfield fascinated Katie with his descriptions and stories of military life and his daily routine on board an aircraft carrier. She didn't follow all the technical details that he talked about but he was living and working in a world that was absolutely foreign to Katie and she was captivated to hear about it.

For three months, at least once a day, they either saw each other, or spoke to each other on the phone. During this time Mike would try to get Katie to go to bed with him and finally, when she kept refusing his propositions, he proposed marriage instead. Katie gladly accepted his proposal and she and Mike went to Foxboro for a weekend, to meet her father, Mark, and her stepmother.

It turned into a happy, carefree visit as Mike charmed everyone with his personality and his stories. By the time they were ready to leave on Sunday, Katie's father was walking around with his right arm across Mike's shoulders and they were both addressing each other by their first names.

Katie and Mike were married at St. Mark's Church in Foxboro and, after the ceremony they drove to Omaha, Nebraska, to meet his family. From there, they went to San Diego, Mike's duty station. At first, Katie's life in San Diego was intoxicating. The climate of southern California was like heaven, especially for anyone born and raised in New England. She admired the Navy's "CAN DO" attitude and their social life seemed to consist of nothing but tennis, bridge, parties and celebrations.

That time, from planning for her wedding until the second year of her marriage, turned out to be the happiest time of her life. During her wedding preparations her father was relaxed, pleasant and generous about the bills. He was alive and lively, working with Helen and enjoying all the details that necessarily accompany a wedding. Katie often thought that he was much like the father she adored before her mother died. When her father waltzed with her at the wedding reception, the poignancy of the moment brought tears of joy and sorrow to both of them.

She left for San Diego married to a handsome naval officer and full of love for the whole wide world. It was Katie's first trip out of New England and she was absolutely enchanted with California. The bright, warm sun bathed her body, her mind, and her soul. The color and the smell of the exotic flowers overwhelmed her. She would tell everyone, "We don't have too many palm trees on the Foxboro Common."

After they got settled in San Diego, their lives took on a daily routine similar to all married couples. Mike would report to the Naval base every day and he would be gone until evening. Katie would meet with the other officer's wives and play cards or drink tea. Their weekends would be filled with social events, parties, picnics, and occasional weekends in Mexico. The parties were of every description for any kind of a reason and party time was from early Friday evening through late Sunday afternoon. Their social life was fast, wet, and shallow.

During the first few months of Mike and Katie's marriage, their relationship was more of a courtship than a conjugal couple. They were excessively solicitous of each other and never made a decision without seeking the other's opinion, no matter what was being discussed. As they relaxed and began to be more comfortable with each other their marriage became more of a partnership and Katie was delighted to be both a wife and a helpmate.

Katie lived inside her state of bliss for almost two years before she started to ask herself questions. During this time, the only real disagreement that the two of them had was over having a family. Katie wanted to get pregnant while Mike was absolutely opposed to becoming a father. There were discussions but no arguments. Occasionally, Katie would wonder about the amount of alcohol Mike would drink at these parties. He seemed intent upon drinking everything in sight. She quickly dismissed any of her observations because she was also drinking more than she had ever drunk before and she just didn't want anything to interfere with their marriage.

It is too bad that reality sometimes sours the nectar of happiness.

One Saturday night, at the Officer's Club, both she and Mike began to drink even more heavily than they usually did. Mike got so drunk that he passed out and his friends had to carry him home. They both had been drinking hard but this was the first time Mike had gotten falling down drunk. Katie undressed Mike, got him into bed, and fell into a stupor herself.

She awoke early Sunday morning with a splitting headache, a dry mouth and a queasy stomach. She took three aspirin, put on a pot of coffee, and headed for the bathroom. After a hot shower and two cups of black coffee, Katie began to feel a little better. She looked in on Mike who was still passed out and then went and sat on their small balcony.

She thought to herself, "Damn, this is absolutely stupid. It's insane. I have done nothing but become a social butterfly since I got here and I'm drinking too much booze. I used to enjoy working out and jogging and now I don't even bother. I have no purpose and I'm cutting down on my chances for having healthy babies. This has got to stop. I also think that Mike has to cut down on the booze."

Katie decided to start on a new path and she also decided not to tell Mike about her decision. That was because she had learned that, although he was her husband and her knight in shining armor, there were a few chinks in his suit of mail. She was aware of them but she figured that Mike had discovered some of her shortcomings and, since he never mentioned her faults, she wouldn't mention his. They had had no overt quarrels yet and Katie had no thoughts that they ever would. That was soon to change.

Katie still considered Mike very charming and engaging but she also began to think of him as a bit selfish and irresponsible. His attitude about having children was one example. Mike categorically admitted that the only reason he didn't want to be a father is that he didn't want the responsibilities of being a parent; he wanted to be able to have a social life, which included drinking and partying.

She also noticed that there were two sides to Mike. Most of the time he was pleasant and easy to get along with but there were times when he would pout and lose his temper. And she was not sure when, or even why, he would have these outbursts. She was still learning about him and she was sure that he was doing the same about her.

Late Sunday afternoon Mike woke up and came out on the balcony where Katie was reading the newspaper. His hair was mussed, he needed a shave, and his eyes were bloodshot. Katie said, "Well sleepyhead, Good Morning to you."

Mike scratched his head and replied, "Boy, I must have eaten some bad food last night. I feel awful."

She innocently asked, "And what did you think about the beverages?"

"I thought they tasted pretty good, didn't you?"

"Oh yes, so good that I woke up with a bad hangover this morning. Listen, I have made a pot of chicken soup and I have baked some bread. Why don't you clean up and we'll eat?"

After they had eaten they sat on the balcony enjoying the sun. Mike had opened a can of beer and Katie was sipping a coke. Katie thought that this might be a good time to broach a subject she had been thinking about all day. "Mike, would you mind if I applied for a job at the base library?"

He slammed his can of beer down on the table so hard that beer sloshed from the top. He shouted, "What? Are you trying to shame me in front of my friends? Do you want them to think I can't handle money and that my wife has to work? No one else in the squadron has his wife working. I won't have it. NO! NO! Absolutely not."

Katie was stunned at his reaction but she wasn't going to cower and just defer to his outburst. She replied, "Calm down Mike. All I did was ask you a simple question. I have no intention of 'trying to shame you in front of your friends' as you put it. It's just that I need to be doing something, I don't like being idle. I didn't mean to upset you and I certainly don't want to embarrass you."

Mike cooled off almost immediately. He grinned and said, "I'm sorry, Katie. I guess I lost my temper. I am a little concerned about our finances. Maybe we should tighten our budget."

That ended the conversation but it marked the beginning of a change. Although they still shared conversations, laughed at jokes, had sex, and gave every indication of a happy couple, a small crack had developed between them. Katie tried to be more careful in what she said when she spoke to Mike while Mike seemed more distant and preoccupied. It was the start of a long slide that started slowly but went faster and faster as it continued downward.

***

When Katie had gotten settled in San Diego she made it a point to stay in touch with her family. There would be phone calls every week or two, usually made by her, to talk with her father, Mark, and Helen. Whenever she spoke with him, her father was outgoing and pleasant. Occasionally, Mark would call her just to talk and she and Helen would exchange long, chatty letters on an infrequent basis. Everything on the "home front," as Katie called it, seemed normal.

A few days after Mark left for Canada Katie got a short note from Helen saying that her father and Mark had had an argument and Mark had left home. Helen did not go into detail and, after much thought, Katie decided not to mention Mark's visit. She reasoned that her father was upset and he probably didn't want to talk about it. Helen had been kind enough to write to bring her up to date. Katie would not discuss the incident unless either Helen or her father brought the subject up.

As a result of this family rift, the tone of their phone conversations appeared to change, or so it seemed to Katie. Her talks with her father were less casual and more guarded. He would ask her how she was feeling and if she was having any problems. That was something he had never asked her before. Katie wasn't sure she was correct, but it seemed to her that there was a different attitude in their relationship and this puzzled and bothered her. She didn't want him to become remote and distant again.

In turn, she began to be concerned about him and she would ask Helen if anything were wrong. Helen, not wanting to speak out of turn, would assure her that her father was doing well and that nothing was going on in Foxboro. Still, she felt uneasy. On the other hand, Helen's letters remained long and upbeat so Katie was unsure whether she was correct or not.

One day Katie got a letter from Helen saying that she and Katie's father were flying to California to visit Helen's second cousin and they wanted to stop by for a day or two to see Katie and Mike. Katie called Helen immediately to get the details of the trip because she was so pleased and excited. She wrote their itinerary on her calendar; they would arrive on a Wednesday afternoon and depart on the following Sunday morning. She was so happy that she turned the volume up on her radio and danced around the apartment.

Katie had a busy afternoon. She first made reservations at a hotel for her father and Helen and then she sat down and made a list of things to do and places to visit. When she was finished, she looked at her list and she decided that, if they only slept three hours a night, they could do almost everything in about a month. She wrinkled her nose and knew that her travel tree had to be pruned.

When Mike got home, there was a sumptuous meal waiting for

him. Katie remembered how well he and her father had gotten along and she wanted Mike to be pleased that they were coming to visit. So, she made his favorite dish, beef stroganoff, and his favorite dessert, lemon meringue pie.

Katie waited to see what Mike would do. If he got a beer from the refrigerator, opened it, and then came and talked to her, he was in a good mood. If he took his beer and wandered into another room, he was not in a good mood. After he was settled, Katie found him sitting in front of the television watching the sports channel.

She decided to try to cajole him into a good mood. She said, "Hi, Honey, how was your day?"

"Hi, Katie, it was going good until some shyster Jew lawyer called me to tell me that I owed his client two hundred dollars. I told him that his client and I had settled between us and he said, 'NO! His client had not settled and wanted full payment on the bill.' He was nasty and I don't appreciate being bothered at work by these bloodthirsty bastards."

Katie was a little concerned. She had noticed that Mike occasionally came up with debts that needed to be paid immediately and she didn't know where they came from or what they were for. He always said that they were for the car, a black Desoto convertible that Mike took care of with love and joy. He spent hours every weekend washing and waxing the car and then driving around the neighborhood waving at people.

She asked, "What are you going to do? What was the bill for?"

"Don't be concerned, Katie. The bill was for something I bought for the car a while back and I forgot to pay for it. I have settled with the lawyer. I mailed him a check but we are going to have to be very careful about our finances for a while."

She didn't quite understand why these financial crises ever came up. She was always very careful with their money, her father had taught her to be prudent and frugal. In spite of that, these emergencies seemed to crop up unexpectedly. Her first thought was that maybe she could talk Mike into letting her go back to work. However, now was not the time to discuss their finances and she really wanted to talk about the visit of her father and Helen.

After a dinner that he enjoyed, along with a few more beers, Mike seemed more relaxed. Katie served him pie and coffee and then said, "Mike, Helen and my father are coming to visit us."

Mike put his fork down and leaned toward her as he spoke. "Did they give you any reason for this visit?"

"No Mike, but don't forget that we haven't seen them since our visit to Foxboro. Helen is coming to California to visit a relative of hers, so they thought they would come and see us also. They won't be staying with us very long and I am looking forward to their visit."

"And that's the only reason they mentioned for coming here? Who did you speak to?"

"I only spoke to Helen and that's what she said. What other reason besides visiting us would there be?"

Mike leaned back and picked up his fork. "None, I guess." He thought for a second and added, "Good. Let them come visit us. It will be a good thing." Having said that, he asked for another slice of pie.

As time sluiced the days off of Katie's calendar, she began to get more excited about the upcoming visit. Although she was not completely aware of it, Katie was lonely. She had left her nest permanently and she missed her family. More important, she was not sure whether she was doing well or not. She was still in love with Mike but they were not as completely meshed together as they once were. Their lifestyle seemed to be going at a faster pace but it was not as deep as it once was. There were shadows looming in the background and she was concerned about them. As a result of these submerged doubts, she was looking forward to seeing Helen and her father. She was hoping that this visit would reassure her that she was on the right path.

The visit did not go as Katie had either planned or expected. It veered off course from the very beginning when the plane carrying her father and Helen arrived almost eight hours late. The Boston to Chicago flight was delayed because the plane developed a mechanical problem just before takeoff and the Chicago to San Diego flight was delayed further in Chicago. Katie's visitors arrived tired and unhappy.

Mike had taken the day off and had made a reservation for dinner that evening at the Officer's Club. When it became apparent that Katie's father and Helen would arrive late, Mike cancelled the reservation and, after he rescheduled it for the following Saturday night, he became extremely quiet. The result was that, when Katie's father and stepmother finally showed up at 9 PM, there were four glum people.

Katie had fretted all day until they arrived and then, after greeting them, she became concerned. Her father and Helen were tired and she was worried that they were hungry. So, despite a few mild protests, she insisted that they all go to a nearby Chinese restaurant to eat something. The meal did wonders for them.

Katie, her father, and Helen all drank hot tea. Helen was a recovering alcoholic and Katie had cut down her drinking to the point where she had only an occasional glass of wine. Knowing Helen's history, Katie would not drink while she was with Helen. Mike was the only one who drank anything alcoholic and he limited himself to two Martinis.

More important, as they talked and ate everyone seemed to revive and their glumness disappeared. By the end of the meal each of them had the feeling of peace and happiness that food and laughter always bring. Helen and Katie's father said goodnight outside Katie's apartment and left for their hotel saying they would be back in the morning when Katie would make breakfast for them.

However, their breakfast date was never kept because Katie was involved in a traffic accident and she ended up in the hospital. Early the next morning, Katie got up and started her preparations for breakfast. She wanted everything to be perfect and that was when she noticed that she did not have as much sharp cheddar cheese as she needed. She decided to go the grocery store on a quick errand and get more cheese and, in addition, some more coffee cream. Ordinarily, she would have ridden her bike to the store, some three blocks away, but she was in a hurry. So, she grabbed the keys to the Desoto and drove over. There wasn't much traffic and that surprised her. She hoped she could get her shopping done and get back to the apartment quickly.

On the return trip, she was stopped at a red light and, after the light turned green, she started to accelerate. She was almost through the intersection when a tractor-trailer ran the red light at high speed and rammed the Desoto's rear quarter.

The force of the crash spun the car around and the Desoto skidded out of control until it hit a telephone pole broadside. The impact bent the car in the middle and partially wrapped it around the pole. Her seat belt saved Katie from being thrown out of the car but the initial shock of hitting the pole knocked her out.

When she came to, she didn't understand where she was or what had happened to her. She could hear voices but she couldn't follow what they were saying. She had a headache and she ached all over. She groaned as she lifted her arm and, all of a sudden, Helen was standing over her.

"Katie, Honey, you had us all so worried. Your father and Mike and I have been sitting here for hours waiting for you to regain consciousness. The doctors say that you are going to be fine. Is there anything you want? Water? Anything?"

Katie murmured, "Where am I? What happened? Is it time for breakfast?"

Mike came over to her and said, "Katie, a truck ran a red light and our car was crushed. They had to use the Jaws of Life to get you out of the wreck. You didn't break any bones and the doctors think that you will be up and about in a few days. You did have us worried for a while."

Katie was still confused. "But what about breakfast? I haven't made it yet. And where is my father? Isn't he hungry?"

Her father immediately came over to her. "Here I am, Katie Dear. Don't worry about me being hungry. The main thing is that you are going to be all right."

"But I promised to make breakfast for you and I want you to enjoy your visit."

Her father stroked her cheek with the back of his hand and replied, "Katie, just being with you is enough for me and Helen. All the arrangements you made are fine but just knowing you were not seriously injured is good enough. Now, you must rest and we will talk later."

The rest of their visit was a blur of incoherent episodes for Katie. She was under medication and drifted in and out of consciousness while she kept trying to remember what had happened to her. At the same time, she underwent a series of tests while her doctors kept her under observation to make sure there were no internal injuries. She slept a lot. It took her quite a while to reconcile what had happened with what had been scheduled to happen.

All of her plans, all of her trips, were scrapped. Instead, Helen was her constant companion from early morning until early evening the next two days. Mike took her father to the Naval Base with him and then they would come to the hospital and visit her in the afternoons and early evenings. By Saturday the test results showed that she had not sustained any serious injuries and the doctors advised her that she could go home on Sunday. She was beginning to feel better and she wanted to go to the Officer's Club with them on Saturday night. When she got out of bed she was dizzy and she ached all over; she just wasn't up to it. Mike, Helen, and her father went to dinner without her.

Early Sunday morning, Helen and her father came to say goodbye before they continued their trip. They seemed quiet and subdued. Katie attributed their mood to the fact that they were leaving while she was still in the hospital. She was discharged later in the day but it was a full month before she began to feel better.

***

One morning, as she was getting ready to go jogging, the phone rang and, much to her surprise, it was Alma Buoni on the other end of the line. She told Katie that she was calling because she didn't know whom else to talk to. Katie's father and stepmother were in France and wouldn't be home for two weeks. Grandma Barker was being taken out of her small house and moved into a nursing home and someone in the family should know about this. Mrs. Buoni's message upset Katie and she said that she would buy tickets and fly to Boston immediately. They talked for a few minutes longer and then Katie, telling Mrs. Buoni that she had to make reservations, hung up.

Katie made all the necessary arrangements even before she called

Mike to tell him what she was doing. For once, there were no comments from him about their expenses. Early the next morning, he drove her to the airport and she flew to Boston to see her grandmother. When Katie arrived at the nursing home, her grandmother didn't recognize her, or even acknowledge that she was by her bedside. She stayed there for three full days talking to her grandmother and remembering her when she was alive and vital and a major part of Katie's life. Then, sobbing, she kissed Grandma Barker goodbye and left, aware of what inevitably would happen.

She flew back to San Diego late Friday night and she was somber and quiet on the drive home. When they reached their apartment, she told Mike not to bother carrying her luggage in, she would get it in the morning after she woke up. She was exhausted and all she wanted to do was get into bed and sleep.

Katie slept until after one in the afternoon on Saturday and, when she awoke, Mike was drinking a beer and watching the sports channel on the television set.

"Hey, sleepy head," he greeted her, "I was going to wake you up in a day or two if you didn't rise before then."

She replied, "Wow! I really slept. Seeing Grandma Barker in that nursing home really got to me. She has changed so much even from the time that you last saw her."

They talked about her trip for a while and then Katie took a shower and had something to eat. She went to the car to get her suitcase and, as she was lifting it off the back seat, she noticed a pink cloth under the driver's seat. Thinking that it was a cleaning rag that Mike had left in the car, she put the suitcase down on the cement and reached for it. What she picked up was a pair of women's panties and a bra.

Katie was stunned. She had never dreamed that Mike would be

unfaithful and the bra and panties she found hit her like a punch in the stomach. She sat down on her suitcase, put her elbows on her knees, and buried her face in her hands. She quietly wept as she was overcome with bitter, negative thoughts, outrage, guilt, anger. She had tried to be a good wife and a helpmate, why couldn't Mike have talked with her if there was a problem? What had gone wrong? Was she to blame?

All of a sudden she felt a tiny hand on her shoulder, and a child's voice piped up, "Mrs. Oldfield, are you all right?"

She looked up to see Madeleine, the six-year-old daughter of one of her neighbors. She wiped the tears from her eyes and hugged the girl. "Yes, Madeleine, I'm fine, I just got some bad news, but seeing you makes me feel much better."

She carried the suitcase and the bra and panties into their apartment wondering how she was going to give Mike a chance to tell his side of the story. She wanted to believe that there would be an innocent explanation for having women's underwear hidden under his car seat but she was almost sure that Mike was cheating on her. As she went towards the bedroom to unload the suitcase, Mike was still looking at the television. She dropped the underwear on his lap without saying a word. When she returned, he looked at her and asked, "Where did you get these?"

"From under the driver's seat in the car."

Mike shrugged, and then he said, "Well, I guess you caught me flagrante delicto."

Katie waited for him to say more. After a few moments of silence, her emotions began to rise again. In a cold tone she asked, "Is that all you have to say to me?"

Mike replied, "What else is there to say?"

Her temper began to show. She yelled, "What else is there to say?

Damn it Mike, you broke our marriage vows and you cheated on me! You make me feel cheap and unwanted and all you tell me is that I caught you? This is no game. I gave you everything I have and you have hurt me."

Mike finally broke away from watching the television and looked at her. He replied, "Katie, Honey, you shouldn't feel that way. I married you and I love you. It's just that sometimes, as a man, I need a change. My straying doesn't mean anything. I truly love only you."

Katie answered angrily, " Mike, that's total bullshit. Your fooling around means everything. It means you love yourself much more than you love me. You certainly are not honoring me with your affairs. You are showing me contempt. That is certainly not love or respect. So, stop treating me like an idiot by telling me you love only me." With that, she walked out of the room.

The next few weeks were even more tense. Katie was aloof and cold and rejected all of Mike's pleas that he loved only her. When Mike realized that Katie was not going to easily forgive him he began to change his story. He started to tell Katie that it really was her fault he went astray because she was not satisfying him when they had sex. That accusation made her even angrier.

After thinking about her situation, Katie did two things without bothering to consult Mike. She went to the base library and got a full time job as a librarian. She also saw a lawyer about getting a divorce. When she told Mike that she was thinking of leaving him, he solved his problems by quickly volunteering for another tour of duty in Vietnam.

While Mike was gone, he would write to her and she would dutifully reply. At first, the letters were formal and impersonal, but, as Mike's turn to rotate home approached, his letters took on a different tone. He wrote that being close to life or death had made him aware of what was important to him. He admitted that he was wrong and he asked her to forgive him. He would never disappoint her again and he would love, honor, and cherish her.

At first, Katie was unyielding and unforgiving. However, as time passed, and her anger subsided, her reasoning began to exert more influence on her judgements. Despite Mike's faults, she loved him and did not want a divorce. With his absence, and his pleas for another chance, Katie relented. She was willing to try to save their marriage.

They decided to get away from their friends just to be alone with each other. As a result, when Mike returned, they went to Banff for a three-week vacation. It was a happy interlude and, during their time together, they could not get enough of each other and it was during this time that Tyler was conceived.

When Katie told Mike that she was pregnant, he was not as pleased as she was and, six months later, he began another affair. One night, after he had been drinking, Mike drove his new convertible off the road over a cliff. Both he and his passenger, the wife of one of his best friends, were killed instantly. The autopsies showed that Mike was well over the legally drunk limit and that his passenger, who was pregnant, was carrying his child.

6

When Katie called and told her father and Helen that Mike had been killed in an automobile accident, they were both shocked by the news. Helen told her husband that she should be with Katie as she coped with being pregnant and being a widow. Helen quickly prepared to fly to California. Although Katie had not given them many of the details, both of them had suspicions about what had happened; they knew a lot more about Mike than Katie realized.

Helen arrived just after the funeral and Katie's demeanor was what she expected. Whatever Katie was feeling inside, on the outside she was aloof, composed and not willing to talk about Mike. Helen stayed until after Tyler was born and she and Katie grew even closer to each other just by respecting their mutual silences. They would sit over coffee or tea and chat, or they would shop for baby clothes, or go to a movie or a concert, or just walk the beaches. For Katie, it was a healing process, for Helen, it was a helping process, for both, it was a peaceful interlude.

At the start, Helen avoided any reference to Mike. She wanted to wait until Katie was willing to voluntarily talk about him. However, since they were both interested in each other, they had a mutual basis for talking about other subjects. Katie knew Helen as her third grade teacher and then, years later, as her father's wife. She wanted to know more about Helen as a person. At first, Helen was reluctant to talk about herself but, as they exchanged confidences, she hid nothing of her background from Katie.

Helen Schultz was born and raised in Ayer a small town northeast of Boston. Her only sibling was an older sister who died of pneumonia and, as a result, her parents wanted to keep her sheltered from harm. They only succeeded in keeping her sheltered from life. She attended Catholic schools until she graduated high school and went to Simmons College. She graduated eager to learn but knowing hardly anything about the world. Foxboro was one of the towns that offered her a job as an elementary school teacher. She visited the town and the school and, after her interview, she accepted the job. After she had rented an apartment she decided to buy a new automobile, so she went to a Ford agency on Route 1. The salesman, Peter Jordan, was also part owner of the agency and he overwhelmed Helen. He was twenty years older than Helen, nicely dressed but not flashy and he was well mannered and polite. He wooed Helen, literally sweeping her off her feet, and they soon married and moved into his house on Phyllis Road.

Once they were married, Helen realized that she had made a mistake. He was a wife beater and she became a victim of spousal abuse. She was terrified of her husband and ashamed of her choice of partners. One of the cruelest injuries, because of his beatings on her body, was the loss of her ability to have children.

In time, she came to believe that she was responsible for her husband's anger and cruelty, so she never said a word to anyone about the beatings that she had to endure. Instead she became an alcoholic.

Peter Jordan died of cancer five years after they were married. Helen finally got some good out of the marriage; she inherited the house, a large life insurance premium and a share of the automobile agency. She also legally went back to her maiden name. However, the damage to her life had been done. She couldn't face living without drinking.

One night the Foxboro police pulled her over for drunk driving and, when she was brought to the police station, she called the only person she could think of for help, her school principal. Helen liked and respected her principal and she didn't know anyone else to turn to. The principal came down to the station and got Helen released. The next day she told Helen that she either had to get help or that she would have to resign. That is when Helen joined Alcoholics Anonymous.

All of Helen's personal history was new to Katie and it made her feel closer than ever to her. It also made her eager to learn more about her stepmother. She said, "Helen, our home on Phyllis Road was the only home I knew until I got married. Did you move to Phyllis Road before my mother and father bought their house?"

"Oh no Katie, your mother and father were living there before I moved in. Interestingly enough, since our houses were so near to each other, your mother was one of the neighborhood women who came over to greet me after I got settled."

"Did you meet my father about the same time?"

Helen replied, "No. I never met your father until after your mother passed. That was a long time after you had left my classroom. I knew of him, from your mother, but we were never introduced to each other."

Katie asked, "Well, how did you meet him?"

Helen had to smile, "You don't know? Your father isn't one of the greatest communicators is he? He has a tendency to keep everything bottled up inside himself and that is not good.

"You asked how we met? In a rainstorm in Shaw's parking lot. I had a flat tire and your father offered to help me. I was smart enough to let him drive me home. That's how it began for us."

Katie was surprised, she said, "I didn't know that."

Helen reached over and held one of Katie's hands. "When your father proposed to me I asked him if I shouldn't come over to the house and meet with you and Mark and he told me that wouldn't be necessary. I've often felt that was a big mistake on my part, I should have insisted on it. It also shows that your father is not as aware of other people's feelings as much he should be."

"Why do you think you made a mistake?"

"Two reasons, Katie. When I had you in third grade, you were lively and happy. When I came into your house you were so grave and reserved and Mark was so quiet that my heart ached for both of you. I should have tried to get to know both of you on your own terms the moment that I accepted your father's proposal.

"I also think that maybe Grandma Barker wouldn't have felt she was no longer needed if I had met her before I moved in. After all, I was not only replacing her daughter, but her grandchildren were going to be guided by someone besides herself. She was a lovely person and I tried to keep her close to you and Mark but she felt that it would be best if your upbringing was left to your father's new wife. I wish she had stayed closer to you and, also, to me.

"Katie, you were so very young when your life was turned upside down, I don't think you knew everything that was happening. Your father was facing other difficulties when your mother died. After she passed, he not only struggled with her death he was also had problems at work. For a very short time, he started to drink. That didn't last long but it shows how upset your father was.

"You probably were unaware of any of this."

"You're right, I never realized anything other than my mother's death."

"Sometime or other you and your father should talk about that critical period. It would be good for both of you to be frank with each other. You would have a chance to see your father as a human being who had personal problems. He has his faults and his shortcomings, as we all do, but he has always tried to be honest and sincere. On the other hand, he is extremely stubborn and it is difficult for him to change his mind. He has been generous, warm and loving to me but he can be exasperating. I think about you and Mark and your father constantly and I wish I could resolve the differences that exist among you."

It was after that conversation that Katie began to look at her father not only as a parent but also as a person. For children, parents are role models, protectors, disciplinarians, and, sometimes, even friends. Parents are their signposts as children start their lives and, as a result, they rarely dwell on the human side of their parents. Children shy away from thinking of their parents as having either sex, or bodily functions, or passions. Children enshrine parents in their imaginations and they separate them from human fallacies, human passions and human shortcomings. Katie took her father down from his shrine and began to treat with him honesty, not awe.

After thinking about her father for several days Katie asked, "Helen, why is my father so hard on Mark?"

Helen, who was drinking coffee at the time, put her mug down and sat so silently that Katie was not sure she had heard the question. Finally, Helen sighed and replied, "Katie, this is a subject of much disagreement between your father and me. I have seen Mark grow from a child into a man and I love him as if he were my own flesh. He is a son that any father should be proud of. But your father is obstinate, pigheaded, and above all prejudiced. He feels that Mark, by going to Canada instead of joining the Army, has hurt and dishonored not only him, but also his father. Your father has taken the virtue of patriotism and raised it to the level of religion. I don't agree with your father: I think he is carrying his emotions much too far.

"You have to go back to the time that your father was a young man. World War II was at its height when your father was drafted into the Army. The whole country was united and it was almost unthinkable to say that we should not be fighting to save our country. No one would have thought to challenge either our government or what we were doing. Your father volunteered for the paratroopers, but he was turned down. He ended up as a clerk in a large warehouse dispensing equipment and keeping records. When his father, your grandfather, was killed in action, he began to solidify his thoughts on what patriotism should be. It may be that his not being able to avenge his father's death made his feelings stronger. I don't know, I do know that, through the years, his pride in being an American gets louder and more shrill.

"The Vietnam War came along and your father saw people, whom he disagreed with, start criticizing the government for getting involved in Vietnam. He felt it is disloyal and unpatriotic to challenge our government in wartime, and those 'peaceniks' at first made him uncomfortable. As the war got messier and more devastating, they became more vocal and your father got angrier. Both sides lost all sense of reason and civility. Then Mark, who truly believed that we should not be in Vietnam, told your father he wouldn't fight for his country.

"Your father made two mistakes. He lost his temper and, while he was angry, he ordered Mark out of his house. Your father knows he shouldn't have done what he did but he doesn't know how to correct his mistake. Especially when they both still disagree about Vietnam.

"Believe me, though, your father still wants to hear news about Mark. He loves him; he just doesn't understand him. Especially, when Mark believes in a cause that your father feels dishonors the ideals that he has defended all of his life."

Katie sighed, and said, "It is quite a mess, isn't it?"

It was after all these conversations took place that the harmony and rapport between Helen and Katie allowed them to finally discuss the subject that was on both of their minds. They could both begin to talk about Mike without either of them flinching in self-defense.

One morning, after dawdling over their coffees, Katie suddenly asked, "Helen, how familiar are you with the details of Mike's accident?"

Helen paused for a few seconds before replying, "Susan, my second cousin whom we came to visit, sent your father and me all the newspaper clippings about the accident. Also, your father obtained copies of the autopsies. So, to answer you, I know a lot about the accident."

For the first time in all the weeks Helen had been there, Katie broke down and started to cry. For ten minutes she wept uncontrollably while Helen cradled her. She stopped, snuffled, wiped her nose and eyes and said, "I am so sorry. I just lost control. It is hard to lose someone you love."

Helen said, "Yes it is. You have been remarkably brave to keep control as long as you have."

"Oh Helen, I'm not brave and I'm not in control. At night, I cry and I curse and I realize that I am lost and empty. Our marriage ranged from happiness to hatred but I loved Mike. Yet, I'm haunted because he died along with his pregnant mistress. Was that his fault or was that my fault? Did I drive him away or was that his nature? Along with trying to understand his death, I am wrestling with my conscience."

Katie stopped speaking and began to silently cry again. Helen got up, kissed the top of Katie's head and went into the kitchen and made a pot of tea. When she returned, she poured Katie a cup of tea and added some sugar and a strong shot of whiskey. After two servings, Katie started to feel better.

Over the next several days Katie began to speak about both the good and the bad times of her marriage. Once she started talking, she couldn't seem to stop. It was similar to releasing the air from an over inflated tire, as she talked the pressure inside her became less and less. She still had her grief and her self-doubts but, at least, she could think about them in a calmer way.

It was this inner calm which helped Katie decide to tell Helen of her deep seated emotional despair. She could not come to grips with Mike's infidelities. She was a bubbling cauldron of rage, humiliation and doubt. Why hadn't Mike honored her the way she had honored him? How much was she to blame for his promiscuity? Could she have prevented Mike's tragic death? She was in turmoil over these questions which would never be answered; and all the while she was carrying Mike's child. It was this torment that disturbed her so much.

After listening to Katie and hearing her deep doubts, Helen decided to tell Katie about her own run ins with Mike. She had not planned on saying anything about them but, to ease some of Katie's concerns, Helen felt that she was obligated to speak out. She was not trying to vilify Mike because, in many ways, he had been likable.

Her intent was to show Katie that it was Mike's own thoughtless and irresponsible attitude that was his problem; what happened was not Katie's fault. Both Katie and Mike were victims of his actions. Helen wanted to acquaint Katie with Mike's negative traits without destroying his image because Katie still had many loving memories. On the other hand, Helen didn't want to bungle her opportunity to help Katie resolve her problems. It would be a delicate task to tell the truth without disparaging the dead, so Helen had to wait for the correct time and opportunity.

Katie herself supplied Helen the opening. One day, as they took a break from going over a list of names for boys and girls, Katie asked, "Helen, you never said anything about what you and Dad thought when you read the details of Mike's accident. It must have come as a total shock."

Helen looked at her and replied, "Katie, it was not a total shock. By this time, your father and I were both totally disillusioned with Mike."

"Disillusioned?" Katie echoed, "How can that be? I was under the impression that my father was very fond of Mike. Look, this was when Mike and I came to Foxboro to announce our engagement." She reached behind her and got the picture of her father and Mike, each with one arm around the other's shoulder.

"Yes, Katie, that is how it started out. Your father was very proud to have Mike as his son in law. Especially since Mike was in the Navy and had served in Vietnam. Your father believed Mike was doing what he would have done if he were younger. Mike replaced Mark in your father's affections. Then, certain things happened that you undoubtedly knew nothing about and we both became disappointed with Mike."

Katie shook her head almost in disbelief. "Helen, what are you talking about? What did I not know about? What things happened?"

Helen took a deep breath, and then asked, "Did you know that

Mike ran up gambling debts and that, over time, he borrowed a large sum of money from your father?"

Katie was completely surprised. She asked, "Gambling debts? Are you sure? I can't believe it." Then she thought for a second and added, "Yet, Mike would occasionally tell me that he had an unexpected expense for his car, and we always seemed to be living on the edge of our income. When did all of this begin? If Dad was giving Mike money why didn't Dad let me know?"

"That was part of Mike's devious charm," Helen replied. "He started calling your father shortly after both of you got to San Diego. Mike told your father that you were running up some small bills buying clothes and that his pay was being held up because of a computer glitch. At first, they were small sums.

"Soon, Mike was asking for fairly substantial amounts of money. When your father began to question Mike, he said that you were almost out of control when it came to spending money.

"What was your father to do? He didn't quite believe Mike but he didn't quite disbelieve him. Should your father call you and ask you what you were doing? If you were spending recklessly would you admit it? He was in a quandary and he was upset over it.

"He needed to know what was really happening, so he hired a private detective in the San Diego area to find out if you were running up debts. Three weeks later, the detective's report came back and your father was furious after he read it. Not only did it say that there were no outstanding bills in your name, the report also stated that Mike was gambling, drinking, and womanizing.

"It was after he read the detective's report that your father decided that he was not going to give Mike any more money. However, your father wanted to talk to Mike face to face. That was the major purpose of our trip to California, it was our attempt to see if we could help. I did want to visit my cousin but, more important, we hoped to be able to help you if you needed support of any kind. Instead, you had that terrible car crash and that changed all of our plans."

Helen stopped talking and, for a few minutes, both of them sat silently. Finally, Katie sighed and said, "I knew Mike was drinking too much and I suspected he was womanizing. With his squadron's flight schedules being rotated fairly often, he could come and go at odd times. However, I had no idea that he had a gambling problem. I feel so embarrassed that I didn't know anything about any of this.

"Did Dad ever get to talk with Mike?"

Helen answered, "Yes, and it was an ugly scene. The Saturday evening we went to the Officers Club your father told Mike that he knew the money he was giving him went for gambling debts and not for clothing bills. Your father purposely didn't mention anything else in the detective's report other than Mike's gambling debts. He wasn't trying to have an argument he just wanted to make his position clear. When he told Mike that he wasn't going to give him any more money, Mike didn't appear to get upset. He drank a little more but he was civil and friendly and talked quietly.

"However, when we got back to your apartment, everything changed. Mike got aggressive and nasty and he and your father got into a shouting match. Finally, Mike punched your father, with all his might, in the stomach. The force of the blow caused your father to sink on the floor.

"I will never forget this. He sat there retching and Mike laughed, got himself a beer, and said, 'Old man, you and your bitch better leave before you really get hurt.'

"I helped your father to his feet and we left. He was so humiliated that he has built a wall of hate around Mike. He refuses to talk about him and he is not pleased that you are carrying Mike's child.

"Katie, I feel so badly for you, your father, and Mark. You all deserve the happiness of each other's love but, the way it is right now, each of you is totally disconnected from the other."

They sat quietly and held each other's hand. Katie was depressed and saddened by Helen's revelations about the events that, until now, she had not known had taken place. After she thought about it, she finally decided that she would rather be told about them than be ignorant of what had happened.

They spent the rest of the afternoon talking about how foolish men could be.

What Helen had not told Katie was how the fight had begun. She thought that what she was relating to Katie was bad enough without making matters even worse. When the three of them got back to the apartment, Katie's father had gone to the bathroom. The moment he left the room Mike had come over to Helen and attempted to kiss her. When she resisted he tried to put his hand under her skirt. She didn't want to make any noise and she was resisting him when Katie's father came back into the room and saw her trying to push herself away from Mike. When he went to Helen's rescue, Mike turned on him and purposely hit him in the stomach.

7

Near the end of October, Katie heard that one of her coworkers at the library was planning to bake a large batch of cranberry bread. That conversation reminded Katie of the many times that she and Grandma Barker had baked cranberry bread in her kitchen. During a staff coffee break one day, Katie had a chance to talk to Mrs. Menefee, the woman who was going to do the baking. Mrs. Menefee told her that she had five sons and twenty grandkids and that she had been baking bread for over twenty years. She was going to bake about eighty loaves and give them as Christmas gifts to her friends and family. She baked them early and then froze them until the Christmas season.

As they discussed the work involved in baking, cutting the cranberries, sifting the flour, chopping the nuts, and oiling the pans, Mrs. Menefee invited Katie to help her and, at the same time, bake her own loaves of bread. Katie thought that was a good idea and she gladly accepted.

She arranged her schedule to be off on a particular Friday and to open the library on the following Saturday morning. Then, she asked Mrs. Buoni if she would take care of Tyler until she was finished with her baking. Her request started the usual tug of war between Mrs. Connors and Mrs. Buoni over custody of Tyler and ended with Tyler in the guardianship of both at the same time. She gave them Mrs. Menefee's phone number if they needed to contact her.

It was cloudy, cool, and raining as Katie drove to Mrs. Menefee's house which was in East Foxboro, several miles from Foxboro Common. As she was driving along the country lanes she didn't pay much attention to the weather. She was mentally checking to make sure that she had brought enough ingredients to bake all the loaves she and Mrs. Menefee would need. When she arrived, they both unloaded the car and began the work they had been anticipating. The next few hours were filled with their activities as they measured and mixed their ingredients, baked their breads, let them cool, and removed them from their baking pans. Both women were pleased with their efforts as the kitchen filled with the tantalizing aroma of baking. They were so engrossed in their tasks that they lost track of time.

Late in the afternoon, they took a break, had a cup of coffee, and cut slices from their first cranberry loaf. They sat down and relaxed as they tasted their freshly baked bread with cream cheese when Katie glanced out the window and exclaimed, "My goodness, it's snowing."

They both rushed to the window to see a heavy mantle of snow covering the entire landscape. Mrs. Menefee exclaimed, "This wasn't predicted. I wonder how bad a snowstorm we will get. Katie would you like to stop now to make sure you can get home without any trouble?"

Katie replied, "Oh no, Mrs. Menefee, now that we are midway, I would prefer to finish today instead of starting over some other time."

Mrs. Menefee agreed, so Katie called Mrs. Buoni to find out how

Tyler was doing. First, Mrs. Buoni got on the phone to tell Katie how good Tyler was under her care and then Mrs. Connors had to get on the phone and tell Katie how good Tyler was under her care. Katie thought to herself that she should have had twins so that Mrs. Buoni and Mrs. Connors could each have their own "grandchild." Before she hung up she arranged for Tyler to spend the night with either of his "grandmothers" if she were late.

By 9:00 PM the baking was finished and Katie helped Mrs. Menefee clean up the kitchen. She left shortly after that, pleased with what they had accomplished but she felt tired. After brushing the snow off her car she started her trip home. As she left the driveway, she suddenly realized that it was a different drive over to Mrs. Menefee's house than it would be on the way back. She had driven in daylight and the road had been visible. Now, it was night, the roads had no streetlights and she had to rely on her headlights. She wasn't familiar with any of the country lanes she was driving and the falling snow made it difficult to see the road itself. Katie had to drive slowly.

Even being careful didn't save her from having an accident. As she rounded a curve with a downward slope, the car skidded on the ice and she slid off the road into a ditch. For her, it was a slow motion horror trip, as she clutched the wheel with both hands while the back end of the car swung around and spun the car out of control. The front end came to a stop on the shoulder almost at a right angle with the road.

Katie sat in the car trembling in fright. She knew that she had not been hurt but the vision of her other accident flashed through her mind as the car was sliding. After a minute or two, she took a deep breath and began to force herself to function normally. She tried driving the car back onto the road without success. The back wheels spun and could gain no purchase. The car would have to be towed out of the ditch.

"Damn it!" She muttered. "What a stupid thing to do. What the Hell am I going to do now?"

She looked at her gas gauge to see how much gas she had. The tank was nearly full. She couldn't remember how far the nearest house was but she knew the road she was on was fairly deserted and not traveled too often. Although it was snowing, the temperature was just above freezing. She decided that her best course of action would be to stay in the car and wait until someone drove by. She could flag help by flashing her headlights and blowing her horn. She shut off the lights, tuned the radio to WEEI, and listened to the news about the unexpected snowstorm sweeping Eastern Massachusetts.

Katie sat there for an hour Eastern Standard Time although it seemed much longer than that because she was on Katie Distress Time. No traffic came down the road as she waited and she began to be worried. She again thought of whether or not she should leave the car and walk when she saw a pair of headlights driving towards her. When the vehicle got closer, she rapidly began to honk the horn and switch the headlights off and on. The vehicle stopped just in front of her car. It was one of the town highway department trucks. Katie felt an inrush of relief.

A man walked over to the driver's side of the car and Katie rolled the window down as he approached. He asked, "Are you injured?"

Katie was surprised to find that the man talking to her was Mountain Man. For some reason she was a little embarrassed as she replied, "No, Mr. Booker. I'm not injured, just annoyed that I skidded off the road and got stuck. I tried to be careful but I didn't succeed. Now, I don't know how to get out of this mess."

Mountain Man replied, "Don't be too concerned Mrs. Oldfield, you're not the only one having trouble. The ice is making driving treacherous and quite a few other people have skidded off the road.

You're not hurt and your car is not damaged so it shouldn't take much to set things right."

Mountain Man's soothing words calmed Katie and made her feel a little better. She asked, "How will I be able 'to set things right'"?

"Well, the first thing I can do is drive you home. When I finish plowing, I will pick Mark up and both of us will come back here and free your car and bring it over to your house. That is, if you will give me the keys to your car."

"Mr. Booker, if you did that, I would be grateful. Especially since I'm scheduled to open the library tomorrow morning."

"Mrs. Oldfield, I can't promise you a time, but I will get your car over to you as early as I can. Although, I'd be very surprised if you see a crowd on the library doorstep when you get to work tomorrow morning."

He helped her out of her car and into his truck. Katie had never ridden in a heavy-duty truck before so the twenty-minute ride to her house was a new experience. When she climbed into the cab she was surprised at how high over the road she was in comparison with her automobile. The cabin was hot and noisy, as Mountain Man had the heater going full blast. The chair bench was covered in plastic and it was not soft, which made for more bouncing than she was used to. The headlights made the snowflakes sparkle as they fell through the light beams and the yellow light on the top of the cab turned the falling snow into gold flakes as the light rotated.

As the truck started down the road, Katie heard loud static and then the voices of men talking over a radio. She saw the radio mounted under the dashboard along with a hand held microphone that had a coiled cable running to the radio. Mountain Man turned the volume almost completely down and said, "That's what we use to keep in touch with each other. When the superintendent isn't around some of the guys talk about everything except work. I don't use the radio, I only talk when they call me."

With the radio almost off, Katie heard another sound; it was a portable radio that was on the seat between them and it was playing a Sibelius symphony. Katie listened for a second and then asked, "How often does this guy Sibelius call you?"

He chuckled and replied, "Not as often as I would like. That's my way of passing time pleasantly during the hours I'm plowing."

"Does anyone know you listen to classical music?"

"Oh, I wouldn't tell anyone that. I call it 'country and western from a different country' and let it go at that. I'll turn it off if it bothers you."

"No, I enjoy the music of that 'other country.'" There wasn't much more conversation between them, but Katie enjoyed the trip because of the new experience of riding in a snow storm and listening to the music. When they arrived at her house, Mountain Man escorted her to the door, took her car keys, and then left.

Katie took a hot shower and fell into bed. Before drifting off to sleep, she remembered that it was because of Mountain Man that Mark had first come over to her house; she also was curious about a man who would plow snow in a dump truck while listening to classical music.

She awoke early the next morning with a start, wondering where Tyler was. Then she remembered that Tyler was with one of his "grandmothers" and she relaxed. She looked out her window to see a six-inch blanket of snow on the ground. She immediately saw her car sitting in her driveway. The driveway had been plowed and the car had been backed in so that it was facing the road.

As she drove from her house to the library she saw that the highway department was clearing the snow from around the Common. After all the town roads had been plowed, the entire downtown area was cleared of snow by the highway department. Two front end loaders scooped the snow into the town dump trucks. The trucks would offload the snow in an empty field near the high school and then returned to the Common. Although clearing the Common added longer hours to an already overworked highway department, the residents expected the Common to be clear of snow and the workers were always glad to earn the overtime pay. After the roads were plowed and salted and passable, it took the highway department a few days to catch up on their regular work and resume a normal routine.

***

Katie and Brenda Quinn valued and enjoyed their friendship. They met less than a week after Katie moved to San Luis Obispo from San Diego. She was working in the main library when Brenda came in to return some books. Katie couldn't mistake her height and her flaming red hair, she had to be one of her new neighbors she had seen when she moved into her apartment. Katie introduced herself; they chatted for a while and Brenda invited her for coffee at Brenda's apartment after Katie got out of work. Their personalities matched each other and, from that time on, they became close friends and secret sharers. They provided support for each other as they each worked through their individual problems with the help of the other.

Katie, the widow, had a marriage that had exploded with bad feelings and then, suddenly, her husband had died. The aftermath had been almost as unpleasant. Working at the base library, where everyone knew the circumstances of Mike's death, was extremely difficult. No one ever said anything to her either directly or by inference, but she knew she was the subject of much discussion. That is what made her change jobs and move up the coast to San Luis Obispo.

Brenda, the divorcee, had a background that was very different from Katie's. She had no family background, either good or bad, that she could recall. She had been dropped off just after she was born and the authorities never found her mother; they suspected that Brenda was born out of wedlock to a young girl. She had been raised in orphanages all of her juvenile life. Her memories of her younger life were stark and grey with no highs or lows. When she was fourteen, an elderly couple, with no children of their own, adopted her and she took their last name of Quinn. Four years later, they both died and her brief period of family happiness was the only bright spot in her childhood. Their joint wills left enough money for Brenda to get an education. She became a dental hygienist and got a job in Minot, North Dakota.

It was while she was working there that she met the man she married, John Karen. He was a podiatrist whom she met when she went to his office as a patient. They got married and, three years later, the marriage imploded when she discovered that her husband was bisexual.

One day she came home from work and her husband told her that he wanted a divorce because he had met a man he wanted to live with. Brenda was stunned, disgusted, and furious.

After the divorce she began to wonder how much of the responsibility for the failure belonged to her. Had she been a good partner? Had she been a good wife? Could she have been more sharing? Had she been selfish? Because the marriage had failed she got different answers every time she examined her questions.

One day she decided that she would never know the answers to any of those questions and all she could do was to start over and try harder. She legally changed her name back to Quinn; then, she walked into a travel agency and looked for the farthest place she could go for the least amount of money. Thus, she had arrived in San Luis Obispo a few months ahead of Katie.

In a very short time they knew about each other's personal and family histories. They served each other as companion, confessor, and confidant and both became stronger and calmer because of their friendship.

Before Katie made her decision to return to Foxboro she and Brenda talked about all their options. They didn't want to break up their friendship and Brenda really had no personal ties to San Luis Obispo. They discussed the possibility of Brenda moving east after Katie got settled and they left it at that. There were no plans made, no deadlines established, just future possibilities. They were so close that neither wanted their friendship to end.

From the moment that Katie arrived in Foxboro, she and Brenda kept in touch with each other. When her phone was installed in her house Brenda was the first person Katie called. Once Brenda had her number they began to call each other whenever they got the urge to talk, sometimes three or four times a day. Their spontaneous phone calls ceased after they both received their monthly phone bills that reflected their ongoing conversations. They agreed to alternate calling each other and they managed to reduce their calls to almost one a day. They each talked about their daily routines, their problems, their activities, and their hopes. In addition, Brenda insisted on having photographs of Tyler and Mark, and Katie's house. Besides the phone calls, there were long, chatty weekly letters between them. They both were aware of how much they missed each other.

Brenda invited Katie to fly to California and Katie invited Brenda to fly to Massachusetts. Katie won out on logic because it would cost more for her to fly with Tyler than it would cost for Brenda to fly alone. After many discussions it was finally arranged for Brenda to visit Katie some two weeks before Thanksgiving and stay until the Sunday after the holiday. Brenda and Katie were both thrilled at the prospect of seeing each other again.

***

Katie wanted to thank both her brother and Mountain Man for returning her car but, for the next few days after the storm, she did not see or hear from them. On the following Thursday she dropped by Mark's boarding house and left a message under his door to come over Friday evening for dinner. She was eager to talk to him and she had many questions that she wanted to ask.

During dinner they talked about the early snowstorm and its effects on the town. She fed Mark his favorite meal, a fresh pork roast, mashed potatoes and gravy, and pumpkin pie. When they were relaxed and comfortable, Katie said, "Mark, your friend Mountain Man is a complete mystery to me. You work with him so maybe you can tell me something about him."

Mark asked in surprised, "Mountain Man?"

Katie laughed as she replied, "Sorry. That's what the librarians call him. I mean Tom Booker."

"Tom? He's a good friend but I don't know too much more about him than anyone else does. He doesn't talk a lot about himself but his actions are loud."

Katie was now really interested. She asked, "What actions are you talking about?"

"Well, there are two that come to my mind immediately. When

I first joined the highway department I had many problems. There's a guy who has been on the highway department for years. He's big, strong, fat and dumb and he is a bully. We all call him by his nickname, P J, which stands for Portagee John. When you first join the highway department he makes it a point to come over, introduce himself to you as PJ, and shake your hand. He tries to crush it until it hurts and then he'll let it go. He enjoys showing that he is stronger than you are.

"Most of the crew are afraid of him and they just leave him alone. After I was hired and he found out that I had gone to Canada, PJ started to bait me trying to get me to fight. I tried to avoid him because it would have been a mismatch. He's much bigger than me and he has been in many bar room brawls. However, one day he was meaner than usual and he said, 'I'm going to beat the living shit out of you just for the fun of it.'

"All of a sudden, Tom, who had been sitting there and listening to all of this for about a week, got up and stood in front of PJ with his hands on his hips. He was in a rage and he looked it. He said quietly, 'PJ, you're going to have to go through me first before you get to him.'

"That stopped PJ in his tracks. PJ knows that Tom is very strong and he also knows that Tom had been in combat in Vietnam. Tom was a lot more than he wanted to tangle with, so PJ told him, 'Aw, I was only kidding him. I wanted to see what he would say.' He got up and left the room."

Katie was taken completely by surprise. "Tom Booker served in Vietnam? I never thought of that. His beard and long hair made me think he was a hippie."

Mark laughed, "Sis, Tom is not what I would call a hippie. I think of a hippie as someone who protests against something in a negative way. I'm much more of a hippie than he is. However, I admire Tom. I learned from him not to apologize for what I believe in. I grew my hair longer for a ponytail after I met him and started working with him.

"I wouldn't call him a hippie. He doesn't protest; he just wants to be left alone. I would call him more of a dropout; someone who has completely given up on the system and is just trying to survive."

Katie replied, "I wonder if you're right. You know I've never met a dropout before. I wonder what pushes a person into giving up and dropping out?"

Mark said, "I don't know. I can tell you that he has been like a big brother to me even if I went to Canada while he went to Vietnam. He knows that and he says nothing about it. He told me once that everyone has to follow his own conscience no matter where it takes him."

Katie said, "You said two actions come to mind. So far, you've only mentioned one."

"The second thing I can tell you is that he has been after me, for a long time, to get both a class-two driver's license and a hydraulic license."

"Why, what would those licenses do for you?"

"Well, with a class-two license I could drive a dump truck and my pay grade would go from laborer to driver and the raise would be significant. And, with a hydraulic license, I could operate a backhoe or a bulldozer or a front-end loader. He has been working with me during lunch hours teaching me how to handle all that equipment and I soon will be getting both of those licenses. I think he is quite a guy."

Katie sat quietly for a few minutes. Her initial cobweb image of Mountain Man was wiped away by Mark's description. Not that her first impression mattered because she really knew absolutely nothing about him until the night of the snowstorm. Now, her interest in him was reaching the level of curiosity. Nothing about him added up; he was a truck driver who read incessantly and listened to classical music and helped people in trouble. He was a mystery. Finally, she said, "Mark, I didn't realize that he had protected you. Do you know anything about his family?"

"Not really. Tom mentioned once that he was born and raised in Michigan and for him that was a major announcement."

Katie spoke up, "If he wants to remain secretive that certainly is his right and I can easily respect that. I do want to thank him for helping me. What do you think of my inviting him here for Thanksgiving? Do you think that he would come?"

"Sis, I would enjoy having him here for Thanksgiving and I think he would be glad to come. Believe me, I know what it is like to have a holiday come along and be by yourself; it is sad, depressing. He may be a loner but he is a human and he really is a person who cares about other people. In fact, I have me a hunch that you would like Tom."

Katie refilled both their coffee cups before replying. "Let me think about it. No one should be alone on a holiday, but I have other people coming and I wouldn't want your friend to be uncomfortable and not enjoy himself. My best friend is flying here from California for a visit and Mrs. Buoni will be here. Mrs. Connors may be here depending upon whether her daughter goes to her mother in law's house or stays at her own home."

After Mark left, Katie thought about his attitude towards Tom. Mark seemed to regard him as a big brother. She found herself interested in learning more about the man she had referred to as Mountain Man. She needed to thank him for helping her so, she decided to invite him for Thanksgiving.

***

A few days later, Tom came into the library to browse. When Katie noticed him, she went to the small refrigerator the staff used for their lunches and retrieved a cranberry bread that she had placed in the freezer. She had brought it to work specifically to give to him. Katie placed it under the counter and when Tom came to check out two books, Katie was ready. As he handed her his library card, she purposely let it slip from her fingers and fall to the floor at his feet.

As he stooped to retrieve it, Katie slipped her invitation into the top book and she put the cranberry bread, wrapped in cellophane with a ribbon on it, on the counter. When he saw the bread he looked at Katie and she said, "Mr. Booker, this is my way of thanking you for driving me home and then getting my car out of the ditch."

He smiled, showing a full set of white teeth in the middle of his beard, and said, "Mrs. Oldfield, that is very kind of you and I appreciate it but, in a way, you rescued me. I had been plowing for about ten hours and I was getting sleepy. When I stopped to help you it was a welcome change that gave me a chance to relax. It may be that I owe you a loaf of bread."

Katie answered, "If you bake it I will eat it. In the meantime, I hope you enjoy Les Miserables," she said, pointing to the top book.

Not realizing that she was referring to the invitation that she had placed inside the book, he airily replied, "Oh, I will. I read it once before but that was many years ago." He picked up the books and left.

Two days later, he walked in and went over to where Katie was sorting the books to be returned to the shelves. He said, "I enjoyed Les Miserables very much. I don't have an oven to bake bread but I do have a florist," and, with that, he handed her a single rose.

Katie was a little flustered she certainly had not expected anything in return from him. She weakly replied, "Thank you."

"Listen, I appreciate your Thanksgiving invitation and I accept your offer. My only question is whether you want me to bring something or not?"

"No, all you have to do is show up."

"I'll be there."

After Tom left, Katie placed the rose in a small vase and put it out on her desk. She knew the rest of the librarians were curious about what was going on between Katie and Mountain Man. The rose was placed in a conspicuous spot to keep the rest of the librarians guessing.

8

Thanksgiving is the quietest, the sweetest, and the most unaffected of all our holidays. That is because Thanksgiving has been able to resist the commercial viruses that have ravaged all of our other holidays. Centered on celebrating the goodness of life with family and friends Thanksgiving has been able to withstand the heat of commercialism. Although it may be slightly scorched by all the hot advertising, Thanksgiving has not yet caught on fire. May it always remain the same.

Christmas has been exploited, and expanded, from "the twelve days of Christmas" to the "twelve months of Christmas." Corporations show no shame in hawking their wares every day of the year while drowning out the religious and spiritual aspect that once was the central meaning of this holiday. If Jesus ever returned to Earth, there would be an immediate corporate frenzy to get Him to endorse their products. Corporations would be oblivious to the reason for His return. Nor would they care; their only interest would be for Him to sign their contracts. Large corporations do not suffer from moral standards.

Halloween used to be young children, dressed in homemade outfits and faces painted with their mother's cosmetics, going around their neighborhoods to simply play "trick or treat." The holiday has been stolen from children and is now in the hands of misguided parents who want to include themselves in the celebration. We presently have factories in third world countries designing expensive costumes for the parents as well as the children. What used to be innocent offerings to youngsters now have to be scanned for razor blades and poison. Halloween has become the second most commercial holiday, only exceeded by the Christmas commercial cornucopia.

The Fourth of July is losing its Independence and its significance. Because of their costs, the smaller towns and villages across the country are discontinuing their fireworks and giving up their parades. These celebrations, along with major sports events, are being transferred to larger cities. The day has gone from showing our political past to showing off our commercial skills. Businesses and manufacturers mark all of their goods down on the Fourth of July. If any of our Founding Fathers returned for this day they would believe the only reason we celebrate is to sell cars, furniture and appliances.

This heavy emphasis on commerce milking the original meaning out of our holidays may be the main reason that people try to keep the Thanksgiving holiday a simple celebration.

***

Brenda Quinn arrived at Boston's Logan Airport late on a Thursday evening, two full weeks before Thanksgiving. Katie met her at the airport and the ride home was full of animated, high pitched talk as both Katie and Brenda brought each other up to date at the same time.

Neither seemed to care that it was harder to hear than it was to talk. They were just happy to be together again.

When they reached Katie's house, Brenda rushed in, hoping to find Tyler awake. Mark, who was babysitting, informed them that Tyler had fallen asleep on the couch an hour ago so he had tucked him into bed. Brenda was disappointed but she knew that she would get to see Tyler in the morning. She tiptoed into his room to look at him while he slept. Then, Katie introduced Mark to Brenda and the three of them chatted over tea and pastries. Mark excused himself because he had to go to work Friday morning and Brenda and Katie quietly talked for a long time. Finally, Katie showed Brenda where the small guest room was and they both went to bed.

Tyler woke Brenda up early Friday morning by coming into the guest room and hugging her until she came to and began to hug and kiss him back. Katie had arranged to take Friday off but she had to work on Saturday so the day was spent at home talking and relaxing. Katie wanted Brenda see how her lifestyle had changed since she had returned to Foxboro, so that evening, Katie and Brenda prepared supper for Mrs. Buoni, Mrs. Connors, and Mark. Mrs. Buoni and Mrs. Connors entertained everyone by telling stories about Katie, Mark and Tyler. Brenda enjoyed the evening.

Katie had asked Mark to show Brenda around on Saturday while she was working. The next morning, he picked Brenda up early and took her for breakfast. They went to a small, family owned restaurant near the Common; the customers were mostly local residents and this morning they included several of Mark's coworkers from the highway department. When Mark and Brenda entered, some of them began to heckle Mark. Two of them whistled and one said loudly, "Why would a cute redhead like you want to be seen with a bum like him?"

Mark escorted Brenda to a back booth and Brenda could see that Mark was embarrassed. He said, "I'm sorry, Brenda. I apologize for them, they are rude. I hope that didn't bother you too much."

Brenda leaned across the table and put one hand on Mark's hand. "Mark, that doesn't bother me at all. They were just teasing you so pay no attention. If they didn't like you, they probably wouldn't tease you. It certainly won't stop me from eating a big breakfast and, while we eat, you can tell me what your plans for today are."

Mark answered, "Just the same, that's not right. My so-called 'friends' should have shown you more respect.

"Anyhow, you'll have to help me decide. You've never been in this area before and there is a lot to see. We could go to Plymouth and see Plymouth Rock and a replica of the Mayflower; or we could drive to Cape Cod and look at the ocean. This time of year the cape is almost deserted and it is quiet and, in its own way, quite attractive."

Brenda asked, "And what is your personal preference, kind sir?"

Mark replied, "Well, if I were by myself, I'd drive to a small town in Rhode Island called Little Compton. It isn't famous like Plymouth or Cape Cod but I enjoy the drive down and there's no traffic. I take the back roads. It's slow, I pass through old towns and there's no rush. It's much less commercial than other places and it is peaceful. I don't know whether you would like it or not."

"Well, we are about to find out because, if that is what you would like to do, that is what I would like to do. So, on to Little Compton."

After breakfast as they were ready to leave the table, Mark paused for a second and suddenly said, "He was not correct."

Brenda asked, "What are you talking about?"

"What my 'friend' said when we first came in. I don't agree with him; you are more than cute, you are attractive."

She noticed that Mark appeared nervous as he spoke. He wanted to tell her what he thought but he didn't want to appear fresh or aggressive. She laughed as she replied, "Thank you, Mark, every girl likes compliments. I think yours is an especially nice compliment, so I won't question your sanity. That was a good breakfast and we are off to a pleasant start. On to Little Compton."

Thus began a day that brought them close to each other. At first, Mark did not say much, but, as Brenda began to ask him personal questions, he responded slowly. Soon, he was chatting as much as Brenda, and she was never at a loss for things to say. As they passed through Barrington, Warren, and Bristol, Mark enjoyed telling her about each of the towns' histories. Barrington long ago had a large brick works factory that brought laborers over from Italy to make the bricks. Warren was the original home of Brown University and Brown was called the College of Rhode Island. Bristol hosted the oldest continual Fourth of July parade in the country. By the time they reached Little Compton and then went on to Sakonnet Point they were almost out of breath from talking.

When they returned from their trip, they picked Katie up and drove to the Red Wing Diner. Brenda had her first taste of fried clams and she enjoyed them but she would not try the steamed clams that Katie and Mark ordered.

As they walked to their automobile, Katie noticed that Mark's arm was linked through Brenda's arm and that they leaned towards each other. All of a sudden, she sensed that there was an attraction between them. That made her feel happy for them and, at he same time, she also felt a sudden tinge of sadness; she had no partner.

That evening, as they were having a cup of tea before going to bed, Brenda asked, "Katie, why hasn't Mark ever married?"

"I don't really know, Brenda. He is good natured and a sweet person. I suspect he is afraid of being rejected but I've never asked." Then, looking straight at Brenda she added, "He would be a good husband, don't you think?"

Brenda grinned and replied, "Now who's doing the matchmaking? You're right though, he is really a sweet person, not pushy and edgy like the guys we met in San Luis. But I can't tell what he looks like. Why does he have that bushy beard and long hair?"

"I don't remember what he looks like either. He copied the beard and hair from his friend Tom, who I used to call 'Mountain Man.' Why they look like that is beyond me. Why don't you ask Mark to trim down and shave?"

'Do you think he would?" Brenda asked.

Katie replied, "He may not for me but I'll bet he would for you."

They both smiled as if they each had a secret; they then straightened up the kitchen and went to bed.

From that Sunday, until the Wednesday evening before Thanksgiving Day, it was a busy, joyous time for Katie and Brenda. Katie had requested time off but her boss asked her to work a few hours each day and, while she was gone, Brenda would take care of Tyler. In the evenings, Mark would come over right after work and eat dinner and then would sit around and visit until late. Katie could see that Mark and Brenda were building themselves a nest of happiness and she felt good for them. On Friday, Mark invited both of them to a movie but Katie, sensing that three was a crowd, demurred. Brenda and Mark went together and when they returned they brought Katie a hot fudge Sundae.

Thanksgiving morning, Mrs. Buoni was at Katie's door by 8:30 with a huge platter of Italian cookies. She got there even before Mark arrived; he was coming over midmorning to take Brenda and Tyler to the Foxboro/Mansfield High School football game. Katie, Brenda, and Tyler hadn't finished breakfast so Katie invited Mrs. Buoni to have coffee with them. When she was settled, Brenda asked, "Do you know if Mrs. Connors will be eating with us today?"

Mrs. Buoni answered, "No, she won't. Arlene is going to be in New Hampshire with her daughter. I came over early because I wanted to help prepare the meal."

Katie was pleased to see her. She suspected that Mrs. Buoni was feeling a little lonely and she didn't want anyone to be lonely, especially on this day. Besides, she really could use some help in preparing the meal and Mrs. Buoni was an excellent cook.

As the four of them sat at the table nibbling Mrs. Buoni's cookies, there was a knock on the door and Mark walked in carrying a huge bouquet of flowers. Katie almost gasped, Mark was clean-shaven and his hair was short and parted. "Hi everyone, the flowers are for our table. Happy Thanksgiving."

Mrs. Buoni was the first to say anything. "Mark, I forgot how handsome you are. You look so good, just like I remembered."

Katie couldn't get over how much better he looked. She glanced at Brenda who was staring at Mark as if she had never seen him before. Brenda asked him, "Mark, when did you get your hair cut?"

"Yesterday afternoon. I decided to let all of you see that you had invited the handsomest man in Foxboro over for Thanksgiving. How do I look?"

Brenda, Katie, and Mrs. Buoni all expressed their pleasure with his new look. Even Tyler, who liked to pull on his beard, was pleased. Soon, the three of them departed for the football game.

After they left, Katie changed into blue jeans and a sweatshirt and she and Mrs. Buoni got busy rearranging the furniture, setting the table, and preparing all the traditional foods associated with Thanksgiving. At the height of their activities, the doorbell rang and, when Katie opened the door, she saw Tom Booker standing there. He had a large pumpkin pie in one hand and a box of chocolates in the other, but what caught Katie's eye immediately was his appearance. He was not completely clean-shaven like Mark but he had trimmed his beard and cut his hair. His hair was still rather long but it was much too short for a ponytail. He had a pencil thin mustache and a very small Van Dyke beard. He looked distinguished, almost good looking.

Her instant thought was that he looked more like a French Poodle than an Old English Sheep dog. Then she felt embarrassed that she had made such a comparison because she was delighted with his present look. She almost blushed at her irreverent sense of humor as Tom said, "Happy Thanksgiving, Mrs. Oldfield. I know that I may be early, but I wanted to see if you needed any help. You probably do have dessert but I brought a pie for everyone and I brought candy for you."

Katie covered her confusion by quickly replying, "Please, call me Katie and Happy Thanksgiving to you. You look so different and so handsome that I almost didn't recognize you. I'm glad you're here because I could use a hand.

"That pie looks delicious. You didn't bake it yourself did you?"

"Oh no, I know how to eat but I don't know how to cook. What I did do was go to that fancy grocery store, S.S. Pierce in Brookline, and buy their pie and their candy. I hope you like chocolates."

Katie answered, "I do like chocolates and I thank you. Actually, if you wish to help, Mrs. Buoni and I would appreciate it. You won't learn how to cook but you will earn your meal and our gratitude."

Tom pitched in to do some of the menial chores, peeling vegetables; lifting and moving heavy items, washing pots and pans, and making himself useful. He did whatever was asked of him promptly but he hardly said a word.

His silence was broken when Katie plugged in an electric frying pan and immediately the kitchen lights went out. Her temper got the better of her, she muttered, "Damn."

Tom said, "Looks like you've overloaded a circuit. Where's your main electric panel?" Katie led Tom down the cellar stairs, using a flashlight, and she showed him the panel. He opened it and inspected the inside.

"My goodness, this still uses fuses. I can see which fuse blew but I can't tell what room is associated with each circuit. Luckily there are some spare fuses so we can replace the blown fuse. Before I screw a new fuse in, lets go upstairs and shut off a few lights and anything you're not using right now."

Shortly, after moving the frying pan to a different circuit, Tom had everything on that needed to be on and all the unnecessary lights and appliances were shut off. When the activities returned to the preparation of the holiday meal, Tom said to Katie, "You know, you use a lot more appliances than were around when this house was built. For your own safety and convenience, you should consider having your house rewired sometime in the future."

Mrs. Buoni was excited and pleased when Tom solved the problem. She was impressed that he seemed to know what he was talking about. None of the mechanical or electrical problems she had made sense to her but here was someone who could fix them. She timidly asked, "Mr. Booker, could you help me? My washing machine just quit in the middle of washing and I have a tubful of wet clothes and I don't know what to do."

"Mrs. Buoni, if you promise to call me Tom I'll be glad to help.

If Katie doesn't need us right now, I'll take a look at your washing machine."

They left and were back within a half-hour. Mrs. Buoni was smiling as she told Katie, "Tom fixed my washing machine. He took it apart and put it back together and now my clothes are going to be clean."

Tom looked at Katie and shrugged. "Her washing machine is a Sears. It is old and needs a new part. I got it to work but the old part should be replaced. I'll order a new part and install it."

Just then, Mark, Brenda and Tyler came trooping through the door, the three of them were flushed from the cold. "Hey," Brenda yelled, "we beat Mansfield. The Patriots aren't the only football team in town. Now that we are back, is there anything we can do to help you with dinner?"

They were told that there was nothing to do. All the preparations were completed, and the dinner was ready to serve. Katie slipped out of the kitchen as the others started putting the food on the table. She appeared a few minutes later wearing a burgundy colored dress and a pearl necklace and pearl earrings. She radiated beauty and happiness; it was a day to put aside problems. She said, "Before we eat, I think that we should all hold each others' hands and say, very simply, what we are each most thankful for. I will begin.

"I am thankful that I am home in Foxboro with my brother and my friends. I hope and pray that no one is alone or hungry today."

She turned to her son and asked, "Tyler, what are you thankful for?"

Tyler replied, "I am thankful for my mother, my Aunt Brenda, my Uncle Mark and my Grandma Buoni."

Brenda said, "I am grateful that my best friend, Katie, invited me for Thanksgiving. I am overwhelmed with happiness."

Mark was silent for a second before he spoke. "I am grateful that my life is changing for the better. I am on the threshold of peace and love."

Mrs. Buoni was on the verge of tears. "Thank God Katie came home and brought her son Tyler into my life. God is good."

That left Tom as the last person to give thanks. He had been taken aback when Katie had said that she wanted everyone to give thanks. He had certainly not paid attention to thankfulness for a long time. As he thought about what she asked from each person he knew that he couldn't object to Katie's request on religious grounds. She was asking only for personal testimony and that had nothing to do with formal religion. Tom had to reach back to thoughts he had not called forth in a long time. While the others were talking, he watched each of them and listened to their words. The pause, before he began to talk, was long.

Finally, he spoke in a low voice, "Katie, I am thankful that you invited a stranger into your house to celebrate Thanksgiving with you and your family. Your thoughtfulness makes me realize that there are still good people in this world. I may have forgotten that and I am thankful for the reminder."

Everyone was silent for a while, savoring their personal thoughts and feelings. Then, the feasting began. Whether sharing their feelings contributed to their hunger was moot, the fact is that everyone gorged on the Thanksgiving dinner. Turkey, stuffing, yams, cranberry sauce, mashed potatoes, gravy, vegetables and pumpkin pie all disappeared as fast as an ice cube in an oven. When dinner was over, everyone felt bloated. Everyone, except Tyler, said to himself or herself that they should learn to eat less. After a banquet, it is always easy for a glutton to promise to go on a diet.

During the meal, Katie looked around several times to see Tom looking at her. She didn't feel uncomfortable or self-conscious because she had been hoping that he would think that she was attractive. She would smile or nod and he would return the favor and turn back to whomever was talking.

Afterwards, everyone crowded into the small parlor and, all of a sudden, Mrs. Buoni started singing "Silent Night". She had a surprisingly clear voice and, slowly, Mark, Brenda, Tyler, and Katie, joined her. The rest of the evening was spent singing Christmas carols and savoring the togetherness of Thanksgiving. Even Tom joined in singing some of the traditional songs. By 9:30, Mrs. Buoni, Mark, and Tom began to get ready to leave.

Tom pulled Katie off to one side and said, "I want to thank you, Katie. It has been years since I've had a Thanksgiving as simple and as pleasant as this. It reminded me of my childhood."

Katie was touched by his sincerity. She replied, "Tom, thank you for coming. You did me a favor and I wanted to show you that I was grateful. I'm pleased that I could repay your kindness. I enjoyed having you here."

Tom laughed, and said, "Katie, I'm stuffed with food and gratitude. It has been a long time since I have enjoyed myself as much as I have today. Take care of yourself and thank you for making my Thanksgiving so enjoyable." He left and Katie shut off the lights and went to bed leaving Brenda and Mark sitting together in the living room. She found herself thinking about Tom before she fell asleep.

***

Saturday morning Mark came over to join Katie and Brenda for breakfast. Mark seemed fidgety and nervous during the meal and

Brenda was extremely quiet. At first, Katie thought of saying something but then, she decided to wait until one of them told her what was going on between them. Finally, Mark announced, "Katie, Brenda and I are thinking of becoming engaged."

Katie replied, "I'm absolutely pleased for both of you. I knew that you two were in a world of your own; but what do you mean by 'thinking of becoming engaged'?"

Now it was Brenda who was eager to speak up, "It sounds crazy but we were attracted to each other immediately. Maybe it was because you had spoken of Mark so often that I knew him even before we were introduced. At any rate, we are in love and I am going to move to Foxboro. Getting a job is easy for dental hygienists so that won't be a problem. After I get back here we will start making formal plans.

"Katie, I never thought anything like this could happen to me. I hope you are happy for us."

"Oh, Brenda, I am delighted. My best friend and my brother are going to get married. I couldn't be happier."

Then she thought for a minute, grinned, and added, "I thought there was something going on and, when Mark came out from behind that bush of his at Thanksgiving, I was sure. And to think that in San Luis Obispo you were always trying to fix me up.

"Mark, what are your plans? Will you stay with the highway department?"

"At least for a while, Katie. I plan to start my own handyman business, you know, mowing lawns, painting, small fix-ups, home repairs and remodeling. After I establish my name and my business I will be able to quit, but not for a while."

In a surprised tone Katie asked, "Do you know how to repair and remodel houses?"

"No, not completely. But when I told Tom what I was thinking of doing he said that he would work with me to get me started. There isn't much that he can't repair or figure out. He said that he didn't want any money but, if he helps me, I intend to try to pay him."

Katie was surprised. "You discussed all of this with Tom?"

"Yes, he likes Brenda and you and when I told him of my plans he was very encouraging. He thinks I can make a very decent living as a handyman. Several guys from the highway department have their own part-time businesses. Tom thinks I can do a better job than most of them. I think so, too."

Katie was awhirl with jumbled thoughts. She believed that Mark would succeed in his business because he was serious and industrious and her new found friend, Tom, would help him. She was glad that Mark was putting his past behind him and getting on with his life. He and Brenda would be good for each other.

After breakfast, Brenda and Mark left to go look at apartments and they were gone most of the day. That evening, Brenda treated Mark, Katie, and Tyler to dinner at the Red Wing Diner. Since she was flying back to California early the next morning, it was her way of saying, "goodbye, for the time being" to all of them. They feasted on clams and lobster and enjoyed themselves.

Later, after Tyler was in bed, and they were in their pajamas, Katie and Brenda had their last talk before Brenda left. Brenda told Katie how much she had missed her and Tyler after they left California. She did not have anyone to confide in and, as a result, even her dating was not as much fun. All the men she went out with were cold, self centered, and sex driven. That may have been one reason that Mark, who was gentle and caring, made her realize what a treasure he was. Good men were hard to find. For the first time in years, she was looking forward to her future with Mark and being close to Katie and Tyler.

Katie told Brenda that she was settling in to her new life and that she was glad that she had returned to Foxboro. She still had to reconcile her father and Mark but that would come when her father and Helen returned from Florida.

When Brenda asked her if she had been dating anyone Katie told her that she had not. When Brenda asked her if she was interested in dating anyone Katie told her she was not. Then Brenda asked, "Well, what about that guy who came over here on Thanksgiving, Tom? Mark talks about him all the time. He seems like a genuinely warm person and, without his winter coat, he is handsome."

Katie covered some of her present thoughts with a few white lies. "I don't really know much about him. Mark says that he never talks about himself. It's as if he has not only dropped out of society, he's dropped out of life. Besides, I'm not really interested in men right now. The wonder and romance went out of my marriage and all I remember is the hurt. I'm not ready to take another chance. Men may be a biological necessity but they surely are a mixed blessing."

They talked for a while about their futures. Brenda was optimistic while Katie was hopeful. It was early the next morning when they stopped talking and went to their beds.

9

Early Sunday morning Mark showed up to take Brenda to Logan airport. Katie decided not to accompany them, as she was sure they would rather say good by to each other with no one else around. She hugged Brenda, told her that she enjoyed her visit, and could hardly wait for her return. Brenda cried a little and then she was gone. The day deflated for Katie. It seemed to her that the weather was bad, that Tyler was cranky, and that there was nothing that she wanted to see at the movies.

When Mark came over to her house, later that afternoon, he also was in a sour mood. Katie decided that she was not going to hang around being downcast. She made tuna fish salad sandwiches and while the three of them were eating she said, "When we finish, everyone dress warmly because we are going to drive over to La Sallette Shrine and get there just before they turn on the lights."

Mark smiled at the thought but Tyler immediately asked, "What's La Sallette Shrine?"

Mark replied, "Tyler, you will love La Sallette Shrine. It is a place that has Christmas lights, thousands and thousands and thousands of Christmas lights. It is beautiful and it is fun."

The Patriots of Foxboro

Mark was correct about what La Sallette Shrine was but he was wrong about the number of Christmas lights. La Sallette was a huge Catholic seminary that covered hundreds of acres in Attleboro. To help defray their costs, and to celebrate the Christmas season, La Sallette Shrine had, for years, put up a light display; and, every year since the start, the display had gotten larger and larger. Soon, the lights were strung over acres of gardens, paths, and around a small lake. There were well over two hundred and fifty-thousand lights, of all sizes and all colors, in both the religious displays and the children's displays. At specific locations throughout the outdoor pavilion, there were stands to buy votive candles for departed loved ones.

To attract people to their spectacular panorama, there were free parking lots. There was one for cars and one for the buses that came from all over the eastern United States and Canada. Inside one of the buildings closest to the parking lots were rest rooms, a cafeteria, and a gift shop. The hallways, inside the building, had tables selling lottery tickets and chances on automobiles, vacation cruises, and other high end prizes. The gift shop sold votive candles, rosaries, and related Catholic articles from trinkets to expensive silver crosses. There was something in the gift shop for everyone's taste from catholic to Catholic.

Mark, Katie, and Tyler arrived at the parking lot just before dusk. The day had been gray and humorless and as they got out of the car the wind made them feel glad that they had bundled up in warm clothing. The lights were always turned on the weekend after Thanksgiving but the larger crowds didn't show until after the first day of December and hardly anyone arrived before it got dark. As a result, there were very few people around as the three of them climbed the marble steps of a steep hill that overlooked the entire seminary. At the top of the hill was an outdoor altar with a huge granite cross looming over the scene.

As they reached the crest and turned to look at the parking lot, a gust of wind cut through their warm clothing and made them begin to feel the cold. They stood staring through the gathering darkness that was making it almost impossible to even see the huge seminary building in the distance. The cold began nibbling on their fingers and toes and Katie began to wonder if she had made the right choice.

Just then Mark pointed to someone standing five feet away from them and said, "For crying out loud, look who's here. Tom. Have you come to see the lights too? Come over and join us."

Tom moved to where they were standing. "Hello Mark, Tyler, and Katie, yes, I came…."

Just then every light in the display came on and instantly transformed the murky darkness into a blazing panorama of colors, thousands of colors. The change was from inky blackness to a brightness that almost hurt their eyes. It was a spectacular sight that stretched for acres. The four of them gasped both in surprise and delight. Tyler jumped up and down and said, "Let's go and walk through the lights."

The four of them made their way down the steps and began a journey of wonderment through the many paths of lights. After an hour of excitement they walked around a small pond encircled by a replica of a large set of rosary beads. By that time, the crowd was getting larger and the cold was beginning to penetrate their fingers and toes; they needed to get indoors.

Tom turned to Tyler and asked, "Would you like to get a hot chocolate?

Tyler replied quickly, "Boy, would that taste good."

They went into the cafeteria, got coffee, hot chocolate, and snacks and sat at a table to warm up and recap their adventures. Tyler was the most talkative since this was the first time he had ever seen such an elaborate display of lights and he was excited and happy. However, Mark and Katie had a lot to recount and even Tom, the usually silent one, joined in the conversation.

After their conversation slowed down, Mark said, "I wish that I had shown this to Brenda before she left for California. I think I'll go to the gift shop and buy a souvenir for her."

As he got up to leave, Tyler asked, "Uncle Mark, can I come along?" That left Katie and Tom sitting there quietly. After a while, Katie decided to open the conversation. She began by asking, "I guess you know that your rooming house will be losing one of its clients shortly?"

"You mean Mark? Yes, he is looking forward to a happier time. When I came over to your house for Thanksgiving and saw him and Brenda it was obvious that they were melting towards each other. Knowing Mark, it was pleasant to see them both happy."

That remark surprised Katie. She hadn't thought he had paid attention to Brenda and Mark. Tom continued, "I was glad to see you this evening because I thought of something after I left your house on Thanksgiving.

"The way your house is wired you might have trouble when you go to put up your Christmas lights and decorations. It is an older house and it was built before appliances became so plentiful. Katie, you really should think about having your house rewired sometime in the future. It is not unsafe but, if you want a larger television or a separate freezer, you will need some extra circuits. Even now, you could use some extra outlets."

"How much would that cost?"

"I'm not sure, Katie. But you can find out by getting a couple of estimates. Try Connors Electrical or Schultz and Sons. They are both honest and do good work. Get them to give you an estimate and compare their prices."

They chatted for a while longer until Mark and Tyler returned and then the four of them went out to the parking lot, got into their two cars and left.

When Katie got to the library the next day, she was in for a surprise. She was asked to fill in for the head librarian for the next two weeks while she went into the hospital for an operation. She was happy to do the job but it meant a lot more work for her. She worked longer hours and was not near the front desk. As a result, she did not see much of Mark and she had to delay starting her Christmas decorating. After she resumed her normal duties, she had Mark over for dinner to find out how he was doing and to ask his help in putting up her Christmas lights. He told her that he would be glad to help but that she should start soon because he was going to fly to California to spend the holidays with Brenda. That pleased her but it took her by surprise.

Katie began to examine all the old Christmas decorations that Grandma Barker had used for many years. The lights were so old that they were useless but the tree ornaments were loved and well remembered by Katie and Mark. To use all the ornaments Katie went out and bought a Christmas tree too large for her small living room and strings of inside and outside lights.

Mark trimmed the tree and put it up, helped decorate it, and strung the lights as she requested. When she went to turn on the lights her troubles began, as the circuits would blow fuses instead of lighting the lights. She began to string extension chords from other rooms in an attempt to balance the circuits. Mark made two trips to the hardware store to buy extra long extension chords and his job would be to yell "on" or "off" when she changed fuses in the basement. After many hours of frustration, the Christmas decorating was finished. The extra work and efforts were not lost on Katie, she was convinced that she needed more electrical outlets.

With Mark gone, Christmas was pleasant but much quieter than Katie had expected. She and Tyler went to church, opened their presents, and then they went for a walk in the Sharon Bird Sanctuary. Later, she had Mrs. Buoni and Mrs. Connors over for dinner. During the day, she called Brenda and Mark to wish them a "Merry Christmas", and, after they opened their presents, Brenda and Mark called her back. As she went to bed, she briefly wondered what her father and Helen and Tom had done to celebrate Christmas.

New Year's Eve was spent drinking wine with Mrs. Connors and Mrs. Buoni. She had allowed Tyler to stay up and bang some pots and pans together as the ladies drank their toast. After Katie tucked Tyler into bed, she went out on the porch and looked up into a cloudy sky; it was chilly as she stood outside. Katie took several deep breaths and then said a prayer that the New Year would bring her peace, happiness, and maybe, even a little love. Then, she went to bed and fell into a deep sleep.

10

Mark Givens was smitten with the deadliest, most delightful virus known to humans, love. And, since it was his first exposure to the virus, it affected him the same way that smallpox affected the American Indians; he was completely ravaged. Like all viruses, there were unpredictable side effects. When he was with Brenda he was at a symphony, when he was with Katie he was at a concert, with anyone else he was at a solo performance. Whenever he was alone he was at a drum practice; he was in sheer misery.

While Brenda and he were together he was euphoric, after she returned to California Mark's mood changed. He began to wonder whether Brenda still loved him or if she was changing her mind. It was not that he had a jealous nature or was suspicious of people; he had a very open personality. It was just that love makes a person do odd things and think funny thoughts. Despite talking with Brenda on the phone every day, and receiving her assurances that she had not changed her mind, Mark was in the agony of the ecstasy of love.

Originally, their plans were that Brenda would go back to California, cut her ties there, and return to Foxboro. They didn't discuss time because everything was to be done speedily so that they would be quickly reunited. Neither of them knew how long they would be apart and their urge to be together again began the minute they parted.

When Mark could stand it no longer, he asked Brenda if he could fly to California to be with her for Christmas. He said that they would be with each other again and then they could drive back to Massachusetts. Brenda was going through the same pangs of loneliness so she was thrilled with the idea. Mark took a leave of absence from the highway department and flew to California.

From the moment they were reunited at the airport, they both felt that their commitment to each other was absolutely the right choice. Amidst the deplaning crowd, they hugged and kissed until they were the only ones left standing at the gate entrance. On the way to her apartment, Brenda brought Mark up to date on her plans. She had made all the necessary moving arrangements, the only problem she was having was giving notice to all of her employers. She worked part time for three dentists and one had been on vacation. When he returned, she had given her notice and in two weeks she would be free to head to Foxboro. In the meantime, there was nothing to do but visit the area and enjoy each other. They did both.

They toured the Hearst Castle at San Simeon, the flower gardens at Lompoc, and they wandered through the Thursday evening farmer's market in San Luis Obispo. On Saturday, they strolled among the barbeque stands in Santa Maria and then they drove to the Monterrey Peninsula for the rest of the weekend. In truth though, they discovered each other, physically and mentally, much more than they explored California. They started sleeping together from the first night after Mark arrived.

They would call Katie every evening and tell her about most of their activities. From their excitement, she could tell that they were happy. She suspected that they were having sex but they were certainly old enough to decide for themselves and it was none of her business. Katie was pleased that the two of them had found each other.

Originally, Brenda had planned to drive straight through from the west coast to the east coast, but that was before Mark flew out to be with her. When she finally had all of her business taken care of, she and Mark discussed their travel plans and what routes to take. Mark surprised her by saying that he didn't want to rush home. He wanted to stop off in Las Vegas, get married, and then drive slowly to Foxboro on a honeymoon tour. Brenda was thrilled and agreed with Mark's proposal and plan. As a result, Mr. and Mrs. Mark Givens arrived in Foxboro a week after they told Katie they would arrive. However, they did call every evening to tell Katie where they were so she wouldn't worry.

Mark went back to work immediately while Brenda applied for a job as dental hygienist with several Foxboro dentists. They rented a small, furnished apartment near the Common and soon had an established routine.

Katie did not know that they had gotten married until they arrived in Foxboro; they kept that fact as a surprise until they saw her in person. When they did return, in early January, she was pleased to see them and thrilled with the news of their wedding. It was a happy, but not unexpected, announcement.

***

A few days after New Year's Eve, Katie and Tyler were shopping at Shaw's, a grocery store just over the Foxboro line in Sharon, when she heard a voice say, "Good Morning and Happy New Year, Tyler and Katie."

She turned around to see Tom standing there. She had forgotten that he had trimmed his beard and mustache and his ponytail. He was much more pleasing to look at, almost debonair in his appearance. Katie was pleased to see him.

"Tom, Happy New Year. I hope you had a good time on Christmas and New Year's Eve."

"I did. I went home to see my mother and father. On New Year's Eve we ended up at a square dance." He laughed, "I couldn't keep up with any of the old folks.

"How were your holidays? Tyler, what did you get for Christmas?"

He listened as Tyler listed the books and the clothes he had received as well as the name of the person who had given him each present. It was not a long list and there were no toys mentioned, just books and clothes.

Tom looked at Katie and asked, "And Katie, was your Christmas a good one?"

Katie answered, "Yes, it was in a quiet way. However, I did have some trouble getting ready for Christmas. That reminds me, you were right about the house needing more outlets. I had extension chords everywhere because of all the inside and outside lights I put up. Right after Christmas I got an estimate from Schultz and Sons and it is expensive."

"Do you remember the price?"

"I surely do because it was much more money than I expected. The cost was over three thousand dollars."

Tom looked at her and said, "That's not right. Something is wrong. I would like to look at the estimate and see how they got such a high figure."

Katie felt relieved because ever since Schultz and Sons had been to her house she had become concerned whether she and Tyler were in any immediate danger. The estimator had suggested that she needed to act quickly.

"Tom, if you would look at it I would appreciate it. They indicated that the wiring might be a fire hazard."

"When would be a good time for you, Katie?"

"The sooner the better. If you are free this evening why not come over for dinner?"

He accepted the invitation and then he asked about Mark and Brenda. She told him that Mark was enjoying his visit in California and that the two of them would be coming back to Foxboro in a week or two.

At six that evening, Tom showed up at Katie's house carrying a large package wrapped in Christmas paper. He handed it to Tyler and said, "Santa left this under my tree by mistake. You might as well have it because I am now a little too old to play with these things."

Tyler looked at his mother who hesitated a second and then nodded. He took the package, opened it, and discovered a big, red dump truck. He looked at it with wide eyes, thanked Tom and sat down and started playing with it.

Katie said, "Thank you, Tom. You didn't have to do that."

He replied, "I guess I didn't but that's the nicest time to give presents, when you don't have to. Your son is a well mannered child, so why not? I loved a dump truck when I was growing up and I'm sure he will too. Since you work at the library you know that I enjoy reading, but children need play time every bit as much as they need learning time."

Katie watched Tyler sitting on the floor putting things into his truck and driving them around. He was in his own world. "You may be right.

I've never thought of that before. I loved dolls when I was his age. I guess children should have time to play."

During dinner, Katie and Tom were wary of asking each other any awkward questions. Luckily, Tyler, who was thrilled with his present, rescued them. He asked Tom simple questions, like where did he live and did he have any brothers or sisters. After Tom answered all of his questions, Tyler told Tom about Brenda and his Uncle Mark and how they were going to get married. Katie let him continue because it was an easy conversation and she was learning about Tom. However, when Tyler inadvertently started to refer to him as "Uncle Tom" Katie stepped in, and clearly, explained to Tyler that he was not to call him "Uncle."

Tom laughed and said it was all right with him if Tyler wanted to call him his uncle. The three of them enjoyed the meal with no self conscious attitudes either in the conversations or in the silences.

After dinner, Katie handed Tom the estimate and he stared at it for a long time. He finally asked, "You said he indicated that you were in danger?"

"Yes, but not directly. The man who did the estimate said it was possible that the wiring could cause a fire."

"Did he show you any examples where 'it was possible that the wiring could cause a fire?'"

"No, he just looked around and said that a couple of times."

Tom shook his head and said, "I know the guy who did this estimate. I'm surprised he is working for Schultz because he is not one of the better electricians around. My guess is that he thought that, as a widow, he could pull the wool over your eyes.

"Look, I've examined your wiring. It is old but the insulation is in good condition. You could use a new main electric panel and some new outlets but you're not in any immediate danger.

"This estimate is high and is padded with labor charges. You can get the job done much cheaper than this price."

Because she trusted his judgement, Katie felt relieved at what Tom told her.

"Thank you, Tom. I feel better now that you've looked at the estimate. I will probably get it done when I can free up some extra money; it's inconvenient to keep changing fuses all the time."

They chatted for a while and Katie and Tom soon began discussing classical music. She played a Brahm's symphony that was recorded on an LP record and, afterwards, she told Tyler to get ready for bed. He soon came back from his bedroom, in his pajamas, carrying a well-worn book. He carried it over to Tom and, disregarding his mother's injunction, he asked, "Uncle Tom, will you read me a story?"

Katie, when she heard Tyler's request, started to say something and then she stopped. Tom smiled, pulled Tyler on his knee, and began reading to him. Katie watched for a second and then she went into the kitchen to do the dishes. When she returned in twenty minutes, she found Tyler and Tom in a deep discussion. She put Tyler to bed and then she and Tom sat in the kitchen and had coffee.

Tom said, "Tyler's at an interesting age. He wants to believe in Santa Claus but his classmates tell him there is no such person. Next year there will be no Santa."

"Is that what the two of you were talking about?"

"Yes, that was because of the truck I gave him."

Katie thought for a second and said, "Well, the Easter Bunny will soon be history, too. Until he stops believing in the tooth fairy, I won't consider him grown."

She then shifted the conversation to something Tom had said

earlier. "Tom, you said that you went to see your parents. Where do they live?"

He replied, "Milan, Michigan and, before you ask, Milan is located about ten miles south of Ann Arbor. It is strictly a farm community while Ann Arbor is a college town."

"How long have they lived in Milan?"

"For years and years. That's where I was born and raised."

Katie asked what she thought was the next logical question, "How did you get to Foxboro from Milan?"

It was as if a curtain had descended inside Tom. His mood went from relaxed to tense. He covered the change by curtly saying, "That's kind of a long story, Katie."

Shortly after that, he said that he had to get going. He walked to the front door where he and Katie had an awkward moment. He didn't know if Katie would let him hug her and she didn't know if Tom would try to kiss her. So, they just stood there for a while until indecision won out. Neither touched the other and Tom finally went out the door.

***

For the next few days Katie wondered about the clumsy way they had said goodnight. Since becoming a widow she had turned down, or avoided, all advances. She had no desire for any kind of intimacy and she had been absolutely firm and deft in avoiding any compromising situation. However, this was different; the hesitation had been on her part. She wasn't sure what her reaction would have been if Tom had put his arms around her. It was her uncertainty that puzzled her.

She had to admit that Tom interested her. Physically, he was attractive. With his new look he was distinguished, almost handsome.

She had long ago stopped thinking of him as "Mountain Man" because there was more to him than he allowed people to see. Why didn't he let anyone to get close to him?

His reading habits alone indicated that he was more intelligent than his wild look would lead you to believe. When Mark told her that he liked and respected Tom she began to think of him in a different way. He was friendlier than she first thought but he kept everything about himself hidden. Why? Did he break the law somewhere and this was his way of trying to keep from being found? It puzzled Katie that, with his intellect and intelligence, he chose to work at the highway department. She thought that he probably had a reason for keeping a low profile.

She knew that Mark was working there because it was the course of least resistance for him. He didn't have to account for the time he was in Canada and it was relatively easy to get a job at the highway department. Did Tom have something to hide? Was he hiding from something or someone?

She decided that she had to find out more about Tom and more about her own feelings. The opportunity arose when Mark and Brenda returned. Katie decided to give them a welcome home party and she invited Tom as well as Mrs. Buoni and Mrs. Connors. After Katie knew that everyone was coming, she felt lighthearted; this was the first time in years that she had organized a party of any kind.

The Saturday morning of the party Katie was in the kitchen baking oatmeal cookies when her phone rang. Under the assumption that it was either Mrs. Buoni or Mrs. Connors wanting to help with the arrangements Katie picked up the phone and said, "Hello."

A voice she knew but couldn't immediately place replied, "Katie? It is so good to talk to you."

Katie was taken aback for a second until she recognized that it was Helen speaking. She was flooded with happiness. "Helen? Helen, is that you? I'm so happy to hear your voice. Oh, oh, how did you know to call this number?"

"Arlene Connors called me last night. She is so happy that you have returned and that Mark has married your best friend that she went to St. Mark's church and asked the priest for our Florida phone number in Naples. She said that she doesn't have Mark's number so she gave me your number instead.

"I was absolutely floored by the all the news. I'm bursting with happiness; I just had to call and talk to you. Is now a good time?"

Tears welled up in Katie's eyes. "Helen, any time is a good time to talk with you. I've missed you terribly."

Katie spent the next two hours answering Helen's questions about Tyler, Mark, and Brenda. Each of her questions required detailed responses so Katie did most of the talking. Towards the end, when Helen began to feel that she was catching up on what had happened in the past, Katie began to ask questions of her own. She wanted to know how Helen was feeling and what she had been doing. She asked for the same amount of details in her answers that she had given Helen. After they had finished with their questions, Katie asked the question that had been heavy on her mind from the start, "Helen, how is my father doing?"

Katie thought that she heard Helen sigh before she answered, "Dear, he is doing well, I guess. Physically, he's healthy and active. He plays golf almost every day and he has no big medical problems but he is not a happy man.

"Your father has become more rigid in his views about where the country is heading. He can't wait until the news comes on so he can argue against anyone on television who disagrees with him. He doesn't want to forgive and forget.

"What makes it so hard for me is that I think he was beginning to come to terms with Mark's draft evasion until he had problems with Mike. Before then, your father thought of Mike as his real son and he was proud of him. Mike was fighting the Vietnam War and that allowed your father to tolerate Mark as the son who wouldn't fight. He didn't approve of Mark but as Mark's father he couldn't abandon him, so he was willing to make excuses for his bad decisions.

"When your father became aware of Mike's real character, the realization that he had been made a fool hurt your father. He couldn't forget that Mike was a selfish womanizer who had lied and taken money from him. Worse than that, Mike hit your father and humiliated him and, afterwards, Mike died under very disturbing circumstances.

"Your father has been assaulted with negative feelings for a long time. He is ashamed that he didn't see Mike for what he was when they met the first time. He is upset that you didn't tell him about Mike when you found out what he really was like. He is not pleased that his only grandson is Mike's child. All of this is on top of his anger over patriotism and the Vietnam War. Right now, his thoughts are dense, hard and negative. I feel so sorry for him because he is not happy and I can't get through to him and help him. I hate to tell you this but that's the way it is."

There was a long pause in the conversation and, finally, Katie said, "Helen, that is so sad to hear. I feel badly for my father. We all have scars from the past; I know that you do and you know that I do. Regardless, we all have to live in the present and that includes my father.

"Listen, Tyler is a good child and he is going to grow into a fine man, you will love him when you meet him. He says childish things that make you laugh and he is intelligent. I think that he may change my father's attitude after you two return to Foxboro. I'm so looking forward to seeing you.

"My mother couldn't have been any more caring of me than you have been. You have been so kind to me all these years. I love you Helen."

They each were teary eyed when they got ready to say goodbye. Helen told Katie that she would call in a week or ten days to keep track of everyone and, with that, the phone conversation finally ended.

Katie had to work extra hard to make up for the time spent talking with Helen but she was so pleased with the phone call that she didn't give the inconvenience a thought. By the time her guests arrived, all of her preparations were complete.

Of course, Mrs. Connors and Mrs. Buoni were the first to arrive and Brenda and Mark followed them shortly. Mark carried in a projector and screen to show a movie of their honeymoon trip. Brenda hugged Katie and told her she looked radiant and beautiful. Katie had spent a long time choosing her dress and her accessories because she wanted to look her very best, and she did.

Tom was the last to arrive and, much to everyone's surprise, he was dressed in a blue suit, a white shirt, and a tie. He looked dapper as he came in with a wrapped wedding present for the newlyweds and a bouquet of flowers for Katie. She was aware of his appearance as she took the flowers and put them in a vase and she wondered if Tom had noticed how she looked.

The party was cosy and warm and all the attention centered on Mark and Brenda. They were continually questioned about their wedding and their trip back to Foxboro. Mrs. Connors and Mrs. Buoni insisted on asking about details as they hunted for the sexual intimacy of the newly weds. Tom caught Katie's attention several times as he smiled and shook his head at the persistence of their questions. Katie finally ended the inquisition by serving a buffet dinner.

After the meal Mark set up his projector. He had to move the furniture around to find an electric outlet that he could use and then he had to connect several extension cords to reach the projector. When everything was ready he showed his home movie taken at their wedding. Afterwards, Brenda cut the cake that Mrs. Connors and Mrs. Buoni had baked for the party. Both of the "grandmothers" were so happy that they cried as Brenda passed out slices of cake and ice cream.

Tyler had been allowed to stay up so he could eat some of the cake and, after that, he was put to bed. A little later, the party began to break up. Mrs. Connors and Mrs. Buoni left because they wanted to go to church early Sunday morning. Mark and Brenda also left early because they were newlyweds. Before they went, Mark returned all the furniture he had moved, back to their original locations.

When they were alone, Tom looked around at the table littered with plates and serving dishes and said, "This is quite a mess. I'll be glad to help you clean up."

"That's very sweet of you to offer, but you don't have to. It won't take too long to straighten this out. You aren't obligated."

"Obligated or not, I helped make this mess so I'm going to help clean it up."

Katie smiled, "Thank you, I really do appreciate it. If you carry everything out to the kitchen, I will put the food away and wash the dishes. It won't take that long if we work together."

However, it took a longer time than Katie thought because there was a lot to do. She washed the dishes and Tom dried them. Then, while Katie tidied up the kitchen and living room, Tom washed the pots and pans. When everything was cleaned, Katie brewed a fresh pot of coffee and they sat in the living room. She sighed as she slipped off her shoes, sat in a chair, and put her legs on a footstool. After taking a drink of coffee she said, "Tom, you were right. There were a lot more things to wash than I thought and I'm glad that you helped."

He sipped his coffee and answered, "You really are welcome. I've enjoyed it. I hadn't thought about it in years but I used to help my mother after her parties in exactly the same way. It's strange, how sometimes the past merges with the present."

Katie saw an opportunity to find out a little more about his past so she asked, "How often did your mother have parties?"

"Maybe once a month, maybe more. She was principal of Milan High School and president of the Milan Historical Society so she entertained quite a bit. As her only child I helped her get ready for the party and the cleanup afterwards."

They quietly chatted about little things in their pasts until Tom glanced at his wristwatch and said, "Holy Smokes, it's almost two o'clock. Schaeffer stadium is being renovated and I have a job there at 8:00 AM. I've got to go."

Katie went to get his coat and when she came back Tom said, "Katie, I have a proposition for you. If you will pay for the cost of the materials, and that won't be too much, I will install more electrical outlets and fix all of your wiring problems."

"Do you know how?"

Tom replied, "Yes, and it will be professional enough to pass code. I am not as fast as these commercial electricians but, for your problems, I can do everything that they can do."

Katie was surprised by his offer. She replied. "Tom, that is very kind of you. Do you have any idea of what the cost of the materials will be?"

"I would guess it would cost anywhere from five to six hundred dollars."

"That's a lot cheaper than the estimates I got. But why should you do a job for nothing? I don't think that's fair. What would you get out of that?"

Tom smiled as he answered, "I would get a couple of things. First, I need to keep busy and a job like this would interest me. Furthermore, you're a good cook and you could occasionally invite me over to dinner. Most important of all, it would give me a great deal of pleasure to help the prettiest lady in Foxboro."

Katie was taken by surprise with his answer. She hadn't expected such honesty and she hadn't even been sure that he noticed her this evening. He hadn't said anything about her appearance so she thought that he hadn't paid attention. Evidently, he had and that pleased her.

"I'm not sure that I agree to your terms and I may change them later but I gladly accept your offer to fix the wiring. It has always been a concern of mine.

"However, you have got to go and get some sleep."

She went with Tom to the front door, where he said, "Goodnight" and left. They did not touch each other but there was none of the awkwardness of their last parting; they walked away from each other knowing that they were friends.

11

Human beings are a diverse and unique species. We have evolved from the beginning of the universe into what we are today; and what we are is puzzling. We are a mystery because even when we, as individuals, aspire for the best we, as societies, usually achieve the worst. For example, we are the only species that willingly and wantonly goes to war to slaughter our own kind.

Physically, we have many of the traits of the other species. For propagation purposes we have two sexes, we are protective of our young, we have finite life spans, and we have natural diseases that inflict us. However, we are different in the sense that, as we have developed our intellectual capabilities, our tactile senses have diminished. We do not see, hear, smell, feel, or taste as acutely as some of the animals we keep as our own personal pets.

What we have done is develop our capability for abstract reasoning to such a degree that we are a complex blend of emotions. Kindness and cruelty, love and hate, divinity and depravity are all delicately balanced within each one of us. How we individually handle these divergent feelings defines us as the person we are within our own particular society.

Human beings are at a level that no other species has ever achieved. We have taught ourselves to read and write and talk and, using those basic skills, we humans have unlocked the warehouse of knowledge. We have learned to do both wonderful things and terrible things.

Evolving as we have in different parts of a planet that has many varieties of climates and living conditions, humans are now a diverse physical specimen. We come in all sizes, most colors, and many races. We have so many cultures, so many languages, and so many alphabets, that it is sometimes hard to understand each other. The human race appears to have come full cycle; at first not possessing the ability to communicate, but now having languages so different that we often times cannot conduct a basic conversation.

Long ago, as humans became more numerous, there became a need to establish rules by which they could live with each other. Individuals came together and formed clans. As the clans grew they formed communities and these communities, when they became powerful enough to last for long periods of time, became the bases of civilizations.

Within our own large and complex civilization, individuals still crave companionship, friendliness and the love of others, especially those who mirror comparable values. Anyone who thinks and feels the same as you do is worthy of being admired. As a result, we come together in small groups that have common goals, be it a social club, a church, a neighborhood, or a labor union.

Humans find it much easier to stay within their own race, or color, or religion, or economic status than to stray across these boundaries. An individual who doesn't conform is at risk of being considered as different because homogeneity is much more desirable than diversity.

Both Tom Booker and Mark Givens, for exactly opposite reasons, got into trouble with the most intimate of social groups, their own families. Booker went to war and he was affected by it; Givens didn't go to war and he was still affected by it. They were both guilty of something every human does, they allowed their experiences to govern their social attitudes. Because of their experiences, they became isolated from their families until all family members recognized that forgiving is one of the most important components of mature people. Mark was ready to forgive but his father had to learn to overcome his prejudice; Tom's parents were ready to forgive but Tom had to learn to forget his past.

***

Thomas Booker had come to Foxboro out of desperation. For years he had been like a plastic dinner plate floating on the tide. He roamed aimlessly around the country, drifted from job to job, accepted no responsibility for anything and drank heavily. He was on the brink of falling out of the human race when he finally realized how badly he was sinking.

His epiphany began in Seattle when he recognized that he was almost out of control. What brought him to his senses happened late at night in a dingy, working class bar. He had been drinking his salary away and minding his own business when four or five couples came in and sat down at a large table in the middle of the saloon. At first, the only thing that caught his attention was their appearance. All the women wore formal gowns and they were well coifed and attractive; all the men wore tuxedoes and they were self satisfied and portly. Tom looked at them when they arrived, dismissed them as the type of people he didn't like; he thought that they had come to slum. He went back to his own bitter thoughts.

After a while though, their conversation began to penetrate through to him and what he was hearing angered him. The men were complaining that working for a living in peacetime was not as easy as it was in wartime, and they were citing their own experiences of trying to make money during the Vietnam War.

This infuriated Tom. He was absolutely fed up with fat civilians and their take on the Vietnam War. In a silent rage he looked at their table again and thought to himself, "If I wanted, I could take out every one of those bastards in less than a minute."

Then the enormity of his own thought struck him. "You dumb bastard. What gives you the right to take those fat porkers out? Just because you hate them?" He knew what the answer to his question was and he was truly stunned over what had been going through his mind. He sat at the bar for a minute or two, swallowed the rest of his drink, and walked out into the night.

He went back to his small, rented room, finished off a pint of cheap whiskey that he had under his pillow, and fell asleep fully dressed. In the morning, when he awoke with a throbbing hangover, he went to a local restaurant and drank black coffee. He felt terrible, mentally and physically. It took two full days to purge the poisons from his systems. In the interim, he cleaned his room meticulously, ate carefully and took long walks. He was becoming aware that his thoughts were getting increasingly violent and dangerous. It was then that he realized that he either had to change or he would go to pieces and do something bad.

After his mind and body began to clear, Tom began to think about his past. Not the nightmares he suffered, nor the way he was treated when he returned to this country, nor the way the Veterans Administration seemed so indifferent to the veterans' problems. In his mind, he went back to Nam and his brothers whom he had fought with. He thought about his brothers who came back either maimed, or wounded, or in a casket; he also thought about those who would never come back, the Missing In Action.

He remembered that he had silently told all of them that he would try to see that they had not died in vain. He had vowed to do something to honor them and make them proud of him. They died alongside him; he owed them a lot more than he had been giving.

He had not been keeping his promise.

That's when Tom decided, on a sudden whim, to move to Foxboro. He had never visited Foxboro but his sergeant had lived there and he had talked constantly about his home town. Tom loved and respected his fallen brother; he thought it would be a fitting tribute to start his life over in his home town. When he arrived in Foxboro, he rented a room and began searching for a job. The first place he went to was the Company; however, after looking at the long application form that made him account for each of his jobs since his discharge and the name of his supervisor, he realized that he probably would not be hired. The unexplained time gaps after Vietnam would show that, as an employee, he would not be reliable. All the other applications he would have to fill out asked for the same information. After being turned down three or four times, he decided on a different approach.

He went to the Foxboro Highway Department and asked if they had any openings. Their paperwork was minimal and, after he talked directly with the Highway Department Supervisor, Joel Kinnick, he was hired immediately. The pay was a little less than a good factory job so there usually were jobs available. Although there was a cadre of older men who had been with the highway department for years, Kinnick was always looking for good, steady help. As long as you did your job no one asked about your background.

The superintendent soon realized that he had hired a competent man as Tom easily could handle most of the heavy equipment, the bulldozers, the front-end loaders, the backhoes as well as the dump trucks. The only trouble Tom had was with one of his fellow workers. The man who usually ran all the heavy equipment was called PJ, for Portagee John, and, until Tom was hired, he was the biggest bull in the coral.

PJ was a large man with a big mouth and a small brain. His father had been in the construction business for years and he had tried to teach his son how to run the operation. PJ could handle the machines but he couldn't handle the numbers, they confused him, so he ended up working for the highway department. None of his fellow workers ever crossed him because they were afraid of getting into a fist fight with him. His fists were his rule book.

PJ watched Tom, for about a week, trying to decide when he wanted to pick a fight with the new man; he figured he was much bigger and stronger than Tom. He made several stupid and offensive remarks to Tom but Tom didn't respond. One day, Tom walked over to where PJ was struggling to move a tree stump out of a hole. He pushed PJ out of the way, grabbed it with both hands and almost jerked it free. From that day on, PJ never thought of confronting him.

Tom went about his job quietly not saying much unless asked a direct question. He minded his own business, helped his fellow workers, and kept to himself. The only thing they knew about him was that he went to the library often and that he usually carried a book with him.

He had been there about a year when Mark joined the highway department. The foreman assigned him to work with Tom because Mark knew nothing and Tom was experienced. Tom took a liking to Mark because Mark was honest and open about everything. Tom learned that

Mark had gone to Canada to avoid the draft and that made no difference to him. He respected the fact that Mark had made his own decision and that he was paying the price of his choice without complaining.

He discovered a lot about Mark while they worked together because Mark liked to talk. He found out about Mark's father shunning him and he heard a lot about Helen and Katie. Tom didn't realize it at the time, but he saw Katie, when she returned, even before Mark did.

Tom first noticed her when she started working at the library. He thought that she was an attractive woman but he had no idea that Mark was her brother. He would look to see if she were working when he came into the library and he enjoyed glancing at her as she went about her business. For him, watching the new librarian was a pleasant diversion when he was taking a break from reading or working.

When Mark found out, from Mrs. Buoni, that Katie had moved back to Foxboro, he told Tom. Still not knowing who she was, Tom insisted that Mark visit her and, after Mark kept hesitating, he finally drove Mark over to her house.

Tom was totally taken aback when he saw Katie standing on the porch waving at Mark. The library lady he thought so attractive was Mark's sister. He knew so much about her and yet, he had never met her. After he was introduced, Tom began to think of Katie other than just as the library lady. He noticed how she did her job and how much she tried to help anyone who asked for assistance. It was obvious to him that, along with being attractive, Katie was a caring person.

The morning of the first big snowstorm, the supervisor had pulled him off to one side and told him that one of crew called in sick. He asked Tom if he could handle another route as well as plowing his own. It didn't make any difference to Tom because he would be plowing for sixteen or eighteen hours anyhow and the other plow route was on winding back roads with little traffic; plowing both routes would keep him out of the busy downtown traffic. He didn't realize how fortunate his choice was until he came upon Katie's car in a ditch.

After he drove her home, Tom went for coffee and, for the first time in years, he felt happy and carefree. Even in a dump truck in a snowstorm, Tom was elated to be driving with Katie as his companion. The kinder side of his personality, frozen for such a long time, was beginning to thaw. During the early morning hours, Tom and Mark drove to where Katie's car was abandoned; they attached a chain to the frame and pulled it out of the ditch. Then Mark drove the car to Katie's house where they cleared her drive and backed her car into her driveway.

When Katie invited Tom to her house for Thanksgiving he decided to get his hair cut and his beard shaved; he was subconsciously returning to the fold. When he left that evening, he knew that he was in love with Katie.

Unrequited love has even higher and lower emotional peaks than the requited virus; Tom was completely smitten. He would sit in the library, attempting to do his home work or read a book or a magazine, and just daydream. He began to wonder how he could get Katie to acknowledge that he existed and what life with Katie would be like if they were married.

He also began to think of what he had been doing with his life these past few years. He realized that he wanted, and needed, to talk with his mother and father; there was a chapter he needed to close and a new chapter he needed to open. So, he called and asked if he could come home for Christmas. For Tom and his parents it was the happiest Christmas they had had since he had returned from Vietnam.

***

The Patriots of Foxboro

Their family problems had started just before Tom graduated from the University of Michigan. He had taken his deferments to get a Bachelor's Degree in Political Science and, instead of going to law school as his parents wanted, he decided to join the Army. He felt that he owed his country something for letting him get an education.

His mother and his father had both been opposed to the Vietnam War from the beginning. They felt that the United States shouldn't be fighting a war that the French had walked away from. They also believed that our leaders were using the excuse of Communist expansion as a scare tactic. They felt that all we were doing in Vietnam was pillaging and punishing a backward country; and now their only son was going to be immersed in that Hellhole. They argued with him to no avail and the results were predictable, and disastrous.

Tom went to Vietnam and was there on a long tour of duty. He was heavily involved in combat and was slightly wounded. He was hospitalized, flew home and was honorably discharged. Immediately after receiving his discharge, he returned to Milan. His mother and father were thrilled to have him safely home but they soon realized that their son had completely changed. Tom was an entirely different person. It was as if he was buried in a crypt inside of himself. He drank heavily, smoked pot, and was extremely hard to talk to.

At first, they tried not to notice that he drank and smoked and didn't pay attention to anything they asked of him. However, after a few weeks, their household was tense with almost no conversations except hushed complaints. They spent anxious hours in bed at night whispering with each other trying to figure out a way of getting through to Tom. It was not that his parents had stopped loving him; it was that they had lost him and didn't know how to get him back.

Tom supplied their answer. He told them one morning, during a very silent breakfast that he was leaving. He said that he was going to live with one of his Vietnam buddies in Montana. He didn't have any buddy in Montana but he knew that he had to get out of his parents' home; they didn't understand what he had been through and he couldn't tell them. All he wanted was to get away from everybody and everything. Society had turned its back on him and he wanted to return the favor. He told no one about the mind numbing nightmares that wracked his sleep every night and stole his sanity.

So, Tom left Milan and drifted from one state to another, taking whatever job was available. He paid no attention to the news on television or in the newspapers and when he got tired of either his surroundings or his job, he would move on. It was a restless, lonely life that sent him aimlessly in all directions. He had no plans and no goals and his life consisted of himself, his bitter memories, his drinking, and his pot. He was in a constant downward spiral and it wasn't until he thought of killing those people in the Seattle bar that he realized what was happening to him.

***

As he drove up to his parent's home, he knew that they both would be nervous and apprehensive when he arrived. He was also nervous. He had occasionally called them since leaving home but he had never been back to see them. Their last memories would be of him when he had left to go to Montana. They wouldn't know what to expect from him and, for that, he felt ashamed. He had not been a good son.

His mother opened the front door as he reached for the storm door. She said, "Hello Tom, welcome home."

"Hi Momma, I brought you these flowers."

She suddenly grabbed him and hugged him fiercely. "I'm so glad that you are here for Christmas. Your father and I have repainted your bedroom. I think you'll like it. How long will you be staying"?

Tom's voice cracked as he returned her hug and answered, "I don't know Momma. It's a long drive from Michigan to Massachusetts, about fifteen hours. I'll be here until sometime after New Year's Day.

"Where's Dad?"

"Right here, Tom. Your Mother was able to beat me to the door only because I'm getting old while she stays young.

"Welcome home, Son. Can I help you unload your car?"

"Don," his mother said, "Neither of you are to touch anything in his car until Tom has had a chance to eat and drink and relax."

"Yes, Selma."

They went into the kitchen and Tom's mother made a pot of fresh coffee to accompany the four-dozen chocolate cookies that she had freshly baked for him. The three of them sat there talking about events that had happened in the their past, when Tom was much younger. As they relaxed and corrected the other's memories, the tensions evaporated like steam off a mirror. By bedtime each of them knew it was going to be a happy homecoming and each was glad.

At dinner time the next evening Tom said, hesitantly, "Momma, Dad, I have something to say to you. You told me not to enlist and I did, despite your warnings. You were right; the results have been bad for all of us. I went to Nam and I saw things that no person should ever have to see and I did things that no person should ever have to do. It's difficult to get over something like that and I didn't do well. I'm trying to do better but sometimes it's hard, very very hard.

"Through it all, you tried to help me even when I turned away from you. I was wrong and I am so sorry, so terribly sorry. All I can tell you is that I thank you for being my parents and being so patient. I love you."

There was a moment of silence and then, with tears streaming down their faces, they each hugged one another.

In the following days, Tom would go to his father's hardware store in the morning and help his mother with her Christmas preparations in the afternoon. The day before Christmas he stayed home all day to help her with the dinner she was preparing for the eight guests she had invited. She had made a list of people who would have been alone on Christmas and she had sent them invitations long before Tom had called. Tom was helping her because he thought she looked frailer than he had ever seen her.

As they were working in the kitchen Tom said, "Momma, I've met the girl that I want to marry."

His mother stopped what she was doing, looked at him and replied, "Thomas, I'm absolutely delighted to hear you're thinking of marriage. Why didn't you bring your young lady home with you? I want to meet her."

"Momma, it's not quite that simple. She is a widow with a young boy and she works at the Foxboro library. That's where I first met her and I'm not sure that she knows I even exist."

His mother replied, "You want to get married but the woman you want to marry may not know you exist? You'll have to tell me a lot more before this makes sense to me."

They sat at the kitchen table as Tom told her about Katie and her son, Tyler. Then, he went on to tell her about Mark, Brenda, Helen and Katie's father. When he finished, his mother said, "Tom, your future wife sounds like a sensible person who is trying to make her life better; I would like to meet her.

"However, let me give you some advice. I hope your feelings won't be hurt but if you want her to notice you, you are going to have to be more assertive. Tell her your feelings. You don't have to apologize for your past any more than Katie has to apologize for her marriage. You are a handsome, intelligent man so why not show yourself at your best?"

"Momma, that doesn't hurt my feelings. I wanted your advice and I welcome your comments. I came home to make my peace with you and Dad and tell you about Katie. I hope to marry her and raise a family. I wanted you both to know."

Their days together went swiftly because happiness compresses time just as misery lengthens it. Tom told them more about Katie and that he was taking classes to get a teaching certificate. He didn't mention that he had decided on teaching as his way of giving back to his brothers; he was randomly picked to stay alive while they had not. His parents could see that Tom was trying to put Vietnam behind him and they were pleased and proud of their son.

When the time came for him to leave, he couldn't believe the days passed so quickly and that he had to leave to go back to work. As he made the long drive home, he alternately thought of his peaceful visit with his mother and father and what pleasures could lay ahead for him and Katie. What also delighted him was that, during his entire visit, he had suffered only two of his mind shattering nightmares.

***

The first time Tom came over to Katie's house to work on the wiring was early on a Saturday afternoon. He worked until suppertime when Katie made dinner for him and Tyler. After Tyler was put to bed, they sat in the living room talking and gossiping. Katie was surprised at how easy their conversations flowed, no matter what the topic.

This set the pattern for the next three or four Saturdays; and Tom, no matter how slowly he tried to work, was beginning to get the job finished. He followed his mother's advice and eagerly told Katie about his upbringing. During their conversations, Katie found out that Tom was a graduate of the University of Michigan and that he could have gone to law school, instead, he had enlisted in the army. She soon learned that he still shied away from answering any questions about his time in Vietnam.

Tom told Katie that he needed to work one Friday and one Saturday together and then the job would be finished. He took a day off work and by late Saturday he had everything completed. Katie was pleased as Tom showed her the new outlets and the new light fixtures that he had installed throughout the house. She said, "Tom, this is great, a lot of good lighting and I don't have to worry about blowing fuses. I want to write you a check for your services, you certainly deserve to be paid."

"No, Katie, I don't want your money. I have a better idea. You have a large back yard and I would like to have a small vegetable garden this summer. When I was a youngster in Milan, I used to have one for my family. If you will let me have a small plot, I will enjoy gardening and we will share the veggies. That's what I would really like."

"Tom, you keep avoiding the fact that I want to pay you for your work. Of course you can have a garden in my back yard, I like the idea. I will reserve the right to work in it with you because I have always wanted to grow fresh fruits and vegetables. Tomatoes, corn, beans, berries, oh, I can hardly wait.

"In the meantime, you have no idea how grateful I am. I'm going to go to Shaw's and get some thick steaks for dinner tonight."

"Oh no Katie, now you're ruining my plans. I don't want you to do any cooking tonight. It's my night to celebrate my work. I want to take you and Tyler out to the Red Wing Diner as my guests."

Katie didn't reply at first and Tom looked at her and wondered if he had said something wrong. After a few seconds she said, "How about if we go Dutch treat and I pay for me and Tyler?"

"Katie, why would we do that?"

"Tom, you work for the town of Foxboro and your salary is on public record at the library. I know how much you make and I don't want to be a burden on your budget."

Tom smiled as he replied, "Well, Dorothy Detective, for your information you are also a town employee and I looked up your income. It is substantially more than mine but my offer still stands.

"First, my salary isn't my only income. I make fairly good money as a handy man. Second, I live very frugally thanks to my mother's teaching. And third, Brenda and Mark will probably join us and I want to avoid a lot of confusion when the bill arrives."

Tom's statement that he was frugal rang a bell in Katie's mind, it reminded her of her own upbringing. She said, "OK, Senor Snoop, so you looked up my pay? Well, I guess that's fair enough, if I looked up your salary you should be able to look up mine."

Then, after a second, she blurted out, "Listen, I will accept your offer if you will accept mine. Next Saturday, I will bring Tyler to one of his 'grandmothers' and you and I will go to the Lafayette House and, this time, I pay." Katie couldn't believe she had enough nerve to make such a suggestion. However, she thought that Tom was too self-effacing, he underestimated his work and he refused to take any money. Since she sincerely believed that Tom was under pricing his work this was one way to pay him back.

Tom answered, "You're on, you must be expecting a large raise if you are going to take me to the Lafayette House. I certainly hope your raise comes through, in the meantime, this evening, we are headed for the Red Wing Diner."

It turned out to be an outstanding evening. The four of them and Tyler ordered fried clams and lobster rolls and they ate until they were sated. Brenda still didn't have the courage to try steamed clams.

Then, Brenda and Mark had to come over to Katie's house where she turned on every light and every appliance to show them how pleased she was. After Mark and Brenda left, Katie put Tyler to bed and she and Tom talked for a while. She escorted him to the door where he told her, "Good night" and left, no hug, not even a handshake. Katie wondered if Tom was ever going to try putting his arms around her and giving her a kiss.

12

Helen was as good as her word about keeping in touch. She made it a point to call early on Saturday mornings and she would chat for hours. Katie had the impression that Helen was alone when she phoned but she didn't ask. Mark and Brenda came over for breakfast, at Katie's invitation, and Helen talked to each of them as well as to Tyler. It made for a good start to their weekend activities.

On the Saturday morning that Katie was going to the Lafayette House, she told Mark and Brenda about her date after Helen's phone call. Brenda asked about Tyler and Katie told her that he would go over to one of his "grandmother's" house.

Brenda said, "Listen Katie, Mark and I are going into Boston to sightsee. We will try to get through the Aquarium, Faneuil Hall, and Old Ironsides. Why don't you let us take Tyler with us? I'm sure he'd enjoy himself and Mark and I would love to have him."

Katie answered, " I'm sure he'd like to go but when would you get back? He will probably be tired by the time you got home."

Mark replied, "No problem Katie. We will keep him overnight and you can pick him up whenever you want to on Sunday. Actually, we haven't had him for a while; it will be fun for all of us. We'll take him with us now and you come and get him tomorrow."

Katie had not taken Tyler into Boston very often; the traffic and parking in Boston were things she gladly avoided. She was sure that Tyler would enjoy seeing those sites so she was glad to let him go with Mark and Brenda. After they left, she called Tom to find out what time he had planned on being at her house and to let him know that he could come over earlier if he wished.

When he found that Katie was free, he said to her, "I was just heading out the door. Why don't you join me? I'm sure you'll like where I'm going"

"And where is that?"

"HAH! I can't tell you, we'll be going on a secret mission. Dress warmly because we will be out of doors. I'll be at your house shortly."

When he picked her up he still didn't say where they were heading, but the minute he crossed the town line into Norfolk, Katie said, "We're heading for Stony Brook. I haven't been there for years. Oh, what a pleasant surprise."

Tom parked the car and they walked down the long boardwalk over to the observation platform. Although no warm spring weather had yet arrived, the weather was not cold. There was no wind and not a cloud in the sky and the sun was making the snow smile. It was a day that made you feel happy to be alive. They sat on a bench at the observation platform and looked across the pond, watching nature go about her solemn business of renewing life. There was not another soul in the bird sanctuary; they were alone with each other. They sat there listening to the muted birdcalls and enjoying the beauty and the tranquility.

The Patriots of Foxboro

Tom turned on the bench to look at Katie and he began to talk, "Katie, you asked me a while ago why I came to Foxboro and I didn't answer you. Are you still interested in hearing that story?"

Katie could see how tense Tom was. She took his hand and replied, "I'm interested."

"It is a long story that begins when I joined the army and went into the infantry. The army's job was to teach me how to kill. That was something that went against what my mother and father had been teaching me since I was a child. That's against what every religion believes. I had always been taught that life was sacred. I believed life was sacred. But my kill teachers told me that this was war and I was fighting for everything that was dear to me, so I learned what I was taught.

"I learned to kill with a gun, I learned to kill with a knife, I learned to kill with my bare hands. I even learned to kill with whatever was available. I was taught well and I learned well.

"Then I was sent to Vietnam. Oh Katie, what a hellhole Vietnam was. Heat. Humidity. Confusion. Stink. I was almost immediately deployed into combat and, for me, the heat, humidity, and confusion got worse.

"It was impossible to know who was the enemy. They were all small Asians whose speech you couldn't understand. You couldn't tell friend from foe. There was no front line. The enemy was everywhere, behind you, ahead of you, beside you. A small kid or an old crone could walk by and roll a grenade at you. After a while hate and fear ate you from one end while the battlefield kill ate you from the other end.

"I lost any sense of reason and applied all the knowledge they taught me. I did the thing I was trained to do; I killed. And the longer I was in combat the easier it was to kill. It became easy, so easy, too easy. Killing became a reflex, like breathing.

"Vietnam was shit."

He stopped speaking and just sat there. Katie looked at him and saw tears coming down his cheeks.

She squeezed his hand and said, "Oh, Tom. How awful. I'm so sorry. You don't have to say another word." Katie began to weep.

"No, no Katie, I want to tell you, I need to tell you. Meeting you has been the best thing that has ever happened to me and I keep thinking maybe that was why I survived while my brothers died. I …"

Just then, they heard a dog barking close at hand, signaling that their solitude was going to be interrupted. Sure enough, two children came running down the path oblivious to their presence. Behind them came a man and a woman holding a dog on a leash. The man cried out to the children to be careful and not go near the water. After some noise and disturbance, the family retreated back down the boardwalk and left.

Katie and Tom stood up and held hands as they watched this domestic scene play out. The intrusion of other people broke the thread of Tom's story while the exuberance of the children swept away the horrors that Tom had been describing. The two of them walked around the Beech Grove and Stony Brook Pond talking about small tidbits of their individual lives.

After a while, they returned to the bench and sat down. Tom looked straight ahead of him and said, "It is so peaceful here. I come here often to think. Maybe it is to pray for my brothers. I often wonder whether our society truly appreciates their supreme sacrifices.

"Anyhow, I was wounded in the last firefight I was in and my platoon sergeant, Sergeant Pinckney, died in my arms. He was all ripped open. God, I think about him all the time; he was my brother and my best friend."

Tom sat, staring out across the pond, with tears streaming from his eyes. A few minutes later he blew out his breath, wiped his face, and smiled at Katie. "I'm sorry; I'm not a baby but I loved those guys. We lived and fought together. We never questioned what we were doing, we were just trying to stay alive in that God Damned Hellhole.

"I was sent to a hospital in Saigon to recover and then I was evacuated back to the states. It was only then that I realized that people were blaming the soldiers for what the politicians had gotten us into.

"I was stunned. I got off a plane filled with wounded soldiers. We had fought for our country and we had all left behind friends and brothers who had died for our country. Yet, just after I arrived, these people were screaming 'Baby Killers' at us, the survivors. One woman walked up to me and spit in my face.

"What had we done to deserve such hatred? We did no more than the men of World War I and World War II. We had answered our country's call. I wonder what our accusers would have done to stay alive if they had been in Vietnam? Those bastards never had to live in fear or see their friends blown apart. I cursed them on behalf of my dead brothers for passing judgment on what we had done. Why weren't they spitting in the faces of the politicians that sent us there?

"I might have been able to overlook the hatred and scorn except that they made my nightmares worse. The government had turned my kill button on but I don't have an off switch and I can't forget what I've been through. Every time I went to sleep I was haunted by the fear of dying and the deaths I was inflicting. I saw my friends dying and I saw myself killing just to stay alive.

"My nightmares made my drug and drinking problems worse. Added to all of this was the fact that, after we took off our uniforms, the government forgot about us. We became invisible to the very people who sent us to Vietnam. I couldn't get the help I needed and I couldn't stop the torment that wracked me. For a long time, I was dangerous, angry at the world and moody. I was a mess, no good to myself, to my parents or to anyone else.

"I can't change my past mistakes, Katie, but I can look to the future. All I want now is to lead a normal life and be a better person."

Tom stopped speaking and just sat quietly. Katie had never thought about the burdens he carried. She was stunned to hear them and find how deeply he had been wounded. Then, she thought of how lightly she and the other librarians had talked about him as "Mountain Man." She was ashamed that she had been so frivolous in her initial judgment. Without thinking, she leaned forward, kissed him on the cheek and asked, "And is your plan working?"

"Now, Katie? Well, I don't have nightmares as often as I did and I have been free of drugs and alcohol for almost five years. I don't hate the world and I have a goal to keep me moving forward. I want to be a high school teacher and help young men and women choose their correct paths. If I could do that, I think my brothers would be proud of me.

"What I will tell you is this, I would give anything to have my record prettier than it is. I made many, many bad decisions and I'm sorry about them.

"I hope you can forgive what I was and see what I can be."

Katie had to overcome her own emotions before she could speak. She thought to herself, "You survived Vietnam but you paid an awful price for your survival. All you've ever asked for is a chance to forget what you went through and to get on with your life."

When she finally had control of her voice she quietly said, "Tom what is there to forgive? You went to Vietnam and fought because you thought that was your duty."

Katie paused, and added quietly, "For that alone, I admire you."

It was beginning to get chilly but it was not cold enough to be unpleasant. They both sat on the bench and watched the birds; some were slowly wheeling through the blue sky, others were flying direct flights. The serenity that surrounded them softened their thoughts.

After a while, Katie spoke again. "You are not the only one who made mistakes. I saw us slowly sliding into a full scale war and never questioned why.

"When Mark left for Canada, I started to think more about what was happening in Vietnam. Until then, I had assumed that any decision made by our government was in the best interests of our country. All a politician has to do is shout 'Patriotism' and everyone stands at attention and salutes.

"Of course Mike, his squadron, all our friends, and even my father, were for our military campaign. I was surrounded by people who didn't question what we were doing. Mark's stand was painful for him so I began to wonder if what we were doing was right or not.

"I watched the news on television, read the newspapers, and listened to what was being said by our elected leaders and our generals. The government insisted that we were fighting the Communists while the military said that we were beating the enemy.

"I didn't see any of that. What I saw, when I finally looked, was our young sons and daughters dying for their country. I began to wonder why we were even there. The body counts, the napalm bombings, the Agent Orange spraying, were these the answers to a Communist threat?

"I finally began to wonder if there were really a Communist threat? Do you spread democracy by setting up puppet governments? Weren't we really spreading chaos? I wondered if we really and truly knew what we were doing?

"And you were in the middle of that? You have no need to apologize to me. I am grateful and thankful to you. You are a hero to me."

They sat and held hands. There was peace within both of them. After a while Katie said, "I'm getting chilly. Let's go home. Would you mind if we didn't go to the Lafayette House? I'd rather stay home and cook dinner for us. If you don't object, I'll call and cancel our reservation."

Tom looked at her and replied, "Katie, as long as I am with you I don't care where we are. If you are going to cook I want to help."

With that they went shopping at Shaw's and bought two huge steaks and more food than they could possibly eat at one meal. They went back to Katie's house and she broiled the steaks while Tom set the table, made a salad, and prepared the fresh vegetables.

During all of this time they talked about their childhood, their high school days, and their alma maters, Boston University and the University of Michigan. They were so busy chatting that their meal got cold and they didn't notice. The hunger for love is much more acute than the hunger for food.

It wasn't until after they had cleaned up the kitchen that Katie returned to their personal conversation. They were together on the sofa in the living room and Tom had his arm around her shoulder Katie asked, "Tom, did you ever get around to telling me why you came to Foxboro?"

Tom chuckled and answered, "I told you that it was a long story and I have taken the long way around, but no, I never got to why I came to Foxboro. However, I have talked so much about me that I decided to give it a rest. You have to be a little tired of me by now."

"No, to be perfectly honest, I'm intrigued. You're a survivor and I want to know the rest of your story so you certainly have my permission to continue.

"And I must warn you that, if you don't tell me, I won't offer you any dessert."

"That's just plain blackmail, but I'm a sucker for pie, so you win.

"My turnaround started when I realized I was wasting my life. I was drunk in a seedy bar in Seattle when a group of well dressed, well fed people who were slumming came in to sneer at the lowlife. These pudgy know it alls made me so angry that I thought of attacking them. Luckily, I was so drunk that I didn't carry out my plan, but after I sobered up, I was scared.

"I realized that I was slipping closer and closer to doing something insane and dangerous. I began to think of my dead brothers in Vietnam and I wondered why I was wasting the life I had been spared. They didn't come back and I did and, because of that, I owed them. I owed them my life and I needed to stop screwing it up and do something they would approve of. Those thoughts about my friends hit me hard. I had to honor their memories even if no one else did.

"I made a trip to Washington DC and I went to the Wall. I looked up each of my brother's names, touched every inscription and I cried for all of them. Lord, how I cried for them, and for me.

"My platoon Sergeant Pinckney had told me that he was born and raised in the town of Foxboro. I loved and respected him so much that, after I finished talking to him at the Wall, I decided to start again in his hometown as my tribute to him. When I got here I found no one by that name living in Foxboro. Evidently, they had moved on a long time ago. I picked out a job that had no pressure and where no one would pay attention to me, the Foxboro Highway Department. I moved into a single room in a boarding house, lived by myself, and went straight.

"About two years ago, I went to a Foxboro football game and an odd thing happened to me. The band of the opposing team played the 'Star

Spangled Banner.' It was the worst rendition that I ever heard in my life. Every horn was off key and the tempo was almost a funeral march. It didn't make any difference; all of a sudden I went under the grandstands and started to bawl. I had suddenly discovered that I was proud of my service and that I had nothing to be ashamed of. My brothers and I had done what we were asked to do to the best of our ability, and many of them had died for our country. If there was any shame associated with the war it belonged to the politicians who allowed it to continue and the people who blamed the soldiers for doing their duty.

"A short time after that, your brother came to work at the highway department. At first, I paid little attention to him. He had elected a different path than going into the service. He had made his choice and he had paid his price. The truth is that every one of our generation paid a heavy price for a misguided political decision.

"Anyhow, I listened and watched as Portagee John started to ride Mark about being a coward and a draft dodger. PJ is a stupid bully who never went into the service and had used draft deferrals to stay a civilian. That annoyed me.

"Your brother didn't back away from PJ but he wasn't sure how to handle him. He tried to reason with him and that was a big mistake. Bullies don't understand reasoning and take it as a sign of weakness. Your brother is not weak and he wanted to try to get along with PJ. I began to admire him for trying to be friendly with PJ but, truthfully, I was sure that it wouldn't work.

"I also knew that it was about time that I put PJ in his place. Strength is the only thing that bullies understand; if you are stronger than they are, they stop bullying. So, it was no surprise to me when I stepped in just as PJ decided that he was going to beat Mark up. It was something I had planned to do when Mark was finally in over his head.

"Because Mark was paired with me quite a bit, I got to know a lot about him and his family. Your brother has become like a younger brother to me. He went one way while I went the other but I don't find myself getting angry about it. He followed his convictions and he paid for it. He told me all about your father, your stepmother, Helen, and you. I heard a lot about you long before I ever met you. For that alone, I will always be grateful to him."

Katie was taken by surprise. She had no idea that Mark had ever talked about her to a complete stranger. "Well, I guess I will have to thank him for introducing us. I hope what you found out wasn't completely bad."

"Oh no, Katie. You have no idea how much your brother loves and respects you. I knew you from the library while Mark had told me how you had helped raise him. I had two different views of you; however, I didn't connect the two until the morning I first saw you standing on your porch. When I realized you were his sister I felt, for the first time in years, that my life could be sweet."

Katie looked at Tom and, without thinking, they came together and kissed. What neither of them realized was the bond that they had subconsciously formed. For years, they had been fighting their personal battles alone and for years they had each refrained from any kind of intimacy. Today, by the pond at Stony Brook, their minds, thoughts, and hearts had aligned with each other without them being aware it had happened. They were each a powder keg of emotion ready to detonate.

Their kiss lit the spark that set off an explosion of passion. They wound up in Katie's bed making love. Sometime in the early hours of the morning, Katie was awakened by Tom; he was still asleep but he was moaning and talking. His body would twitch as he muttered,

"No!" or grunted, "Keep down!" Katie rubbed his shoulder and kept reassuring him that everything was all right. She knew that he was living his nightmare. After a while, Tom settled back into a deep sleep. Katie kissed his shoulder, snuggled against him, and, before she fell asleep again, she thought, "Oh my god, how many more victims are there like this in our country?"

***

When she awoke, it was daylight and she was in bed by herself. Once she realized that Tom wasn't there, she panicked. Where was he? She jumped up, put on her robe and slippers and opened the bedroom door. Much to her relief she smelled coffee, obviously he was around somewhere. As she entered the kitchen Tom was pouring a cup of coffee for her.

He handed her the cup and said, "Good Morning. I was just getting ready to deliver this to you when I heard the bedroom door open."

Katie felt a little embarrassed. She had never had a lover before and she wasn't sure of what to do or what to say or even what her feelings were. "I didn't see you when I woke up and I was concerned where you were."

Tom replied, "You didn't think that I had left did you?"

"I wasn't sure."

Tom put his coffee cup down, came over to her, and put his finger under her chin so that they were looking at each other. "Listen to me, Katie Oldfield. I have no intention of ever leaving you. I love you and I want to marry you.

" As far as I am concerned today is not too early for a wedding, we can do it this afternoon. Will you marry me?"

"Yes, No, Yes. Damn it, I'm confused. Yesterday was such an enchanting day for me and last night was fun. Are you proposing marriage just because we had sex?"

"No, Katie, I most certainly am not. I'm proposing to you because I have fallen head over heels in love with you. You're the woman I want to spend the rest of my life with. I want to live with you and raise Tyler to be our son. I want us to have more children. Katie, all I can tell you is that I love you."

Katie took Tom's hand which was under her chin, kissed it, clasped it with her two hands and brought it to her heart. Her emotions were as mixed as a banana in a blender. She felt strongly about Tom but she wasn't sure whether she was in love.

Even though the pain had subsided, the scars from her marriage ran deeply through her. The humiliation and embarrassment of her husband's infidelity still echoed in her thoughts. She could not reconcile his protestations of love for her with his willingness to break her heart by sleeping with every female he could lure into bed. These negative feelings lay deep inside her subconsciousness and they bothered her. They haunted her and made her unsure of herself.

"Tom, I think I love you but I'm not sure. You are dear to me, but I'm just not sure. Marriage is a deep commitment and I can't marry you until I'm sure of myself.

"I'm not being coy, I was hurt once before. I need time. Please don't be angry with me."

"Why should I be angry? You're honest, you've always been honest, and I can understand your hesitancy. I'm disappointed we're not going to get married today, but that doesn't stop my feelings; there is always tomorrow. Make no mistake Katie, I'm in love with you. You're the woman I want to be with forever.

"In the meantime, what the Hell are we going to do about breakfast?"

Katie squeezed Tom as hard as she could. She said, "Honey, I don't want to hurt your feelings. I just want to be careful. Be patient."

She stopped and then she added, "But you don't have to be patient about breakfast. If you'll let go of me I will fix both of us a blue plate special."

As she was making toast, eggs, and bacon, Katie was deciding what she wanted to do and, while they were eating, she said, "Tom, I want you to move in with me. I want to be able to chat with you, cook for you, snuggle with you. All the things that couples do I want to do with you.

"I know that sounds crazy wanting you to be near yet refusing to marry you, but I need time. I have to talk with Tyler and tell him that you are moving in. He will be glad to have you here. I also have to speak with Mrs. Connors and Mrs. Buoni otherwise they will get the story completely wrong and who knows what they will say."

Tom spoke softly, "I'll bet they have already noticed that my truck is parked in your driveway. They probably have been on the phone with each other talking about me being here all night. They do love to gossip."

"I'm sure you're right. They are the unofficial town criers of Foxboro. They are not malicious, they love me and Tyler but they also love to talk about us. Once I tell them that we will be living together they will talk about it and then move on to other, more important, town events.

"Finish eating so that I can go pick up Tyler."

They parted and didn't see each other for a few days until Katie called Tom on the phone and invited him to move in with her.

Living together proved much easier than either of them expected.

Tyler accepted the fact that Tom was living in his mother's house without any question; in truth, he was glad to have him around. He knew Tom, loved him, and he welcomed him. With Tom around, there were less sermons and more horseplay and more roughhousing.

For Katie, it was a reawakening of herself as a person and as a woman. She had forgotten the joy that accompanies sharing life with a partner. She gave herself completely and, in turn, she was rewarded by Tom doing the same. For both, ordinary tasks became adventures; daily chores were enjoyable activities; sharing thoughts and ideas was the nectar of companionship. For Katie and Tom, life turned from chalk to chocolate.

Tom, who had never fallen in love before, believed heaven had arrived before he left this earth. To someone who has been to Hell and back, the path to happiness is never taken for granted.

Every morning before Tom got out of bed, he would kiss Katie and say, "I love you. Don't you think today would be an excellent day for us to get married?"

Katie would laugh and ruffle his hair. She would reply, "Wasn't I scheduled to get my hair done today?" or, "Aren't they having a sale on marriage licenses next week?" or anything else that deflected a direct response to his question.

However, her fear of making a bad commitment started to slowly ease as she began to appreciate the depth of Tom's love for her. Katie quickly realized that she and Tom were both fortunate.

***

A short time after Katie and Tom started to live together, Helen Givens decided that she needed to return to Foxboro. She wanted to be with her family. She always secretly thought of Katie and Mark as her children and had loved them as if they were and she was desperate to see Tyler, whom she had held as a newborn. She made her decision one Saturday morning after talking to them on the telephone.

John had bought their condo in Naples only a few years before. He had made a fortune and he wanted to get away from the New England winters and play more golf. He could do that in Florida. He would keep himself working as little as he needed while playing golf as much as he wanted.

It was a different story for Helen. Although she loved the climate of Florida she didn't mind winter in New England. During the time she was gone, she missed her friends, her activities and her charities. While John played golf she played bridge, joined several book clubs, sketched birds and soon tired of bettering her mind. She needed to be a part of her community.

She found a civic group that asked volunteers to participate in one on one English conversations with Hispanics to better their speaking capability. Helen spoke fluent Spanish and she wanted to help these immigrants overcome their language barriers, so she volunteered to join the program. This became her main activity while she was in Florida and she helped many women learn to speak English more fluently. However, at the time she made her decision to go back to Foxboro, Helen was speaking with only one woman and her student was leaving for her home in Texas in a few weeks.

She waited to discuss her plan with her husband until one evening after they had eaten dinner at their country club. They were driving home in his maroon Bentley when she said, "John, I would like to fly back to Foxboro as soon as I can. Would you mind?" She was willing to explain why she wanted to return to Foxboro if he asked; however, he rarely did.

He was quiet for a while, thinking over what she had said; then, he replied almost as if answering a different subject. "You will have to check on my mother because I'm getting mixed messages about her health from her nursing home. If you leave early I will have to drive from Florida to our house by myself. That's no big problem, though."

"I take it that you want to see Katie?"

"Yes, I'm eager to visit with Katie and see Tyler."

Helen had never hidden her contacts with Katie and Mark from her husband. He would occasionally ask her questions about them and she would always answer his question exactly. Helen was a loyal wife who loved her husband while, at the same time, she understood the motivations of her "children." It bothered her that John's pride couldn't allow him to shower his son and daughter with the same love and respect that he showed her. She kept trying to heal the breech with kind words and gentle hints.

She would never do anything behind his back but, sometimes, she had a difficult time maintaining her dedication to her husband while trying to guide him to accept both of his children as they were, not as he thought they should be. It was a delicate balancing act for Helen as she understood her husband's viewpoint but believed he carried it to the extreme as far as his children were concerned. Helen was in the difficult position of loving three people who were, for no real reason, at odds with each other.

13

As we live our lives and go about our business, every day brings small changes. These changes are usually so negligible that we are not even aware that they have taken place; but they have. Our personal world, like the amount of daylight in a twenty-four hour period, changes imperceptibly each day. No matter how stable we believe our life is, whether at home or at work, our North Star yaws and we veer ever so slightly. It always takes a while before we realize that our direction has been altered.

For example, parents don't notice the growth of their children, on a day to day basis, even as their offspring pass from infants to adults in front of them. The children's daily growth did not catch the parental eye but, without it, their children would not have changed.

Unlike most other people, John Given's world changed quickly after he left the Company. As he made more money, his outlook on life changed considerably. When he first started handling his own finances, just before his marriage to Helen, he was not quite sure that he was doing what was best for himself. His office was a small, unused bedroom in his house. As his financial decisions proved correct, he gained more confidence in his own judgements and his ventures became larger. He began to invest outside of his portfolio of stocks and bonds, in real estate, and his successes continued. He had to move his business out of his house into a small office on the second floor of a building near the Common on Bird Street. It was directly above a hardware store and it had its own separate parking, entrance door and stairs in the back of the building. Over the course of years, he amassed a fortune in land, stocks and bonds; he was a self made millionaire.

His success in making money led him to be more assertive in his opinions on other matters. He began to believe that there was no problem for which he didn't have the correct answer. As long as he limited his self congratulations to his financial abilities he was correct, he knew what he was doing. However, in all other matters, he was as fallible as everyone else.

His problem was a common human failing; he had two sets of standards. For his financial dealings he used reason; he would dispassionately analyze all his information before coming to any conclusion. He wasn't aware of it but, for all other matters, his decisions were based on his emotions. Because he was now both a little stubborn and a little arrogant, he was prone to making mistakes when it came to dealing with people.

John Givens was a decent person. It just was that his personal experiences in life, along with his inherent stubbornness, made him more inflexible than most. One of his major problems was that he couldn't give credence to anyone who opposed the war. He couldn't understand how people could consider themselves patriotic if they didn't support our effort in Vietnam. In his eyes, they had to be either hypocrites or damn fools, or both. Supporting our fighting forces took complete precedent over disputing whether the government was right or wrong. An individual's views on the Vietnam War was the first and most important criteria John Givens used to evaluate anyone.

He was not a cardboard figure. In most other matters he was a completely honest person who could admit when he made a mistake. He also cared deeply for those that he loved and respected. He showered Helen with courtesy and respect. He would ask for her opinion and listen to what she had to say before he made up his mind. That allowed Helen to understand his decisions even when she disagreed with them.

He was conflicted about his children, especially Katie. She had been the child that he had lavished his affections on and, when she married a man who seemed to be everything that Mark was not, he was completely satisfied. It was years later before he realized the truth about her husband. After Mike stole his money, humiliated him and then beat him up in front of Helen, John's relationship with his daughter changed.

It was not that he held her responsible for Mike's actions but he did have a grudge against her. Because he hated Mike so much he lost his sense of reasoning and he believed Katie should have told him earlier about Mike's lack of morals and bad character. He completely overlooked the fact that Katie hadn't know that he had secretly kept in touch with Mike. He also overlooked the fact that she had her own pride to consider and her own problems to wrestle with. He was so angry about his own dealings with Mike that he wanted nothing to do with Mike's son even though Tyler was his only grandchild.

His feelings towards Mark were also mixed. After Helen and he were married she encouraged him to try to get closer to Mark, while Mark was growing. He tried and, to his surprise, he was disappointed. He wanted a football player and his son was a checker player; he wanted a leader and his son was a follower. His son was not what his father wanted him to be and that added to his negative attitude towards Mark when they started to disagree over the Vietnam War.

John was at odds with his children but he still felt some responsibility for them so he was glad that Helen kept in touch with them. When Helen mentioned flying home to Foxboro, he had no objection. He could drive back, by himself, a few weeks later and, in the meantime, he would manage his business affairs and play a few more rounds of golf.

***

When Helen's plane landed at Logan airport late one Saturday night, only Katie and Mark were there to greet her. They had decided that offspring, spouses and live-ins would not accompany them as it was the first reunion for the three of them in many years. They wept unashamedly, hugged and kissed each other, and held hands for a long time. Katie thought Helen still was a handsome woman but she looked older and tired.

On the drive home, Helen kept asking questions about Tyler. She was looking forward to talking to him and she wanted to know all about him. Katie tried to keep her answers short and she even attempted to change the subject once or twice. Her reluctance stemmed from the fact that, in their phone calls, she hadn't told Helen that she was living with Tom. Now that she and Helen were face to face she didn't know how to bring the subject up.

Mark inadvertently solved her problem by blurting out, "Katie, why don't you have Helen over for breakfast and, then, she can visit Tyler and meet Tom?"

Katie cringed as Helen looked at her and asked, "And who's Tom?"

Mark answered immediately, "He's my best friend and Katie's boyfriend."

Helen asked, "Will he be there in the morning?"

This time Katie spoke before Mark could make things any worse, "Tom lives with me and he will be there when you arrive for breakfast." Instead of a barrage of questions in front of Mark, Helen reached over and held Katie's hand. Katie understood that Helen and she would talk about Tom in private and she was relieved not to have to say any more during the ride home.

Tom and Katie had quickly become comfortable with each other. While they snuggled, they reached for each other by recalling their pasts and then talking about their futures. Katie wanted to have more children and Tom said that was all right by him as long as Katie set an upper limit. Tom surprised Katie when he told her that he would shortly be leaving the highway department. He was working towards getting a teaching certificate and when he completed the rest of his requirements he wanted to be a high school teacher and counsellor. His goal was to help younger people choose a direction that would make them happy. Afterwards, when Katie thought about it, she was proud of his goal and pleased that they were partners.

Recently, Katie had stopped being flip in her answer to Tom's morning proposal. She was beginning to consider "when" and not "if." Her fear of making a permanent commitment was melting as she and Tom discovered the joy of uniting their individual personalities. They began to act, and react, as if they had been together a long time.

They were lying in bed, snuggling, when Katie told Tom that Helen would be over for breakfast to see Tyler and meet him. He was amused and asked her, "So, this morning I finally get to meet Helen? Is there any subject that I shouldn't talk about?"

"No Honey. All you have to be is honest with her and I know you will be."

"Can I invite her to our wedding?"

"No, you cannot. She has more manners than to ask about us getting married. You are not to bring the subject up, all you have to do is refer her to higher headquarters."

On Sunday morning they both arose early as they anticipated a busy, pleasant day. They were not disappointed. Helen arrived long before she said she would carrying clothes and gifts for Tyler. Katie had just finished making cinnamon buns so the three of them sat down for coffee. Katie didn't say much, allowing Helen and Tom to talk with each other. When Tyler woke up, Helen abandoned the adults as she put on her grandmother role. She was in a world she had dreamed of many times, being with her grandson.

Until Mark and Brenda arrived, most of her attention was focused on talking with Tyler. When Helen and Brenda were introduced, the five adults sat around the kitchen table as Tom and Brenda asked Helen about Mark and Katie's childhood. As a result, breakfast was a long, disorganized, laughing and learning experience for everyone. Eating was not as important as meeting. After the meal everyone went into the parlor and the reunion continued.

It was some time after noon when Tom suggested that everyone get some fresh air and exercise by going to Capron Park in North Attleboro. This diversion was welcomed and after a long walk in the brisk air they all returned to Katie's house. They no sooner had gotten inside when Mrs. Buoni and Mrs. Connors rang the front doorbell and joined them. They said that they had seen Helen driving her car and they hoped that they were not intruding. They were made welcome and, of course, they joined in the conversation. More time passed in recalling the past.

Finally, Helen looked at her watch and said that she was taking everyone out to dinner. They all trooped over to the Red Wing Diner and the celebration continued. The most notable event of the meal was that Mrs. Buoni and Mrs. Connors drank enough wine to become tipsy. They sat at the table grinning and giggling. When they returned to Katie's house, Helen made sure that Tom and Mark walked each of the pixilated ladies into their houses. Then, she said that she was tired and was going home, and she asked Tom to escort her to her car.

As they walked she said, "Tom, this has been the happiest day I have had in years. To have Mark and Katie together has been my dream for a long time. To have them both together and happy is something I wasn't sure I could ever hope for. Now, I have them and my grandson close by. I consider myself fortunate.

"I don't know what the future holds for you and Katie and it is none of my business. I do know that you have been good for her and that is all I need to know. She is as relaxed and animated as I have ever seen her. You both seem so happy together.

"I just want you to be aware that I'm so happy for the two of you."

With that, she kissed him on the cheek, got in her car, and drove home. What she hadn't told him was that one of the reasons she was so happy was that she had also found out that Brenda was pregnant.

***

As Tom and Katie snuggled that evening, Tom was surprised that Katie was not saying much. She usually started chirping the minute the light was turned off but, tonight, she was barely answering his questions. Tom rubbed her back, between her shoulder blades, and asked, "Honey, is something wrong?"

Katie snuggled a little closer and was silent for a while before she replied, "No, Tom Dearest, nothing at all is wrong. It's just that I have been thinking about a couple of things. First, today has been a day of total happiness for me and I was trying to savor it. Mark, Helen and I are at peace with one another and that means so much to me. It is something I have wanted for a long time.

"Helen told me that she was surprised when she found that we were living together but, before she left, she told me that she likes you very much. I'm so grateful for today.

"The other thing I was thinking about was something that I have to tell you."

"You're not planning on kicking me out are you?"

Katie was quick to respond. She nipped his shoulder and said, "Quit acting like a dunce and pay attention. Are you going to propose to me tomorrow morning?"

"Don't I every morning?"

"No. Believe it or not, twice in the last three weeks you haven't asked me to marry you."

Tom chuckled before he replied, "I didn't know you were keeping track."

"Of course I am. Everyone wants to be loved. Now please hush and let me finish what I'm trying to tell you. This is important.

"Watching you today when you were talking to Helen and Tyler made me realized how lucky I am to have you. It has taken me a long time to admit it to myself but I love you Tom. I love you with all of my heart and soul.

"If you aren't going to propose to me tomorrow then I'm going to propose to you. I want you near me for the rest of my life."

Tom hugged her so hard she felt almost crushed; then he eased his grip. "Sweet Katie, I've been waiting for you to say that. I loved you long before I met you; you are the dream I've always looked for. I knew that when I found you. You are all I could ever want or need. I want you as my wife and my friend forever. I'm so happy, I can't, and won't, wait until morning to ask you.

"Katie, will you marry me?"

"Yes, I'll marry you any time you want. But when? My father isn't back from Florida and I haven't met your parents yet. Should we marry before I meet them? I don't want your mother and father thinking of me either as a prostitute or as a whore because we're shacked up."

Tom replied almost before Katie finished speaking. "Katie, they don't think that at all. They know that we are living together because you haven't agreed to marry me and they understand your hesitancy. They are anxious for us to marry and they are eager to meet Tyler. Our happiness is a lot more important to them than whether we had a contract to live together when we first started out.

"We will have much more of a problem with your father than with my parents."

Katie sighed and said, "I think that you're right. From what Helen says he seems more stubborn and determined in his ways than ever. I wonder what we should do; Honey, do you have any suggestions?"

"No, not really. However, I suggest that we talk with Helen and get her opinion. If anyone can give us advice about your father it would be her."

***

Monday morning Mark went to work a little late because he had lingered over coffee with Brenda. He was in a completely relaxed frame of mind. This weekend he and Katie had been reunited with Helen and he had found out that he was going to become a father. His small, handy man business, with occasional help from Tom, was doing well. He felt fortunate to have a wife like Brenda and friends and relatives who loved and respected him. Things were going well for him.

He parked his pick up truck on the grass strip in front of the highway garage yard and then climbed the stairs to the locker room on the second floor. Each man had his own locker to hold his work uniforms and personal items. As he walked into the room, he heard Portagee John talking in a loud voice but he couldn't understand what he was saying.

He soon found out. PJ pointed his finger at him and said, "Your shirt tail relative and another guy, Swenson, came in early because a truck tipped over near Main and Route One and spilled its load. I'm the one that should a been called in for that overtime, not them. I got more seniority than anyone else."

Before Mark could answer one of the men sitting there asked, "PJ, ain't your beef with Kinnick? They only came in because the super called them."

"I'll talk to him later. You guys gotta learn to ask him if he offered the overtime to me first. I've got seniority over all of you. I should always have first choice."

Mark almost laughed out loud but he didn't say a word. He knew that the superintendent tried to follow the seniority list when it came to handing out overtime, but his job depended on his performance and following seniority was not his highest priority. Maintaining the city's highways was. He also knew that PJ would never talk directly to the super about overtime; he only picked on people who were scared of him.

PJ continued, "I ain't greedy. I'll share my overtime with you guys. But things ain't been run right around here for a long time. The supervisor has forgotten how valuable I am and our foreman don't know shit from sugar. Us guys do all the work and they take all the credit. That's why we got to stick together and that includes anybody's shirt tail relative who sneaks in for overtime."

Mark flared internally and was about to reply when the foreman, Jason Drew, walked through the open door. Drew was a relatively new hire and he, after talking with the supervisor, would set up the daily work schedules. When he first started, there were rumors about him. One was that he had worked for a large construction firm until he was discovered in bed with the owner's wife. Another was that he had been fired because he had stolen money from the company. Whatever the rumor, he was not welcomed when he arrived because all the old timers in the highway department thought that they should have had the job he was hired for, and not him. Once he began work, his personality made him even more unwelcome. He encouraged favoritism by having workers tattling on each other and he rarely said anything pleasant; he built his own ego by insulting others. He enjoyed reminding everyone that they reported to him. No one who worked in the highway department liked him and most feared him.

Drew was a short, bald man who wore a brown fedora hat to cover his bald spot and he sported a large, walrus mustache which he unconsciously stroked while he talked. When he entered the room it became silent. He might have been standing outside just listening to the conversation; that would be something he would do. Rather than taking a chance of getting on his bad side, everyone stopped talking.

He stood in front of the room for a while not moving or saying a word. He liked his crew to be nervous. At last, he cleared his throat and said, "Well, I'm glad all you beauties got here on time and are ready to go to work." With that, he handed out the individual assignments and told each driver which truck to use. His usual routine was to gave the easiest work to whomever had been doing the most snitching; however, he occasionally changed the pecking order around just to keep his "beauties" nervous.

Mark's assignment was to clear the brush from the sides of Lakeview Road and paint the fences white. He asked the man assigned with him to get the tools and materials while he checked out the truck. It was parked next to the wall at the far end of the garage. He lifted the hood and checked the oil in the engine and in the power steering, he checked the water in the battery and the radiator and, finally, did a visual inspection of the all the belts and hoses. Then, he checked the outside tires by hitting them with a hammer. If the hammer bounced back crisply, he knew the pressure was sufficient. He was always thorough in his inspections.

He got under the truck to close the reservoir to the air tank and to check the inner tires on the dual axles with a ball peen hammer. As he was getting up next to the garage wall, he saw a pair of work boots. They were large enough to only belong to one person, PJ.

PJ said to him, "Listen Mark, I just found out that your shirttail relative is making nice-nice with your sister. I have seen her and she is a good looking broad. What...."

He got no further. Mark, still upset by his earlier remarks, exploded. He pushed PJ John against the front fender of the truck, and grabbed his shirt with his left hand. His right hand brought his hammer right beside PJ's temple. He had moved so quickly that PJ had no time to respond; his body was draped over the fender and he had no leverage. He was completely at Mark's mercy and he knew it.

"You son of a bitch. Shut your mouth or I'll crack your skull with this hammer. Do you hear me?"

PJ heard him and he was so scared all he could do was shake his head.

"Goddamit, what my family does is none of your business. I don't want to hear you talking about my sister or Tom ever again. You won't say anything in front of Tom so don't you ever speak in front of me. From now on, I will always have something to defend myself. Don't you ever come near me again.

"Do you understand me?" He was so furious that he was shaking.

PJ barely shook his head. Mark stood up, holding the hammer in his hand, and PJ staggered around the front of the truck and, without saying a word, left the garage.

After he was gone, Mark climbed into the truck, on the driver's side, and for a few minutes, he continued to tremble. He had never threatened anyone in anger before. He was surprised at his audacity and shocked that he had done such a thing. When his breathing returned to normal, he decided that would always have to watch out for PJ but that he would never again have to be afraid of him. That was a good feeling.

He sat there until his work partner came up to him and asked if they were going to sit in the garage all morning or were they going to go out and do town business? Mark started the truck and they drove to Lakeview Road and began their work day.

14

That Monday evening, Katie and Tom went over to Helen's house to tell her that Katie had finally accepted the latest of Tom's daily proposals. Helen squealed in delight when she heard the news and hugged and kissed both of them. She made a pot of tea and served it with her home baked cookies. After a while, Helen broke the euphoria by asking, "What are your plans for the wedding?"

Katie replied, "We're completely up in the air. Tom's parents will come here from Michigan. We want Dad to be at the wedding but we don't know when he is coming back to Foxboro. This is going to come as a surprise to him and I'm not sure how he is going to take the news.

"What do you think?"

Helen said, "I talked to your father last night and he told me that he has both a business meeting and a St. Mark's vestry meeting two weeks from today, so he will definitely be back in less than two weeks from yesterday. However, you're absolutely right, your wedding plans will come as a total surprise and he doesn't do well with surprises.

"Don't misunderstand what I'm saying. He is honest and he has a heart of gold; you have to live with him as long as I have to know how sweet he is. The problem is his stubbornness. He has to think about change a long time before he will consider making a change.

"Since he joined the vestry a few years ago he has become even more of a conservative. When he finds out that you two have been living together before the wedding, he will probably react without thinking. We're going to have our work cut out for us if we want him to share our happiness. I'm sure he will, eventually, because he does love you Katie, and he wants you back in his life. He has to overcome his negative feelings about Mike and realize that other people have as much right to their ideals as he has to his."

From then on, until the day John Givens was due to arrive, the five of them, Helen, Katie, Tom, Brenda, and Mark, would talk almost exclusively about the upcoming wedding and how to handle John's homecoming. All of them were hoping for serenity but they were unsure of what to expect. They would discuss different scenarios about how he might react to the news of the wedding and no one was optimistic. It was a time of uncertainty, but it wasn't all lost time. Two positive things occurred during this period.

The first was that Helen, with some initial gentle prodding from Tom, talked with Tom's mother and father several times. She was pleasantly surprised to find how much his parents loved Katie; both of them understood her initial reluctance to make a long term commitment and both had no trouble accepting her unconventional independence. Helen spent a long time telling them about Tyler and she looked forward to meeting the two of them in person.

The second event that took place was that Katie went to see her doctor and she found out that she was pregnant. She was both thrilled and dismayed. Her only concern was that it would now be harder for her father to reconcile himself to her future plans. Tom was absolutely delighted when she told him she was pregnant and he wanted to let Helen and his parents know immediately. However, when Katie told him of her concerns, he agreed not to say a word until Katie herself broke the news. For a while, Katie told no one but she did ask Tyler if he would like to have a little brother or sister. Tyler was too young to really understand the significance of her question.

***

Helen was in daily contact with John and, on the Sunday he was due to arrive home, she invited Katie over to their house. She had spoken to him on Saturday night and he figured he would be home at the latest by 2:00 PM the next day. Katie arrived around eleven o'clock and she and Helen started cooking the food and baking the cookies he liked. Katie wanted him to be in a good mood so that she could talk with him and tell him her news. Such was not to be.

John did not arrive until almost 9:00 PM. Helen and Katie were extremely worried when they didn't hear from him and they were relieved when he did show up. Starting late in the afternoon, when they hadn't heard a word from him, they pictured him as being in an automobile accident. When he did arrive, he was in a foul mood. He gave both of them a perfunctory kiss and hug and refused to eat anything. He sat silently at the kitchen table while they poured him a cup of coffee and put a plateful of cookies in front of him. After he took a couple of sips of coffee, he broke a cookie in two, and started to talk.

"Today has been a bad day for me. I've been on the road for almost 14 hours and I've had all kinds of problems; I hadn't been on the road an hour when my front right tire blew out. After I got it changed, traffic was tied up twice for hours because of accidents. Then to top it off, some damn, stupid Massachusetts state trooper pulled me over and handed me a traffic ticket for going five miles faster than the speed limit. That son of a bitch picked on me because of my car. There were cars going faster than I was. That cowboy bastard didn't have to pick on me. That ticket is going to cost me a heck of a lot of money."

Katie studied her father while he was talking, she was happy to see him but she thought that he had gained weight and showed more signs of age than she had expected. She had never heard him swear before; she thought it was because he was so upset and tired.

Helen tried to cajole her husband into a better mood. "John, you bought that Bentley knowing it showed that you had money. It puts a target on your back. If that trooper had to meet his quota he probably decided to nick the rich and save the poor."

"You're probably right, Helen, but it is absolutely irritating to see cars speed by me and then have this statie pull me over. I'm going to find out if there is anything I can do about that damn Robin Hood and his lousy ticket."

Helen did her best but she could not lighten John's mood. He was too tired and too annoyed to budge off "unhappy" and there was nothing that Helen could do about it.

Katie recognized that small talk was almost impossible. She began to feel annoyed that, after such a long separation, he couldn't get over his pique long enough to acknowledge her presence. Then, she got mad because she realized that this was no time to try to tell her father about Tom and their wedding plans; and she had so much wanted to tell him that she was entering a new phase of her life. So, after a couple of attempts at conversation, she told her father that she was glad that he was home and she left. Everything that should have been said was left unspoken.

Early the next morning, John Givens drove down to the police station and went in to see Captain Bill Callahan, the Chief of Police. They had known each other for years; John had met Callahan when he first joined the Foxboro police as a rookie and John had been on the Board of Selectmen when Callahan was chosen as Captain. Even though they did not see each other socially, they had worked together many times on town matters.

The chief listened sympathetically to John's story but he told John that there was absolutely nothing he could do. Callahan told him that the State Police were an organization unto themselves and that they refuse any appeals from local police concerning tickets they had issued. John was just going to have to pay the fine and swallow his anger.

He left the chief's office almost as furious as he had been last night. As he walked to his Bentley, a town dump truck pulled into the parking lot and parked near him. PJ stepped out of the cab and started to walk towards the building. He stopped when he saw John Givens heading for his car. PJ recognized him as Mark's father and, although he had never met him, he had seen him around town for years. Since Givens was a person of influence and power, PJ automatically feared and disliked him; he was a person of authority who should be avoided.

However, PJ was still smoldering from Mark's attack. Along with that burning ember of hate was his dread of Tom and his own lust for Katie. This witch's brew of evil emotions made PJ brave enough to do something he rarely tried; he decided to cause trouble head on.

As John Givens came close, PJ smiled, waived his hand and said, "Hi there, Mr. Givens. Haven't seen you around for a while. I work with your son, Mark, and Tom, the guy who is shacked up with your daughter. I wonder if you know the date they are going to be married? I want to buy them a present."

Givens was visibly surprised. He had seen PJ for years but he had never spoken to him and the news about Katie took him totally aback. "I'm sorry, I don't know what you are talking about." With that, he walked around PJ, got into his car, and drove away.

PJ was so pleased that he had upset someone he forgot that he was supposed to deliver a letter to the chief of police. He got back into his truck and returned to the highway garage where the foreman promptly chewed him out for bringing the letter back.

***

John Givens stormed into the house looking for Helen who he found in the living room knitting a sweater for Tyler. He loudly said, "What the H--?" and then he stopped before he finished the word. He had never before sworn when they were alone and he was talking with her. He drew a deep breath and started over. "Is Katie living with someone who works in the highway department?"

Helen looked at him and replied, "Yes."

Her husband sighed and then muttered, "What is wrong with that girl? First, she picks out a real louse for a husband and then she gets hooked up with some airhead whose only source of income is by driving a truck for the highway department. He probably is some long haired, hippy peacenik who has no idea of what makes this world go round."

Helen stopped knitting and said, "John Givens, you sit down and listen to me. When you get upset you tend to lose your balance. You know nothing about Katie's man. I do and I know his family and I can tell you that you are completely wrong in every detail."

"You know what is going on?"

"Of course I do, John. I told you that was the reason I decided to come home from Florida early. I wanted to be with Katie and Tyler."

"Do you approve of what Katie is doing?"

"Do I approve? John, that's not even a fair question. I wish she were doing things differently but she is living her life as best she can. Her past is dictating what she does and I understand that. She certainly doesn't need my approval to seek happiness and love.

"Before you make any judgements you should get to know your daughter again and you should meet Tom. He is a wonderful person."

Helen's husband shook his head and asked, "How can you say that? You just met this guy. You probably know only what he wants you to know about him. Mike made himself wonderful too and he fooled everyone. This Tom you tell me about is probably a lot like Mike."

"John, John, John, at least I've met Tom. You know nothing about him and already you've made up your mind. You're not being fair and that is not like you. Meet Tom, talk to him, and then decide for yourself. You may be right but you could also be wrong.

"Katie is as happy as I have ever seen her and she is so anxious for you to be a part of that happiness. That was one of the reasons she was over here when you came home last night. She wanted to talk to you and tell you about Tom, but you were in no mood to listen to anybody. She left angry and hurt. Katie so much wants your love and your approbation; the least you owe her is fairness."

John looked at her for a while. Then, he said, "You certainly have a way of letting me know what you think. OK. I'll meet with Katie's friend and talk with him but I want to meet him by myself."

"Why by yourself?"

"Because if I meet him with you and Katie around I may not be able to find out what he is really like. He could mask himself in social chitchat. That's what happened with Mike and that won't happen again. I want to meet him one on one and pick my own topics. Then, I'll be able to see for myself what he is made of. But, I don't expect much from a highway department worker."

Helen said, "John, I'm not sure that's a wise idea. Tom will be at a distinct disadvantage when you first meet him. He'll be expecting to meet you on pleasant terms to establish a relationship with Katie's father and you'll be looking to find fault with him."

"That's exactly right and that's the way I want it. I'm not going to make the same mistake that I made with Mike. I'll meet him under my terms and, that way, I'll be able to tell what this guy is really made of."

***

Two days later, on Wednesday, they met at John's office after Tom got off work. He was a little late as Drew, late in the afternoon, had him drive a load of sand to one of the elementary schools. He arrived a little apologetic but hopeful that he would gain John Given's good will. On the other hand, Givens was hopeful that he would plumb the shallow depth of Tom's personality along with the narrow breadth of his character. Because of Given's approach, their meeting met none of these goals and ended in chaos.

When Tom entered his office John Givens was standing at the window. Givens introduced himself, shook Tom's hand, and asked him to sit. Tom noticed a carafe of water and one glass close to his chair. Givens sat opposite him with a huge, old oak desk separating them. Tom was a little curious to see only one water glass, as if he were about to be grilled, but he was completely startled by the first question addressed to him.

"How well do you know Portagee John?"

"Well, enough to know that he's bad news."

"Why do you say that?"

"Mr. Givens, PJ is a stupid bully who will pick a fight with anyone smaller than he is. Why do you want to know about him?"

"Because he was the one who told me quote, 'that Tom is the guy who is shacked up with your daughter' unquote. Now what do you have to say about him?"

Tom noticed that John Givens was slowly drumming the fingers of his right hand on the desk. He answered, "That doesn't change my opinion of him. His facts are right but his feelings are entirely wrong."

Givens started to drum his fingers a little faster.

"And exactly what does that mean? If he is such a low life why do I have to hear this information from him?"

Tom thought for a minute; he didn't want to antagonize Givens but he certainly meant to protect Katie. "Mr. Givens, what PJ doesn't understand is the love between Katie and me. Your daughter and I are planning on getting married.

"As far as finding out about us, Katie went over your house the night you came home to tell you that we were going to get married. She said that you were in no mood to talk to her."

"Well, I was a bit upset but she should have tried harder."

From that point on, Tom knew they would disagree but he had no intention of backing down. He simply said, "Mr. Givens, don't you think that your expression, 'Tried harder' is a two way responsibility'?"

The finger drumming stopped as Givens responded, "What do you mean?"

"Katie loves you. She came back to Foxboro to be near you and she has waited all winter for your return.

"She wants you to get to know your grandson and all you want to do is talk to me about someone called PJ. How long has it been since you have even spoken with Katie?"

The drumming began furiously. "Who the Hell are you to tell me about my daughter? What do you know? You are some pinhead liberal that works for the town because you probably can't hold a job. You are a loser just like her first husband was.

"I'll say this much for you, you aren't too smart but you don't let that get in your way when you talk. As far as I'm concerned you can go back to the town garage and join the rest of those losers who work there."

They sat looking at each other for a few seconds. Tom was angry and wanted to lash out at Givens but he knew that Katie would be upset if he did. Finally, he did speak. "Mr. Givens, I came here to tell you that Katie and I are going to be married and that both of us want you at our wedding.

'I feel sorry for you Mr. Givens; you have a lovely wife, two marvelous children, and a grandson who should be the apple of your eye. You don't appreciate what is available to you. You can't be very happy and that's your own fault."

Givens stood up quickly and pointed to the door. "Get out! Get out! You son of a bitch! Get out of my office!"

As Tom left and closed the door, Givens started to come around his desk. He spied his wastebasket at the corner of the desk and he kicked at it with his foot. His other foot slipped and his body went into the air and fell back to the floor with a heavy thud, and left him in pain. He lay stunned and unable to move. After a few seconds, he began moaning for help.

Tom had started down the stairs when he heard a loud bang and then silence. He was reaching for the outside door when he thought he heard a moan. He decided to go back and see what was happening. When he opened the office door he saw Givens lying on the floor, wedged behind his desk. Givens leg was bent at a grotesque angle; Tom could see that his left leg was broken and that there was blood oozing down his pant leg.

"Help me, help me. I'm in pain and I can't move."

Tom untied Givens tie and quickly used it to make a tourniquet. Then he called for medical help and, without moving Givens, he tried to comfort him. Givens kept repeating, "Don't leave me, don't leave me."

Shortly, an ambulance arrived and, after moving the furniture out of the way, Givens was taken to Norwood Hospital. When Givens was in the ambulance and on his way, Tom called Helen and told her what had happened. Then, he called Katie and gave her the same message. He set the latch on the door handle to lock, then he shut the office door and went home.

***

The next few days were chaotic for the family. Helen and Katie remaining at the hospital with John until after his operation. He was heavily sedated and didn't talk much. The surgeons straightened his leg, and because of the multiple fractures, used stainless steel screws to align the bones. With all the concern over John's injury there was little talk about his meeting with Tom. When Tom told Katie that he knew nothing about how the accident happened, hardly anything was mentioned about the meeting itself.

Saturday night Helen, Katie, Tom and Tyler went to the Red Wing

Diner for supper. Helen and Katie had been at the hospital most of the day while Tom and Tyler had gone fishing and then went for a walk in the Moose Hills Wildlife Sanctuary. This dinner was the first time they had all been able to get together since the accident. As they relaxed, Helen said, "Tom, this has been an awful week for all of us. John is beginning to recover but he is taking a lot of pain medication. He won't say a word about his meeting with you. Did you two have a disagreement?"

Tom replied, "I guess you could call it that, Helen. He got angry and ordered me out of his office. It was an odd meeting. I had expected that, as Katie's father, he would be asking about us; you know, how we met, what are our goals, us as a man and a woman about to get married. Instead, he began by asking me about a guy who works at the highway department. This guy told him that Katie and I were living together and that set him off. I tried not to get into an argument with him because he is Katie's father and your husband. I failed completely because he ordered me out of his office. I was leaving the building when I heard him fall and I went back to see if he needed help."

Katie put her hand over Tom's hand and said, "I'm so sorry you were the target of his anger. I was hoping to tell him myself about us but he was in no mood to talk when he first came home. Lord knows how he'll react when he finds out that I'm pregnant."

Tom patted her hand. "Katie, we'll be married shortly. Now, that's a fact that he will have to accept. I think that we should make our plans with or without your father's consent. We now have Tyler and our new one to consider."

Katie nodded her head, "You're right. I love my father but you and I have to live our lives whether he is dragging his feet or not. I wish he weren't so stubborn.

"What do you think Helen?"

"I'm not sure what to say. You two should definitely plan your wedding with or without John. On the other hand John may finally be doing some thinking instead of reacting. He has said nothing about his meeting with Tom but, before I left this evening, he asked me to ask Tom to come visit him at the hospital. To be perfectly honest, he asked me twice and I have no idea why."

Katie immediately asked, "Tom, you will go see him won't you?"

"Of course I will, Katie. He's your father and I'd do almost anything to bring you two together. I will go see him first thing in the morning and I'll try to be pleasant and upbeat."

Sunday morning, when visiting hours began, Tom walked into John Givens' private room. He was lying in bed with his left leg encased in a heavy plaster cast and suspended in the air by counterweights. When Tom entered, he was wearing glasses and reading the Boston Globe. He looked up, put the paper down and took off his glasses. "I was hoping that you would come by. I'm glad to see you."

Tom walked over to the bed. John Givens wasn't the angry, swearing person Tom remembered; he looked like a tired, middle aged man lying in bed. Tom handed him two of the expensive cigars that Givens occasionally smoked and asked, "How are you feeling?"

"Better than I have been but I still don't feel well. Part of the reason for that is that my accident was stupid and it was my own fault. After what happened between us, when we first met, I wasn't sure you would show up. Thank you for coming, I really am glad to see you." He paused for a second or two as if he were not sure how to continue; then, he began again.

"Tell me, do you have a temper?"

"I most certainly do, Mr. Givens. I have a very quick fuse that used to get me into trouble. I have to be careful about my temper."

"How do you handle it?"

Tom thought for a while. "Two ways, I guess. The first is to keep my mouth shut until my anger subsides and then I try to think of something humorous to say. I'm sure that if you can't laugh you can't enjoy life. Why do you ask?"

"Because I was angry with you even before I met you and that's what led to our confrontation. My temper got the best of me and that's my fault not yours. I know I'm stubborn but I would like to be fair. That's one of the reasons I wanted to see you. I want to apologize."

"You don't really have to."

"I think I do because there is more to the story than just that. You saved my life. I could have bled to death if you hadn't come back to find me. I'm grateful to you."

Tom said, "You can say I saved your life but you may be exaggerating. I think you would have been able to reach the phone and get help. Either way, you got the help you needed."

"I maintain it was thanks to you. Anyhow, there's more that I have to say to you. I was angry at you before we even met. I thought that I had reason to be angry. My daughter and you were living together without being married and, since I was on the vestry of St. Mark's, I took that as a personal insult.

"Not only that, when I found out that you worked at the highway department, I assumed you were a longhaired hippy with no education. That seems to be mostly the type of people that work there. I guess I also had my experiences with Katie's husband in my mind because, when you showed up at my office, all I wanted to do was to humiliate you; and all you did, even though we argued, was to save my life.

"I knew that I had to find out more about you. I called my friend, the Foxboro police chief, and asked him to run a search on you. At first, he refused by saying that was illegal but I twisted his arm and he finally relented. What I discovered about you absolutely surprised me; and it made me feel ashamed of the way I acted.

"You graduated from the University of Michigan and volunteered for the Army even though you could have stayed out. You earned a battlefield commission and a silver star in Vietnam. Most young men wouldn't volunteer, they would have remained in school. Why would you join the Army?"

Tom shook his head before he answered, "That seems so long ago. At the time, I felt that I owed my country something. That's how my mother and father raised me. Even though I could have stayed in school and avoided military service, it didn't seem right. Everyone has an obligation to pay back a little for what they receive. I felt it was my duty. God, what innocence."

John Givens was pleased; Tom was rising in his estimation. "That's exactly how I feel. Our country needs, and deserves, our loyalty. I wish more people felt like we do.

"Let me ask you another question, why haven't you and Katie gotten married?"

"Mr. Givens, that's a complicated question. I wanted to get married immediately. However, Katie has wounds and scars from her marriage and they are deep. Her pride and self assurance were almost destroyed. She was hesitant about me because she didn't want to make another mistake. It took her a long time to make up her mind.

"I also have had problems. Vietnam clouded my thinking and what I've done for much too long. My life has zigzagged with no apparent goals. Our love has helped us both realize what is important in life. We are committed to each other and we will marry soon.

"Another reason we haven't wed is that Katie has been waiting to talk to you. You are her father and Tyler's grandfather. She wants your love and approval for both her and Tyler. She moved back to Foxboro for that very reason. So, in a way, I'm indebted to you; I'd have never met Katie if she hadn't returned.

"I can honestly tell you that Katie has sweetened my life. I've never been happier. She has become my North Star; I navigate by her love. You have to be proud to be her father."

John Givens replied quietly, "She was the apple of my eye. My mind is filled with memories of her as a child and as a young girl. I may not talk about any of them but I have never forgotten them.

"Has Katie told you about what her husband did to me?"

Tom answered, "She has told me what she knows. There are probably some incidents that she doesn't even know about. Helen, who has always been your loving and loyal wife, has intimated to me that there were episodes that she didn't tell Katie. It's sad that Mike's personality has caused so much pain for all of you. Think of what Katie had to put up with for so many years.

"Mr. Givens, have you ever talked to Katie about her marriage?"

"No."

John Given's reply to the question was so curt and so cold that the conversation came to a complete stop. Both men sat silently thinking about what the other had said. Tom considered asking John Givens why he had never discussed Katie's problems with her. Givens wondered if he should have talked with Katie despite his hurt feelings. Deep inside himself he knew he that should have.

Their silence lasted for a while. Finally, Givens said, "Maybe I should have talked with her." Then he quickly asked Tom something that he had not even asked Helen, "Tell me, what's Katie's child like?"

Tom was happy to answer, "You'd be well pleased with your grandson; he's a delightful child. He's shy until he gets to know you and then he will pester you with questions that will make you laugh and wonder what made him think of what he did. He is inquisitive and bright.

"You'd also be proud of Katie as a mother. She gives Tyler free rein to use his imagination but she also teaches him that he has boundaries. Manners and respect are part of his upbringing. Believe me, he will restore your faith in humans."

Again, there was silence between them. It lasted so long that, finally, Tom added, "When Katie and I are married, I'm going to legally adopt Tyler. I love him that much."

Givens didn't respond. Tom thought that he might have dozed off when, all of a sudden, he inquired, 'What do you think of my son?"

Tom was so startled that he asked, "What?"

"What do you think of my son? You work with everyone at the highway department, you know PJ, so what do you think of my son?"

"I like him very much."

"How can that be? You are a veteran who has fought for his country; my son refused to enter the service and abandoned his country. Under those conditions, how can you like him?"

"Mr. Givens, I look at things differently than you do. For example, which is worse; you abandoning your country or your country abandoning you?"

"What do you mean by that, 'Your country abandoning you'"?

"Just this. Thirty-six hours after I left the hospital in Saigon I landed in San Francisco. I hadn't even left the airport when two women spat in my face and called me a 'child killer.' In Detroit, a man asked me if I weren't ashamed of myself for spraying Vietnam with Agent Orange.

Meanwhile, my friends and brothers were still over there fighting and dying. That was only the beginning of how most of us Vietnam veterans were treated.

"When I got home, I visited a VFW post near Ann Arbor and one member told me that it wasn't a real war I had been in and that I shouldn't bother to apply for membership.

"What was even worse, as far as I was concerned, was that after I took off my uniform and put on civilian clothes, the government paid no attention to me. The Veterans Administration was a shambles; I needed help and was given the run around.

"For a long time I was angry. I felt that my dead brothers and I were being blamed for the mistakes of the politicians and leaders. I'm not angry anymore but I still feel the same way about our politicians and leaders. I think we fought and bled for no real purpose and that we were shamefully treated afterwards.

"All of this took place before I met Mark; I don't agree with what he did but I'm not sure that he wasn't more correct in his judgement than the politicians."

"How can you, as a veteran, say that? He betrayed his country."

"He didn't betray his country, he betrayed the government that was supposed to represent his country. There is a big difference between the two. Didn't our founding fathers do the same thing against their government?"

Givens looked at him and said, "I don't understand the difference."

"OK, let me try to explain. I was born and raised in Michigan and I love my home town and my home state. As a child I didn't give a damn who was governing Michigan, I never even thought about it. What I did hear was that America was the home of the free and the land of the brave, and I believed it.

"Then, while I was growing up, I learned about our town and our state governments from my mother and father; our national government seemed far away and remote from us. My parents would talk about the caliber of the people who were in our local office and that ran the gamut; some were good and some were bad. However, while they were in office, they all had an impact on our lives. As Michiganders, we could agree, or disagree, with how our state was being run and still love Michigan. No one ever considered his neighbor a traitor if he opposed the state government."

Givens interrupted him and said, "It isn't the same. The states are part of the federal government. Our federal government represents the will of all of the people and it should speak with one forceful voice."

"Does it really? I'll admit that the federal government should represent the will of the majority, but most of our administrations don't; instead, they interpret what they think should be the will of the majority. There can be a huge difference between the people and the government. Just look at our history.

"The United States was founded because of this difference. The British government thought its colonists should be taxed and they ignored the colonists' requests for discussions. Look at what happened because they wouldn't listen."

Givens was quick to respond, "That was over two hundred years ago, when communications were slow. Our government isn't like the English government, we wouldn't disregard the rights of our people."

"Wouldn't we? Didn't our august government do exactly that when it declared that black people were not American citizens?"

Givens got a little feisty. "What in Hell are you taking about?"

"The Dred Scott decision, it made the Civil War almost inevitable. Chief Justice Taney of the United States Supreme Court wrote that slaves, even if they were born in this country, were property, not citizens."

"Why do you keep delving into the past? That was at least 100 years ago. We don't act like that any more."

"Oh, don't we? OK, let's look at the recent past. During World War II we interned 120,000 Americans of Japanese heritage illegally. We then followed that with the shameful witch hunts of the McCarthy era. What that shows is-"

Tom was interrupted by a furious outburst from Givens. "Jesus Christ, what are you? An anarchist? Sometimes our government has to act swiftly for the sake of the entire country. You have the luxury of second guessing them. That's not fair."

Tom felt himself losing his patience so he took a deep breath before he continued. "Mr. Givens calm down. I'm neither an anarchist nor a second guesser. I believe in our government but I also believe that governments, whether in peace or in war, should be accountable for what they do. When they act out of fear, or stupidity, or misunderstanding, they are subject to making costly mistakes.

"The federal government may be more removed than my Michigan government but I feel that they must be held as accountable as my Michigan government is, no matter what their motivation. That attitude certainly does not make me an anarchist or a traitor.

"Why isn't it the same way on the federal level as it is on a state level? The federal level is even more important because our lawmakers are more powerful and further away from their voting base. When they make mistakes, like getting involved in Vietnam, our country, our people and the world, suffers. I think a person has a right to protest what the government is doing without being considered unpatriotic."

By this time, Givens had recovered his composure. "You think that going to war in Vietnam was a mistake?"

"Mr. Givens, I was in that war. I saw my brothers wounded, maimed, and killed. They, and their families, are the ones who suffered for our mistaken policies. I survived and I still don't know why. It took me years to overcome my fears and my hate. The Vietnamese lost over five million people. Does anyone realize that there are over 58,000 names on the Vietnam Memorial Wall; men and women who died fighting for this country? Five million Vietnamese, 58,000 Americans. Does anyone care? Doesn't a death toll like that allow someone to ask, 'What did they die for?'

"What's even more shameful to me is that the politicians never declared war. All during this time, our government didn't even have the courage to formally declare war and make everyone share whatever sacrifices were necessary. Our whole society did business as usual while its youth was fighting in a pigpen of filth and heat. Then, society took its wrath out on the same front line grunts. We lost so many while gaining so little.

"To answer you directly, I think that what we did in Vietnam was an absolute mistake."

John Givens lay there quietly for a while. He had never seen such a passionate argument against the war from someone who had fought in it. Then he said, "Listen. When I came home after World War Two, I was regarded as a hero. Everyone who went to serve their country was treated as a hero. My father fought and died for this country. I fought for this country and I expected my son to do the same. He refused.

"I am ashamed of him; it isn't asking too much to expect your son to honor his obligation to his family and his country. That's how I feel. I don't care how we got involved in Vietnam or whether we should be there or not. What I do know is that my son didn't fight for his country."

Even if he didn't agree with Givens, Tom could understand his feelings. Givens was correct that the country's attitude at the end of World War II was different from the attitude at the end of the Vietnam War. He decided not to argue with the man who was soon to be his father in law. Tom honestly believed that patriotism was to the soul what heroin was to the body; an overdose would turn a quiet person into a raging fanatic.

He said, "Your homecoming certainly was different from the one that the Vietnam veterans received. A lot has happened between the two wars; and not for the better. Watergate, the Gulf of Tonkin, and the assassination of Kennedy have made people distrustful of the federal government. Our nation seems resigned to hearing half truths and duplicity coming from Washington and that's not the way it should be; we seem to have lost communication and trust with Washington."

Givens replied, "Boy, you can say that again."

At that moment, Helen came in carrying a hot fudge Sundae in a plastic container. The three of them talked for a few minutes and then Tom excused himself and left. He had been at the hospital longer than he had planned and he had promised to go walking with Katie and Tyler. He was eager to leave, he wanted a breath of fresh air.

15

They were hiking in the Blue Hills Reservation. Tyler was skipping ahead of them and Katie didn't call for him to wait unless it appeared that they would lose sight of him. They were holding hands and Katie was listening intently as Tom described his conversation with her father. When he finished, she was quiet for a few minutes before she asked, "What do you make of what my father said? Is it possible he is changing his mind?"

"I have been wondering that myself. I honestly think that he wants to get right with you. I have no doubt that he loves you and that he is sorry he lost touch. It seems to me that asking about Tyler is a good sign; but who really knows?

"Mark is another story. Your father talks as if he is unable to forgive Mark for doing something he considers wrong; your father is emotionally tied to his father's sacrifice and to his idea of patriotism.

"It kind of reminds me of the split between Ben Franklin and his son, William. Because William sided with the British, Ben never forgave him. That was a shame because William was his only son and, as a youngster, he was with his father when Ben flew his kite in the rain."

"I didn't know that. What do you think will happen between Mark and my father?"

"I don't know Katie. Your father is an unhappy man inside his own cage and I don't think he knows where the exit is. Until he can find it in his heart to forgive Mark he will remain on the inside looking out. On the other hand, I'm almost sure that he will reconcile with you.

"For me, though, there is a more important issue. It is between you and me. I want to marry you quickly, I always have. Since you are pregnant time is against us; I don't want whispers about you or our child. I love you as my partner and I adore you as the mother of our child. We should go ahead with our own plans. I'm not trying to be disrespectful but we have our life together to live."

Katie stopped and faced Tom. She looked around to see if anyone was near them. Besides Tyler, who was sitting on a rock waiting for them to catch up, they were alone. She kissed him on the cheek and replied, " You're right. You make me feel so happy and so secure; you are the jam on my slice of bread. I love you. This is what I wanted to tell my father the night he came home. I guess that's why I got angry, he wasn't interested in listening. So be it if it has to be. I want my father to come around but, whether he does or doesn't, we have to plan for each other. We are our future. What do you want me to do?"

"I would like you to decide when and where we should marry. We could get married here in St. Mark's with your family and friends or we could go to Milan and get married with my family or we could skip both families and get married by ourselves. The only thing I ask is let's do it quickly."

"Honey, I agree. Let me talk to Helen and I'll set a date. Oh, I'm so excited."

Monday morning, when Tom got to work, he bypassed the foreman and went directly into the highway supervisor's office. They talked together for almost half an hour and, as a result, he didn't see Mark arrive and leave on his daily assignment. Since he wanted to talk privately with Mark, at lunchtime Tom parked his truck at the end of the highway garage away from the other incoming trucks. When Mark drove in, he honked his horn and motioned him over. After Mark got into the cab, Tom handed him a submarine sandwich and a Coke.

"A catered lunch? I'm flattered, confused and concerned. Are you trying to borrow money?"

"No. Something more difficult than that; I'm going to try to improve your mind. I know that Katie and Brenda talk with each other every day, but I don't know what you are told. Things are happening quickly so we need to talk."

"OK, but I think I'm up to date on everything."

"You probably are but it never hurts to check. One thing you don't know, because it just happened, is that I spoke to Kinnick and turned in my resignation."

Mark looked surprised as he replied, "You're quitting the highway department? You didn't speak to Drew, you went right to the supervisor?"

"I didn't bother with Drew; he's a loud mouthed jerk. I talked to Kinnick to let him know what was going on. He is the person that hired me and he is the one that should know that I'm working until the end of this week, taking my two weeks vacation, and I won't be back.

"Kinnick shook my hand, thanked me for my work, and wished me luck."

"Where are you going, Tom?"

"I guess you weren't told everything. I've completed all of my education classes and I have accepted a job in the Mansfield School

System. I start with them in five weeks. We want to be married before I start my new career. With that as our target, Katie and I have set the date for our marriage four weeks from this coming Saturday. We are going to drive to Michigan to meet my mother and father at the end of this week."

Tom was totally taken aback at this news. "Damn, Brenda told me some of this but I didn't know things were moving so fast. Does that mean that Katie and my father have settled their differences?"

"Not by a long shot. I'll tell you all about that in a minute or two but first I have a question to ask. Will you be my best man at our wedding?"

"I'd be delighted to be your best man. Thank you. But won't that present a problem? I mean with my father?"

"That's an iffy question and I think the answer is probably yes. Katie was over your father's house the Sunday he arrived from Florida because she wanted to tell him that she was pregnant and that we were going to get married. He wasn't in a good mood and he didn't give her a chance to talk and, when she left, she was angry with him. She hasn't talked to him since and I've seen him twice. She's over her anger but her attitude has changed. She hasn't spoken to your father, she's waiting for him to come to her with an olive branch instead of her going to him."

As Tom paused Mark spoke up quickly, "That's strange to hear because I feel exactly the same way that Katie does. For so long, I would have done anything to have a good relationship with my father; especially when I was alone in Canada. I still want that relationship but it isn't as urgent as it once was. I have developed other ties. I have a wonderful wife, I'm going to be a father, I've got a decent job and my side business is doing well. If my father wants to heal our rift, he will have to make the first move. I don't suppose he is interested in doing that though, is he?"

Tom replied, "To be perfectly honest, Mark, I don't think so. The last time I talked with your father I got the impression that he might get together with Katie and Tyler. He probably is waiting for Helen to help him out of his awkward position.

"However, when it comes to you, he is absolutely stubborn and completely unreasonable. His father's death has frozen his logic. He believes you can either be a patriot or a protestor; but you can only be one or the other, you can't be both. With that point of view, he's all tangled up in history and duty. Until he learns to accept other people's choices he is going to continue to miss out on enjoying life.

"In a way, I feel sorry for him."

Mark replied, "Tom, you feel sorry for almost everyone. I knew him as a parent who was always distant and cool. He seemed so much more aware of Katie than he was with me. I always envied the way he treated Katie and I guess that's the reason that I thought my father was unlikable. That may be why, when we finally had an open dispute, it was such a dramatic confrontation. If it weren't for Helen, his stubbornness would make him even harder to get along with.

"Anyhow, enough of my father, we'll just have to wait and see what happens. When did you say you were going to Michigan?"

"The end of this week. I'm excited for Katie and Tyler to meet my mother and father. Although she has spoken to my parents over the phone, she's nervous because of her pregnancy. She doesn't know what my parents will think of her. I do. They love her now and their feelings will only deepen.

"Come to think of it, my mother could easily have been Helen's twin sister. Both are loving, no nonsense women. I'm looking forward to introducing Helen to my mother when my parents come to Foxboro for the wedding."

As Tom finished speaking, Mark began to gather the napkins and the wrappings from the sandwiches. He said, "You've been a good friend to me and I'm pleased you asked me to be your best man. This is a new start for you and Katie and I'm happy for both of you.

"Now, I'm going to gas up my truck and get ready for this afternoon's exciting work assignment. Thanks for the catered lunch; once you start your new job I don't suppose we'll be doing this any too often. Oh well, I can always start packing my own sandwiches."

With that he left.

***

When Tom got home that evening, Katie told him that Helen had phoned and wanted to speak to him. He called her back and she told him that John had come home from the hospital and that he was eager to speak with Tom. As Helen was talking, he heard her husband in the background and then he heard John's voice on the phone.

"Tom, I want to talk with you. Would you be able to come over tonight?"

"Mr. Givens, I'll clean up and eat and be over your house in about two hours if that's all right."

"Yes, I'd like that very much. Thanks for accommodating me."

After Tom hung up he asked Katie, "Honey, is there something going on? Your father wants to talk with me. Do you or Helen have any idea what this is about?"

Katie answered, "No, I don't know what is going on and he hasn't said a word to Helen. That's unusual; although he has asked her about some of our wedding details and what we are planning after the wedding."

"Well, I'll know more in a little while."

When Tom got to John's house, Helen greeted him warmly and showed him into the den. John was sitting in a chair with his broken leg encased in a plaster cast propped up on a stool; it was a much smaller cast than the one he had in the hospital. There were two wooden crutches standing against the wall. He pointed to his leg and said, "This cast is going to drive me nuts until they finally cut it off. Before I left the hospital, they gave me a smaller cast; what they call a walking cast. It may be smaller but it still is not going to help my golf game.

"However, since my Bentley has an automatic transmission, I should be able to drive myself around when I get used to this plaster anchor."

Tom tried to ease the conversation along by replying, "Mr. Givens, look at the bright side. Your smaller cast is still large enough for all of your friends to sign their full names. Once you're able to drive you will be able to be mobile, even if it is slow mobility."

Givens immediately answered; he was glad to talk because Tom had inadvertently begun by bringing up one of the topics that he had planned on talking about. "Listen Tom, you're going to be part of the family so you should start calling me 'John'."

"Mr. Givens, I'll try but I can't promise. I don't even call my father by his first name and, being Katie's father, I put you in the same category that he's in. I guess it's a case of parental respect."

Givens replied, "Well, see if you can call me 'John' because it would make me feel a lot more comfortable. I have to tell you that I've been thinking about our conversation since the last time we talked; you made sense on many of the things you said about Katie and me. You were right that I wasn't more considerate of Katie's feelings. I put my own ego first, never thinking of what she had gone through. Helen has told me the same thing over and over but, until I heard it from you, it never registered. It has now and I feel bad. I'm hoping that you will help me set things straight"

"I'll do what I can, Mr. Givens."

"Good. Can you bring you and Katie and Tyler over here for dinner? I really want to get close to her again. You were also right in what you said about Tyler. Why should the sins of the father be carried over to the son? I would like to get to know my only grandchild."

Tom was delighted to hear that John Givens was beginning to change his outlook; he knew that Katie would well up with tears when she heard the news. That made him feel good just thinking of what her reaction would be. "Mr. Givens, er... John, Katie will be delighted when I tell her. Our only problem is that we are leaving at the end of the week to go to Michigan. Pick a night this week and we will be glad to come over for dinner."

After they settled for Wednesday evening, John continued the conversation. "Listen, I've been thinking about you and how you are going to live after you get married. With your education and your personality and your brains, I can't figure out why you went to work for the highway department in the first place. I want you to work with me in my business. I have no doubts that you'll be able to learn the ropes and be successful. Eventually, you will become my partner."

Givens friendliness and generosity surprised Tom. He wasn't sure why Given's stubbornness was being replaced with so much sweetness and light. Whatever the reason, Tom wanted to avoid either doing business with, or being beholden to, his future father in law. He appreciated the spirit but he wanted to avoid the entanglement.

"Thank you Mr. Givens,..." He saw the look on the older man's face and immediately corrected himself, "John, I will not be working at the highway department in a few weeks. I have already given my notice. I will be working as a teacher and a counsellor in the Mansfield school system, but I really do thank you for your kind offer. I appreciate it."

"Helen told me that you were leaving your job. However, you won't be making the kind of money teaching that I'm offering you. I have a good idea of what you will make as a starting teacher and I'm prepared to triple that salary. That's how sure I am that you will do well in my business."

"I thank you John, that is a very generous offer and I appreciate your confidence. However, I'll be doing something I want to do and that, I think, is very important; I'll be working with young people and giving them guidance."

"And you think that giving guidance is more important than money?"

Tom smiled at the way the question was asked. "Maybe not three times as much but I want to do something I feel comfortable with. Katie and I have discussed this thoroughly and we will have enough money to get by. Working with young people is important to me, important enough for me to turn down your generous offer; I thank you, but I must decline."

Givens was surprised and a little exasperated; money had always been one of his key motivators. Most of the time he could win his arguments using cash, but here was someone who was not moved by his golden carrot. Although he didn't like being refused, it began to dawn on him that his soon to be son in law had his own convictions. He didn't like being turned down but he began to respect Tom as a man of principle.

Givens decided to change he subject. "There is one more matter that I want to talk over with you. I assume that Mark is going to be at the wedding. Do you have any suggestions for me?"

Tom looked at Givens. He didn't want to hurt her father's feelings but protecting Katie was his top priority. He chose his words carefully, "John, you should do nothing that would embarrass Katie or ruin her wedding day. If you can't see your way to forgive Mark, you shouldn't come to the wedding."

Givens sat quietly for a while before he asked, "Mark will be at the wedding?"

"Yes, he will be at the wedding; he is going to be my best man."

Givens wondered just how stubborn Tom could be; he certainly was his own man. "You sure are blunt."

"I'm sorry John, but this is our wedding day and I want it to be perfect for Katie and me. Katie wants you to be there and so do I; you are part of our family. However, this is a day of happiness. It should be a day of letting go of the past, a day of starting over, and that's how it should be remembered. The past is done, gone, finished. Embrace Mark the same way you are embracing Katie.

"Please John, come to our wedding."

Givens was churning inside over a tight tornado of swirling emotions. He loved his daughter but he could not overcome his belief that his son had violated his father's honor. He wanted to be at Katie's wedding but he did not want to disrupt her happiness. At the same time, he could see that Tom would do whatever it took to protect Katie. He realized that she was getting a strong man.

"Tom, I'd like to but I can't change my feelings for Mark; at the same time, I don't want to spoil Katie's day. I guess the best thing to do is for me to be out of town on the day of the wedding. You'll have to help me come up with a plan."

"I will if you want me to, but I'd much rather be helping you come to the wedding."

Leaving it at that, they discussed their Wednesday night meeting and ended the conversation.

***

Helen spent most of Wednesday nervously getting a clean house immaculate and cooking and baking as if for the arrival of kings, queens and crown princes. She so wanted this reunion to go right; and it did. When Katie and Tom and Tyler arrived, Helen greeted them and then ushered them into the den where Givens was seated with his crutches nearby. Tyler shyly walked over and handed him a wooden cane. He said, almost inaudibly, "Grandpa, my Momma and I thought you could use this. Here."

His grandson was a lanky, young lad with a mop of light brown hair similar to Katie's color. The sins of the father had absolutely nothing to do with this young boy. Givens couldn't believe the emotional swell of love he felt for his grandson. John Givens mouth worked as tears welled in his eyes.

He reached behind his chair and came up with a football that he offered to Tyler. "Tyler, thank you for your gift. Let me give you one in return. This has been autographed by all the New England Patriots and I got it a few days ago."

Tyler reached out and clutched the ball with both hands as if he had received the Holy Grail. He smiled as he looked at the names and read them wordlessly and immediately thought how jealous his two best friends would be when he showed them his prize. In his quiet voice he said, "Grandpa, thank you."

"Tyler, you are completely welcome. Katie, Tom, how glad I am to see both of you. Katie, come give me a kiss and help me up, and we will go into the dining room. I hope all of you are hungry as Helen has prepared a meal that will take us a month to eat as long as nobody stops to talk."

He was right. When they sat at the table, they chomped, they chewed, they chowed and they chugged until they almost choked; they crossed the boundary and gorged themselves. When they were through with the main course and the many side dishes, they remained at the table almost panting in exhaustion. Nobody moved for a few minutes until John said, "Helen, take Tom and Tyler into the living room and have dessert. Katie and I will join you after we talk."

Katie hovered over her father as he still was a little shaky using his crutches. When he was settled in the den, she got coffee for both of them. John Givens didn't know where to begin to talk of the past so he started with the present. He began the conversation with the question, "Katie, did Tom tell you what I offered him Monday night?"

She answered, "Yes, he did, Dad. When he returned to our house he told me what you two had talked about and what you had offered him."

"Did he tell you that he had turned down my offer of money and a partnership in my business?"

"Yes, he did. To be perfectly honest, we discussed your offers in great detail. Tom asked me if I wanted him to reconsider his answers to you. He might have changed his mind if I had asked him to; I didn't."

Her father shook his head and said, "I don't understand why both of you feel the way you do. You could quit work and stay home with Tyler and there still would be enough money for you to be able to do almost anything you wanted."

"Dad, your offer is very generous. Three times what he would make as a teacher would mean a life of ease and comfort for both of us. You have to know Tom to understand his decision. He isn't after money. It's hard for me to tell you what he is after, but I'll try.

"Vietnam and his experiences since he came back hurt him. I'm not a psychologist but I live with him and I can tell you that they burned him deeply. He has been searching himself trying to sort things out and he started to think things through sometime before we met. Without sounding pompous, all I can tell you is that Tom has personal goals besides earning a living. He wants to make a difference and help young people. Dad, I can't begin to tell you how proud I am of him. His love has brought me back to life."

She sat quietly thinking about how the two of them had meshed with one another since they began living together. When they cuddled in the morning, they would each discuss their days' activities and, when they cuddled in the evening, they reprised their days' events. The intimacy of lying in bed with Tom pleased Katie as a female; talking with him as a partner pleased her as a person. Katie thought of her unborn child and her loving mate and she felt blessed. She had left the parched desert of loneliness. She thought, "It must be that I'm getting close to the Garden of Eden."

She had drifted away from the conversation for a while as she realized that her father had asked her something. "I'm sorry, Dad, what did you ask me?"

"I asked if you knew that Tom was leaving the highway department when you first met him? He seems strong willed when he makes up his mind and I wondered how the two of you got along."

"I didn't know anything about Tom when I first met him. You wouldn't recognize him now from his prior appearance because he had long hair and a beard. I guess he kept his beard and hair that way to keep people away from him. He was called 'Mountain Man' and it was a long time before I got to know him.

"You're right that he is strong willed, but he also is a kind, compassionate man; and he is totally honest. We don't always agree but we don't have to; since there is respect on both sides, we get along extremely well."

"That means that you are happy?"

Katie sat a long time without answering. Finally, she replied, "I'm sorry I took so long to reply. Yes, I'm happy. I'm happy and fortunate.

"That's not what took me so long to answer. I just this minute realized that, had I met Tom years ago, I would not have appreciated his virtues because what you see is what you get. He is honest, open, without guile. Those are marvelous human qualities but not endearing to young girls. In a way, I had to go through what I did to realize how much I love Tom and just how happy life can be."

John Givens decided that this was the time for him to speak about the past. "Katie, I guess I didn't do much to make it any easier for you. I'm sorry for that. I got so wrapped up about what Mike was doing to me that I didn't pay enough attention to Mike's other victims. Helen was one and she is so close to me that it fueled my anger. I never thought about you also being the victim of whatever Mike was doing. Helen scolded me constantly but it never registered.

"The fact is that I got worse as my hatred built up. I got to the point of thinking that you were partially to blame because you never complained about Mike. That was stupid to rail against you for being loyal and uncomplaining when my problems were of my own making. Hate certainly short circuits people's thought processes.

"It was only when Tom started pointing out the same things that

Helen had been saying that I began to look at you the way I should have years ago. I am deeply sorry for the way I treated you.

"I have always loved you, from the very time you were born until right now. As my daughter, you have brought love and joy into my life, and I want that to continue. If you can overlook my negligence I promise it will never happen again. I want to be part of your life along with Tyler and Tom."

They each held the other's hand and sat quietly. After Katie thought that she could control her emotions and her voice, she replied, "Oh Dad, that was such a bad period for all of us. Each of us made mistakes in what we thought and we made errors in judgements that seem insane now. The important thing is that we are starting over. I'm thrilled that you and Tyler will have a chance to know each other. It is important for a family that all generations help grow their offspring to be good persons and good citizens. Dad, I do love you."

They began to reminisce about their adventures when Katie was growing up. Katie would tell a story and her father would embellish it or Katie would correct her father's impression about a particular event. Talking about the past brought them together for the future.

After a short pause, Katie's father asked, almost shyly, "Katie, what are your financial arrangements for your wedding?"

"Dad, Tom and I are going to pay for everything. He has refused offers from his family to help with the expenses and I feel the same way. We are going to pay for everything ourselves. We are both insistent on that."

John Givens thought to himself, "Well, I'm going to talk to Helen about that." He sat still for a moment and then said, "Katie, we have to go back and join the others. If you and Tom are going to leave for Michigan at the end of this week you will be busy preparing for the trip."

Katie took a deep breath and replied, "Dad, there's one other thing you should know. I'm pregnant." She was not sure how her father would react to that news.

"Well, I'm not surprised." He thought a second and then added, "Nor am I too concerned. Your man, Tom, has impressed me. You have made a good choice and the two of you are a fine couple. I guess that I will be having two grandkids instead of one. Let's go back to the others."

He hadn't included Brenda in his census of upcoming grandchildren. It was an oversight that he would think about later that evening.

When they stood up, John tottered a little, and then kissed Katie on the cheek.

16

Milan, Michigan is not quite as famous as its older and larger sister city of Milan, Italy. However, that doesn't bother its inhabitants in the slightest; they feel equally as pleased with their Milan as their Italian counterparts feel with theirs. Michigan may not have as much history, population or pasta as Italy but it certainly has as much civic pride.

The Michigan Milan is a very small city twelve miles south and two miles east of Ann Arbor. Milan is insulated, and well hidden, from that university metropolis by acres and acres and acres of tall corn fields. It is an agricultural community that has remained bucolic and isolated from the "town and gown" atmosphere of its much larger neighbor to the north.

When Milan was founded, in 1831 by John Marvin, he called it Tolanville, after his son-in-law. It was later renamed after the more famous city in Italy but its founders still have two residential streets that bear their names, Marvin and Tolan Streets. The city does not have much of an industrial base; it is home to the Milan Federal Correction Institution and the Milan Dragway. Its most outstanding physical feature is that the town lies across two Michigan counties. The local bakery has its counter in Washtenaw County while the ovens, a few feet away, are in Monroe County. Despite the different tax rolls, Milaners consider themselves Milaners, not county dwellers. As such, this small city has the advantage of rural living while being able to drive down the rural roads to partake of the sophistication of Ann Arbor. There are no strangers in Milan and hardly any personal secrets. The inhabitants of Milan hope that it remains that way.

It was turning dark when Tom slowly drove his car into the driveway of his parent's home. His mother and father dashed from the house because they had been anxiously looking out the windows, awaiting the arrival of their son, Katie and Tyler. Both Selma and Don went to the passenger side of the vehicle to embrace Katie, leaving Tom sitting bemusedly behind the steering wheel. They were both delighted to meet Tom's future wife and their new grandson in person. Tom remained seated in the car, he was weary from the drive. It was only as an afterthought, when the hugging of Katie and Tyler had been finished, that his parents got around to greeting him. He wasn't upset by their apparent initial neglect of him; their immediate acceptance of Katie pleased him. They unpacked their luggage, ate dinner and retired early. It was the beginning of a pleasant, ten day interlude for all of them.

When the three of them woke up the next morning, Tom's parents were in the kitchen waiting for them. Selma and Don took their orders and made breakfast. All five ate heartily. What made this breakfast so enjoyable was that, during the entire time, every one of the adults wanted to talk. Each told stories about the other, and they tattled on one another's foibles. Tyler was included in these conversations but he couldn't be prompted to say much; it was a few days before he overcame his shyness and joined in. It was a long, leisurely meal filled with good will and laughter.

After the meal, Don said that he was going to work for a few hours and Tom decided to join him. Thinking about his own experiences at the hardware store, he suggested to Katie that Tyler come with them. Tyler liked the idea so the three of them left. Katie and Selma sat in the kitchen making a list of what needed to be done for the party that was going to be held at the Booker's home that evening. Selma and Don had invited a few of their close friends over to meet Katie. As they were making a grocery list, Katie decided to broach a subject that was bothering her and she took her direct approach by asking, "Mrs. Booker, you do know that I'm pregnant don't you?"

"Yes, Katie."

"Does that bother you?"

Selma put her pencil down and looked at Katie. "Does it bother me? To answer you directly, no, it doesn't bother me. Do I wish that you were not pregnant? Yes, but that wish isn't as important as the fact that you and Tom are happy. You have no idea how good you have been for my son. Don and I are glad to have you as our daughter, we love you, and we are thrilled at becoming grandparents."

Katie had to wait until her emotions quieted and she could control her voice. Then she said, "Mrs. Booker, thank you. Tom wanted to get married from the moment we got together so, from that point of view, it is my fault. I wasn't sure I was ready for marriage and I didn't want to repeat what I had lived through before. It seems silly now, especially since I'm pregnant.

"However, I do want you to know that I love Tom with all of my heart and soul. He is one of the strongest willed men I have ever met; yet, he is gentle and tender with me and Tyler.

"I just didn't want you or your husband to think that our wedding is the result of a cheap affair."

Mrs. Booker leaned forward and held Katie's hand. "Katie, Dear, we never thought that for a second. Don and I knew about you even before you had ever heard of us.

"When Tom came home last Christmas he told us that he was in love with a librarian, you, but he didn't know if you were aware that he existed. Since that time we have learned about you, Tyler, and your father. Helen and I have talked with each other on the phone.

"Don and I have admired and loved you from the first time we heard of you. Of course we know what is between you and Tom is not a cheap affair. Loving you seems to run in the family genes.

"Now, let me get back to practical matters. How do you address your stepmother when you talk to her?"

"Why, I call her Helen."

"In that case, I hope you will be comfortable calling me Selma. In any event, let's finish this shopping list and get ready for tonight's party."

That afternoon, after the women finished shopping and the men returned from the store, they gathered to discuss their day. Tyler was excited about the tools and gadgets he had tried at the hardware store and it took a while for him to stop and catch his breath. Over sandwiches and soft drinks, Selma described what had to be done to get ready for the party. She didn't believe there was too much to do as only a few friends had been invited.

She was wrong. The party started earlier and lasted later than she expected. It was a noisy, bustling party thrown in honor of Katie and Tom. In a small community, free food and drinks and a chance to meet friends and greet newcomers will always draw a crowd. Katie was overwhelmed by the number of people she was introduced to and shook hands with. She enjoyed herself but by the end of the evening she was tired.

When they finally were snuggling in bed, Tom asked her if she had had a good time. She replied, "Yes, but I think I met every person who lives in the Lower Peninsula. My right arm is stretched a foot longer than my left."

Tom replied, "That was more of a crowd than my parents anticipated. They all just wanted to meet the newest member of the Booker family. Don't forget, my mother and father have lived in Milan their entire lives. I'm sorry that so many of their friends showed up."

"Tom, don't say that, it was a good party. I was only kidding. You should be pleased that your parents have so many friends. I honestly enjoyed meeting them. There were even a couple of women who reminded me of Mrs. Buoni and Mrs. Connors. They are a lot like the people in Foxboro.

"Did you have a good time?"

Tom replied, "Yes, I had a really good time. I've known most of these people all my life and to have them come over and meet you makes me happy. I'm sure it also pleases my parents."

Katie replied, "From that point of view, I guess you're right. Listen, on a different subject, let's make breakfast for your parents tomorrow. It will come as a complete surprise and it is something I would like to do for them."

As a result, when Don and Selma came into the kitchen the next morning, they found Katie, Tom and Tyler waiting for them. Katie and Tom took their breakfast orders and made breakfast. All five ate heartily and their routine followed the pattern of the previous morning except that there was a subtle difference in the conversation; they were more willing to talk about themselves. Each would openly express their thoughts without any concern of being misunderstood. Their love and respect for each other began gluing them together.

The pattern for breakfast was set for the remainder of Katie and Tom's visit. Each couple would alternate making breakfast and then everyone would linger around the table and chat. The rest of each day would be filled with household chores, business activities, and dropping over to friends' houses for visits. The evenings would be spent in quiet visits with friends or playing cards at home. Katie and Selma would bake cookies or cut up fresh fruit for a light bed time snack at the end of the card games.

It was not until almost a week passed before Tom was able to take Katie and Tyler on any sightseeing trips around Milan. He had been anxious for them to see the lovely landscape of farmlands, wooded areas, lakes and streams that surrounded the entire area. He also took them to Ann Arbor and showed them around his alma mater, the University of Michigan. Tyler was impressed with the size of the football stadium, especially when Tom told him that the entire population of Foxboro or Milan could be put in the stands behind either goalpost and they wouldn't be noticed. Katie liked being on the central campus better than standing at the top and staring down into a huge athletic field; she enjoyed the activities on the Diag and watching the students stream by. The Law Quadrangle, with its Gothic architecture, took her fancy.

It was during these outings that Katie, even though she was enjoying herself, started to feel that she wanted to return home earlier than she and Tom had planned. Her mind was on the preparations for her wedding. Much to her surprise, when she mentioned her concerns to Tom, he agreed, he was anxious to get acquainted with the new people and the new environment where he would be working. After they discussed their thoughts with Tom's parents, they decided to leave on Tuesday instead of on Saturday. On Monday, their last day in Michigan, Tom drove them around Barton Hills and then took the Huron River Drive to the town of Dexter for lunch. The three of them enjoyed the slow pace of their sightseeing, the scenery, and the chance to relax.

When they got ready to leave, the parting was hard. Even though they would shortly be together again at the wedding, this had been a special occasion for all of them. Katie and Selma kissed and embraced and cried tears of joy and tears of sadness. The joy came from their meeting and the sadness came from their leaving. It was impossible to tell which tears were for which emotion. Tom and Don felt the same emotions but they managed to keep their tears in check while they shook hands. Tyler had had a good time and he was oblivious to the sadness of adults. He was pleased to have found a new set of grandparents and he was looking forward to the trip back home to Foxboro.

***

Before Katie left on her trip to Milan, she had a long talk with Brenda and Mark. She didn't want to leave before telling them about the results of her meeting with her father. Brenda and Mark were pleased to hear that the two of them had reconciled and, when Katie told them that he had been friendly to Tyler and that she had told him that she was pregnant, Brenda came to life. She asked, "Katie, do you think your father could be changing his mind about Mark?"

Katie answered, "I'm not sure, it is so hard to tell. He seems to soften his attitude and then harden it again. He can be reasonable, sometimes, and then he can be inflexible. Tom says that his patriotism is a disease that leaves him normal in remission and dysfunctional when he's infectious. I think Tom is right."

After Katie left Foxboro, Brenda began to wonder if she could breach the gap between Mark and his father. She and Helen had been together several times but she had never met Mark's father. She was curious how he would react if they were to meet. The more she thought about it, the more she wanted to try to speak with him. Brenda always had an optimistic, direct approach to her problems.

The Tuesday after Katie left Brenda went to the coffee shop early, got two coffees to go, and walked up the stairs to John Given's office. He had just arrived, settled himself in his chair and stored his crutches, when she walked in and said, "Mr. Givens, I would like to talk with you, if I may."

He was surprised but he answered, "Won't you sit down? You'll have to excuse me for not rising, but my leg is in a cast."

Brenda put his coffee on his desk. She replied, "Thank you. That's no problem. Your coffee has two sugars and double cream, just like you like it."

Now, John Givens was puzzled. "Who are you and how do you know how I like my coffee?"

"Mr. Givens, my name is Brenda Quinn Givens; I'm Mark's wife, your daughter in law."

"OH." John Givens wasn't sure what else to say. He looked at this tall, slim, redheaded woman and then took the top off of his coffee. He stared at her in amazement for a second and then he thought, "I wonder what she wants?"

He continued to look at her for another second or two. He was still completely nonplussed and speechless. Finally, he began to respond to his surprise. He volunteered, "Won't you be seated?"

After Brenda sat down and began sipping her coffee, he wondered if she was going to cause trouble. He said the first thing that came to his mind, "I knew my son had married. As his wife, you must hate me."

"Hate is a very strong word, Mr. Givens. Why would I hate you?"

"Well, being married to my son, you would get his side of our relationship without knowing anything about mine."

"I have heard his side of your relationship and I still don't hate you. Why would I?"

"I wouldn't want you to; but I'm sure that he gave you the impression that I'm a mean, heartless father."

"No, Mr. Givens, Mark has never said anything about you like that. He has disagreed with you but he has never disparaged you; you are his father. Something you probably don't know is that Katie and I have been best friends for years, long before I met Mark.

"When I did meet Mark, everything fell into place for us and we are happy together. He has always accepted his share of the blame for the split between you. Whatever else may be said about you, Mark has never said you were mean and heartless."

John Givens nervously asked, "Well, what would you say?"

"I don't know. I'm not sure. I'm not a psychiatrist. I'm a person who wants everyone I love to get along with everyone else. If I had to say anything, I would say that you are a person who has missed opportunities to resolve problems."

He could feel his anger stirring at the thought that he was going to get another lecture. He asked, in a harsh tone, "So, you think my relationship with my son is all my fault?"

"I don't think anything like that. You and Mark went your separate ways long before I met him. I can't change that and I'm not here to talk about the past. I want to talk to you about the future; I do hope you'll listen to me."

John looked at Brenda and then he had to smile. The tone of her voice, along with her button nose, her open face and her red hair, assured him that there were to be no discussions about the past; she was more of a peace advocate, not a trouble maker.

"Anyone who fixes my coffee correctly is worth listening to." Then he switched subjects for a second, "I'm sorry, but what did you say your name was?"

"Brenda Quinn Givens."

"Well, Brenda, you said that Katie is your best friend?"

"Yes, we met when she first moved to San Luis Obispo. We palled around together until she decided to return to Foxboro. Before she left we talked about the possibility of my moving here. I missed her and Tyler so I came east to visit her; and that was even before Mark and I met. Katie had told me about her brother but talk can only stir interest, it can't generate chemistry. It was only after I met him that I realized that he was the mate I had been looking for. I consider myself lucky having Mark and I only wish that you felt the same way."

John sat there drinking his coffee and, suddenly, he asked, "By the way, how did you know how I drank my coffee?"

"A couple of days ago, when I decided to meet you, I asked Helen."

"Does she know you are here?"

"Heavens no, Mr. Givens neither she, nor Mark, nor Katie have any idea that I'm here. Coming to meet you is my own idea."

"Brenda, why would you want to meet me?"

"Mr. Givens, there are several reasons why I decided to talk to with you. The most important one is that I'm pregnant and I want you and

The Patriots of Foxboro

Helen to be joyful and active grandparents. It would mean a lot to me. Your wife is looking forward to her new grandchild."

John spoke out louder than he had planned. "Good lord, you're pregnant, Katie's pregnant; Foxboro is turning into a maternity ward. I ---." He stopped for a second before he dropped what he was going to say. Then, he continued, "Congratulations."

"Thank you, I hope you really mean that because my pregnancy is why I'm here. You see, I was raised in an orphanage and I can tell you chapter and verse about childhood loneliness. I wasn't abused or molested but I was neglected. The lack of family and love on a child is devastating. I felt like I was born and raised in a buried casket." Brenda sat quietly for a few moments. Ordinarily, she wasn't this sombre.

Then she continued, "I don't want my baby going through that. What I want is for our child to have the love and guidance that only a family can provide. I came to ask you if you wouldn't help; I think you would make a fine grandfather for our child."

John was quiet for a while. There was something about her honesty and straightforwardness that appealed to him. She certainly was direct. He found himself pleased with her honest approach. Still, he had his reasons for thinking of Mark the way he did; her suggestion did nothing to ease the pain that his son had caused.

To avoid giving Brenda an answer, and because he was interested, John asked her more about her childhood. Before they realized it, they had spent fifteen or twenty minutes chatting. Brenda looked at her watch and said, "I've got to get ready for work, Mr. Givens. I appreciate the time you have given me."

"Brenda, I have enjoyed talking to you."

"Mr. Givens, before I go, I want to ask you a couple of questions. You don't have to give me an answer, I just want you to think about them."

"Well, what are they."

Brenda paused, not knowing if she would start a landslide or not. "Your father was an honorable man who died for our country. I wonder if you've ever wondered what he would have thought of Katie's husband, Mike?"

John Givens was totally taken by surprise. Such a thought had never crossed his mind. He simply said, "No, I have never thought about that."

Brenda could tell that she had surprised him. She decided to press her luck a little by adding, "Well, if you do, also think about what he would say about Mark."

She stood, as did John Givens by holding onto the desk with both hands and pulling himself up. She reached across the desk and shook his hand. She smiled and he did also. They both enjoyed their conversation and each realized that, although neither of them had changed their minds, they liked each other.

***

Portagee John was in a rage. That was not an unusual state for him; however, this time, it was a particularly deep rage. He had just been chewed out for being stupid and negligent by the foreman because he had backed his truck over a jerrycan of gas that had been lying on the ground, crushing it and spilling the remaining gas. The entire crew heard and saw his tongue lashing and, when he came into the locker room, everyone avoided speaking to him.

He was like a rabid bull. He sat in front of his locker, rocking back and forth, swearing at the universe and the goddam stupid foreman who was as ignorant as shit. He wanted someone to talk to him so that he could pick a fight and use his fists. No one was dumb enough to do that. As the men changed and went home, he heard the talk that Tom Booker was leaving on vacation and then for another job. He already knew that and it had pleased him to think that he would be able to bully people again; but today he was too angry to enjoy the fact that he would ultimately triumph over his most hated enemy.

As he was getting ready to leave he noticed a jacket lying on the floor. The name over the pocket read "Mark." Without thinking, PJ threw it into his locker and left the building. He drove to the Common and went into the hardware store that was located on the first floor, just beneath John Given's office. He was looking for a new chainsaw to buy for his side business. He saw one that he really liked but it was expensive and that made him even angrier. He left the store and went to a bar on Mechanic Street for a beer.

Hunched over his beer, hating everyone in Foxboro, PJ bemoaned the fact that he could not afford a new chain saw. He began to wonder how he could steal it and, suddenly, it dawned on him. His imagination, which was as active as a piece of petrified wood, began to stir. He could break into the hardware store, through the back door, steal the chainsaw, and leave Mark's jacket on the floor. That would almost make him even with that sneaky son-of-a-bitch. He was so pleased with his brilliant plan that he had a few more beers.

Over the next few days, he listened to the talk at work and he enlarged and honed his plan so that two of his worst antagonists would be defeated and nothing would point to him. He, Portagee John, would get even with both Tom and Mark. He considered his plan as complicated as the plan for the invasion of France; and, for him, it was.

Six days after Katie and Tom left Foxboro, PJ went over to their house just after midnight. He parked his truck on Neponset Avenue and walked over to their home, staying mostly in the bushes and woods to avoid being seen. He was not used to walking and he was panting when he reached their porch. He took out a claw hammer and a crowbar that he had brought from his tool box and he split open a panel on the front door of their house. He reached through the door and unlocked it. With his heart beating wildly, he slipped into the house and shut the door behind him. After a few seconds, he realized he was inside and no one knew it. He began to breath easier, he had reached his first objective.

He spat on the floor and the walked into the kitchen. There was a dish on the table; he hit it with his hammer and smashed it into pieces. The noise seemed so loud that he stopped and waited. After a while, he decided that breaking the dishes was too noisy so he began to open the kitchen cabinets and breaking the doors off their hinges.

Then, he took his hammer and punched holes in the wall as he walked down the hallway. He had just reached the living room, when the telephone began to ring. PJ panicked. He wondered if the beam from his flashlight had been seen by a neighbor who was calling to find out what was going on. By the second ring, he was running for the door. He ducked along the route he had taken to get to the house and when he reached his truck he had regained his composure. As he opened the door and threw his tools and the flashlight on the floor, he was elated. He was sure he felt like god would feel; he had desecrated the house of his enemy and had proven his power over him. Booker would be furious and he would never be able to figure out who was responsible. PJ enjoyed the feeling of revenge and was convinced that it was well deserved. Now, he would carry out the second half of his plan and nail the other son-of-a-bitch.

He drove his truck to Cocasset Street and parked close to the Common. He took Mark's jacket, wrapped it around his hammer, and walked down one of the driveways leading to the back of the hardware store. He knew that he would not need a flashlight because there was enough lighting for him to try to break in. He knew he had to be quiet and careful, but the thought of a free chain saw for him and a prison term for Mark was a powerful incentive.

The door was old and made of steel but the doorframe was wood and would split easily. He started to quietly pry the frame apart when, suddenly, he heard the sound of a car coming down one of the driveways. PJ threw himself on the ground behind some trash barrels as a police cruiser made its way through the small parking lot without stopping. After it left, he stood up and looked at the smelly trash that was stuck on his clothes. "Goddam those two bastards, this is all their fault," was his only comment.

He knew that he would have to change his plan; he had to get out of there before he got caught. He was in such a panic that he left the jacket and the hammer where he had dropped them. When he got back into his truck, he remembered his hammer. He started to build his cover story. Even though his initials were on it he would say that he didn't know where it was; it had been stolen from him about a month ago. He wouldn't accuse anybody but it wouldn't be hard to figure out who had stolen it from him. After all, Mark's jacket was in the alley. He was disappointed that he hadn't gotten his new chain saw, but he still had had a good evening. PJ drove home and took a hot shower, thus cleansing himself of all his sins.

***

The next morning John Givens drove into the same parking lot and found his reserved parking space almost blocked by two patrol cars.

He slowly got out of his car and hobbled over to where a patrolman and the police chief were standing and talking.

John went up to them and looked around. He saw some broken wood around a door frame, a hammer lying on the ground, and a highway department jacket with the name of "Mark" stitched on it. He turned cold inside but he managed to say, "Good Morning Bill, what are you two doing here this morning?"

The chief replied, "Hi John. I'm trying to figure out what went on here last evening. The hardware store reported damage to their door casing but they also said that the door had not been opened. Obviously nothing has been taken from their store. Is this a crime scene? It may have been an attempted break in; it may have been a drunk, who came back here to piss, and was just acting up.

"I was just about to tell Fred here that there's not enough evidence to charge anyone with anything. Fred'll take this stuff to the station and hold it for a while; it sure seems to be much ado about nothing. I've got bigger problems to deal with than this."

Callahan was sure that John had seen the name on the jacket but he didn't say a word about it; it wasn't his problem and he didn't want to get involved. He got into his patrol car and left. John waited until the patrol officer picked up the jacket and hammer and drove off in the other patrol car; then, he went over and looked at the damaged casing. There wasn't much to see, just some splintered wood above the lock and the broken pieces lying on the cement.

John mounted the stairs clumsily, using his crutches carefully, to his office and then slumped into his desk chair. He was upset. Without any thought, he had automatically jumped to the conclusion that his son, Mark, had tried to break into the hardware store. At first, he was unhappy but, the more he thought about what had happened, the angrier he got. Not only had his son ducked out of his civic responsibilities, he was now breaking the law and disgracing his family again. John now was feeling shamed for himself and ashamed of his son.

He vowed that he would not try to reconcile his differences with Mark even if it meant that he would not attend Katie's wedding.

17

Katie had been napping in the front seat when she slowly came awake. The car was on Interstate 95 near Foxboro and Tom was driving. Katie watched him for a while and was satisfied at how cautious a driver he was. He would activate his turn signals and look in his mirrors before changing lanes and he would never exceed the speed limit by more than five miles per hour. She decided that she was lucky to have a partner that she both loved and respected. She was happy that they were soon to be married. She leaned over and patted his knee. Tom glanced sideways, he had not known that she woke up.

"Sweetface, if you don't mind my asking, why am I being pummeled?" Tom had started calling Katie "Sweetface" one morning towards the end of their visit in Milan. When Katie asked him why he was calling her "Sweetface," he told her that he really wasn't sure except that he enjoyed looking at her in the morning while she was still asleep. He added that, if she objected, he wouldn't call her by that name any more. After she replied that she rather liked it, he would call her either "Katie" or "Sweetface" whichever came to mind first.

"You are not being pummeled; you are being patted for being such a good driver and for having such a lovely mother and father. I really enjoyed getting to know them."

"Honey, they feel the same way. It was really a pleasant visit and, now, we will be back home soon. I think we'll unpack and either go out to eat or I'll get a pizza. There's no sense cooking this evening."

After Tom parked Katie's car next to his truck, he looked at the house and asked, " Am I wrong or is our front door ajar? I know it was locked when we left because I tried to open it myself. Katie, you and Tyler stay here a second."

He walked up to the door slowly, looked at it, and then peered through the two windows that faced onto the porch. He came back to the car, got in, and said, "Someone has ransacked our home. We'll drive to Mrs. Buoni's house and call the police. I don't want to disturb anything until they have looked around."

The police did come, they did look around, they did file a report, and then they left. It wasn't until Katie went inside that the magnitude of what had happened hit her. She walked through her kitchen that had most of the cupboard doors on the floor, down the hallway with the walls gouged with holes. She kept repeating, "Why? Why? Why would somebody do this?"

Tom called Mark and he and Brenda came over immediately. Tom suggested the women and Tyler go over to Mrs. Connors' house and, after they left, he and Mark threw out the cabinet doors and cleaned up as much of the debris and damage as they could. Katie called Helen from Mrs. Connors to let her know what had happened. They ate supper with Mrs. Connors. It was a quiet, dismal evening.

After they were in bed, Katie snuggled against Tom and began to cry. "I feel dirty. My privacy has been violated and the sanctity of our house has been breached. I feel filthy, I feel slimed. I don't know why I feel this way, but I do and I just hate this feeling.

"Why would anyone do something like this to us? There are nothing but sentimental things in our house; absolutely nothing has any commercial value. There is nothing here but my grandmother's old furniture. I love it because it was hers but they're worthless to anyone else. Why break and smash my dreams and my memories? Nothing was stolen. Why would someone want to trash our nest? We've never done harm to anyone. Why? Oh why?

"And our wedding is so close. Oh, Tom, I feel so hurt."

He held her close to him while she sobbed. After a while he said, "Katie, please don't cry; it breaks my heart to have you so unhappy. Tomorrow, Mark and I will start to repair the cabinets and the walls. I've asked him to take all of next week off from work and he has agreed. We won't have everything fixed by the time of our wedding, but the place will look a lot better.

"Listen, I'll try to make something good come out of this senseless destruction. While we fix the damage, Mark and I will take that small, spare room you use for storage and fix it up as a nursery for our new child; it will be just the right size. That will make something good come from this act of stupidity."

That thought calmed Katie down and she stopped crying. She lay with her head on Tom's shoulder and, in a moment or two, she asked, "Do you want me to take time off from the library to help?"

"Sweetface, you were going to take the last three days of next week off, anyhow. It probably would be good for you to also stay home Monday and Tuesday. You'll be able to help and see the progress yourself instead of wondering what's going on while you're at work. Will you be able to get the time off without any problem?"

"Yes, that will be no problem and the public will be better off if they are not exposed to me. I don't like anyone right now and I don't think I will be of any use to anyone until this episode is over and we are married. I've changed. Now my marriage is so important to me and, six months ago, I was afraid to even consider it."

***

The next morning Katie, Tom, and Tyler went over to Brenda and Mark's apartment to have breakfast with them. The plan was that, after they ate, Tom and Mark would go to a lumber yard, buy the materials necessary to repair the house, and then get busy. Helen would join the women later and the three of them could work on the details of the wedding. As they were driving to the lumber store, Mark began to ask Tom about some of the details of the break in.

"Do you have any idea when your place was broken into?"

"No, it's impossible to tell when the attempt was made."

"You have no idea who could have done it or why?"

"No, I don't."

Mark thought about it for a few seconds before he started talking again. "You know, something odd happened to me while you were gone."

"What was that, Mark?"

"A couple of days ago a Foxboro cop drives over to the town garage and hands me a highway department jacket with my name on it and a hammer. He asks me if this is my jacket and my hammer and then he says that he found both items behind the hardware store that faces the Common. He wants to know if I knew how my jacket and hammer got there. I tell him that I had no idea that one of my jackets was missing and that the hammer was not mine.

"To tell you the truth Tom, I didn't even know I was missing the jacket. Anyhow, the cop says that I was lucky because it looked as if I was going to break into the store but I changed my mind and, because of that, they don't have enough evidence to prosecute. He told me to watch my step because they were going to keep an eye on me if there were any burglaries.

"What do you make of that?"

Tom replied. "That is strange, very strange."

After they loaded Mark's pickup truck with the materials they bought, Tom asked, "You said the cop gave you a hammer?"

"Yes, I guess he thought it was mine since the jacket had my name on it."

"What did you do with the hammer?"

"Nothing. I just put it into the toolbox in the back of the truck."

Tom said, "Let me look at it."

"Sure." Mark unlocked his tool box and rummaged through it for a while. Then, he handed Tom the hammer the cop had given him.

Tom looked at it for an instant before angrily saying, "SON OF A BITCH!"

"What's wrong, Tom?"

"That fat bastard. Look at the butt end of that handle. What initials do you see inscribed?"

"Why, PU? PI? DAMN, PJ! That's what it is, PJ!"

"That's correct, Mark. Now, it begins to make sense about what has happened; it looks like PJ went on a rampage against you and me. I don't care what he tried to do to me, but I won't allow him to bother Katie or Tyler. I'm furious. That fat, fucking slob is going to hear from me.

"I'll tell you what I'm going to do. I'm taking that hammer and personally returning it to PJ. I'm going to give him a message he won't forget. If he ever comes near Katie again I absolutely won't be responsible for what happens to him.

"In the meantime, we have work to do back at the ranch. Let's go."

By noontime they had straightened out the mess in the kitchen, cleaned the house, and began to repair the walls. When they looked at the damage they had decided to reface the kitchen cabinets and had ordered what they needed for that job. Tom told Mark to go back to his apartment and have lunch while he went to the town garage to confront PJ. Mark asked, "Tom, I could go with you couldn't I?"

Tom shook his head "No," and then added, "Mark, you still have to work with him, I don't. I want all of his hate and his attention focused on me, because I'm going to absolutely rip him a new asshole. I intend to give him a message, loud and clear and delivered by me. He is to stay away or face the consequences. It is my responsibility to protect Katie and I'll do it alone. You go get lunch, I'll join you afterwards.

"Don't tell Katie or Brenda where I am going, just say that I'm doing an errand. Bring me a sandwich back at the house and I'll be along when I can."

Tom drove his pickup truck over to the town garage and parked beside the other cars and trucks. It was a warm, sunny day and, through his windshield he could see PJ holding court at a picnic table with three of the older highway workers. He took the hammer and slid the handle up his long sleeved shirt on the inside of his arm and then closed his fingers around the steel head; it was almost hidden from sight. He walked over to where they were sitting and, as he approached, he was greeted by a series of derisive greetings by the others.

"Hey, the teacher wants his job and his truck back," said one.

"Were you fired or did you just miss us?" asked another.

"We just voted and you can't come back," said the third.

Tom replied, "Gentlemen, and I use the term loosely, I have showered since I left the highway department and that makes me ineligible to return. So, relax.

"Anyhow, I want to talk to PJ privately, so if you would leave us alone for a few minutes I would appreciate it."

The three of them, knowing that PJ and Tom disliked each other, were glad to get away from the table. They wanted no part of what might happen.

Tom slid into the seat opposite PJ who had both arms resting on the table. Tom kept his hands on his knees. Tom stared at PJ a while before he spoke softly; there was fury in his voice. "PJ, you fat, useless bastard, I'll bet you never expected me to show up. You should have known better you dumb son of a bitch. You messed with me and you are going to have to face the consequences."

Tom slid the hammer into his hand and, swinging it hard, smashed the table with it. The hammer dented the wood, inches from PJ's hands. The noise scared PJ and he jumped. Tom left it lying on the table between them. He then spoke even softer with more fury, "PJ, I am returning your hammer. Now, I can't prove in a court of law that you were the one who broke into my house but I don't need a court of law. I don't want a court of law. Both of us know that you went into my house. For you, that is forbidden territory.

"In a way, this one time only, you are a very lucky son of a bitch. I'm changing jobs and won't see you again so I will overlook what you did. Believe me though, I will not forget what you did.

"Listen to me, PJ and listen to me closely. I don't like you and if I ever have to come after you again, you will absolutely regret it. I am not threatening you. I am only telling you what will happen.

"Stay away from me, my family and my friends. Butt out of my life and save yourself a problem. Remember what I am telling you, if I ever have to look you up you will regret it."

Tom got to his feet and walked to his truck. As he drove away, PJ was still sitting at the table just staring at his hammer.

***

That evening Katie, Tom and Tyler went over to her father's house for dinner. Helen had invited them before they left on their trip to Milan and it had been planned as a pleasant get together where Helen would find out the details of their trip. The evening did not go as planned. From the very beginning of the meal, the atmosphere was quiet as everyone was wrestling with their own negative thoughts. The invasion of Katie's house and the malicious damage cast a pall on the conversation. Each person was steeped in their own cup of unhappiness.

John was especially somber. His leg was paining him and his thoughts were bleak. He had not told Helen about Mark's jacket being near the scene of the possible break in and he didn't want to talk about it. That was partially because he thought that Mark could be guilty of breaking the law. When he was told that Katie's house had been vandalized, his first thought was that Mark had done it. His mind was churning over and over with the thought that Mark had gone crazy.

Helen was not feeling well either physically or mentally. All day she had been concerned why Katie's house had been desecrated. She kept wondering why a small house on an unpaved road was the target of such a hateful act. Was it a random selection or did someone have a grudge against Katie or Tom? The thought that her daughter, her grandchildren and her son in law could be in danger disturbed her.

Along with her negative thoughts was the fact that she was feeling rather strange. She had a slight headache and sometimes she felt a little dizzy; she found that she had to force herself to remember what she was doing. She was uncomfortable and unhappy.

Katie was upset. A stranger had gone through her home without her permission and, for no apparent reason, had done gratuitous damage. She didn't know who it was or why that person had done such a thing. The wanton desecration of her privacy shocked her; it didn't make sense and she felt sullied. Even though Katie felt safe when Tom was home, not knowing who had been in her house and why they had been there bothered her. She was aware that it would be a long time before her fears disappeared.

Of the three of them, Tom was the closest to being in a good mood and even he was sober. After his confrontation with PJ he had gone back to the house and continued the repairs. When Mark returned from lunch, both of them kept working while Tom described his confrontation with PJ. He just had time to clean up before he and Katie went to dinner and he didn't tell Katie about his run in with PJ. He had decided to explain what had happened to everyone at the same time at dinner.

During the meal, everyone was quiet; the break in had stopped both the flow of happiness and the conversation. Whatever talk there was concerned only the vandalism and not the wedding. Everyone felt uncomfortable and there was very little banter around the dinner table. Tom decided that he would try to change the mood by telling them what he had discovered, so he said, "Today, I found out who broke into our house."

Kate was the first to ask, "Who?"

"There is a guy who works for at the highway department who is called Portagee John. He doesn't like either me or Mark and he decided

The Patriots of Foxboro

to try to get even with both of us while Katie and I were in Milan."

John Givens was surprised and he inquired, "PJ? Why would he do something like that? How could breaking into Katie's get even with Mark? That doesn't even begin to make sense."

Tom sighed; he had wanted to tell his story without mentioning Mark but he knew that, to make his encounter with PJ credible, he would now have to go into all the details. "Listen, Mark and I were on the way to the lumber yard when he told me that, while we were gone, his jacket and a hammer were found behind the hardware store facing the Common. It was a possible break in scene. He didn't even know his jacket was missing until Foxboro's finest gave him back the jacket and the hammer, which they assumed was his. Not knowing that Katie's house had been broken into, he just put the hammer in his truck.

"When he told me what had happened to him, I asked to see the hammer. It had PJ's initials on it. At lunch time, I confronted PJ. I gave him back his hammer and told him to stay away from everybody in this family or else he would have to deal with me. Believe me, that's something he doesn't want to do. We will have no more trouble from PJ."

Tom's story seemed to relieved Katie in the sense that it now wasn't a random act committed by an unknown person. It was now a stupid act committed by an extremely nasty, not too bright, person. She didn't like it but it was something that she could live with.

John Givens sat stoically and silently, thinking about what he had just heard. He wasn't even sure that he wanted to believe Tom's narrative. He had concocted his own story about Mark's jacket and the hammer and he had convinced himself that Mark had tried to break and enter into the hardware store. Now, he was being told by Tom that someone that everyone disliked was the culprit. He decided, because of his disappointments with, and his disapproval of Mark, that he would stick with his own version of what happened. He knew he was wrong logically but emotionally he felt good; his past feelings were justified. Mark had to bear the responsibility for disgracing the family.

Tom's revelation did nothing to change the stillness that surrounded the dinner table. There was not much discussion of the trip to Milan and no chit chat, just moody silence. Everyone seemed isolated from everyone else. After dinner, Katie helped Helen clear the table and clean up the kitchen; both of them seemed preoccupied and there was little conversation between them. Katie wondered if Helen was feeling all right and, when she asked, Helen assured her that she was doing well. Katie wasn't sure but she didn't pursue the subject any further. They all said, "Goodnight," and she and Tom and Tyler went home. There wasn't much conversation on the drive home. A pall of unhappiness seemed to have envelope them.

***

Tom came to bed about a half hour after Katie. She was reading a magazine when he got under the covers. Katie asked, "What have you been doing?"

"Nothing much. I was reading about the Red Sox. Why? Did you miss me?"

Katie put her arm around Tom and pulled herself close to him. "Listen Honey, I was thinking about us." She called him "Honey" as her personal form of endearment, meant only for Tom. It was after he started calling her "Sweetface" that she thought of giving him a loving code name. Katie really didn't think her face qualified as particularly sweet but she was not going to fight happiness. So, she picked a name for Tom and enjoyed the intimacy of using it just to identify the man she loved. She felt that using private names for each other was to give both of them a verbal tattoo for personal identification.

"What I was thinking was that if I had gone to the University of Michigan instead of Boston University we might have met years ago and married earlier and could have been together so much longer. What do you think?"

Tom thought for a while before he answered. "I'm not sure I agree. I love you right now. If we had met in high school I would have loved you; if we had met in a hospice, while our beds were side by side, I would have fallen in love with you. We match and fit like a jig saw puzzle.

"Listen, our love for each other is not the problem. What I don't know is that, if we were younger, would I have been mature enough to be honest with you and not hide my doubts and fears from you? Love needs passion to start and maturity to last; if both partners aren't honest with each other, their chemistry will disappear.

"There is also the question of whether you would have been able to see me then as you see me today? What would you think if we had met as teenagers? Would you be as impressed with me as your mature judgement is today? We were both so young and naive; we were so prone to human error."

"Darn you, Tom, you are always so practical. You may be right though, we both might have been too young to realize what we now have. I guess there is no sense looking back. I'm so happy with what I have that I wonder about our future. I'll try to make it good for both of us.

"I love you and your warmth makes me glow with happiness. This I do know, when we are together God knows both our names."

Tom kissed her and said, "You mean Sweetface and Honey? Whatever He calls us, I love you with all my heart, Katie." Then, he started to move his fingers up and down Katie's arms.

"Don't start that, yet. Maybe later. I have to tell you something you should know. I haven't mentioned it before because I didn't think it was important. Now, I know it is. What I never told you is this; I have a long history with PJ and it isn't very good. His younger sister and I were friends in high school and I liked her. She was bright, good looking and sweet. She moved out of the house after we graduated and I think she got married and moved to California. Anyhow, while we were going to school, PJ was always trying to hit on me. He stayed within bounds because I slapped him hard a couple of times and his sister told his mother and father on him.

"After I came back, he came over to the library a couple of times and tried to date me. I kept turning him down and, one day, I finally got tired of his dirty suggestions. I told him that I would call the police unless he left me alone. That scared him away. He's an unfeeling pig; he'd pick his nose at his own mother's funeral.

"All of this took place before I knew that you could easily take care of him. Little did I realize that you, Honey, the man of my life, would provide Tyler and me so much protection.

"I was surprised when you said that it was PJ who had vandalized our house. Knowing the name of the person who broke into our house is much better than not having a clue. You know who you are dealing with. At least some good will come from his stupid attack. The nursery for our baby will be ready and our kitchen will look much nicer when you and Mark finish facing the cabinets.

"Now, if you are still interested, you can start again where I told you to stop."

They both continued to make amends for having such a disappointing evening.

***

The phone rang about 4:00 AM. It awakened Tom on the first ring and, before it rang again, he had picked it up. Even though he had just quit the job, he automatically expected to hear the voice of the highway supervisor calling about an emergency. Because of that, he did not recognize who was speaking.

A voice asked, "Tom? Tom is that you? Are you awake?"

At first, Tom shook his head wondering who was talking. All of a sudden he realized that it was John Givens on the other end. He replied, "John? Yes, I'm awake. What's wrong?"

By this time Katie was awake and, when she heard Tom speak her father's name, she slid over to the side of the bed and sat beside him. He tipped the handset away from his ear so that Katie could hear what her father said. There was no response for a while and Tom again asked, "John, what's wrong."

After another long pause, John replied, "Tom, I'm at Norwood Hospital. Helen has had a stroke."

Katie cried out "Oh Dear God!" and clutched Tom's arm.

Tom put the phone in his other hand and put the arm closest to Katie around her shoulders. He asked, "How is she doing?"

"I don't know. I'm frightened. She is in a coma and the doctors are running tests on her. I don't know what to do."

"Do you want to talk with Katie?"

"Yes, please. If she is awake I'd like to talk with her."

Tom handed the phone to Katie. She grabbed it quickly from him and held it to her ear. "Dad, how is Helen?"

"I don't know, Katie. She is sleeping now and the doctors won't know anything until she wakes up. This is terrible. I don't know what to do." His voice trailed away and there was silence on the line.

Katie waited for him to say something and, when he didn't, she said, "I'll be right over, Dad. When did this happen?"

"About ten o'clock last night. Helen collapsed and I called an ambulance. They let me come to the hospital in the ambulance with her. I've been here ever since. She hasn't recovered and I don't know what to do. Please hurry, Katie."

"I'll leave immediately, right after I get dressed. Just keep praying and telling Helen that we love her." Katie hung up and turned to Tom. She leaned into his outstretched arms and put her head on his shoulder; tears welled in her eyes. "Honey, you heard my dad. Helen has had a stroke. I'm scared for her, I'm scared for myself, I'm scared for my dad. I can't bear the thought of losing another loved one. I've got to go to her. What should I do?"

"Go, Sweetface, go. You're needed at the hospital. Get dressed and drive your car over there. I'll handle everything here. I'll get Tyler up at the regular time, feed him, and make sure he's off to school. I'll notify Mark and Brenda and the grandmothers.

"Your job is to get to the hospital, comfort your father, and be with Helen. All I ask is that you let me know what's happening whenever you can."

Katie hugged Tom and gave him a grateful kiss. When she arrived at the hospital, she found the room where Helen was and asked the floor nurse if she could go in. The nurse told her that Helen was in a room by herself and that she could visit her; then, Katie asked how Helen was doing. The nurse replied that Helen was resting comfortably under a sedative but Katie would have to talk to the doctors to get more information. Katie had expected that general answer she received but she had hoped to learn a bit more.

The door to the room had "DO NOT DISTURB" and "NO

SMOKING" signs taped on it. When she went in, she saw Helen lying under the covers with an oxygen mask on her face, electronic monitoring devices were attached to her, and a drip pole was administering liquids into her arm. Her father was sitting in a chair facing the bed and his head and arms were resting on the mattress. His left leg was out to his side so he could bend forward. He was sleeping in this position. Katie slid around the bed to the only other chair in the small room and sat down without disturbing him. She stared at Helen who lay in bed with her eyes shut. The light was very dim and there wasn't much to see; Katie sat watching Helen and praying for her.

She had no idea how long this tableau of silence and sadness lasted. It ended when her father raised his head and saw her sitting on the other side of the bed. He whispered, "Katie, I'm so glad your here. How long have you been in the room?"

She looked at her wrist watch and replied in a low voice, "I'm not sure how long I have been here maybe a little more than an hour. How are you doing?"

John Givens looked at Helen before he replied, "Not well at all, Katie. I'm afraid for Helen and I'm at loose ends; that's why I'm so glad that you're here."

"Dad, nothing is going to happen until Helen wakes up. Let's go for a cup of coffee and sit where we can talk."

Katie tiptoed and her father hobbled out of the room and she got coffee out of a vending machine. They sat down in a waiting room and Katie asked, "Dad, tell me what happened?"

"I don't really understand. After you and Tom and Tyler left, I asked Helen when she was going to bed. She said that she was a little tired and would go shortly. I went out of the room and, shortly after that, I heard a noise. I came back and Helen was lying on the floor. I put a blanket over her and called 911. They came immediately and brought her to the hospital. I have been by her side since we got here and the doctors started to run tests. They think that she has had a stroke but they won't tell me any more than that until she wakes up and they finish running tests and evaluating her vital signs.

"I'm scared, Katie. I don't know what I would do without Helen. We've been married almost twenty-five years and she has been my constant love and companion. I don't want her to die; I want her to live so we both can enjoy life.

"I just keep thinking these thoughts over and over and over. I can't get them out of my head."

"Dad, we're just going to have to wait until we hear what the doctors have to say. There's no sense in thinking or saying anything until we know what is going on. Let's just concentrate on praying and hoping for Helen. She needs our positive thoughts, not our worries.

"I love her and need her as much as you do. However, until we hear from the doctors, I'm going to concentrate on praying for Helen. It's not easy, but I'm praying for her to be at my wedding. You can help by also praying for her."

Katie hugged her father and she carried their cardboard coffee cups back to Helen's room. They sat in their chairs across the bed from each other and watched Helen. Both of them were inside the steam room of their minds, sweating out all possibilities. Each longed for Helen's good health but were haunted by the possibility of death. Katie thought that time stood still and dragged by at the same time. She noticed that her father fell off to sleep huddled against the back of his chair. He looked old, needed a shave, and seemed pitiful. Her mind wandered and she too began to doze off.

All of a sudden, Katie sat bolt upright. She thought that she heard a noise. Again, there was a small moan. Katie got to her feet and looked at Helen's face; her eyes were open and she lifted one arm slightly. Katie took her hand and kissed it as tears started to run down her face. She leaned over Helen's face and softly asked, "Helen, can you hear me?"

Helen nodded her head up and down. By this time, John Givens was on his right foot, standing with his crutches under his arms, and he was sobbing almost uncontrollably. He kept repeating, "My darling Helen, my darling Helen."

It was at this moment that a man in a white jacket, with a stethoscope around his neck, walked into the room. He looked at the three of them and said, "Good Morning, I am Doctor Sanborn. It looks as if Mrs. Givens has revived and that is a good sign, a very good sign. But, I would like to examine her so, if you don't mind, could you two step out of the room? I will let you know when you can come back."

They made their way out into the corridor; Givens wiped his eyes and regained his composure. He said to Katie, "Helen is awake. She's coming back to me. Oh, thank God."

Katie was also relieved but she was still had fears. She wanted to hear what the doctor had to say about Helen's prognosis before she would relax. She told her father that she had to call Tom and let him know what was going on and she went to find a pay phone. Tom answered on the first ring and Katie began by saying, "Helen has just regained consciousness." She then told him, in detail, everything that had happened since she arrived at Helen's bedside. When she finished answering all of his questions, she wanted to know what was going on at his end of the phone.

Tom explained that Tyler was in school and would be picked up by Brenda and delivered to the grandmothers who were fighting over him as if he were a winning lottery ticket. He told Katie that he would call Mark and Brenda when they finished talking. Then Tom said, "Mark, is upset, of course. He wants to go over to the hospital to be with Helen and I have been discouraging him. What do you think?"

"I agree with you, Tom. Dad is extremely emotional and I don't know how he would react if he saw Mark. They both have been through the mill and both are up tight right now. Ask Mark not to come but that I will call when I have the doctor's report. There are enough problems without stirring up new ones."

"OK, I'll pass that on; speaking of your father, how is he doing?"

"He needs to rest; he is beat emotionally and fatigued physically. After we talk with Doctor Sanborn, I'll ask him to go home and sleep. I'll call you shortly after we see the doctor.

"Honey, you have no idea how thankful I am that I have you. I love you."

"Sweetface, you have no idea how pleased I am to be able to help you. Let me know what's going on when you can and give my love to Helen. Keep some of it for yourself because I truly love you."

Katie rejoined her father and, as they were waiting in the corridor, Doctor Sanborn came out of Helen's room and joined them. "Good news for both of you. All symptoms and tests indicate that Mrs. Givens suffered a mild heart attack. She is still relatively young and she can have a full, active life. Her chances for a full recovery are promising but she is going to have to change her life style. She will have to alter her diet, eat more fruits and vegetables and less fried foods. She will also have to follow an exercise regime and get plenty of rest. She and I have discussed this and she is more than willing to comply. I'm sure that we can keep your wife and your mother around for a long time."

The happiness that stirred in both of their faces was apparent along with the drain of physical energy that almost buckled their knees. They had been in a pressure cooker because of Helen's condition and now the valve had been opened and their fears and anxieties evaporated. Neither could speak for a minute or two. Doctor Sanborn continued, "I would like to keep Mrs. Givens in the hospital for the next few days to run a few more tests and to check on her physical condition. I would hope that she could go home on Saturday."

Katie almost wailed, "Dr. Sanborn, Saturday is too late. I am getting married on Saturday and I need Helen to be at the wedding."

The doctor replied immediately, "Mrs. Oldfield, I didn't know that. Yes, I can change my schedule and have Mrs. Givens ready for discharge on Friday afternoon instead of Saturday.

"Congratulations on your marriage, I wish you the best. In the meantime you both look tired and Mrs. Givens need to rest. So, if you can say, 'Goodbye' to her and get some rest your selves, it would be good for everyone.

"I will be monitoring her closely so you have nothing to be concerned about."

With that, Doctor Sanborn left. John made his way in first to talk with Helen and came out five minutes later. He told Katie that Helen was eager to see her and that he was going to get a taxi, go home and fall into bed. Katie entered the hospital room and was pleased to see that the oxygen mask was no longer on Helen's face and that she was sitting up in bed looking tired and pale. Katie came to the edge of the mattress, reached for Helen's hand, and kissed her on the cheek.

"Helen, you scared me terribly. I was so afraid of losing you and I love you so much. How are you feeling?"

Helen smiled wanly. "I feel a little tired but I don't know why.

I don't know what happened; I had just finished cleaning up after everyone left and I just passed out. When I woke up, here I was in the hospital with everyone hovering over me. I'm sorry, darling Katie."

Katie replied almost sharply, "What in heaven's name do you think you have to be sorry about?"

"This happened so close to your wedding day; I don't want to spoil your plans."

"Helen, the only way you can spoil my plans is if you didn't show up. You have no idea how much I need you and love you. Last night, while I was sitting by your bed, it struck me that you and I have discussed our relationships with other people; we talked many times about me and Mike, me and Tom, you and Dad, you and Mark. Somehow, we never talked about us, you and me.

"I don't know why I never talked about us. I may have been afraid to bring the subject up. Anyhow, last night, I thought about how you entered my life, not as my teacher but as my father's wife. When you first came into our house, I didn't understand why you were there and I guess I resented you. You were not my mother and you were a stranger in our home.

"As I matured and realized that, along with life there is death, I realized how lucky I was to have you. Even though you didn't birth me, you treated me as your own daughter and you couldn't have been kinder to me. I'm grateful for you and, if I ever have a daughter, she will be named 'Helen.'"

Helen squeezed Katie's hand and said, "Katie, I'm the one I considered fortunate. Although I couldn't have children I got the nicest girl in the world as a daughter and a good man as a son.

"I'm going to have to change my eating habits, no more fried foods and no more luscious desserts and I'm going to begin a program of heavy exercising. That is little enough sacrifice to be around to see all of my future grandchildren. I have been blessed.

"Listen, under no condition will you postpone your marriage this Saturday. Whether I'm there or not, you are to go through with it. Please, Katie, promise me that you will."

Katie nodded her head "Yes," and Helen shut her eyes and lay there quietly.

Katie looked at her for a few seconds, smiled, kissed her on the cheek, and left for home.

***

As she parked in her drive, she saw that her brother's car and a car with Michigan license plates were both parked beside the house. Obviously, Tom's parents had arrived. This surprised her because Tom had not mentioned anything about his parents in their many conversations during the day. She quickly entered the house to give all of them the news about Helen. When she entered the door she was even more surprised to find the grandmothers, Mrs. Buono and Mrs. Connors, also awaiting her return. "Of course," she thought, "Everyone wants to know how Helen is."

All of them, except Tom and Brenda, were seated and eating. Tom put down the loaf of sliced bread he had been carrying and quickly came over to her. He put both arms around her and said, "Sweetface, you've had a long day. I'm glad you're back."

By that time, his parents were eagerly greeting her. Katie hugged them gratefully basking in their warmth; the aura of love for each other and the joy at being alive enveloped them all. They made room for Katie and Tom served her a bowl of beef stew. She suddenly remembered that she had not eaten since she left early that morning and she was famished. The stew was excellent and when she asked Tom who made it he laughed and told her that he had. He reminded her that, when he was younger, his mother had taught him how to cook.

While Katie ate, she told everyone that Helen was resting comfortably after having a heart attack and that her prognosis appeared good. She answered every question patiently, even though many of the questions duplicated what had just been asked. She knew that each person was individually trying to come to grips with Helen's condition. It took a long time before the grandmothers decided they had enough information and it was Mrs. Connors who changed the subject by asking Katie if she were going to change her wedding plans. This immediately started a debate between Mrs. Buono and Mrs. Connors whether there should, or should not, be a change in the plans.

Katie listened to the discussion about her wedding for about two minutes and then her emotions overcame her manners. Since early this morning she had been fighting to keep calm while being frightened for Helen. She had struggled all day with fear and worry; and she had gone without rest or food. Now, all she really wanted was to snuggle against Tom, to be held, and to talk with him. Her own love batteries needed recharging.

She took her spoon and tapped it against her water glass until all the talking stopped. Then, she said, "Helen and I have talked about my wedding. There will be no change to the date; it will be held this Saturday. I have had a trying day, so if you'll excuse me, I am going to take a shower and relax." She got up from the table and walked out of the room.

Katie returned a half hour later with her hair wrapped in a towel and wearing a terry cloth robe. Tom was sitting in the plush, red sofa while his mother and father were each in the two matching chairs.

Everyone else had gone. "Oh dear," she said, "I feel bad; I didn't mean to send people home."

Tom laughed as he answered, "You didn't, Brenda did. The minute you left she told everyone that you needed to rest and that, unless anyone had any questions, we should break up. She sent Tyler with the grandmothers and she and Mark went home. She told me to tell you to call her in the morning but that you should get a good night's rest. I walked the grandmothers home and they were arguing over which of them was going to have Tyler sleep over.

"Come sit with me a few minutes and then I think that you should follow Brenda's advice."

"I will in a second Tom, I have apologies to make first." Katie walked over and kissed Tom's mother and father and said, "Mom and Dad Booker, welcome, I'm happy you're here. Our house is in a mess and I've been at the hospital all day. Please excuse me if I sounded bitchy. This has been a full day and I didn't even know you were in town. It probably wouldn't have made any difference, there was nothing that I could have done differently, but I wish Tom had told me that you were coming."

Mrs. Booker spoke up, "Katie, Don and I are glad we came, especially when we got here and found out that Helen was having a health problem. We want to help and we won't be in anyone's way. We had decided to come to New England and meet Helen and your father before the wedding. We thought that we could visit with you and your family or, if it proved inconvenient, we would go sightseeing.

"It really was a spur of the moment decision and Tom knew nothing about our arrival until after the last time he spoke with you at the hospital. We were completely taken aback to find that Helen was in the hospital so, this once, he is blameless."

Katie sat beside Tom and nestled against him. Her face was working as she was near tears. "Mom and Dad Booker, I apologize to both of you for being snotty.

"Tom, I guess I haven't been thinking straight today. Of course you would have told me that your mother and father were coming, if you had known. You have been the beacon that has given me the strength to get through today. I have been ungracious to many people today; including your mother and father."

Tom leaned down and kissed her toweled hair. "Hey, that's nonsense. You've taken a pounding today and kept on ticking. You may owe all of us a dish of ice cream but you don't owe me any apologies."

His mother picked up the idea. "Nor do you owe us any apologies; we showed up at an inconvenient time. Ice cream does sound good, especially since Don and I brought some cookies we baked. Who wants some?"

Dessert brought on a much sweeter mood. Katie detailed the vandalism done to their home and showed them the newly painted nursery for their grandchild. Tom's parents described what they hoped to do while they were in the area; walk the Freedom Trail, visit Old Ironsides, and walk down Bearskin Neck in Rockport.

Shortly, Tom could see that Katie was getting sleepy so, he suggested that they call it an evening. His parents quickly agreed and left for their motel, Gaard's, on Route One. Before Katie went to sleep she remembered to ask if Tom had called her father. He told her that he had spoken to her father after he had gotten home and that, although her father was tired, he was in good spirits. Katie was asleep before Tom finished answering her question.

18

After John Givens got a taxi and arrived home, he undressed and fell into bed without washing his face or brushing his teeth. He had just survived the worst day of his life. The acids of fear and despair had been dripping on his soul since Helen had collapsed. Until the doctor's diagnosis, he hadn't know whether she was going to live or die. Minor irritants bothered him also. His left leg ached and he felt awkward whenever he had to move.

The uncertainty of what might be going to happen left him in a screaming free fall of fright over both of their futures. He didn't want Helen to die and he didn't know what would happen to him if she did. He kept going over scenario after scenario under endless possibilities. Even though Katie had tried to ease his anxieties, he was in constant agony.

This was even a more brutal experience than when his first wife, Alice, had passed away. Alice's death was sudden, totally unexpected, and a shocking experience. However, the finality that death brings forces the survivors to accept reality. For his second wife, his hopes pushed him towards Helen's life while his fears dragged him towards her death.

He went to bed completely exhausted.

John Givens awoke early the next morning more rested and more hopeful about the future than he had been last night. True, Helen had suffered a heart attack but Doctor Sanford had been optimistic about her prognosis. His leg was not aching; he actually felt good. With that in mind, John showered and shaved and went to the hospital to see her. He got to her room just as she was finishing her breakfast and she greeted him with a smile. "Hi, Honey, you're a little late for a piece of dry toast but there's some skim milk you can have."

He was not in the mood for banter so, as he kissed her, he didn't rise to her bait. Instead, he asked, "How are you?"

"I feel fine, John. Have you had breakfast?"

"No, but I'm not hungry. If I get hungry, I'll get something later from the hospital cafeteria. For the time being, I just want to be here with you. Are you OK?"

"Yes, John, I'm fine. I feel good and I'm glad you're here; I have a lot to talk with you about. This episode has made me think about our life together and what lies at the end of it."

John got upset. He quickly said, "Don't talk like that Helen. You are going to live and we will have a happy life together."

Helen patted his hand and smiled before answering softly, "John, dearest, don't be unhappy. I'm going to live, I plan on staying alive for a long time. I want to live and this morning I feel rested and ready to begin my new life.

"But, one thing about being in a hospital after having a heart attack, is that you have time to think. My time was last night.

"I first thought, 'I was lucky and I was blessed. I have survived.'

"However, it also dawned on me last night that I'm a mortal and that, eventually, my time will come."

The Patriots of Foxboro

John quickly interrupted Helen. "Don't talk like that. You will live with me for a long, long time. We have a lot to do together."

Helen waited a while before replying, she wanted to have John calm and reasonable, not angry or defiant. "Oh, I'm definitely planning on that, Dearest; I intend to be with you for quite a while. I wasn't thinking about my death as much as I was wondering about the rest of my life.

"All I'm saying is that everyone, including you and me, takes their lives for granted as if it never ended. Wouldn't you agree with that?"

John replied, "Well, I guess that's true. I was never concerned about your health until yesterday, and then I was very worried."

"That's what I mean, John. I was unconscious and I could have passed away but I survived and I'm here with you. That's what started me thinking. Right now, I am alive but, when I do pass, what will I have left behind? I am a bridge between the past and the future. How will I be thought of? To be remembered for a some worldly trinkets is no tribute to me as a person. Have I done any good or helped anyone? I need to feel that I have contributed something to the lives of the people I know and love.

"That's when something occurred to me that I should have thought of before. Do you know what the three most important words in the world are?"

"What?"

"I love you. People don't use those words often enough. It's the most universal feeling on our planet and people are too inhibited to admit it. Those three simple words could purge almost all the hate and fear that surrounds us. From now on, I intend to tell the people I love my feelings more often. And that starts with you, John. I love you."

"I love you, Helen."

"Does what I've been saying make any sense to you, John?"

"I guess so, Helen. Why are you asking me that?"

"For this reason. I have been married to you for almost twenty five years and, because I love you, I never asked you to do this before. However, before Katie gets married, I want you to talk with Mark."

Helen could see John react almost physically. She thought, "If he were a turtle he would have pulled his head completely under his shell."

"I can't do that, Helen."

There was an ominous silence for quite awhile. Helen decided that she wasn't going to say a word; it would be up to John to explain himself.

Finally, John began again. "I'm not sure I can do that. He broke away from me when he wouldn't support either our country or my father's memory. I have lost all respect for my son."

Helen quietly said, "Tell me this, John; did Mark break away from you or did you break away from Mark?"

"I don't follow what you're saying."

"I'll try to explain but I want you to listen without getting defensive or angry. First, I know your feelings about your father's sacrifice and I totally agree with you. Any person who has ever taken time out of his or her personal life to serve our country is a patriot. Each and every one of them deserve our respect and appreciation. I feel as strongly about this as you do.

"There were many people who thought that being involved in a war in Vietnam was not our country's finest hour. Mark was one of them. He didn't come to that conclusion quickly; it took him a long time to decide that, and only after he asked many questions about what we were doing over there. You commented about him not being able to make up his mind yourself."

"Yes, I argued with him and he wouldn't listen. I tried but no matter what I said I couldn't convince him that he was wrong."

"John, I'm not sure that there is such a thing as right or wrong when it comes to discussing Vietnam. Each person has an individual viewpoint; each person believes he, or she, is correct. The only thing that is important is to respect the other person's right to that opinion whether you agree or not." Helen was about to continue, when John interrupted her.

"How can you say that, Helen? Our finest young men and women were sacrificing themselves for our country and Mark was denying them his allegiance. Don't tell me that you could ever consider his denying our fighting men and women as being right?"

"I don't believe Mark denied the sacrifices of our young men and women. He felt that they shouldn't be called on to make their sacrifices because of stupid errors of judgement by our leaders. He felt that our government was morally wrong in fighting for an unworthy cause. Mark believed our elected leaders should stop yelling 'Patriotism' instead of admitting their mistakes. Many people felt the same way."

"Helen, no one has the right to criticize the government when we are at war."

"Do you really believe that, John? Were we at war? Did we go through the formality of declaring war and imposing sacrifices on everyone?

"More important, can't you be loyal to your country and still question whether your elected leaders are right or wrong? Does being at war shift a democracy into a dictatorship? I certainly hope not."

"Helen, you are overstating your case. Everyone has to support the government and show their patriotism."

"Oh? Let me ask you this; it's true that Mike supported our country. Did you consider him to be patriotic?"

"You know that when I found out what he really was like as a person I hated the son of a bitch. I have nothing but contempt for him. He certainly was no patriot. Why are you asking me about him?"

"Just this, Dear. Mike fits your standards for patriotism but his personal morals were so bad that you are disgusted by him. Mark doesn't fit your standards for patriotism yet his morals and scruples are as honest and true as yours and mine.

"It may surprise you, John, but Mark considers himself as patriotic as you believe you are. What he was saying is that we were in a place we shouldn't have been in and that the bloodshed was caused by cynical politicians, preying upon the country's patriotism. He truly believed the death of our youth was senseless and should be stopped. And he may well have been close to the truth."

John sighed and then spoke in a low voice, "Well, I still feel he avoided his obligations."

"I know you do, Dear, and I know this isn't easy for you, but I would still like you to talk with Mark before Katie's wedding. I'm not trying to be dramatic, but this heart attack has reminded me that all of us have only a finite time to be together. I don't know how much time is on our calendars or how long you and I have and the number is not that important. What is very important is that we enjoy our time together. I want both of us to watch our grandchildren grow, I want us to be bathed in our love for each other and our families.

"I want you to give the bride away and I want Mark to be Tom's best man. That's what Katie wants and, absolutely, that's what I want. Am I asking for too much? That will be up to you to decide.

The Patriots of Foxboro

"Please consider it for Katie's and my sake."

John Givens sat in the chair by Helen's bed for a long time without saying a word. Finally, he struggled to his feet, positioned his crutches, kissed Helen on the cheek, and said, "You should have been a lawyer. I have to think about your case. I will follow some of your advice immediately by telling you that I do love you. I have to think about everything else.

"I'm also going to go eat some breakfast." With that, he left.

***

Brenda was concerned about Mark. Even though she knew that he was an extremely placid person, he had been quiet ever since Katie had told him of Helen's heart attack. She knew that was because he was so worried. Even after he had been informed of Helen's prognosis, he was much more subdued than usual. Brenda could easily understand his fears and anxieties and she wanted to help; but she wasn't sure what she could do.

During the night, she decided on a course of action; she would get up early and make Mark some oatmeal and raisin cookies. She figured that would dispel some of his gloom and cheer him up. She was right. When Mark woke up and entered the kitchen, filled with the smell of freshly baked cookies and freshly brewed coffee, he grinned from ear to ear. He clasped her from behind, kissed her on the neck, and said, "Thank you, Honey. I love you."

They both sat down and began munching the cookies. "You are the best baker I ever married," Mark said.

"I'll bet you told all your wives that," Brenda replied.

"No, not all of them. But yours are really good, Honey."

"Thank you, I appreciate the compliment. What are your plans for today?"

"I'm not sure, Brenda. I will stay here until I hear from Katie. She is going to go to the hospital early to see Helen and then call me.

"I never knew my mother, the woman who gave birth to me, she died in the hospital. Helen has taken care of me, all these years, and I regard her as my mother. I love her and I'm so worried about her. Right at the time Katie and I are so happy, Helen gets sick. Life seems unfair sometimes.

"I can't even begin to imagine what your life was like without having a family to support you."

Brenda ran her hand through Mark's hair. "It was difficult. It was different. Now, I have you, Katie, Tom, Helen, and my new baby. All of us make my past worth what I went through. You and I will pray for Helen and cling to our loved ones. What do you think?"

"Brenda, I'm so happy you are my wife and my partner. Life finally has been good to both of us. You're right, I'll pray for Helen and help my loved ones.

"After I hear from Katie I'll go over to her house and keep working on repairing the damage. I'm sure that Tom and Katie will go to the hospital early this morning. I can either continue working or be available to take Tom's parents into Boston, depending on what Tom wants me to do. We're so close to the wedding and I'm ready to do whatever I can to help. Is there anything you need or want today?"

"No. I want to help too, and I'm available. I'm excited because, in the past, I never dreamed that Katie and I would become mothers within days of each other. I want this wedding to go well for everybody."

"I do too, but I'm concerned. Not so much for Helen, even though her heart attack bothered me, but for Katie. So far as I know, my father has not said if he intends to be at the wedding or not. Tom still insists that he wants me to be his best man so, how is this going to work out? I don't know. Nobody seems to know."

Brenda said, "I hope it all gets sorted out soon. In the meantime, how is the work at the house going?"

"Actually, pretty well. I'll have it finished when Tom and Katie return from their honeymoon. In a way, PJ did them a favor. The kitchen will be much brighter with the newly restored cabinets. The place looks great."

"But that jerk PJ gets away with it and nothing happens to him."

Mark shook his head, side to side, and answered, "Not exactly true. The guys at work have completely lost their fear of him and now they, if they want to, make fun of him to his face. It's a different atmosphere than it used to be."

"Why is it that way?"

"It's kind of simple, Brenda. The majority of the crew that work for the highway department are older veterans of World War Two. They are decent people who just want to do their jobs; they don't want trouble and will go out of their way to avoid confrontations. They never argued with PJ and slowly they let him dominate them physically. Soon, that was the way it was at the highway department; No one ever crossed PJ or made him angry. When Tom started to work, he made it a point to stay away from trouble. When he had had enough, he stood up to PJ and exposed him as a bully and a bag of wind. After that, everyone recognized him for what he was and, now, they have no fear of him at all. It's amazing how one person can change everyone's attitude."

"But, won't that all change when you go back to work next week and Tom isn't working there any more?"

"No. He tried to fight one of the guys about two weeks ago and the guy did something he would have never dared to do before Tom got there. He reported PJ to the Highway Department Supervisor, Kinnick, and that was the end of that problem. Kinnick told PJ he would fire him right on the spot if he heard of any more threats. Believe me, PJ is walking a fine line. His reign of terror is over. That may be one of the reasons he tried to get back at us the way he did."

"And you think Tom is responsible for the change in attitude towards PJ?"

"Brenda, I know he is."

"But, he seems so mild and quiet."

"Don't let him fool you, he fooled me for a while and, at first, he completely fooled Katie. He is mild and quiet but he also is much different from what you expect.

"Look what he has done for me. I was concerned when I first met him. He went to war, I went to Canada. He fought, I fled. That didn't make any difference to him, he was willing to help me. He told me to defend what I really believed in without apologies. He made me focus on what I want to do, not on what I had done. He talks, he does not lecture, and he doesn't look down his nose at anybody.

"I've thought about it after we became friends and there are two things to remember. He is strong and he is smart. He has paid his dues for his past mistakes and he wants to help people. The Mansfield school system is going to be a much better system with him in it."

"You really like him, don't you?"

"Oh yes, I think of him as an older brother. Believe me, he is someone who enriches the life of everyone he touches. There are not many like him. When you get to know him as well as the rest of the Givens family does, you may want to divorce me and marry him."

"No way, Mark, I'm satisfied with what I found lying by the side of the road. You happen to be my husband and the father of our child. I chose you, I love you, and we will never get divorced. That might be subject to change if you become very, very wealthy and start fooling around; until then, give me a kiss before you eat any more of my cookies."

***

By an odd coincidence, at the same time that Brenda was asking Mark about Tom, Katie happened to be asking Tom about Mark. They had gotten up a little earlier than usual so that they could both visit Helen. After that, Tom would be free to either visit with his parents or continue work on the house. As they sat drinking coffee, Katie said, "Honey, in less than a week I'm getting married and I need your help. I know three people who will be in attendance, you, me, and the priest. I'm almost sure Helen will be there but, right now, I'm not sure of anyone else. Are you still planning for Mark to be your best man? And, if so, what are we going to do about my father?"

"Sweetface, outside of the fact that I haven't changed my mind about having Mark as my best man, I don't know any of the answers to your questions. Your father was supposed to tell me what he intended to do, but that was before Helen got sick. Let's see how Helen is doing this morning and then I'll try to find out who will be at our wedding. I'm sure that you would like to know."

Katie replied, "I may sound as if I'm kidding, but I'm concerned. I want this to be a happy day for you and me and our child. It certainly isn't Helen's fault but her heart attack has made our family problems all the more difficult. I don't want to postpone our wedding as time is closing in on us; on the other hand, I don't want tensions or bad feelings to ruin our day. I guess I am worried but, Honey, I don't like to burden you with my problems."

Tom hugged her and then rubbed her back, "Katie, the day you don't tell me your problems is the day that you will be a burden to me. Even before the ceremony, we are a team. Your problems are automatically our problems. Anything else is nonsense. You have no idea how precious you are to me.

"You and I will get these matters resolved and our child will not be born out of wedlock. Is there anything else on your mind?"

Katie kissed Tom and said coyly, "Yes, Honey, there is but don't ask me that question again until this evening."

When they got to the hospital and entered Helen's room they were surprised to see her sitting up in bed, with her glasses on, reading the Boston Globe. Her hair was combed and her lipstick was fresh. She looked up from the paper and said, "Well, good morning sleepyheads. What took you so long to get here?"

Katie was pleased to see Helen alert and more like her normal self; she kissed her and said, "Good Morning, I didn't know that we had to be here by any certain time. Tom has a present for you."

Tom walked over to the bed, pulled a brand new Red Sox baseball cap out of a paper bag, and handed it to her. "Here, Helen, your old one is moth eaten and faded; use this new one when you do your gardening.

"I take it you're feeling well this morning?"

Helen took the cap from Tom's hand and put it on her head. She answered, "I'm feeling good and I'm not waiting until I start gardening to wear my new cap. I shall wear it out of the hospital. Thank you very much. What made you decide to get me a new one?"

Tom smiled as he replied, "Well, I noticed your old baseball cap hanging by the back door when I was over at your house. I decided then that you deserved a new one for this season; it would cheer you up and, possibly, help the Red Sox. I hope it makes a difference for both of you."

Helen shook her head up and down. "I'm sure it will. Tom, you haven't called your family and told them about my being sick, have you?"

"That's a two part question that I'll answer this way; I didn't call them but they do know that you had a heart attack.

"Without telling anybody, they arrived a few days early to meet everyone and go sightseeing. We didn't know they had arrived until after they checked into the Gaard motel. They were shocked by our news and now they feel guilty that they didn't call ahead of time.

"They are going to have brunch with Mark and Brenda and then they are going to drive into Boston and walk the Freedom Trail by themselves. They are concerned. They don't want to interfere with anything but they want a complete report on you and they want to know what they could do to help."

"And what did you tell them?"

Tom said, "Helen, I told them the truth. There's not much they can do and, right now, things are a bit loose."

Helen frowned as she asked, "In what way are they loose, Tom?"

"The last time I spoke with your husband he wasn't sure if he would be at our wedding or not. He hasn't gotten back to either Katie or me to let us know what he has decided. Both of us want him there but we also insisted that this is Katie's wedding and we want Mark as my best man.

"Has he said anything to you?"

"No not really. We had a long discussion about the very same thing just a while ago; and I'm sure he is thinking about what I said to him. He is worried about me and I gave him an earful concerning what I want for our future.

"He left to get breakfast without saying much. I know he is having a difficult time trying to decide what to do. Tom, it may be a good idea to track him down and talk to him; he values your advice. I'm sure he's in the cafeteria.

"While I'm thinking of it, why don't you ask John to meet with your parents? I feel bad for them. I can meet them after the wedding but there's no reason for John to wait. See if you can get him to meet with you, Katie, Tyler and both of them. Any night would be good. If necessary, I'll also urge him to meet them."

Tom patted Helen's hand and left her and Katie. He walked into the cafeteria and noticed John Givens sitting by himself at a small table against the wall. Tom walked over and asked Givens if he would like a cup of coffee and, after receiving a "Yes" response, he bought two cups and returned.

As he sat down, Givens said, "I've been thinking of you; I'm glad your here. I need your advice."

Tom replied, "I'll be glad to talk with you but I don't believe I can give you much advice. You and I don't agree on many things."

"Maybe that's true, but you always make sense and you tell me exactly what you think. You certainly aren't afraid of disagreeing with me and, right now, I need someone to talk with."

"In that case, I'm your man. I'll listen, I'll talk, but I don't hand out penances; that's someone else's job. So, how can I help you?"

"What am I going to do about Katie's wedding? Should I go? Should I not go? I don't know what to do."

"Mr. Givens, er, John, I'm not sure you are defining your problem correctly. You would go to Katie's wedding without any hesitation if your son wasn't going to be there. You should think about resolving your relationship with Mark. That's the key to deciding if you'd be comfortable going to the wedding."

"Listen, Tom, Helen has been telling me the same thing. I was so scared when she got to the hospital that I would do almost anything for her. But, the facts are the facts and they can't be changed."

"That's true, facts can't be changed. However, one thing can be changed, though, and that is your attitude."

John Givens looked surprised. "What does that mean?"

Tom answered, "I'll tell you. When you were Mark's age, before you were drafted, what was your world like? World war II was being waged wasn't it"

"Yes."

"And, almost everyone and everything was dedicated to winning the war. The whole country was united and everyone trusted our federal government."

"Of course."

"Think about that. Back then, almost everything was different from it is today. For the most part, everyone agreed that the war was just. There were no weapons, until the end, capable of killing hundreds of thousands of non combatants instantaneously. There was no television to show one end of the world what was happening at the other end as events unfolded.

"Life seemed to go by a little slower and things were a lot less complicated back then. Won't you agree?"

"Yes, I guess you're right, Tom. So what?"

"Well, think of what Mark's world was like before he was drafted. The scene in America was nothing like it was when you were young.

In that span of time between the two of you, many attitudes and many things had changed. Nowadays, news can be flashed around the world instantly and facts are not nearly as important as speed. The rational decisions we should make are fed by emotional sound bites. What happened to truth and integrity?

"Between the two conflicts our President was assassinated. John Kennedy, Robert Kennedy, Martin Luther King, all were murdered by other Americans. What a terrible waste of humanity. The Ohio National Guard fired on, and killed, college students. Our government has deceived its own people. Nixon lied and the Gulf of Tonkin incidents were no real basis for escalating the war in Vietnam.

"Is it any wonder that today people are so skeptical and so distrustful of our government and, for that matter, each other?"

John Givens looked puzzled. "Tom, you are a combat veteran and Mark is a draft dodger. Are you defending him? Do you agree with what he did?"

"Whoa! Let me try to answer those questions one at a time. First, I guess in a way I am defending him. He did something that I don't think you are giving him any credit for. He followed his conscience. That is one Hell of a lot more than most of our politicians do. He simply followed his conscience and he paid his price for doing it.

"As for me, I followed my conscience, along an opposite path, and I paid my price. I don't fault him for doing what he thought he had to.

"Now, whether or not I agree with what he did, that's a more difficult question to answer. If you had asked me the day before I enlisted, I would have said that I disagreed with him. If you had asked me the day after I was discharged, I'm not sure but what he might have been right and I might have been wrong."

Givens started to lean forward and speak; but Tom raised his hand, palm up, and said, "Wait, let me finish. Forget whether we should have been in Vietnam or not. Forget how we veterans were treated when we returned home. I'm only talking about me personally.

"I went to Vietnam and killed to stay alive. All of us did. I learned to feel superior to those yellow bastards; I hated them. The more we hated and killed, the better our own chances were of surviving.

"When I was a civilian again I had trouble adjusting to civilian life. It took me years to realize I would have no peace until I cleansed my soul of everything I had learned in Vietnam. They fought us the way we would have fought them if they invaded our country.

"It took a long time for me to get rid of my hate and to realize that those yellow bastards I had fought were just like me. Not physically, but they were as loyal to their country as I was to mine.

"Just as an aside, a very important aside, I feel that God sent me Katie because He thought I was finally trying to do the right thing. I'm in love, at peace, and I want both you and Mark to come to our wedding."

Givens obviously heard what Tom had been saying but there was no way of knowing if he was getting the message. He fiddled with his coffee cup for a while and then he spoke, "Well, OK. Maybe you're right. Maybe people and things change from one generation to the next. But, the basic values that we live by shouldn't change; and that's my problem. I believe that Mark should have honored the family tradition of patriotism. After all, my father gave his life for our country."

Tom thought about how he wanted to answer Givens. He certainly had no intention of disparaging Givens father's supreme sacrifice; on the other hand, he wanted Givens to reconcile with his son. To keep him focused, Tom asked, "John, I wonder if your father would have handled your problems with Mark any differently than you have?"

John quickly replied, "I'm sure he would have done things differently and better than I did. My father was extremely cool headed and honest; he often told me I was too hot headed and stubborn and I guess he was right.

"Do you know that you are the second person who has recently asked me what my father would do?"

"No, I didn't know that. Who asked?"

"Brenda."

Tom was completely surprised. He was almost incredulous as he asked, "Mark's wife? Brenda? She never said a word to Katie or me that she had talked to you. When did this conversation happen?"

It was now John Givens turn to be surprised. "She didn't tell any one that she came to my office to talk to me? She treated our meeting as a private discussion? That makes me like her all the more; she is some lady.

"When did I talk with her? She came to see me while you and Katie were in Michigan. She made quite an impression on me with her openness and her flaming red hair. She wanted me to know that she was Katie's best friend, Mark's wife, and that she was pregnant. As the only grandfather, Brenda told me that it was important for her child to have loving and caring parents and grandparents. She wanted me to reunite with Mark.

"I guess she was raised in orphanages and with foster parents. She suffered through a cold, miserable childhood and she didn't want her children going through the same experience. I can't blame her for feeling the way she does; good for her.

"She was so open and frank that I couldn't help but like her. And, to tell you the truth, I have been thinking about what she said."

Tom smiled. "She and Katie go a long way back; they have been good for each other for years. You're right, Brenda is something else. She is always upbeat and pleasant. You'd have to hate people to dislike her."

They both sat quietly wrestling with their own thoughts which were the mirror image of the other. Tom wanted John to be at peace with Mark as well as with Helen and Katie; however, he didn't want to push John. It would have to be a decision John made himself; he was stubborn enough to resist almost all outside influence.

John wanted desperately to be at peace. He had recently become aware that, if his attitude didn't change, he would be alienated from his future grandchildren. Now, with Helen's heart attack, his love for Helen was forcing him to look at his life in an entirely different manner than he had before. His future looked clouded; and his, and Helen's, mortality weighed on his mind. He was like the driver of a skidding automobile; he was very scared of the motion but he absolutely dreaded the stop. Givens didn't know what to do or how to do it.

Surprisingly enough, it was John Givens that broke their silence. In an attempt to change the mood, he asked, "How are your parents doing?"

"They aren't doing too badly but, of course, they are concerned about Helen. They came east early for the sole purpose of meeting the two of you before the wedding. They can go sightseeing since they have never visited this area before, but that's only their fallback plan. They really were looking forward to visiting you and Helen.

"In fact, Helen mentioned that to me this morning. She suggested that Katie and I host a dinner over your house with my parents. She wants everyone to be comfortable at the wedding so, she thinks the sooner we meet the better, and I agree with her."

John Givens was quick to respond, "That would be a good idea. If that's what Helen wants, that's what we should do. Do you agree?"

"Yes, I feel that it would be beneficial for everyone. If you think about it, my parents went through exactly the opposite experience that you did. They didn't want me to enlist in any of the armed services and I went ahead and joined the army. You wanted Mark to enlist and he went ahead and left for Canada. They would learn about Katie and Mark from talking with you and you would learn about me from talking with them. Listening to other parents talk about their children can sometimes help you understand your own.

"You're eager to get back to Helen, and I'm anxious to get back to work at our house, so, I'll talk to you later. I'll set up a time for all of us to meet and we'll go from there."

***

After they said goodnight to Tyler and tucked him into bed, Katie and Tom sat at the kitchen table. The newly painted cabinets were without doors because the new ones had not yet arrived but, outside of that, the kitchen looked normal, clean and neat. They had each briefly talked about their day at supper but, with Tyler out of hearing, they could talk more freely. Katie had a pad of paper in front of her and she was studying it; her listing of things that needed to be done before her wedding.

"So tomorrow we're cooking dinner at my father's house for your family and us?"

"Yes, after Helen talked to your father I spoke to my parents. They wanted Helen to be present but, since the wedding is only five days away, they realize we have to use what ever time is available. They hope that Helen will be out of the hospital in time to meet them. The doctor says she could be released early. However, we have to make our plans on what we know we can do not on what we hope we can do."

Looking at her pad, Katie said, "OK, there will be six of us, my father, your parents, Tyler, you, and me. You and I will prepare the meal, clam chowder, broiled lobster, and raisin pie for dessert. Then what?"

"After the meal, we clean up and vacate the scene as soon we can. I want my parents and your father talking about us."

"Do you think it will do any good?"

"Sweetface, I honestly don't know. It is worth a try. Your father still hasn't said what he is going to do but Helen's heart attack frightened him. He is doing some heavy soul searching. Besides, he will enjoy meeting my parents and maybe some good will come from the three of them getting acquainted."

"Tom, it would please me so much if we could put aside all family differences."

"It would please me too, but don't get your hopes too high. We'll just have to wait and see what happens when the three of them meet.

"By the way, did Brenda ever tell you that she went and talked with your father while we were in Michigan?"

"No, absolutely not. This is news to me. What did she say? How do you know that she did?"

"Your father told me when I talked with him this morning. He said that she wanted him to get to know his grandchild and that she wanted him to come to your wedding?"

"That's Brenda. Right to the point. I'll have to thank her for trying. How did my father react?"

"I'm not sure. It got him thinking about what she said. The odd thing is that even if he didn't like her message he likes her; he likes her very much. I think her directness got to him. That may be why this meeting with my parents could do some good. Your father's life has just been turned upside down by Helen's heart attack and that couldn't have come at a worst time for him."

"Tom, do you think that my father might come to our wedding?"

"Katie, I know you would be thrilled if he did but I don't know the answer to your question. He has to do something but he isn't quite sure what; right now, he's dead in the water.

"He has made his peace with you but he has to decide what to do about your wedding. That really means that he must look at how he has dealt with your brother; and that's where his past is catching up with his present. He can't undue what has happened but it is like an anchor preventing him from moving forward. We'll just have to wait and see."

Katie almost moaned, "Wait and see? Our wedding is coming up on Saturday and I have no idea of who is going to be standing where. I don't like the idea of not having everything ready."

"Sweetface, you have a right to be upset but things will work out. Your father will work his way through this. His love for Helen will melt his paralysis."

"You sound as if you feel sorry for him."

"In a way, I do. All these years he has been hard headed, stubborn, short sighted in his dealings with his children; all kinds of adjectives can apply to him. However, I can also say that he is an honorable man of high principles who truly believes in doing the right thing. His world is spinning apart around him. I don't agree with him but I do feel sorry for him."

"Oh Honey, you're right. I should give some tolerance for my father's problems. You are so considerate of others that you make me feel a little ashamed of myself; you should not have to remind me that there must always be room for compassion. I hope my father can resolve his problems both for his and Helen's sake. I'll leave it at that. So there.

"Now, let's concentrate on what we need to do between now and Saturday. There are a few details left that we need to resolve."

"Such as what?"

"There are two items that you are taking care of and which you haven't given me a definite answer about. The first is the food at the rehearsal dinner after the rehearsal."

"Sweetface, I thought that was put to bed. The grandmothers have insisted that they were going to prepare everything for the rehearsal dinner and it will be held at St. Mark's. You said that they are excellent cooks and they will be able to take care of whatever number of people show up. What else is there to do?"

"Hah! You have forgotten one step. We need to supply them with whatever food they need to cook. I will ask them to give you a shopping list and you will have to buy everything and deliver the food to them."

"OK, I didn't realize I needed to do that. No problem. What's next on your list of in-completes?"

"Our honeymoon. You said that you were going to pick out a place for us but, so far, I've not heard where that place is. Surely, you intend to tell me so that I can be there with you?"

"Yes, Smartypants, my intention is to have you with me on our honeymoon. I only finished the reservations this afternoon. We will be spending a week in Newport."

Katie smiled, "Newport, Rhode Island? What a good idea. We will be able to tour all those mansions and walk the beaches. How marvelous. How did you ever decide on Newport?"

"Well, if I'm to be converted into a New Englander, I have to be indoctrinated and brainwashed. Newport is an old, established part of New England history. Historic, scenic, with plenty of good restaurants. Being converted, especially with you as my partner, isn't so bad. Actually, I had to choose between Bar Harbor and Newport and I decided on Newport. Is that all right with you?"

"Honey, I like your choice. It will be fun exploring an old seaport with you. You will soon be mispronouncing your words like the rest of us Bostonians.

"I have a couple of more questions for you. Now that Helen's heart attack is worrying my father is there anything that you should be telling your parents? Are you going to warn them, ahead of time, about what to say concerning my father and Mark?"

"No, I hadn't thought anything about that. We told them what had happened in the past and what the present situation is. I'm hoping that your father and my parents will learn about each other, and about themselves, from this meeting. They are older than us and supposedly wiser. So, my feeling is let everyone speak their individual minds and let the chips fall where they may."

19

The next morning, Wednesday, Brenda, Mark and Tom's parents came over to Katie's house for breakfast. She had arranged this meeting to make sure that each of them was kept up to date on what was happening. She also wanted the chance to talk with everyone and find out how they were doing.

Katie's days were stretched. Before she had her heart attack, Helen had been taking care of all the wedding details; now, she was one of the details herself. Katie spent as much time as she could at Helen's bedside besides running errands for her. She was glad to be able to repay the person she loved and respected but it took up a great deal of her time. She relied on Tom to relay messages and run their errands and he did; but he himself was busy with his own agenda. He was taking care of Tyler, repairing the damage in the house and working to familiarize himself with his new job and his work associates.

In the meantime, nothing was coordinated as everyone went their own way. Katie would drive to the hospital early in the morning to be with Helen. Tom would join her after getting Tyler up and ready for school. Mark worked on the house while Brenda went to work.

She worked as many extra hours as she could so that they could buy necessities and niceties for their unborn baby. Tom's parents went sightseeing after inquiring if they could be of help. The result was that while no one was at cross purposes, Katie had the impression that cooperation could be improved. She wanted to make sure that nothing was overlooked and that everyone was all right.

When Brenda and Mark entered the kitchen, Katie hugged Brenda and said, "Thank you so much for asking my father to come to our wedding."

Brenda looked surprised as she answered, "How did you know that I went to see him. You were in Michigan and I haven't told anyone that I spoke to him. I didn't even mention it to Mark because I didn't think I had accomplished anything."

"Yesterday, my father told Tom that you came to his office to visit him. You made more of an impression on him than you realize. He likes you."

"Does he like me enough to attend your wedding?"

"Tom and I don't know the answer to that yet but he hasn't said that he is not coming. Helen's heart attack has really scared him so maybe some good will come from all of his anxiety."

Tom's parents arrived a few minutes later and Katie gave them all the latest update on Helen's condition including the fact that she might be home late Thursday instead of Friday. The news was welcomed and the breakfast meal was a pleasant diversion before a busy day for all of them.

Towards the end of the meal Tom asked his parents, "What are your plans for today?"

Tom's father answered, "Well, Selma and I are planning on visiting the Old North Church and Harvard campus, places we haven't seen before. Both are famous and fascinating. You said that everyone would be busy today. Is that all right with you and Katie?"

Katie replied for both of them, "Of course. Helen is looking forward to meeting you both, but she wants to be in her own home when she does; since she is not sure what day that will be you should go ahead with your sightseeing.

"The only thing that I would remind you is that you should leave yourself plenty of time to come back early to Foxboro. You are invited to have dinner tonight with my father and Tom and me."

This time, Selma answered, "Yes, Don and I are looking forward to meeting your father. But, wouldn't it be better for us to wait until Helen is out of the hospital and able to join us?"

Tom spoke up, "Mom, not according to Helen. She feels bad that she hasn't been able to meet you personally and she thinks that asking you to spend your time sightseeing is sort of an insult to both of you. The sooner you meet her husband, the better Helen will feel about your stay in Massachusetts. She will feel much better knowing that you are meeting all the people she loves."

Selma replied simply, "Helen is an extraordinary woman. Katie, please tell her that I admire her very much and that Don and I are looking forward to meeting her personally.

"Now, about what time do you want us back in Foxboro and where should we be?"

Katie thought for a second and then said, "Those are interesting questions. We've never thought about them. Let's see, Tom and I will be over my father's house early in the afternoon, while he is visiting Helen, to start preparing the meal. Then Tom will have to run errands and pick up Tyler. The three of us will be leaving shortly after dinner so that you two can talk with my father. That's the schedule.

"I guess the best thing would be for Tom to meet you over at our house about five. You can follow him in your car from there to my father's house; it isn't very far away. When you leave my father's house you will have your car to go back to your motel. Is that all right with you?"

Tom's parents agreed that the plan was sensible. They finished eating and everyone got ready for their day's activities. Brenda went to work and Tom's parents left to go sightseeing. Tom told Katie that he and Mark would clean up the kitchen and she left to go to the hospital. As Tyler was getting ready for school Mark said to Tom, "Brenda didn't tell me that she had spoken to my father. I guess she figured that she wasn't successful. That was brave of her to confront the lion in his own den; she will do anything to make sure our child doesn't have to go through what she did while she was young. Brenda is a caring person and a good wife. She makes me feel good.

"You know, I've noticed how easily you and your father talk to each other. That must be a good feeling to be able to discuss anything without having to be careful in what you say."

"Mark, it wasn't always like that. When I first came home from Vietnam talking with my parents was almost impossible. It was like snaking our way through a minefield. It's only since I met Katie that my mother and father and I have been able to reestablish our ability to talk with each other."

"Was that Katie's doing?"

"No, not entirely, but she certainly helped. It was up to me; I had to change and let go of the hate and fear that I carried around. I was doing that when I met Katie. I guess my point is that people can change and that could include your father. So, we will see if our wedding and Helen's illness helps a miracle to occur. In the meantime, we'll just keep working and hoping."

With that, they cleaned up the breakfast dishes and, when Tom drove Tyler to school in his truck, Mark came along. After they dropped Tyler off, they went to the lumber yard and bought extra items for the house repairs. Then they went grocery shopping for the grandmothers. They dropped off enough food at both homes to feed the Yankee Division if it happened to bivouac at the reception. Finally, they returned to Katie's house, unloaded the repair items, and discussed what next needed to be done. Tom left to go to the hospital.

Helen was sitting up in bed and talking with Katie when he entered her small room. Her hair was combed and she was wearing lipstick; she looked bright and alert. What struck Tom most was the amount of flowers in the room. Every time John came to visit Helen he brought in two or three bouquets and, because she hadn't been in the hospital long enough for any of the bouquets to wither, the room resembled a flower shop.

"Good Morning, Helen," Tom said as he kissed her cheek. "What are you going to do with all of these flowers when you leave this joint?"

"If you are asking if you can have them for your wedding, forget it. I've arranged with the nurses when I leave tomorrow. Some will go to special patients who could use some cheering up and some will go to the children's ward. They will all be used for a good cause.

"Katie tells me that you and she are just about set for the wedding."

" She's right in that all the details have been taken care of. All we have to do now is show up at St. Marks' Church on Saturday with or without these flowers. All we really need is for a few more of the important cast of characters, like you, to show up. Yes, we are both ready, and anxious, for Saturday to arrive."

"How about this evening?"

"Katie and I are also ready for that. Is John?"

"Yes, he is. He has been asking me about your mother and father; questions I can't answer. 'How long have they been married? How did they meet? Are they enjoying themselves?'

"He seems eager to meet them. I wish I were going to be there this evening. However, I'm thankful that I'll be home early enough to be at your wedding. Both of you are so precious to me."

Katie squeezed Helen's hand. The three of them chatted for a while until Katie looked at her watch and said, "My goodness, Helen, we have to go. Tom and I have to go shopping and then prepare dinner. Will Dad be here shortly?"

"He'll probably show up about an hour after you leave. He'll come marching in with flowers; I keep telling him he is crowding me out of the room but every time he walks through the door he has more bouquets. His concern for me is touching."

Katie and Tom stood up and moved to Helen's bedside. Katie held Helen's hand and Tom's hand and was silent for a moment before she spoke, "Helen..," then she paused. "I don't know why I never called you Mom. You really have been my mother." She paused again. "Mom, Tom and I wish you were going to be with us tonight. You have been so kind and so forgiving to both of us. We will leave now but our love will be left in this room. You are forever in our hearts."

The two of them walked out; the three of them were teary eyed and happy.

***

The preparations for dinner were carried out without any problems. Tom and Katie got to her father's house with all the food they had bought for the meal. After walking around, Katie decided that the house needed cleaning. Tom didn't think it did. He was convinced that her judgement was based on the fact that Helen hadn't been home in five days; during that time, her father hadn't been home long enough to make any kind of a mess. Nevertheless, they vacuumed, dusted, wiped and cleaned as if the house was filthy. When they finished, it was just as clean as when they started.

They worked together on the necessary preparations for dinner until Tom picked up Tyler, ran some errands, and returned to Katie's house to wait for his father and mother. They then drove back, in two cars, to her father's house. The preparations were complete.

There was only one thing wrong. Katie's father didn't show up on time. After waiting a while, Katie passed some hors d'oeuvres and drinks while they asked Tom's parents to describe their day. Even so, John was so late that everyone started to become apprehensive. No one said it but each of them thought that, because of his cast, he might have been in an accident. Just as they began to be really concerned, he crutched through the door carrying a bouquet of flowers in each hand.

"I am so sorry I'm late, I do apologize. I couldn't help myself; traffic was slow on the way home and, to make things worse, I got stuck behind a three car accident that blocked the road. I feel bad that I kept you waiting so long.

"I have a bouquet for each of you ladies. Helen wouldn't let me leave them. She said that she has more than enough flowers and she wanted Tom's mother and Katie to have these. So, here they are as a present from Helen and an apology from me." He handed a bouquet to each of them.

They both thanked him and Tom formally introduced John to his father and mother. Katie got him a plate of goodies along with a drink and all of their anxieties slipped away. Everyone relaxed and the conversations consisted of the three parents talking about their children and their offspring corroborating, or correcting, the stories.

The discussions continued over the meal of toss salad, clam chowder, boiled lobsters, mashed potatoes and broccoli. Everyone was sated and satisfied. After clearing the table, Tom and Katie served coffee and dessert. Selma was pleased when she was given a piece of raisin pie. She said, "I haven't had this in years. It is so good, I wonder why I don't have it more often. Katie, this is delicious, did you make it from scratch?"

"Yes, I followed my grandmother's recipe. I made it in honor of Helen; it is her favorite dessert."

Selma replied, "Will there be enough left for Helen?"

Katie laughed as she answered, "Oh, yes. I've baked two pies. Helen will have plenty to eat when she gets home tomorrow."

When everyone finally finished eating, Tom's parents helped Tom and Katie clean up the dining room and wash the dishes; Katie's father was in charge of taking care of Tyler. After the cleanup, Katie, Tom and Tyler said, "Goodnight," and left.

John Givens and Don and Selma Booker retired to the living room and sat in comfortable chairs with a fresh pot of coffee. John said, "As your host, and on behalf of my wife, please allow me to speak first. I can't tell you how happy Helen and I are that our daughter is marrying your son. Tom is everything parents could wish for in a son in law. He is proud of you and you must be proud of him."

Selma reached over for Donald's hand and said, "John, thank you for your kind words. All parents like to believe that their children are loved and respected. Don and I don't always agree with Tom but we are proud of him and we couldn't be more pleased with his choice of Katie to be his partner.

"She stole our hearts from the very first time Tom told us about her. When Tom did bring her to Milan and we met her, I wept with happiness. Don and I were sure that Tom had found a soul mate and that we had found a princess. Katie radiates joy and receives happiness; that is a gift that few people possess."

The three parents sat there relishing the thoughts of their children for a few moments. Finally, John sighed, and continued, "I wish Helen were here with us. She has asked me several times to apologize for not inviting you to the hospital but she does not want you to meet her under those conditions. Hopefully, she will be coming home tomorrow."

"That's totally understandable," Selma said, "I would feel the same way if I were in the hospital. Don and I are looking forward to meeting her. She and I have had several phone conversations and I'm eager to talk with her face to face."

Again there was a slight pause in the conversation. John suddenly blurted out, "Tom told me that you and your wife were against his enlisting in the army."

Don answered, "Yes we were."

John Givens asked, "Would you mind telling me why?"

Don immediately understood why John was asking him that question. Katie had never sugar coated any of the family problems when she told Tom's parents about her background. She never embellished the good things or polished the bad; she just detailed the facts. As a result, Tom and his parents were aware of the rift between John Givens and his son Mark. They also knew of the anguish this caused for each family member.

"John, I don't mind telling you at all. I not only was against his enlisting, I was even opposed to his being drafted when he reached eighteen. And, that was because I thought our government was wrong in sending our youth to be killed in a stupid, senseless fight. It was not in our best interests to grind the future of our country against the Vietnam wheel of death."

Givens was surprised at the strength of Don's feelings. He said, "You know, everything seems to have changed. You and I are of the same generation, we are about the same age, and we both grew up during the Second World War. I'll bet both of us felt the same way about winning that war. And yet, now we hold opposite views about Vietnam.

"I'm not questioning your loyalty, Don, I just don't understand what happened to our patriotism?"

Don smiled, "John, you were in one of the services during World War II, weren't you?"

"Yes, I was in the army for almost three years. My father was killed in combat at Anzio."

"I'm sorry to hear that. I lost my older brother on D-day, at Omaha Beach, and Selma lost her father, who was on board the Lexington, at the Battle of the Coral Sea. I was with Patton's Third Army when it relieved the 101st Airborne at the Battle of the Bulge.

"I tell you this to show you that both Selma and I are aware of what sacrifices patriots have to make to keep our country safe. As individuals, we are not pointy headed liberals who can only wring their hands in times of trouble. As parents, we do not want our children sacrificed on the altar of patriotism unless our country is truly defending its principles.

"Every citizen has the right to disagree with our government. That does not mean we are not patriotic; it does mean that we thought the administration that sent us to war was wrong. John, you mentioned the Second World War; think back to that war effort. It was an effort that involved our entire society.

"Our country was attacked and Congress met and declared war. It was difficult to avoid the draft. There was rationing of food and gasoline. We had specific goals and our entire country was mobilized to meet those goals. Civilians were asked to sacrifice. Certainly, we made mistakes as we struggled but our goals never wavered.

"Contrast that with how we slid into the Vietnam War. We inherited a second hand war without debate and our goals were murky, without clear definition. For most of our population it was business as usual. Life went on as if there were no war; no sacrifices were asked for and only a small percentage of our people, those who served in our armed services, made any kind of a sacrifice. It was mostly the young men and women of our country, our nation's future hopes, who bled and died for a cause that our government never clearly defined. It seemed we just bumbled into a war and the government had to shout 'Patriotism,' to ensure we would keep on fighting.

"War is the scourge of mankind; it turns humans into animals. It shatters beauty and destroys life. We should only go to war if we are attacked, not because our government thinks we are the world's police department.

"That's a long winded answer, John, but I hope it helps you understand the question you asked."

"I found your answer quite interesting. What you said made sense even if I didn't agree with some of your ideas. I remember the pride I felt that my father was fighting for our country. My world collapsed when he died. I didn't know that Tom had relatives who died in combat; he never mentioned them to me. You and Selma must feel the same bitter sweet pride for them that I feel for my father."

"Yes, we do. Absolutely."

"Do both of you know about the rift between my son and me?"

Selma and Don both nodded their heads affirmatively.

"Well, I can listen to your calm statements and understand your reasons for feeling the way you do. The war is over and the fires of hate have been stoked to some degree. I can even agree with you up to a point. However, at the time my son and I began to disagree tempers were flaring. I couldn't stand the sight of those long haired hippies challenging legal authorities and giving comfort and aid to our enemies. They may have had a right to do that but when I thought that my father died so this ragtag group could disrupt our legal processes, I was furious. Then, when my son started to sympathize with them, I lost my cool. I guess as a parent I should have done a better job of controlling my emotions. I just couldn't help but feel that my son was making a mockery of my father's sacrifice.

"I don't suppose either of you ever have had deep problems with Tom?"

This time, Selma answered for both of them. "John, you are wrong, dead wrong. We have had our share of problems; I'm sure that every parent child relationship has rocky periods. Don and I have spent hours discussing our problems as I'm sure that you and Helen have."

John lost a little of Selma's conversation as a piercing thought suddenly struck him. He had never ever had a discussion with Helen about his basic attitude towards Mark. He had not brought the subject up and she had never asked questions. He put the thought aside and brought himself back to listening to what Selma was saying.

"Until Tom enlisted in the army the relationship among the three of us followed a fairly normal pattern. However, as Don told you, we opposed the Vietnam War long before Tom was old enough to be drafted, and, as he neared eighteen, the war began to be more personal for Don and me. We had already lost relatives and loved ones and we didn't want to lose our only son for a cause we didn't believe in. But what were our obligations as law abiding citizens?

"Tom knew absolutely nothing about this but Don and I searched for alternative answers, both legal and illegal, to his being drafted. We discussed sending him to Canada, or getting him enrolled at the University of Michigan, or having him join the National Guard; anything to keep him out of the Vietnam War. We never did a thing because, as it turned out, he got himself accepted at Michigan and went for four years until he graduated.

"While he was at school he heard all the pros and cons of the Vietnam war and he developed his own conscience. After graduation, without even telling us, he enlisted in the army. That came as quite a shock to Don and me but there were no recriminations. It was too late for them, anyhow. So, like all parents, we hugged our son tightly, kissed him passionately, and prayed fervently for his safe return.

"Our troubles really began when Tom finally returned. We had not seen him since he had left almost four years before and we were absolutely shocked at his conduct. He walked into the home he had been born and raised in wearing his army uniform with all his medals, ribbons and patches. He took off his uniform almost when he got in the door and he didn't tell us why.

"It wasn't that he was hostile, he was just uncommunicative. He stayed to himself and rarely spoke. Don and I could hear him cry out, with loud shouts and swearing, every night. We would ask about his nightmares, but he wouldn't talk about them with us. He smoked pot, drank heavily, and let his hair and beard grow long and shaggy. Living with him became almost impossible. He wouldn't listen to us or talk with us. The young man who left us had been transformed into a sullen brute who acted like a cave man. We were beside ourselves with worry over his obvious pain and suffering and the fact that there was no way we could help him.

"Don and I read every article we could find on the plight of returning Vietnam veterans. We became non medical experts on Post Traumatic Stress Disorder. We were shocked to find out how shabbily the veterans were being treated by our own government; such as not believing or treating soldiers who had been exposed to Agent Orange. Finally, we were dismayed by how the veterans were seen by our own people. Instead of thanking them for their service, they were treated as murderers. We thought that our government was ungrateful and that our society was unappreciative.

"Finally, Tom solved our family problems by leaving. For the next few years we heard very little from him; a postcard or a short note from dinky towns all over the country. We thought that we had lost our son because we knew nothing about his health or his well being. So, we treasured those postings as if they were the family bible. We have them in a well worn scrapbook and my tears are dried on every page.

"Then, in early December of last year, we got a call from Tom asking us if he could come home for Christmas. We were so excited and so petrified because we didn't know which son would show up. However, seeing Tom, and realizing that he had worked his way through his problems, made the Holiday season the happiest we had ever had. Then, when he told me that he had found the woman he wanted to marry, your Katie, I realized how fortunate our family was.

"John, life would have been different if Mark had gone into the army. However, if you had gone through the experiences Tom and I had, you may be better off with his going to Canada. All I will say to you is embrace your family."

"You have met my son?"

"Don and I have heard about him from Tom and Katie and we have met him since we arrived in Foxboro. We like him and his wife Brenda very much."

"Let me ask both of you another question. If you were me, how would you handle my attitude towards my father's sacrifice?"

Selma looked at her husband and waved her hand for him to speak. He did, "John, I'll give you my answer and hope that you will listen to what I say without getting angry or upset.

"If I had a son like Mark, I would change my attitude towards him. I don't believe that Mark meant any disrespect to your father; I honestly think that he was following his personal convictions. I may not agree with those convictions but I would assume that Mark truly believed that what he did was right. At worst, he made a mistake and he really has paid for his actions. I would forgive him rather than hold it against him. I would honor the dead but I would also love the living because what is past cannot be changed.

" I know that my brother, Selma's father, and probably your father too, would agree; put the past behind and think of the future. That's why I say that it is time to honor the dead and love the living. As you sit here with us, while Helen is in the hospital, you know that what I'm saying is true."

After Don stopped speaking, there was silence in the room; no one said a word. John Givens sat motionless as in a trance. He stared straight ahead without speaking for a long time. Then, still without talking, he arose, freshened the three coffee cups and sat down again. Finally, he said, "Don, I can see where Tom gets his directness from. Am I upset because of what you said? Absolutely not. I asked for your opinion and you gave it to me and I thank you for that. You certainly presented a different point of view than I have had. I promise you that

I will think about what you have said because I have got to make some decisions in the next day or two."

John Givens changed the subject and for the rest of the evening the three of them discussed less personal issues, sports, politics, their home towns of Milan and Foxboro. It was early Thursday morning before they realized how long they had been talking. John made his way with his visitors to his front door and, uncharacteristically, he warmly shook Don's hand and kissed Selma on the cheek. He had thoroughly enjoyed himself.

***

That morning, Helen woke up even earlier than she usually did. She had not been sleeping well during her hospital stay; her mind was so cluttered with thoughts that it was not allowing her body to rest. She kept thinking, over and over, of the wedding, her health, her husband, Katie and Mark. It was as if she were checking a long shopping list. This Thursday morning was especially important to her as it was the day she probably would be leaving the hospital; and she also wanted to hear how the meeting between her husband and Tom's parents went. All things considered, Helen's thoughts were way ahead of the hospital's schedule.

She was pleasantly surprised, and pleased, when her husband appeared at her bedside with a brown paper bag in one hand. "John, you must have read my mind. I was hoping you would come here early. I'm so glad to see you."

John quickly hobbled to her bedside where he could give her a kiss. "It doesn't seem early to me, Helen. I got to bed late last night; really, it was closer to early this morning and I couldn't get to sleep. So, I decided to come over and talk to you, my beloved wife. We have a lot to talk about.

"Since you prohibited me from bringing any more flowers and I wasn't sure when you would have breakfast, I brought two navel oranges for us. Now that I see your tray, I think that I should have stuck to flowers."

Helen smiled and replied, "You could have come here empty handed and you would have been welcome. I'm dying to know about your party last night. What do you think of Tom's parents?"

"I like them very much and you will, too. I want to take a trip to Milan and visit them sometime or other."

"You really did like them."

"Yes, they are common sense people. You can get a better picture of Tom after you meet them. I don't exactly agree with them but they do make sense and they are very honest. You have talked to Selma a few times, I'm sure that you will enjoy meeting her and Don in person."

"Well, I hope to later today. Tell me about last night."

"To begin with, it didn't start off too well. I got stuck in traffic and was almost two hours late; not a good way to meet your future in laws. Despite that, the meal was excellent and, while Katie, Tom and Tyler were there, the conversation was easy, relaxed and enjoyable. Tyler is such an enjoyable child to be around; he is bright and talkative.

"After they left and there were just the three of us, we had a long, serious conversation. I talked a lot, I listened a lot, I learned a lot. Hearing from both of them, I found out something I had paid no attention to before. They informed me that many of the veterans came back from the war with PTSD, Post Traumatic Stress Disorder. Selma and Don had their share of problems when Tom came home. He returned from Vietnam as a victim of the war and it took him a long time to adjust back to civilian life. I had never really thought about that. If Mark had joined the army he might have been as brutalized as Tom was. Selma and Don opposed the Vietnam War but they really are no less patriotic than I am.

"I also discovered something about myself that really surprised me. Last night, a casual question from Selma, got me thinking about something I had never thought about. She was telling me about the problems that she and Don had with Tom and then she asked me if you and I ever discussed my problems with Mark. It dawned on me, for the first time, that we never have talked about Mark.

"In fact, you have never asked me many questions about him. You ask all kinds of questions about Katie but you only listen to me when it comes to Mark. I know that both of them fill your heart and your mind, so there must be a reason why you will ask about one and listen about the other.

"Now, I know that I am stubborn but I also know that I'm not stupid. After I thought about it, I think I figured out why you never asked. If you treat them both differently, it is undoubtedly because I treat them both differently. If that is true, and I'm sure it is, it must have put a strain on you, all these years."

John stopped speaking for a while. Finally, Helen asked, "Well?"

"I'll continue, but I have to tell you in my own way because I'm still working on my thoughts and I'm not very glib. I'll start by telling you that I love you dearly and that your heart attack scared me, it really did. To lose you would be the biggest hurt in my life; something I would never overcome.

"When my fright about your health started to ease, I find that I have not been fair to you. Even though it was entirely unintentional, I feel bad. You are the center point of this family, you are the fulcrum. We all balance around you. You have always asked for calmness and patience out of loyalty and love for everyone. That is quite a burden you've carried and I'm sorry that I added to it.

"Helen, all I can tell you is that I love you and respect you deeply. There is nothing that I wouldn't do for you."

"What about Katie's wedding on Saturday?"

"I'll be at her wedding. I'd be delighted to give the bride away."

"What about Mark?"

"I will talk with my son, Mark. Any other questions?"

Helen had to wipe the tears from her eyes before she answered, "Oh, thank you, Honey. You have made me and the children happy. When did you decide to change your mind? Last night?"

"Last night helped, but, as you can probably guess, it was a long time coming. Your being hospitalized finished it for me. To be honest, though, I began to rethink how I was living my life after the evening that Tyler and Katie came over for dinner. He is such a happy child; talking to him started to loosen my thoughts as well as my tongue. Especially since that was also the evening I found out that Katie was pregnant again. I started to realize that my feelings for his father should have absolutely nothing to do with Tyler. I was the one missing out on the joy of having a grandson and I was in danger of repeating the same pattern if I didn't change.

" After that, Brenda just waltzes into my office to introduce herself and tell me that she is also pregnant. I found myself admiring her courage and liking her honesty. Then, she said something that stopped me cold. She asked me if I ever thought of what my father would think of Mark if he were alive. I didn't know then and I can't say with any certainty even now. He might not have been as harsh in his judgement as I was.

"So, there I was, juggling these new thoughts and ideas, and you got sick. Helen, I don't want to lose you and I don't want to be left behind. I don't want to be alone. There should have been more room for compassion and love in all of my decisions. That was in the past. All I want now is to live my life with you and enjoy our grandchildren. Now, does that answer all of your questions?"

Helen sighed, "Yes, you have answered all my questions and all my prayers. I love you now as much as I did when we married so long ago. But, I have never been more proud of you then I am right now. We will share our lives for years to come. I'm happy to your wife."

Helen thought for a second and then asked, "Have you told Katie and Mark about your decision yet?'

"No, and I don't want you to say a word to them, either. I want to meet Katie and Tom and Brenda and Mark face to face and talk with them. If you are able to be there at my side that would be even better, but I must do this face to face and personally."

"When and how do you plan on doing that?"

"It shouldn't be too hard. Katie and Tom are not coming to the hospital today because they are sure that you are being released. After Dr. Sanborn makes his rounds and tells us what time you will be able to leave, I'll call Tom and ask him to gather everyone at Katie's house. That shouldn't be a problem."

Dr. Sanborn put a slight crimp into John Given's plan by informing him that Helen would be released immediately but that she was to go directly home and get into bed; complete bed rest and no visitors for twenty-four hours. Dr. Sanborn didn't want too much activity for Helen before the wedding.

While Helen was getting dressed to leave, John called Katie's house. Tom answered the phone and said, "Hello."

"Tom? Good Morning, this is John Givens."

"Good Morning, John. I hope you're calling with good news."

"Oh, I am. Helen is getting dressed to come home as I talk to you. We'll be leaving shortly, but she is on bed rest for twenty-four hours.

"Is Katie there?"

Tom answered, "No, she has gone to drive Tyler to school and then she and Brenda are going shopping. Right now, I'm by myself but Mark is due over here in a while. Why?"

"I'm glad to hear you are by yourself because I need you to help me without anyone knowing. Do you think that you can get the four of you, Katie and you, Brenda and Mark, together? I don't want anyone else in attendance, just the four of you."

"What time would you want for us to be here?"

John thought for a second before replying, "How about 11:45? I'll bring pizza for everybody."

Tom replied, "I can get them all over here by that time. And, I'm not to tell them that you are coming?"

"Yes, I would appreciate it if you didn't mention me. I want to talk with all of you but I would prefer that you are the only person that knows I'm coming until I get there. That way, no one will waste any time speculating on why I'm coming or what I am going to say"

20

At 11:48 that morning, John Givens stood at the door to Katie's house. From the time that he had called Tom until now, he had brought Helen home, made her comfortable, and picked up four large pizzas. They were in the back seat of his car. As he made his way up the steps and moved across the porch he was nervous and a little fearful. What he was going to do would make changes and turn his life around. Despite a pep talk from Helen he was apprehensive about how he would be received. As he was standing there, he noticed that the door was new, not weather beaten; this puzzled him until he remembered that the old one had been badly damaged by PJ. John shrugged his shoulders, took a deep breath to boost his courage, and then tapped lightly on the door.

Brenda opened it almost immediately and stood there staring at him. She was completely surprised to see Mark's father standing on crutches in front of her but the only change to her expression was that her eyes widened. She reacted quickly saying "Mr. Givens, come in, come in." Then she yelled, "Katie, Mark, Tom, look who came to see us." She tried to help him by putting one arm around his shoulders and guiding him from the porch into the house. She was quicker, and stronger, than John realized and she almost caused him to trip before he could move at the speed she was propelling him.

Nevertheless, Brenda got John Givens into the kitchen where he was trying to stabilize himself on his one leg and two crutches when the three others arrived to see what the commotion was about. Katie squealed, "Dad, Dad," and rushed over to hug her father and give him a kiss. Mark came into the kitchen and stopped in his tracks. There was no awkward attempt at a handshake between him and his father because Katie was holding John Givens tightly and he couldn't move. Tom, because he knew who the visitor was, was the last to enter the kitchen. He wisely stood off to the side without saying a word but he listened to everything that was said and watched intently.

When Katie stepped away from her father, Mark was on the far side of the table from John. His father looked at him and said simply, "Hello, son."

Mark answered, "Hello, Dad."

They looked at each other. Mark saw a father who was on crutches and looked older than he remembered. He had put on weight around his middle and his hair had grayed considerably. His father looked tired and less combative, not the angry man with the low boiling point that Mark envisioned.

John Givens saw a son who was taller and heavier than John recalled. He was not Hollywood handsome but he was wholesomely attractive and clean cut. John stared at him and wondered why he had been so quick to judge his son as a failure. He began to realize what his stubbornness had cost him over all these years. A sense of remorse began to well up inside of him. He began to wonder if the breach could be healed. He had to try.

John Givens asked Brenda, "Could you help me by bringing in the pizzas that are on the back seat of my car? I'm not used to these crutches and I need some help. I'm hungry and I hope that all of you are, too."

Brenda changed the atmosphere from the doubts that everyone had to a more positive outlook by declaring loudly, "Let's eat. I'm famished." She brought the pizzas in and began opening the boxes. That was the signal for everyone to sit down and begin handing different slices, from different boxes, to different people. Soon, everyone was chewing their own slice of choice.

John Givens looked around at everyone and, then, decided to begin. "I asked Tom to get you all together so that we could talk. Since I asked for this meeting, and since everyone else's mouth is full, I will begin. I want to bring you all up to date on Helen's condition and answer all your questions."

He paused before beginning again, "I also want to know what I can do for Katie's wedding."

Katie smiled from ear to ear and asked loudly, "You will come to our wedding?"

John was surprised to see how pleased Katie looked. His gloom left him and he began to feel happy and, to his surprise, excited. "Katie, not only will Helen and I be in attendance, but I also plan on being part of the ceremony no matter how slowly I walk down the aisle."

Katie, realizing that her father was talking about giving the bride away, reached for Tom's hand. Tears rolled down her cheeks as she said, "Everything I ever wanted is coming true. I love the world."

Everyone basked in her radiance; happiness is as contagious as the common cold. After a few minutes, Tom said to him, "John, tell us about Helen, how she is feeling and what her condition is."

John explained, in detail, what Helen's doctor had told him. Helen had suffered a mild heart attack. However, with proper care, exercise, and healthy eating, she should be able to lead a normal life and live a long time. Her body needed both exercise and rest and everything she did had to be done with moderation.

When he had finished talking about what had happened to Helen, the questions about her present condition came from everyone at the table. Katie asked first, "Dad, will Helen be able to attend the rehearsal and the rehearsal dinner tomorrow?"

Jon answered, "Doctor Sanborn told her to do whatever she felt like doing but to be careful at first, not to get too tired. She wants to attend; however, she also wants to meet Tom's parents. She doesn't want to do too much tomorrow and not be able to come to the wedding on Saturday. We will just have to see how Helen feels. I can tell you, though, that her immediate goal is to meet Tom's mother and father."

Tom spoke up. "Well, if that is to happen, tomorrow morning would probably be the best time. From noontime on, everyone will be busy and there will be no time to sit and talk."

Brenda asked, "Mr. Givens, will Helen be able to handle so much activity tomorrow without getting too tired for Saturday?"

John looked at her as he replied, "Brenda, I honestly don't know. That is a determination that only Helen can make. I will ask her to be cautious and I know that she will because Saturday is the day that she is looking forward to. She has been waiting for this day for a long, long time."

Mark finally spoke up, "Dad, when can I come over and see Helen?"

"Whenever you can. Helen asked me to invite you and Brenda to come to the house as soon as we finish here. She is looking forward to talking with both of you."

With all the immediate questions answered, everyone's attention was turned on demolishing the pizza. In short order, that mission was accomplished and everyone felt full and lazy.

When John suggested that he had to go home, Brenda looked at him and asked, "May Mark and I follow you so that we can see Helen? I have some oatmeal raisin cookies that I baked for her."

"You are certainly welcome to follow me. Helen will be delighted. I know it's against doctor's orders but I'm sure it will do her good."

Katie spoke up. "Don't you want to see how well Tom and Mark repaired the house?"

"Of course I do." John turned to Brenda and Mark and said, "Why don't you two go on. The door is open; just walk in and see if Helen is sleeping. I will follow you shortly."

Katie and Tom slowly escorted John around while Katie proudly showed her father what had been done to repair and remodel the house she loved so much. John was impressed with the quality of the work but, it had been so long since he had been inside the house, he had forgotten what it had originally looked like. What he primarily gathered from his tour was that Tom and Katie were a happy pair looking forward to living together and raising their family.

***

When John arrived home, he heard voices in the living room. He made his way there and found Helen, Brenda, and Mark drinking tea and nibbling Brenda's cookies. He made himself comfortable and was given his own cup of tea and a cookie and he joined the conversation. He could see that Helen was relaxed and delighted to have Mark and Brenda with her.

Helen said to him, "Hi, Honey. We were just discussing the wedding; I was just asking if there was anything that we could do. Mark and Brenda think that everything has been well taken care of."

John answered her, "Well, if an emergency arises we'll be glad to help any way we can. In the meantime, I'm glad that the four of us are here. I want to say something to both Mark and Brenda.

"You both will soon be parents. You will find parenthood a difficult job to do right and an easy job to do wrong. I know because that's what I did with you, Mark. I made a mistake. I should not have ordered you out of the house when you were so young. I lost my temper and I have regretted it ever since.

"I thought that I had reasons for being angry with you, Mark, but I really didn't. What I did was wrong for a parent; I forgot that loving and teaching are the two most important functions of raising a child. It is probably no consolation to you now, but it was the teaching aspect that I forgot, not the loving. For that, I apologize. I have always loved you."

There was a heavy silence as they each groped and coped with their individual emotions. Finally, Helen said, "Mark and Brenda, this is the man that I have lived with for over twenty-five years. He and I have had our differences in the past but I know that there is no more honest or finer man in the world than my husband. He has developed the wisdom to see his past mistakes and is trying to make amends for his sake and mine.

"What has happened in the past is history, but we can learn from it to shape a much better future. You have no idea how thrilled I am to have the two of you, and our future grandchild, sitting here with us. I don't ever want you to leave; we don't ever want you to leave."

Brenda put her tea cup down and reached for Helen's hand as she said, "You are right, we should all learn from our past. My past has taught me that a lonely child is a frightened child; I wouldn't want any youngster to grow up feeling frightened. That's why I'm so thankful that you and Mark's father will be part of our child's life. I truly believe that no child can ever receive too much family love; it is the nectar that nourishes a child's soul. Both of you will be necessary for Mark and me to raise grandchildren that you will be proud of."

Brenda turned to Mark and said, "You are unusually quiet. Surely you have something to say."

"No, not really. All of you have said whatever I wanted to say better than I would have been able to. I'm just overwhelmed to be back in the house that I grew up in. I haven't been in it since I left. I peeked into my old bedroom and the past came alive. The house holds so many memories for me.

"I can't put in words what it means to be reunited with my father and my mother. As a matter...."

Mark got no further because the phone rang and it interrupted him. There was silence as the ringing continued. John Givens reached over from his chair, picked up the receiver, and said, "Hello." He listened for a while and then replied, "Yes, yes, I'm sure Helen would like that. Look, we're in the midst of a family discussion right now; can I call you back in a few minutes? Good, yes, I promise that I will call you."

He hung the receiver up and spoke to Helen, "That was Don. He wanted to know how you were feeling and if he and Selma could come over to the house later today and meet you; that is, if you feel up to it. You know what Dr. Sanborn ordered. Won't that be too much for you in one day?"

"John, Dear, I've not done much today and I don't feel tired; I really feel good now that I'm home. I'd like to meet Don and Selma in person. That will do me better than bed rest. Why don't we have them over and I promise I'll rest after that."

Brenda looked at Mark and inclined her head towards the door; Mark got her message. He said, "Mom, Dad, Brenda and I have some errands to run. If you want Tom's parents over now call them up. We've met them and they are just as nice as Tom; you'll enjoy them, Mom.

"We have to go. There are several thing we have to pick up for Katie and Tom. Mom, please get some rest."

They both went to where Helen was seated and kissed her goodbye. John saw them to the door, kissed Brenda on the cheek and, this time, shook Mark's hand. When he returned to the living room he phoned Don and invited him and Selma over. While they were waiting, John said, "Mark calls you 'Mom.' He hasn't always called you that has he?"

"No, not consistently until he got back from Canada. He was a little scared and lonely when he arrived so he unconsciously started to call me 'Mom'; I admit that I unconsciously liked it."

John didn't answer Helen but he thought to himself, "You consciously earned the right to be called his mom. It shows how we humans need each other."

When Don and Selma arrived, they brought peach preserves and corn relish that Selma had put up in her kitchen and a half gallon of Michigan maple syrup. Selma, with instructions from Helen on where things were, made a fresh pot of coffee and they sat in the living room and chitchatted. In a little less than two hours they had resolved all the world's problems and they had gotten quite comfortable with each other.

Then, of course, as parents their conversation turned to their children and the upcoming wedding. They each expressed their hopes that the wedding would be a lasting union that would bring happiness to Tom and Katie and grand children to them. Towards the end of this discussion, John became quiet and didn't join in the conversation.

After a while, he said, "We have been talking about our kids, which is all well and good; they are an important part of our lives. However, what about us? We were alive and kicking before we became parents and we still are. One of the things I've learned in the last few days is to love those you have and celebrate life. Believe me, I have never been more thankful for Helen than I am at this very second.

"I'm so grateful that I'm going to ask Katie first, and then, if she agrees, I'm going to ask Father Jonsen to renew our marriage vows right after her ceremony."

Helen, who had no idea that her husband was thinking of doing any such thing, was surprised, flustered, and pleased. Don asked, "I assume that Father Jonsen is your priest at St. Marks'?"

Helen answered him, "Yes he is," and then continued, "John, that is a lovely idea and I thank you, but you never mentioned it to me before."

"That's because I hadn't thought of it until just now. I don't even know if there is a service that will cover a ceremony like that."

Selma, who had been listening, said, "John, that is a beautiful idea. That is so thoughtful and tender.

"I'm sure that Katie would be pleased to have her father and her stepmother reaffirm their marriage vows at her own wedding ceremony."

Don was the next to speak up. "John, you are right. We may be older but we are far from decrepit. We should never take each other for granted. Would the two of you consider us imposing on you if I asked for permission for Selma and me to do the same thing? I want to show her my love and respect the same way you want do for Helen."

Helen laughed and asked, "Isn't this giddy and silly and marvelous? We geezers carrying on like we are teenagers? I'm almost sure that Katie and Tom will welcome the idea of their parents renewing their love for each other after their own ceremony. I'm almost as excited as Katie."

The four born again teenagers were elated about their new idea and they jokingly discussed going on their respective honeymoons together. Shortly after they recovered from their emotional high point, Selma and Don left so that Helen could get her rest.

***

After Helen got ready for bed, she sat on the edge of the mattress on John's side. He had been reading while he waited for her. "John, we have to talk to Katie and Tom tomorrow and get their permission if we want to continue on this silly idea. We shouldn't bother asking Father Jonsen until both of them agree and give their permission. After all, it is their day and they may want to remember it as their wedding ceremony only.

"I'm almost certain that Father Jonsen can find a ritual that would cover renewal of wedding vows. However, we should start with Katie and Tom. I hope they will let the four of us join them at the altar. Wouldn't that be fun?"

John put the book that he had been reading down and took off his glasses. "Katie and Tom are only the first step. Even if they agree, and I think they will, Jonsen can be a stickler for formalities at times. Any deviation, or change, from The Book of Common Prayer sometimes makes him contrary. He does not like change. I don't expect any problems but let's not take anything for granted.

"To answer your question, yes, it would be fun. Not only that, it would be cheaper than our first wedding; no license fee, no rings and no honeymoon costs are involved. It doesn't get any better than that."

"John Givens, you are a big fraud. You are not interested in saving money and don't tell me you are. I know and you know that you have changed your attitude and your feelings. That brightens my life.

"What you are interested in is showing me your love. I am grateful and I return my love to you with all of my heart. I didn't know it at the time, but the luckiest day of my life was when my car wouldn't start in that parking lot, so many long years ago."

"You are only partially right Helen, the luckiest day of my life was when your car wouldn't start. I never was fully aware of my happiness and good fortune until you got sick. That's a mistake I will never make again. I love you. To me, you are the dearest person in the world.

"Now let's put out the lights and go to bed. You need your rest along with your medicines."

***

When the Bookers returned to their motel, they both took their shoes off, sat down on the pull out sofa, and raised their legs on a coffee table. They were not sleepy as much as exhausted. Their physical activities of sightseeing up and down the coast of Massachusetts had tired them physically. The emotional roller coaster they had been riding since they arrived added to their fatigue. They just sat and held hands for a while.

Finally, Selma spoke in a low, soft voice, "Tom, I haven't enjoyed myself so much in years. Tom has selected a wonderful mate and Katie is equally fortunate. I like all three of our future in laws and I'm looking forward to watching our grand children grow.

"You absolutely took me by surprise by asking if we could renew our marriage vows. I hope we can. We have been through good times and bad for almost forty years, yet, the romance is still there. I hope the next forty are just as sweet.

"We may have a problem though. If Tom stays in Foxboro, and it looks like he will, we will have troubles visiting our new family. Katie's house is too small and motels are too expensive. I don't want to be limited in seeing them and our grandchildren."

"Selma, I'll tell you what John and Helen told me. I guess you were out of the room at the time and didn't hear their offer. They told me that we were welcome to stay at their house whenever we were in town whether they were there or in Florida. Katie and Tom would always have a key and we would always have access. That is a heart warming, friendly gesture."

"It certainly is. I think I would have cried if I had heard them when they made that offer. I will thank both of them before we leave, not only for their offer, but for all the hospitality and good will they have shown us. I want them to come visit us soon so that we can return the favor."

"Selma, we will ask them to come to Milan before we leave on Monday. In the meantime, we have a lot to look forward to, especially the wedding. God surely works in mysterious ways."

"I'll say the Amen to that and then I have got to write some postcards to our friends back home. Why don't you watch television for a while and, when I finish, we'll go to bed."

***

Katie, Mark and Tom were oblivious to the fact that their parents were experiencing stirrings of romance and rutting. Both of them were ending their daily activities and preparing for bed thinking that Friday's plans for the wedding rehearsal and the dinner would be routine. It had not occurred to them that romance was contagious and not constricted by age. They would learn that when they awoke.

***

While everyone slept, Thursday night merged quietly into Friday morning and the day started blissfully. At 8:00 AM Katie called Helen to find out how she was feeling and Helen asked her to come over with Tom whenever it was convenient for them. When Katie asked "why?" Helen said that she and John had some questions to ask. Katie replied that they would be over in a while.

Katie fixed breakfast for Tom and Tyler, caught up on a few household chores, talked to Brenda, and then she and Tom went to see her parents. After they got settled, her father said, "Katie, Tom, I have a question to ask you on behalf of myself, Helen and both of Tom's parents. We want to show our love for you, and for each other, by both of us couples renewing our wedding vows at your wedding.

"Now, understand that we are not trying to distract from your wedding. We only want to show our gratitude for having each other. If you don't like this idea, or if you're uncomfortable with it, say so. Tomorrow is your day. The four of us understand how important your wedding is to you and our feelings will not be hurt."

Katie clapped her hands together when her father finished speaking. "Oh," she replied, "Dad, Helen, what a marvelous idea. I can't see your renewing your vows as distracting from our wedding; I see it as strengthening our commitment. Honey, what do you think?"

"What do I think of it? I think that it is sentimental and splendid.

The idea of being at my mother's and father's wedding pleases me no end. If it's possible, let's do it. How do we go about it?"

Helen answered him, "I guess the first thing will be to talk to Father Jonsen. Are you both sure that you are willing to do this?"

"Helen, I'm absolutely sure and Tom is too. Let's call Father Jonsen and set up an appointment."

As it turned out, he was busy until just after noontime. In the meantime Tom had errands to run and Katie stayed with Helen. She called Brenda to tell her about both sets of parents wanting to renew their vows and Brenda just gushed over that fact. When Tom finished his errands, he returned to the house and they all departed to meet Father Jonsen.

When they entered St Marks' one of the assistant rectors handed Katie a note that said that she had had a phone call from Brenda and that it was urgent that they talk. When Katie returned the call Mark answered the phone. "Sis, you haven't been in to see Father Jonsen yet, have you?"

"No, I haven't."

"Good. Listen Sis, would it be asking too much if Brenda and I also renewed our vows along with the parents? We don't want to interfere but it sounds so good that we want to be included. What do you think?"

"I think it's marvelous. I don't see why you and Brenda shouldn't be included. The more the merrier. I'll let you know when we finish talking to Father Jonsen."

When the four of them entered his office, he stood up to greet them. Father Jonsen was a short, bald headed man, in his late sixties, whose empathies had retired years before and were just waiting for him to catch up with them. He clung to the past and he did not like the new liturgy or the newer church philosophies adopted in 1976. In short, he was a conservative.

He began the conversation by asking, "What can I do for you?"

Katie answered by asking, "Father Jonsen, is there a service for reaffirmation of wedding vows?"

"Yes, there is. It is called, 'Anniversary of A Marriage.' Why do you ask?"

"Because my father and step mother want to reaffirm their vows at my wedding."

"At your service? That's a different type of request; I have never been asked to perform both services at the same time. Do you and Tom agree with having both ceremonies at the same time?"

This time Tom replied, "Not only do I agree, I'm going to ask that my father and mother also be allowed to reaffirm their vows at our wedding."

Father Jonsen was shocked. He didn't know how to respond for a few seconds. Finally, he licked his lips and asked. "Are you people playing a joke, or a trick, on me?"

Katie said, "No, Father Jonsen. This is no trick. We all want to show our love for each other. In fact, my brother and his bride also want to reaffirm their marriage. That's a total of three Anniversary services."

"This is turning into a fiasco, a travesty. You want four services rolled into one and one of the couples is on crutches and, possibly, a wheel chair. I don't know how to reply to your request. I will not give you my answer until I call the Archdiocese and talk to the Archbishop. I will get back to you when I can." With almost a wave of his hand, he dismissed them.

There was nothing else that they could do so they left the church and returned to John's house. Brenda and Mark joined them and they all sat around waiting for the phone to ring. They were tense and subdued as they awaited Father Jonsen's decision. Within an hour the phone rang and John picked it up. After briefly listening to the voice on the other end, he handed the phone to Katie, saying, "It's for you."

Katie put the phone to her ear and said, "Hello, Father Jonsen." After that she stood and, sometimes smiling, sometimes frowning, but mostly straight faced, she listened without saying a word for over five minutes. Finally, she said, "Thank you," and hung up. She turned to face everyone sitting in the room; she was grinning from ear to ear. "First, we can have our ceremonies but he wants to make sure that, in his words, 'A mockery is not made of both the sacred ceremony of marriage and my position as rector of St. Mark's Church.'"

"He's not pleased with what we asked but, on the other hand, he is extremely unhappy with the Archbishop. Father Jonsen thinks that the Archbishop was making fun of him. He told me that, when he first told the Archbishop of our requests, the Archbishop asked him what they were putting into the Foxboro drinking water to cause such a wave of romance. Father Jonsen thinks that the Archbishop's levity was not helpful to him in solving his dilemma of how to handle our requests.

"Anyhow, after much discussion, Father Jonsen decided that he will perform our wedding ceremony and the three marriage anniversaries, but he wants everyone to understand exactly what they are to do and how they are to do it. So, he told me that anyone connected with the ceremony, has to be at the rehearsal. The only exception is Helen, because she just came home from the hospital.

"I wish Father Jonsen was more flexible, but that's only a minor comment. The big thing is that the show will go on."

The rehearsal did not start out too well. Father Jonsen tried to have the affirmations take place one at a time after the wedding ceremony. For a while it looked like two platoon football with couples coming in and going out and pairings moving around in the background; all with Father Jonsen calling signals as a frustrated quarterback. And, even though he had given his dispensation to Helen, he occasionally muttered that she should have been there beside her slow moving partner, just like everyone else. The rehearsal began to run more smoothly after Father Jonsen, who was not very jolly even to begin with, listened to a suggestion from his deacon. It was decided that the three pairs of couples would all reaffirm their marriages at the same time with each of them stating their names individually at the appropriate time.

Everyone was a little tired and edgy when the rehearsal was finally finished. It had gone on longer than anticipated and it seemed to lack polish and spontaneity. Each person appeared a little downcast about the ceremony tomorrow. There was an air of tension as they made their way to the reception room, where the rehearsal dinner was supposed to take place. When they got to the reception room, they were surprised. The lights were off, the tables had not been set up, there was no food; the room was empty. When Tom entered the room people were just standing there looking at each other. "Damn. What the Hell is going on?" he said under his breath.

No one seemed to know what to do, the wedding party milled around waiting for direction or clarification. Tom and Katie were perplexed because the grandmothers were supposed to be at the church with the food. On a hunch, Tom had Katie call Helen. When Katie asked her if she knew where the grandmothers were, she replied, "Yes, Mrs. Connors and Mrs. Buoni are both here with a ton of food and two ladies hired to serve and clean up."

"What are they doing there at your house, I wonder?"

"I don't know. I asked Mrs. Buoni and she said, "'Alma told the guy that drove us to come here.' I didn't think anything about it, I just assumed the plans had changed after I was hospitalized."

"Oh Helen, it's a mess here. Please let me speak to Arlene."

When Mrs. Connors came to the phone Katie asked her, "Arlene, why are you over at Helen's house and not down here at the church?"

After a moment of silence Mrs. Connors replied, "Oh my goodness Katie, I'm so sorry. You're right. I forgot I was supposed to go St. Mark's. I just forgot and no one reminded me. What should I do?"

Katie asked to speak to Helen again. "Helen, we will have about twelve people in the wedding party. Is it easier to bring the people to the food or the food to the people?"

"At this stage, bring the people to the food. Our house can handle that number of guests; it will be a little cramped, but who cares? I think that would be the easiest way to solve our problem."

Tom announced the change of plans and almost everyone went directly to where the meal was being served. The only person who made a side trip was Father Jonsen; he stopped at his home long enough to pick up his wife. Despite the change of locales, the rehearsal dinner was a huge success. Mrs. Buoni and Mrs. Connors may not have been too good at remembering where they should be but they were excellent cooks. The unsure rehearsal mood disappeared under a blizzard of lasagna, fried chicken, roast pork, and side dishes. There was enough food left to give each person a doggy bag the size of a bowling ball. The guest who had the best time was Father Jonsen. John Givens gave him some wine that "was exactly like the communion offering." After tasting it, Father Jonsen absolved himself so many times that he left the party in a tipsy condition; he was even smiling and humming to himself as his wife drove home.

***

Later that evening, as Katie and Tom snuggled, she said, "Honey, there is only one other detail that you and I have left to discuss. I don't want to stick around too long after we arrive at our reception dinner. First, this is my second marriage and I don't think the garter trick or throwing my floral bouquet is appropriate. Not only that, I don't like the idea of smooching every time someone bangs a fork on a water glass; it seems silly. I can't dance with my father. So, what I would like to do is quietly slip out at the appropriate time. Would you mind?"

"I think that's an excellent idea. We should tell our parents what we intend to do so they won't be surprised and I'll have Mark put our getaway car in the parking lot so we can go whenever we decide. What we should do is this; both of us should thank everyone and then we will leave when no one is looking. It's our wedding, we can do what we want."

Katie pulled herself even closer to him. "Tom, I'm so happy at this very moment that I'm almost afraid of the future. Helen, my second mother, seems happy and healthy and my father and brother are reconciling their differences. Tomorrow, I marry the man I love, my son gets a loving father and my unborn child and his legal father are united. I can't ask for any more; I don't need any more; I don't want any more."

Tom thought about what Katie had said for a while; he had a lump in his throat. Finally, he hugged her closely and nibbled on her ear before he replied, "Sweetface, I'm glad you give me so much credit for changing your life, but don't forget how you have changed mine. You have washed away all the petty, mean, dirty thoughts that I used to have. Making you happy gives me the greatest satisfaction I've ever had. That has to be my definition of love. And for that, I'm beholden to you, my lovely, beautiful witch. With or without a ceremony tomorrow, I love you and I always will."

They celebrated.

21

Saturday began at midnight and its twenty-four hour cycle unwound at the same, steady pace that the universe had established millions of years ago. It was this constant passing of time that humans were tied to during each of their individual lifetimes. Although the natural clock never varied, humans were usually trying to either speed up or slow down their own lives to stay even with the constancy of the clock.

When all of the individuals associated with the wedding finally awoke on Saturday morning, they followed their usual pattern. They tried to hurry or they delayed their activities to keep abreast of an event that was to take place later that day, on Saturday afternoon.

The domino effect started when Tom, after being urged by Katie, called Mark to find out if he had ordered corsages and boutonnieres for the three couples added to the wedding ceremony. Much to each other's surprise, they both thought the other was going to take care of the ordering. Tom quickly called the florist and got everything straightened out; however, that little oversight caused an added wave of nervousness for the upcoming event. From that point on, the phone lines were always busy as the eight of them called each other to check details, corroborate activities and dispel fears. Soon, each of them was tired of receiving phone calls; however, that didn't stop any one from making them. Katie finally broke the cycle by leaving her phone off the hook. Once the chain was broken, all the phone calls stopped and calm was restored. The wedding ceremony could start without all the feverish anxiety.

The weather on Saturday favored lovers. A late Friday night rainstorm had washed the sky clean and left it a brilliant blue and absolutely cloudless. There was no trace of a breeze and the temperature was moderate enough to walk outdoors without a wrap. The calm air smelled of the freshly watered vegetation and the wet earth; it was an ideal day to get married.

As the time neared, people began to arrive at St. Mark's. Both the invited guests and the wedding curious parishioners started to fill the church. Tom's parents and Brenda arrived and they were ushered to their respective pews. Mark, Tom, Tyler and Helen arrived together and Helen and Tyler were escorted to their pew. Because of the addition of three couples and the expected length of the ceremonies, it was decided not to have Tyler participate in the service; he would sit between Mrs. Buoni and Mrs. Connors. Tom and Mark went into Father Jonsen's office and found him sitting at his desk, red eyed with an open bottle of aspirin and a glass of water in front of him. Neither of them said anything but it was obvious that Father Jonsen was suffering from a hangover. The three of them chatted for a while and then Tom and Mark left.

Just before the time the service was scheduled to begin, Katie and her father appeared at the back of the church. Farther Jonsen, who had been watching for them, walked to the front of the altar and stood there. He waited until everyone in the pews became quiet and were looking at him. "Good Afternoon and welcome to St. Mark's

Church. We are gathered here today to celebrate the wedding of Katie Oldfield and Thomas Booker, and what a gorgeous day for a wedding it is. However, this ceremony will probably be different from all other weddings you have attended. The bride's mother and father, and the bride's brother and his wife, and the groom's mother and father have decided to celebrate the anniversary of their three individual wedding vows. That means that four couples will be standing at the altar.

"I tell you this so that no one will leave prematurely and miss any of the reaffirmation ceremonies. I will announce the end of the service by saying, 'This concludes the wedding ceremonies.' Then we will have the Recessional and the bride and groom will leave, followed by every one in attendance.

"With all of that said, let the ceremony begin."

It did and it went smoothly. The individuals moved from their roles in the wedding party to their positions as couples at the altar. The movements were not as crisp and precise as a Marine drill team; however, they were slow and graceful and meaningful. There were no mistakes of omission or commission and love and happiness radiated back from the altar throughout the church. It was a dignified display of respect for the institute of marriage.

After the ceremony, after the reception line, after the bride and groom had their pictures taken, they joined the wedding party at the Lord Fox. They were warmly greeted by all their friends, relatives, and guests as they made their way to the head table. In the midst of all the noise and activities that accompanied serving dinner and drinks and the glass tinkling tom toms, Tom moved closer to Katie and quietly asked, "Sweetface, Wife, is this the same package that we paid for? I thought that we ordered the least expensive meal, chicken. I know that this dish, filet mignon, was the most expensive meal."

Katie spoke to Helen who motioned both of them to lean towards her. "Listen, when John found out that you were going to get married he wanted to pay for the wedding. He was so pleased for the two of you. Then, when you told him that both of you insisted on paying for everything yourselves, he decided to respect your wishes but he still wanted to do something for you. So, he got in touch with the caterer and ordered an upgrade but he asked the caterer not to tell you that he was paying for the more expensive dinner. He wanted to make you happy without breaking your rules. I hope you won't be angry with him."

Katie waited to let Tom speak first; she had no problem with her father's generosity but Tom might be offended and that would be his right. Tom replied almost immediately, "Helen, that really was a generous thing for him to do. And he did it even before he decided to attend our wedding. He certainly can be full of surprises. We are beholden and Katie and I will thank him before we leave tonight."

As dinner was winding down, Katie patted Tom on the arm and nodded her head. Tom stood up and began tapping his knife on his water glass until everyone was quiet. Katie got up with him and they both stood together, each with one arm around the other's waist. Tom began, "Hello, I'm ringing my chimes to get everyone's attention, not to get you to kiss each other. However, you can certainly do both if you wish.

"First, my wife, Katie, and I want to thank you for helping us celebrate this day which is so important to us. To be married and have your parents celebrate your marriage by renewing their vows is humbling and heartwarming. Today is the happiest day of my life. I'm not just saying these words, I'm talking from my heart.

"Along with marrying Katie, I'm starting a new job. I no longer work for the Foxboro Highway Department plowing streets or emptying trash from the Common. I will be teaching in the Mansfield School System. The residents of Foxboro may think that that is a demotion to take a job in Mansfield. Not me. I see it as an opportunity to help young people.

"A new job, a new wife, a new life. I can say no more. From the bottom of my heart, thanks all of you."

Katie kissed Tom on the cheek and wiped her eyes. She began to speak and her voice was so soft and low that everyone strained to hear her. "I look around and I see all the people who are my friends and my relatives. Some of you have known me all of my life, some of you have known me for most of my life, and some of you have known me for only a few years. The amount of time is not as important as the fact that all of you have tried to teach me right from wrong. Whatever my shortcomings are they certainly can't be attributed to any of you.

"What I want to say is that I am so grateful you took the time to share your thoughts, ideas and ideals with me. You have made my life richer and you have made me a better person than I would have been.

"I guess I'm really not making much sense. I'm not even trying to. I'm so happy I'm delirious. I have a loving family and I have snagged the kindest, nicest man in the whole world as my husband.

"My only wish is that every person in this room and every person on this earth could have as much inner peace and happiness as I have. May God bless us all and may He keep hatred and war out of our hearts."

Katie and Tom sat down amidst applause and a lot of water glass tinkling.

Later on, just before they were supposed to dance as father and daughter, Katie and Tom had a chance to talk with John Givens and

Helen. Katie said, "Dad, my wedding wouldn't have meant as much to me if you weren't here to give me away. Thank you for that, thank you for accepting Mark and Brenda, thank you for reaffirming your vows with Helen. I'm bursting with pride over having a father as caring as you are."

John Givens unconsciously reached for Helen and put his arm around her shoulders. "Katie, Katie, stop before you have me in tears. Helen has been the lighthouse of love for our entire family over all these years. When that light flickered, even for a second, I finally realized what I had had all these years. You are welcome to anything we have not only as a loving daughter, but also as a lovely person."

Tom spoke up. "John, it's a small point to bring up now, but you surprised Katie and me with your generosity. We are truly grateful for the extra money that you paid for our reception meal. You make me both happy and proud to be part of your family."

"Tom, I'm delighted to have you as my son in law. Ordering filet mignon wasn't hard to do. To quote some philosopher or other 'It's only money.' It was one way of showing how much Helen and I care for both of you."

Katie asked both of her parents, "Tyler won't be too much of an imposition to care for while Tom and I are gone, will he? Helen, he won't tire you out?"

"Katie, he will be the best medicine in the world for me. Far better than any prescription Dr. Sanborn could write out. We are going to enjoy having him with us. Don't be concerned; we aren't. Just to show you our confidence, I'll let you in on what we are planning. The day after you and Tom get back your father and I are driving to Milan for an extended visit with Tom's parents."

That news brought a chuckle from both Katie and Tom.

John Givens then spoke up. "Katie, now I have a favor to ask of you. Obviously, I can't dance with my leg in a cast. Would you mind if I have Mark take my place? I would like that."

Katie waltzed with her brother. Both left the dance floor with tears streaming from their eyes while, on the sideline, John Givens also wept.

Shortly after that, Tom and Katie ducked out of a side door and drove quietly away on their honeymoon.

The story of their life together now falls into a chapter that is not yet written.